Part One
Death's Door

The Great Equaliser

The whole world could know your name,
or no one ever notice you.
In privilege or poverty,
no matter if you're wise or true
she comes and makes us all the same.

Some disappear behind the wall,
leaving cradles empty, cold,
Some linger on till blind and deaf,
when finally, she takes the old.
Unfeeling, she will take us all.

And how she takes us, in the end:
resigned or kicking, short or long,
is something of a lottery,
unless we sing the lonely song
of those whose hurts refuse to mend.

Or, holding her in low esteem,
we do her work before its time,
and—God forbid! We end a life.
We justify the violent crime,
interrupting plans and dreams.

Who fears her—inevitable death?
Some crave the sweet release,
while others dread her icy grasp.
Still others in pretended peace
deny her till their final breath.

If left here to pontificate
the cause of their abandonment—
regardless if we do, or gape
in open-mouthed bewilderment—
beyond our sight, she stands and waits.

The Whisperer
A Novel in Six Parts

by A. Ireland King

Copyright 2018 A. Ireland King. All rights reserved.
www.airelandking.com
ISBN 13: 978-1-9803-4935-8

for Grant, my reason

Prologue

I look down at my lifeless body, which lies bleeding into the forest floor. My assailant appears unruffled, aloof, but a sudden moan from the body prompts a second, more frenzied attack. Over and over, the knife is plunged viciously into my torso.

Finally, the assault ends. Hearts pound in the quiet of the evening; breaths gradually slow a little. A blackbird chirrups in a nearby birch tree, oblivious to my calamity.

I get a soft kick to make sure I'm completely dead, and my eyes are pressed shut with a strange air of tenderness. My funeral consists of a few whispered words and a solitary tear.

I look on helplessly as my corpse is dissected, the pieces wrapped in thick black bags. In the gloom, the bags are taken to the deserted building site. Their final resting place beneath one of the trenches is already dug: a narrow, shallow grave, waiting.

My despair grows as the remains are covered: with hardened earth; six inches of cement; and later, brick walls. The building appears steadily—an ironically impressive covering for an unmarked grave—solid and imposing. Final.

I'm often drawn to that place in the long years that follow. I pine miserably for those stolen years. I try to move on by delving into my work. I dig deep to forgive. But questions persist, dragging me back.

Time and time again.

CHAPTER 1

Meredith
Edinburgh is my city. I wander these streets, watching, but nobody sees me. I'm already a ghost.

There's plenty to look at. There's the Old Town, with its medieval buildings and narrow alleys. The Royal Mile, a street full of touristy shops, stretches from Holyrood Palace (official residence of Queen Elizabeth II) all the way to Edinburgh Castle. One of Edinburgh's three cathedrals, St Giles, stands majestic on the Royal Mile, dating back to the twelfth century. There are still cobbled streets; many ancient things endure in the Old Town.

The Georgian New Town is full of elegant gardens and neoclassical structures. Princes Street Gardens slope down from the main shopping street. The impenetrable fortress of Edinburgh Castle stands proud above it all, resting on an extinct volcano.

Arthur's Seat—a hill in Holyrood Park—boasts a sweeping view of the city. There's also Calton Hill at the East End of Princes Street, littered with monuments and memorials.

I'm not much of a drinker, but to me, home smells of mashing grains and boiling wort: beer brewing.

There are beautiful museums, art galleries, theatres and libraries, and that's just the city centre. That's without mentioning the surrounding communities, the universities or the buzzing port district of Leith sitting on the southern shore of the Firth.[1]

So many people, all strangers.

I sit on the first bench I come to in Princes Street Gardens. I won't get any further than this for my last look around. I won't see the gardens come alive for this year's Winter Wonderland.

I was born in Edinburgh fifty-seven years ago, and today, I'm going to die here.

---

[1] firth (noun): an estuary. The port of Leith sits on the Firth of Forth.

Stan

Stan Marshall was having an exceptionally ordinary morning. The East Coast train was running to perfect time, and he was looking forward to his imminent coffee break, in Edinburgh.

People liked Stan—more because of his easy way than anything. He was a friendly chap, bantering with passengers and staff in his London accent. He was good-looking too; five foot nine and thickset, with curly hair that flicked out behind his ears and flopped over his forehead. Best of all there was a twinkle in his eye and laughter in his heart.

Maybe he'd see Emma at the ticket barriers. He'd been flirting, but in his heart of hearts, he knew it wasn't going anywhere. Stan had no problem getting girls, but he rarely got past the second or third date. Maybe it was daft, but he was holding out for something special. Or was he just scared to fall for someone again? No, this had nothing to do with Nora. He wanted something real. When he met the one, he would know, and she'd be worth the wait.

Well, in the meantime he *was* single, so there was no harm in a bit of flirting. He grinned as he thought of Emma's curves and bobbed brown hair, and how easily he could make her laugh.

Stan was interrupted from this pleasant thought by a flashing light ahead. It signalled that he should stop the train and wait for the southbound one to pass, as usual, before continuing on. He whistled a cheerful tune while he waited.

Stan wondered if he should grow a beard.

The light changed and the train heaved on again, rumbling quickly up to full speed to make the final stretch. A patchwork landscape of greens and browns sped by in the clear October morning. Stan checked the clock. 11:34. The train was negotiating the outskirts of the city, as the coffee break approached. 11:37. This familiar stretch of track was bordered by a high bank on the West and a flat wooded area to the East.

Stan had no time to react between the sudden flash of movement and the sickening thump of a body against the front of the train.

Meredith

Am I dead or alive? I jumped, I know that. I definitely jumped, didn't I? It took all my strength, but the adrenaline helped. I thought my heart might give out before I did it, and save me the trouble. It beat hard and fast in my chest, and filled my ears like a drumroll, and then I felt the vibrations in my feet too. No, that wasn't my heart, was it? It was the train. Yes, the train was coming.

I can't hear the drums now. My body feels weightless, its familiar aches and pains gone. There's no firm earth beneath my feet. It's there, but I'm not touching it. I mean, it isn't exactly holding me up. The rear of the train passes by, screeching and shuddering, but I can't find my reflection in the windows. There are only the shabby trunks of the pine trees behind me, hiding their nakedness from the sun's glare beneath sparse branches.

I look down at myself, and it looks like me. I can only see my feet beyond my middle by leaning forward. I'm still wearing the same clothes: the long brown skirt, the black top, and my padded jacket. What's this glow all around me? I touch my arms, my face, my hips, and I'm confused to find everything in its place. I pinch my cheek, hard, but it doesn't hurt.

What's happening? I panic, spinning around until I'm confronted with a mangled body. It's about ten metres down the embankment, wearing the same clothes as me.

Dead? But, how am I thinking? Shouldn't it be dark and quiet? I'm still here, and I'm still me—cursed with an undeniable sense of being. I thought if I could only jump, all this would end. That's all I wanted! How can that be too much to ask? I sit down beside myself, beyond hopelessness, and sob into my hands.

Stan

Stan slammed on the breaks. His heart thudded in his chest, adrenaline coursing through his veins. He swallowed, hard. Never had he imagined that he would actually need his incident training for this eventuality. He scrambled to recall it. Step one – stop the train. Done. Step two – alert headquarters. He punched the button on his radio. He blurted out something about an emergency, and his manager was quickly summoned to the station control room.

'Sharron, I've hit someone! They jumped, I...I couldn't stop...'

'Stan, is the train stationary now?'

'Yeah.'

'Good. I'll stop the trains and send out the emergency services. Get a vague message out to your passengers and keep them on that train. See if there's anything you can do for the casualty. Keep your radio on you, okay?'

'Okay.' Stan was grateful for the reminder of what to do next. He steeled himself, forcing his voice to come out evenly. 'Passenger announcement, this is the driver. There's been a delay due to an unforeseen issue, which will be resolved as soon as possible. For your own safety, please stay seated on the train.' The passengers would be curious; he didn't want them disturbing the scene or causing an uproar.

It seemed to take him forever to run the length of the eight carriages, his lungs burning in his chest. The victim hadn't been sucked under the train, but had bounced off. A quick calculation—emergency stopping distance minus length of train—told him to look roughly ninety metres behind it.

The conductor, Mary, a stout woman with an authoritative air, stood outside the farthest away carriage as he approached, waiting for his instructions.

'A suicide. Keep the passengers inside,' he hissed.

Mary nodded, business-like.

Stan kept running, tasting blood at the back of his throat, drawing great gulps of air that seemed woefully inadequate.

Then he saw her; a large, dark-haired woman. Folded in half over the low branch of an old oak. One leg grotesquely broken. Her ponytail hung below her head, blood dripping slowly from its end. Stan had a powerful urge to run in the opposite direction, but duty propelled him towards the body. When he was close enough to be sure that she was dead—and he couldn't help—he stopped, hands on knees, chest heaving. He vomited profusely, then his ears stopped working and everything went dark.

Meredith

In disgust, I turn away from myself, and see a man in railway uniform running towards me—the driver? His mousy brown hair is windswept, his face pink from exertion. He doesn't see me—he's looking at *it*.

I've made such a royal mess for this poor sod to clean up! Why didn't I think of him before? I know why—because I didn't expect to face the consequences. It hadn't even factored into my plans. He crumples at the sight of my hideous remains, throws up and falls flat out on his back. He lies grey and silent on the grass, his breathing quick and shallow.

There's an urge deep within me to apologise. Of course, it's one of those situations where anything you say would sound trite. *Hi, I'm Meredith. Er, sorry for jumping out in front of your train. Didn't mean to be a nuisance.* Still, I've got to try. I swoop down close to his broad chest, touching imperceptibly, and let my heartfelt regret seep into him.

Stan

'Hello, can you hear me?'

Stan squinted to see the face above him. It was surrounded by white-hot sunlight, like a halo. Then it moved slightly, casting a shadow over his eyes, and revealing itself. The first thing Stan noticed was a generously lashed pair of hazel eyes. Next—well-defined, glossy lips.

'I'm Stacy. Can you tell me your name?'

'Shtan.' Disarmed before this beautiful stranger, he sat up in an effort to appear a smidge more manly. This immediately backfired, blood draining from his face. Everything sounded as though under water, and the urge to vomit almost overpowered him again.

'Whoa Stan, not so fast!' Stacy smiled kindly. 'You need to lie down a bit longer.'

He obeyed.

She had placed something soft under his head and put his feet up on some kind of box, where she now gently but firmly replaced them.

He grinned goofily; even in the state he was in, Stan knew a gorgeous girl when he saw one. Her hair was pinned up in a messy bun, and she was wearing a green uniform. That meant she was one of those people who drive the ambulance. He couldn't think of the word. Or why he was on the ground...then remembering, his eyes widened. 'The woman came out of nowhere! She just-'

'It's okay Stan. There was nothing you could've done.'

Did it really happen? They couldn't be far from the body. Stan was afraid to turn his head and look. In his peripheral vision, a group of people were milling around the scene. There were muffled voices. Focussing on Stacy, he said, 'Tell me something. Tell me...'

'What?'

Stan became aware of his clammy skin, and kicked himself for being so squeamish. 'Tell me something about yourself.'

'Let's see...' Stacy sized him up for a moment. 'I'm twenty-five. I share a flat in Edinburgh with a friend. I work hard and I play hard. My favourite food is Italian. I have a long bucket list and the next things to get ticked off are a bungee jump, and volunteering abroad. I like to laugh. Your turn.'

She liked to laugh. Make her laugh! Normally this would've been no problem at all for Stan, but unfortunately, on this occasion he blurted out, 'You'd laugh at me trying to do a bungee jump.' *What the hell Stan? Use your loaf.*

It worked all the same—Stacy suppressed a chortle.

Stan's brow furrowed and he felt smaller. Was she laughing because he was charming, or hilariously pathetic? He watched as she moved off. She was speaking to a policeman, but kept glancing at Stan. He took deep breaths, trying to get a hold of himself.

Stacy returned and said, 'I think we can sit you up now. The police are going to take your statement, okay? Then I'll see you again when you're done.'

'Good,' Stan muttered, folding his arms. 'Maybe by then, I'll be able to stop making a complete arse of myself.'

Meredith

The area is bustling with activity now; uniformed police, forensics, and paramedics all together in a kind of organised commotion. I'm on the outside looking in, which is pretty much my default position. The living look much as they always did, but each one is surrounded by a subtle glow—an aura—some brighter than others.

I watch the driver; I need to know he's going to be okay. The paramedic is taking good care of him, but he's still an unhealthy colour. He's in shock because of me and utterly bewildered by her. He looks at her in wide-eyed amazement, then delirium takes him again.

His attraction to her must be strong to be felt through his obvious distress. Life goes on, I suppose. A pair of greenfinches twitters its agreement from the top of a gorse bush, naked of its yellow flowers.

I don't know why—she can neither see nor hear me—but I suggest to the paramedic: *give Stan your number*.

I'm confused by a warmth behind me—the sun is still up above—and I turn to face a light equally dazzling. Its source gradually comes into focus in the centre—is he an angel? Wavy, dark hair frames a vibrant face. He has a chiselled jaw and piercing blue eyes. His nose is quite off-centre, but somehow, it suits him. There's a softer appearance to his mass, but he's manifestly real. He's wearing jeans and a t-shirt, and he's looking straight at me.

I can hardly hold his gaze for a second—it's breath-taking and terrifying at the same time. I'm convinced that by simply looking, he can penetrate the depths of my soul. He can see my shame! In awe, I turn my face away. Who is this other-worldly creature, and what does he want with *me*?

CHAPTER 2

Helen

Seventy-nine-year-old Helen Potts sat in her usual spot, a worn but comfortable armchair facing the television. Ginger the cat was curled up on her lap, purring softly and keeping her warm. She'd already been out for her brisk morning walk around the park, and completed the crossword. Body and mind thus exercised, she was now letting *Homes Under the Hammer* wash over her. The TV was like an old friend—a distraction. Not a very effective one, mind you. Helen's thoughts meandered through the mundane, giving a wide berth—as always—to more dangerous territory. The old mantel clock ticked away approvingly, an ornamental plate standing sentry on either side.

Helen fancied another cuppa. She'd have one with lunch—a boiled egg salad. Did they need anything from the shops? What would she make for tonight's dinner? Why was it her turn? Where *was* Meredith, anyway?

Meredith had gone out most days since she stopped working. Helen knew her daughter visited the public libraries, galleries and museums, but how that kept her out of the house all day was a mystery. Perhaps she was out walking—as the doctor (and Helen) had repeatedly advised—but judging by her weight, Helen thought not. More likely she was sitting in a café somewhere eating cake, face in a book.

That morning, Meredith had appeared with her jacket on, holding Ginger and said, 'I won't be able to cook tonight.'

'Why?'

The girl only shrugged. She'd let the cat go, and he'd bounded up the stairs. Meredith came and hovered close to Helen in her strange way. Even after all these years, it felt uncomfortable.

Helen was pouring milk into her favourite teacup (china, painted with sweet peas), wondering how one person could make you feel so crowded. (One very large person, mind you). With effort, she had resisted sighing out loud. 'Do you want a cup, before you go?'

'No, thanks.' Meredith had placed a crushing arm around Helen's thin shoulders. 'Just wanted to say bye.'

Helen was never one for hugs, but she reached over her shoulder and patted the arm. 'Have a good day.' Helen had removed her hand, but the arm remained on her shoulders longer than was natural. She could feel Meredith's breath on her neck. She closed her eyes, waiting for it to be over. But it took too long. Finally, Helen wriggled out from beneath Meredith's arm and clipped, 'Off you go, then.'

Meredith turned and left.

Helen called, 'Enjoy yourself,' to her retreating steps in an attempt to mask her relief.

Meredith

I finally find the courage to speak to the angel. 'Who are you?'

'My name is Michael.'

His voice is too kind, his smile too warm; I can't bear it. What's worse—he glances over at my body and his eyes betray a deep sadness. I don't deserve his attention; and yet, I wish for it. Does he know what I'm thinking? I look away.

'I watch over the living,' he says, gently lifting my head so that our eyes meet, 'including *you*, Meredith.'

My shame deepens; this divine being has been watching over *me*? Guardian angels are a myth, aren't they? One of those lovely things people invent to comfort themselves. Yet what is Michael, if not that? Even if I *could* have imagined him, he probably would've been a woman: winged, dressed in white.

'I'm a whisperer,' he says. 'I speak to the living: in their thoughts, in their hearts, and in dreams. It's like a whisper to them, so quiet it's easily missed.'

'You...spoke to *me*?'

'All your life.'

What a frustration I must have been! 'I'm sorry. I didn't know. I couldn't hear.'

'Sometimes you did. It may simply have seemed like your own thoughts or ideas, but at times I was able to help you along. You didn't need much help with kindness—you're good at that.'

I cringe. Feeling both small and conspicuous at the same time, I manage a feeble, 'Thank you,' which comes out like a question.

Helen

Helen hoisted herself up, wincing at the familiar ache in her hip, and cleared away the remains of her egg salad. She washed the dishes, dried them and put them neatly in their places. She had afternoon activities three days a week: yoga class, walking group, and book club. However, today was one of the free afternoons reserved for housework.

She began to dust the mantelpiece. The sideboard. The little table by her favourite chair. Not that any of it was particularly dirty, but it was important to keep on top of these things. A place for everything, and everything in its place.

Meredith helped with the housework, and contributed to the bills. Her bedroom left a lot to be desired, mind you. Helen had long since given up on it, amongst other things. It still rankled to walk past the closed door, knowing that clothes were probably strewn across an unmade bed, books and drawing materials littering the desk. One thing was certain; Meredith hadn't inherited her laziness from her mother. Helen compensated herself by keeping her own room absolutely spotless.

Meredith

Michael asks me to trust him and takes my hand.

Before I can react to the shock of his touch I feel a jolt in my belly, followed by a squeezing sensation. Indefinable colours fly past us in blurred lines, then the squeezing stops and new surroundings come into focus.

Michael lets go of my hand, wearing an expectant grin.

I stare wide-eyed, trying to make sense of what just happened. We're in Waverley station, hovering high in the centre of the building. From this vantage point, we can see almost everything at once. Watching people is a well-established favourite pastime of mine. After I gave up work, I spent most of my time wandering the city, sitting on benches, noticing things. Sometimes I would sketch—nothing fancy. I always took a book; wherever you are, you can always escape into a good story. This morning, I didn't bring one. I didn't want any distractions.

Waverley station is crowded as usual; a river of souls flows constantly in and out. Some loiter by the shops and platforms, killing time on smartphones. Others are sold on the smell of toasted sandwiches and hot coffee. There are business-types, blustering through with such a sense of self-importance that they barely notice anyone. A number are frustrated by delays due to an 'incident' on the line. Just like the professionals buzzing around my corpse, these people have auras, varying in brilliance.

All of this amazes me, and I forget to be shy. 'How did we get here?'

Michael laughs at my look of wonder. 'You start by concentrating on where you want to go, a person or a place. You sense a channel opening up, and when it's ready, you move.'

'How do you know when it's ready?'

'You feel it. The movement starts from your centre. You gather yourself in, ready to squeeze through.'

'Then what?'

'The final step is just a matter of confidence.'

Oh, just a simple matter of confidence. Funnily enough, I'm not bursting with that; I'm pretty much the last person on earth who could squeeze into a small space.

'You need to believe you can do it.'

It's an act of faith. Great. I close my eyes, concentrating hard on the spot by the railway track where I left my body. I visualise the channel opening from here to there, like a very long straw, stretching to a rain pipe. I screw up my face, willing it to open wider, and it does...but it's not wide enough. I'm too scared to try the next bit, so I give up. 'I can't do it—I'm too fat.'

Michael says, 'No. A spirit isn't fat—it's just an imitation of the body. You can get the weight off if you want to.'

More diets? I can't think of anything worse.

He tells me, 'No one can do it the first time.'

I don't believe him.

'Try again.'

I take a deep breath, close my eyes, and try again. This time the channel feels almost wide enough to fit a body. Okay, I can do this. I scrunch myself up into the middle, and I feel the squeeze. It's like having a blood pressure cuff around your whole body; it fills with as much air as you think you can take, then a little more. The distance between starts to pass by in a streak of colour, but it's taking too long. I can't do this! Everything goes dark, and I'm stuck, crushed into a tiny space. I think I'm going to die for real this time, then Michael takes hold of me and we're moving again. Finally, we emerge by the railway track. I suck in great gulps of air, which I can't possibly need. I'm exhausted.

Michael says, 'You did well,' but I know I didn't.

'Can I just walk, or take the bus, if I want to?'

He laughs, but I wasn't joking. 'Don't worry. You'll get the hang of it with practice.'

I'm doubtful. I look around at the mess I've made, and feel the same old hopelessness, crouching in the pit of my stomach like a beast ready to devour.

Michael asks, 'What are your questions?'

Where to begin?

'Don't be shy, Meredith. You can ask me anything.'

I look at the ground. 'How come I'm still here?'

'You destroyed your body, but not your spirit. You can't kill that.'

I wish I could. 'Am I going to hell?'

'I wouldn't think so, but none of us knows what'll happen when we go on.'

'Wait, *us*? Do you mean that you're...human, like me?'

'Of course!' He laughs again, his lustre confusing me further. Seeing my expression, he becomes serious. 'I walked the earth, and I died. Now I whisper. But we must all go on, sooner or later, when our work is done and the time is right. Some go on the moment they die, others linger for years.'

'Go *on*?'

'Yes. We move on from here, and we never come back. I believe there'll be a judgement before we go to our final resting place.'

I cringe inwardly. Who does the judging—someone more majestic than this shining creature? Are my good and bad deeds to be balanced on some eternal scale? 'When will I go?' Not that it matters, really.

'Impossible to say. But don't fret. It won't be sudden—you'll feel it when the time is getting close.'

'How long have you been here?' Michael's beautiful face falls, and I look down again, wishing I hadn't pried.

He sighs. 'Longer than I care to remember.'

CHAPTER 3

Meredith

Next, Michael takes me home; I let him take care of the travel arrangements, promising to try again soon. A policeman knocks on the front door, but mum is snoozing and doesn't hear. He knocks louder, and rings the doorbell. Mum stirs and gets up, wiping saliva from her chin onto her sleeve. She opens the door, but keeps the chain on, peering suspiciously at the policeman.

'Mrs Potts? I'm Sergeant Jamieson. I need to talk to you. Can I come in, please?'

Mum unchains the door, stony-faced, and gives a terse jerk of her head towards the living room. She leads the way, and lowers herself with a minor grimace back into her chair.

Mum looks a little different to this morning; she's now surrounded by a subtle aura.

She makes no invitation, but the Sergeant sits down on the sofa. 'Mrs Potts, I'm afraid I have some terrible news.' He speaks slowly and clearly, holding her gaze.

Her face doesn't change. 'Go on.'

'A woman was hit by a train and killed this morning. It's likely that she committed suicide. We believe her to be your daughter, Meredith.'

A pause. A blank expression. 'Why do you think it's her?'

'There was a purse in one of her jacket pockets, which contained her identification, and a card naming you as her emergency contact. She was also carrying this envelope. I'll need to borrow it, I'm afraid—for evidence—but you'll want to read it first.' He holds out my pathetic note, waits for her to take it.

But she doesn't move.

The Sergeant raises his eyebrows, holds the envelope a little closer.

Mum glares at the Sergeant.

The poor man looks gobsmacked, but he slips the envelope into a pocket and presses bravely on. 'We'll need you to identify the body, Mrs Potts. Is there someone you'd like me to call?'

'No.'

'I'm afraid I must ask you to come with me.'

Without a word, mum stands and goes to fetch her coat. She sticks her chin out as she passes the Sergeant, pressing her lips so tightly together that the wrinkles above her mouth deepen.

The Sergeant looks bewildered. My mother has been a formidable woman all her life, but there are certain qualities that no one expects of the elderly. Silly, really. You don't turn into someone else just because you get old; a fact most people don't seem to realise until they're old themselves.

For my part, I'm not shocked. I wasn't expecting tears. I know what I am: a parasite that never should've been born. I've finally done something real for her. I've undone her biggest mistake.

I can get into the car without opening the door. Mum sits up straight, her head held high. I've always been an embarrassment to her, and this is no exception. She's mortified, but she won't show it.

Michael comes too, but in the mortuary he shrinks back to the furthest reaches of the room. I suppose he doesn't want to be close to that thing. I don't blame him; I'm disgusting.

The oversized corpse lies covered on the gurney, but not zipped into one of those body bags you see in films. They probably couldn't get one big enough. The left arm has slipped down and the hand protrudes, revealing its ugly scar tissue and chubby, ringless fingers, the nails chewed to the cusp. They've repositioned my leg so you can't tell it's broken.

The Sergeant says, 'Mrs Potts, you must understand—your daughter's injuries are extensive. I should warn you—'

'Yes, yes, I understand. Let's get it over with.' She stands stiffly, her face fixed, making no move to unbutton her coat.

He uncovers the head, *my* head. It's the first time I've seen my injuries up close and I'm taken aback. Both eyes are closed, but one is swollen, purple and encrusted with congealed blood. That whole side of my face is bruised and puffy, the lips burst. The hair is matted with blood but I can't see where it's coming from. Only on the other side of my head can you tell that the dark hair was turning grey. The rest of the face looks jaundiced, except for scarlet gashes on my forehead, cheek and neck. I suppose those happened when I landed on the tree; it's a mercy I can't remember it.

Mum looks for long enough to take all of that in. She's glaring at my dead face, tight-lipped as if to say *how dare you*? She nods curtly, signs the papers the Sergeant gives her and turns to leave, walking smartly in spite of her dodgy hip.

Sergeant Jamieson replaces the cover, whispers, 'I'm sorry,' and follows mum. Through the window I see him helping her back into the car, head bowed, hat in hand. I'm touched by the pity of a stranger, and ashamed, so ashamed that he saw my mother's coldness for me. What's worse, so did Michael.

An emotional tsunami rushes over me, sweeping me away to dark places against my will. I got that scar on the back of my hand and arm when I was eight. I had already tried bumping into things, and being careless with sharp objects. The little cuts and bruises had got me nowhere with mum. I tried scratching my arm till it bled, but she seemed irritated at best. I was determined to get her attention. I would make her cuddle me on her knee and wipe away my tears, whatever it took. I boiled the kettle and poured the water over my skin. I had no idea how much it was going to hurt! There was no acting; the searing pain made me howl (like a banshee, mum used to say). But even as I screamed, I was filled with eager anticipation for the reward that would surely follow.

I was wrong—she was cross with me for being so careless. She handled me roughly, holding my burn under the cold tap longer than I could bear. She lectured me about knowing better, and learning my lesson.

I haven't hurt myself on purpose since then—unless you count my eating problems. Not until today.

Stan

Stan decided to stay at his brother Simon's house in Edinburgh for the weekend; he didn't feel like getting back on the train to London, or going home alone. That said, he didn't want to face the family just yet, either. Simon would be at work, but Carla may be around. He was twitchy, so he walked the streets, heading for the park. Thoughts distilled on his mind as the shadows lengthened.

One pivotal moment can change everything. You come to a crossroads, and the direction you choose is going to determine where you end up. Maybe for the rest of your life.

Do you let yourself get spooked when something terrible happens? Do you let it come between you and your career? Or do you soldier on, knowing that the trauma will pass, safe in the knowledge that it couldn't happen twice? He could carry on as normal, hiding the lead weight in the pit of his stomach. *Stan Marshall is a killer.* He tried not to think about the way the body bounced off the windscreen, and landed, ruined, in the tree. Was he paying proper attention? Could he have spotted her, prevented it somehow?

Then, juxtaposed against the ugly trauma, was the gorgeous paramedic. If only he'd met her in different circumstances! He shivered, hands in his pockets, and his fingers found a little piece of paper. He pulled it out to take a look. Just an old receipt. But when he turned it over, his heart did a somersault. There was a little note with her name and number. She must've slipped it in there! It read: *let me know how you're doing, Stacy.*

Stan was a pretty traditional guy. The dynamic with Stacy was completely upside down. He was the confident one—he could read the signals and take the lead, and girls liked it. But this one? He hadn't a clue. Did she fancy him, or was she just being nice? Had she clocked that he fancied her, and thought he'd do for a notch on the bed-post? Did she do this kind of thing all the time, or was she looking for something real? What if she was just another bully in a beautiful mask?

He passed a couple at the park holding hands. They looked so comfortable together—could he ever be that guy? Then there was a proud dad, pushing a pram. Did he know how lucky he was?

Stan snuck home while Carla was picking up six-year-old Sam from school. He gave the dog a little pat, but left her in the kitchen. If she didn't give him away, he could sit quietly in the spare room till Simon got back. He lay on the bed with a book, reading the same page over and over, his thoughts preoccupied with two women: one gorgeous and a little intimidating, the other horribly dead.

Meredith

Michael takes me to Arthur's Seat, as the sun begins its retreat beyond the horizon of the cityscape. A few walkers linger, and we all watch in the stillness. The skyline turns seamlessly from clear blue to shades of coral, orange and cerise, gradually cooling to silver moonlight.

I expect Michael to say something comforting about mum, but I'm glad he doesn't. If he's been watching me my whole life, then he knows how things are, I suppose. He seems to suffer with me, and I can't help wondering; why would a creature like that—almost a god—care about someone like me? How long is he likely to stick around, now that I'm dead? I appreciate his kindness, I do, but I don't need a friend I can't keep.

Eventually—eyes down—I say, 'Do you think she loves me at all?' Please, please give me a reason to believe she does.

He disappears. The truth was too hard to say, I suppose. But then he's back, holding a book, and my Hannah doll.

I try to take the doll, but my fingers slip right through her.

Michael says, 'Don't worry—it takes time to learn how to interact with the physical.'

He holds her up for me, and I gaze at her stitched features. She was my favourite toy for many years, probably because mum made her for me on her old Singer. She's completely sewn from bits of scrap fabric or pilfered household items. I think her face and body used to be one of mum's doilies. She wears a gingham dress and a matching bow in her woollen hair. Her eyes, nose and mouth are carefully hand-stitched, right down to the detail of her long eyelashes. I got her for my fifth birthday—I remember because I had just started school. Mum was good at birthdays. She always seemed to find the one thing that would be most special. Not this time, but birthdays don't matter much when you get older, I suppose.

Next, Michael shows me the book—it's one of my sketch pads. It's open on a portrait of mum, young and smiling. She looks beautiful. She's looking down to one side, her hair flapping in the wind. I've never seen her smile like that. It's like...pure adoration. I think that's why I drew it; it encapsulated how things should've been, how I wished them to be. I copied it from a photo in our half-empty album—the one with all the pictures of my father ripped out.

'She was looking at you,' Michael says. 'You were playing on the beach.'

I try to smile, but it comes off sad; I can't remember how it felt to be on the receiving end of that adoring smile. 'Was it before my dad left?'

'Yes, before that,' he says, and his smile is full of sympathy. 'Hold onto your good memories, Meredith. She does love you, I know it.'

I'm not so sure, but I say, 'I'll try.'

'I need to put these things back before they're missed.'

I say, 'Goodbye, Hannah doll,' then he's gone.

I'm tired, so tired! But I don't know what to do about it. It can't be a bed I need, can it? Is there no rest now from my thoughts and feelings, always churning? When Michael returns, I say, 'What do we do to recover? Eat? Sleep?'

To my dismay, he says, 'No. We can't do either.'

Those were the small comforts in life, little ways to abate my troubles, but something at least. Now I've deprived myself of any relief at all.

Michael says, 'Sometimes, we just need to be still until we're ready to move again. Meredith, while the living sleep, I whisper. I want to teach you to do it, too.'

'Me?' I can hardly look at him—he's so powerful, so virtuous. 'I can't do what you do.'

'You already have,' he points out.

I can't think what he's talking about.

'Stan. You said you made an apology, of sorts? After you died?'

I nod.

'Well, that's whispering. There are lots of people who need help, and they could use someone like you.'

I study the ground, wondering what *someone like me* means.

'Think about it,' he says. 'You've been a carer most of your life. Your work at the nursing home was amazing.'

I cringe at the compliment, screwing up my face.

'You can do this, you'll see. Will you give it a try? For me?'

'...Okay.'

Since I owe Stan one, we go there first. He's in bed, but he isn't sleeping. He lies on one side, then the other, then on his back. He breathes deliberately, exhaling heavily as though he can blow his troubles out through his mouth. His feet fidget under his duvet.

'I didn't mean to cause him trouble,' I say.

'I know.'

'Can we help him feel calmer, get some sleep?'

He nods. 'I'm going to summon the feeling into myself, then share it with Stan. No lies, just an assurance that everything will be okay.'

Michael closes his eyes, turns his face upward, and is still for a few minutes.

I can watch him now. I still think he looks like an angel; the title of whisperer seems inadequate.

He puts a hand on Stan's head, barely touching, and there's a sound like an electrical hum. Michael says, 'peace,' over and over. It's an invitation, not a command, but there's power in it.

I feel it too; so different to the turmoil inside. I want that peace, but it's elusive to me.

Stan's feet stop moving. His breathing regulates. He turns a few more times while we watch over him, finding his groove in the pillows. He's asleep.

Michael smiles at my look of amazement. 'Do you want to check on your mum?'

'No,' I say, 'not tonight. I just don't...'

'It's okay.'

'Can I see my old folk, at the home where I used to work?'

He takes me there, and we visit each one in my old block. Two have passed away since I had to give up my job, but there are six people here that I know well.

I say, 'If I'm to whisper, the ones I know seem a good place to start, don't they?'

'Definitely.'

'I'm just not sure if I can-'

'Meredith. You love each one of them perfectly; just take your time, and say what comes naturally.'

First is Irene. Her dementia is advanced, and she's become child-like again. She doesn't know her daughter, Sandra. Sandra told me all about Irene: how she loves Elvis, how she likes her hair blow-dried just so, how she always wore red lipstick before the forgetting. I bought her a scarlet lipstick when I worked here, and put it on for her every day. We played her Elvis CDs and I would blow-dry her hair. It took me a while to get it right; every time Sandra visited she would give me tips. Irene didn't say much but she would smile at me and sometimes sing along with the music. I look around for the lipstick. It sits on her bedside table, and I wonder how often she wears it, now I'm gone.

I watch her sleeping for a while. There's not much meat on her bones, and her mouth has a toothless, sunken look. There's a set of false teeth on the table and a walker next to the bed. Her breathing is quiet. I can feel that her spirit isn't far away, and I like being with her. I always did. I know there's much more to Irene that the little I've seen, but I remember our good times, and I feel her energy. I place my hand over her arm and I let the feelings flow into her. Then I speak. *Irene, sweetheart, I've missed you so much.* I wonder if she feels it too. I watch in the darkness, and think I see her lips curl into a little smile.

Next, I go to Peter. He's a much chattier person than Irene, always looking for a laugh. He still knows his family, but many everyday and personal tasks are difficult for him. He manages at home with his wife, but he comes here for a week at a time, for respite. His way of coping is to make light of it all; he makes fun of himself and loves a cheeky joke. Nobody minds—he's harmless. He calls all the women darlin', which I like, coming from him. He's sleeping, too, an extra bulge in the blankets around his middle, his length filling the whole bed. His bald head reflects the moonlight through a gap in the curtains.

Our roles were reversed a couple of weeks before I gave up the job. I helped him into the shower that day. It's important to protect people's modesty, so once we got Peter down to his underpants, I turned the shower on and faced the other way to let him get in. I was already out of puff from the work, when a sudden squeezing pain took hold of my chest. The angina, I thought, or I was about to die. I fell to my knees, then the floor, unable to speak.

Peter wasted no time—he headed straight out the door and down the hall in his pants to call for help. Of course, he joked about it for days after. He kept thanking me for giving him an excuse to let all the ladies see him in his undies. When I returned a smile, he winked and made out it was all an act we had planned together. He said he could've gone full monty for the ladies, but then there would've been *real* heart attacks.

I smile fondly at Peter now, and I lay a hand over his belly. I tell him simply, *I hope you're well, my friend.*

Fiona is on duty—she's alone in the sitting room, drinking tea and watching some old film. When I see her beady eyes and her pointy chin, I want to slap her as much as ever. I go right up to her face and I tell her: *You're a horrible person. You shouldn't be here. You should get a job sitting at a desk.* She flicks one hand as though swatting a fly, and continues watching.

There are four others on the block—three women and a man. I spend time with each of them: remembering our conversations, picturing their wee faces, and passing on my feelings. I can't tell if it makes any difference to them, but I like being here. I like that I can see my old folk again; I thought I'd lost them for good, and it hurt like hell.

Michael seems satisfied with my work, but I suppose he's just being kind. Anyway, it doesn't seem like work to me; I think this could even be my rest, my relief.

'Next time,' he says, 'I can teach you how to use dreams.'

There's so much to learn, but maybe, just maybe, I could learn it. I say, 'I'm ready to practice moving. Will you show me again?'

CHAPTER 4

Meredith

I'm surprised by how quickly I'm getting the hang of moving around. It's still weird, and takes me a lot longer than Michael, but I'm getting there. I've done it successfully several times now. I don't need to know the place if I'm going to a person. I concentrate on Stan, and a channel opens that takes us to him.

He wakes too early in a cold sweat, shouting, 'No!' and I suspect he's reliving the impact of my body against the train. He showers, dresses, and manages a slice of toast.

When his brother appears, they drink coffee in the kitchen and talk about my suicide in hushed tones. Carla is sleeping, and Sam is watching TV in the living room.

Simon listens to the story, wide-eyed, and gives his brother a solid shoulder. 'Mate, that's awful!' He means it. Siblings aren't always friends, but these two seem close.

It makes me wish I'd had a brother or sister—a special friend to grow up with. I have cousins, but I never got to see them. Mum was more or less estranged from her two brothers. I don't think they were ever close like Stan and Simon, but there was some kind of row, too. I don't remember it, but my Aunt Lizzie once hinted it was to do with my father.

Stan says, 'The paramedic, Stacy...'

'Sounds like a real looker.'

'Aw, yeah—stunning. Thing is, she slipped her number into my pocket.'

I had no idea! I didn't see her do that. It can't be anything to do with my suggestion, but it's a hell of a coincidence.

'Get away!' says Simon.

'True story, mate.' Stan's face lights up. He becomes very animated when he says, 'I was thinking about Stacy, how gorgeous she is and how gutted I was that I'd never see her again, when—as if by magic—I found her number in my pocket!'

'You must've made an impression, then.'

'D'you think?'

'Why else would she do it?'

'Well, look what she wrote.' Stan produces the old receipt and passes it to Simon. 'What d'you think?'

Simon considers. 'She must fancy you, or she wouldn't have done that. There's no way she does that with everyone.'

'That's what I'm hoping. I straight up have no clue what is going on in this woman's head. She's really something.' Then he sees the way Simon's looking at him and says, 'but, you know, it's no big deal.'

'No big deal, mate? Time will tell. You gonna call her?'

Stan grins sheepishly. 'Probably, once I figure out what to say.'

Stan offers to take Sam and Maggie—the family's beagle—to the park. Sam squeals with delight, switches off Transformers, and rushes to get dressed.

'Warm clothes today, mate,' Simon shouts.

At the park, Stan finds a seat while Sam chases Maggie around, kicking up piles of leaves. His leg is jittering, and I don't think it's the cold. He keeps fiddling with the phone in his pocket. After a while he takes a deep breath and calls Stacy's number.

'Hello?' says Stacy's voice.

'Hi Stacy, it's Stan. I was just...'

'Gotcha! You've reached Stacy's phone but not Stacy herself. Either I'm busy or I'm ignoring you! Leave a message, and if I'm not ignoring you, I'll call you back. Sucker!' Then a beep.

Caught off-guard, he hangs up, disappointment etched on his face. Then the joke sinks in and he shakes his head, smiling. Next, his brow furrows—what if she really is ignoring him? He sits watching the small boy and the dog running wild, looking from them to the phone and back again.

I think he needs to leave a message. It's hard to explain how I feel that; I wouldn't want him to make a fool of himself or anything. Michael says that truths for the living flow through us, and we need to learn to trust them, and pass them on. So I tell Stan:

Make the call. She gave you the number, didn't she? Why would she do that only to ignore you? Make the call.

Stan takes a deep breath and calls back. He listens to Stacy's cheeky prank again before leaving his message.

'Stacy love, it's Stan – the bloke you rescued yesterday—nah, not the ugly one, the good-looking one, yeah? So listen, I found your number, and I thought you were probably taking the piss like it was maybe for your local Chinese takeaway or something? Anyway, it'd be nice to talk. Plus, I *badly* need to redeem myself, so if this really *is* you, how about lunch? Get on the old dog and bone, and let me know when you're free.' He leaves his number and says, 'Talk to you soon.' He doesn't look nearly as confident as he sounds.

That makes me wonder—what if she really is ignoring him? I hope she isn't toying with him. I ask Michael if we can go and see what she's doing. He agrees, and this time we emerge in a moving ambulance. Stacy sits in the front, and a man is driving. We arrive at an incident on Easter Road involving a cyclist and a transit van. The police are already here, one heading to find the van driver and another near the fallen cyclist, waving the traffic on. As soon as the vehicle stops, Stacy jumps out and hurries to the casualty.

A man I'd estimate to be in his forties lies in the road on his back, some fifteen metres or so behind the blue Transit. A buckled bicycle lies near him on the pavement—no sign of a helmet. There are lacerations to his head and limbs. A younger woman, another cyclist who has stopped to help, is holding a blood-soaked T-shirt over his right shin. She has a hold of his hand.

The policewoman says to Stacy, 'I've just arrived, so I haven't offered first aid. I'll leave him to you.' She turns to the other cyclist. 'I'll need a statement when you're ready.' She then resumes directing the traffic. A crowd gathers as it always does. The police encourage them to move along, with little success.

Stacy works quickly, talking to the man and looking over his injuries. He's very pale and barely conscious. She can't get a response from him, so she turns to his helper. 'Has he spoken to you?'

'Yes, a little bit,' says the girl in a Polish accent. 'His name is Matt. I've been talking to him to try keeping conscious, but...' Her eyes fill up.

'Hey.' Stacy lays a hand briefly on the girl's arm. 'You've done a great job. Can I ask you to move back a bit now, and we'll do what we can for Matt.'

It's impressive watching Stacy work. Her natural compassion makes her comfortable with strangers in their most distressing moments. She uncovers a deep gash on Matt's leg, the bone visible. She applies pressure, bandages it up and elevates the leg. Then she goes to work on his less serious injuries. By the time her partner returns from checking over the van driver, she has Matt ready to be moved onto a stretcher. Each time Matt opens his eyes, Stacy soothes him, using his name and explaining what's happening.

When the paramedics reach the Royal Infirmary with Matt, another call is waiting: an elderly lady in Dalkeith. I'm satisfied that Stacy is definitely not ignoring Stan. She hasn't had a minute.

Stacy's aura is vibrant and rich, and she seems like the kind of woman worthy of a guy like Stan. In the ambulance, I speak his name to her.

Stan is a great guy—funny, honest and good-looking, I say. *It would be amazing to go out with Stan.*

Helen

The previous day's awful events replayed like a dream. Meredith dead? Suicide by train? Numbly, Helen made some tea—in the china cup with the sweet peas on it—and lowered herself into the faithful old armchair. Something out of focus was nagging at her, like an itch just out of reach. She shivered. A bluebottle buzzed angrily at the window, smacking itself repeatedly against the glass. The air itself was taut with irritation; energy vibrating like a low growl, an animal fixing for a fight.

Trying to ignore all of this, Helen switched on the TV and turned the volume up. She had never suspected Meredith would take her own life. She refused to let the question – why – form in her thoughts. She stuffed it away in a dusty old box at the back of her mind. That box could jiggle and thump all it liked, its secrets desperate to break free, but Helen had no plans to confront it.

Instead, she reached out for other thoughts, grasping straws of bitterness and resentment. The bluebottle zinged around the room, vaguely audible above the TV.

Meredith never really loved me. If she did, she would never have killed herself. After everything I've done for her, this is the thanks I get. She abandons me in my old age. Well. Chip off the old block.

Suddenly, the bluebottle thrust itself into Helen's ear. She jerked her head and swatted at the fly, but it was already out of reach.

A trail of shady mutterings followed her back to the kitchen. *How could she be so selfish? Did she think of me at all? I'll bet she did it just to spite me.*

The bell rang and Helen knew it was Lizzie, the only person who would open the door and come in. Was Helen expecting her? What day was it? The confusion rankled —honestly, Helen, wake up!

Lizzie was Helen's closest friend—they'd met as teenagers, and saw each other often. They both walked with the Roving Ramblers, and Lizzie came for tea every Sunday. (Helen didn't visit Lizzie, whose house held bad memories. When Lizzie bought it from her, Helen was clear she would never set foot in it again.)

The chain was on, so Lizzie had to wait. When the door opened, she breezed in with a carrot cake and started up the hall. 'Where's my darling girl?'

Helen followed Lizzie, confused to see her in trousers and walking shoes—quite a contrast to her usual suits and heels. Of course, it was Saturday. Helen should be out walking today too, but everything was upside down.

Finding the sitting room and kitchen empty, Lizzie turned back to Helen. 'Did she like the books?'

'Books?' Helen replied stupidly.

'Yes, darling, for her birthday.'

'Birthday?' Helen staggered back into her chair, aghast. Birthday! Lizzie had been on some residential with her church women's group and left her gift with Helen about a week previously. Helen had hidden it away with her own, and then forgotten the birthday altogether! How could she forget?

Lizzie looked questioningly at her friend. She'd been Meredith's honorary Aunt, and had spent a great deal of time with her. She had cared for Meredith in childhood while Helen worked. Meredith had even lived with Lizzie as a teenager. 'Darling, what is it? Did you forget?'

Helen nodded, horrified.

Lizzie looked as unruffled as her perfectly straight chin-length hair and impeccable make-up. 'Well, no matter—we'll do it now. Is she upstairs?'

'No!' Helen wailed, causing Lizzie sudden alarm.

'Darling, whatever's the matter?'

'Meredith...' Helen mumbled. 'Dead.'

Lizzie opened her mouth and closed it again. 'But...How? When?'

The easy bit first. 'Yesterday.' The rest of it made Helen ashamed—how could she bear it? Lizzie would find out anyway, so there was no option. State the facts. 'She took her own life, by jumping in front of a train.'

Lizzie brought a hand to her mouth with a sharp intake of breath. Her eyes filled up with tears. 'Oh, my darling girl!' She backed down onto the sofa, dabbing her eyes with a hanky to stop the mascara running.

The two women sat without speaking for a while, then Lizzie began doing what she did best: taking charge. She could be overbearing at times, but Helen would need her. There would be a funeral to arrange for a start.

'Have you eaten anything today?' Lizzie began.

Helen shook her head wearily. 'I really can't face it.'

'Well, you must eat something. Take care of yourself before you try to do anything else.' Lizzie left the birthday cake on the worktop and made toast.

'Thank you. Lizzie, go for your walk. It'll take your mind off things.' In truth, Helen wanted to be alone. She wasn't ready to face anyone, not even Lizzie. The only person she wanted when things went south was long gone.

Lizzie raised an eyebrow. 'What about you?'

'I'll be fine. There isn't much we can do until we find out when the body will be released. It can wait till tomorrow, at least.'

'Well, I'll be back tomorrow. But if you need me before then, darling, please call.'

'I will.'

With Lizzie gone, Helen could think. Meredith had turned fifty-seven on Thursday. How had she managed to forget? She had always made a point of celebrating Meredith's birthday, always.

A nasty, incriminating voice called out: *It's your fault she's dead, you miserable old cow! You did this! You should be ashamed of yourself!*

'Shut up!' Helen shouted. She hurriedly bundled her guilt into that dusty old box, with the question why, and marked it DO NOT OPEN.

Meredith

Michael brings me to the magnificent Central Library on George IV Bridge, a place I visit often. There is a local library in Oxgangs but I love the bigger libraries; they give me an excuse to wander the city. I mean…gave me an excuse.

It's different now. I can move so much faster, even without the trick Michael taught me. I don't need a seat or a wall to lean on every few minutes to catch my breath.

I love this place—it was opened in 1890, and paid for by Andrew Carnegie. There's something almost sacred about its majestic high ceilings, its pillars and archways, and the decorative cornice work. I could spend hours admiring the dome ceiling in the centre of the main reading room, which is always bathed in natural light.

In the lending library, there's a man I haven't seen before working at the help point. He must be new – I know all the library staff to look at, if not to speak to. His lanyard reads *Alfie Campbell*. He looks to be in his late fifties to early sixties. He's tall and skinny, and peers through rectangular plastic-framed varifocals that make his eyes appear unnaturally large. His clothes, like mine, are plain and unfashionable: trousers, a cardigan—both brown—and a white shirt. His hairline recedes into an unkempt mop of faded auburn. When he turns his head, his shoulders turn too, so his neck hardly moves. Maybe he has some kind of neck or spine pain. His aura is strong—one of the brightest I've seen.

Even before watching for long, I wish I was alive to meet Alfie. He seems like a kindred spirit; one who could be friends with the likes of me. Socially he's on the outside looking in. Most of his conversations consist of nothing more than the necessary to assist customers. He doesn't look them in the eye. He doesn't make small talk unless to comment on one of their books. He's quite knowledgeable—books being easier for him to read than people.

If I was living now, I could talk to him. We'd be awkward, but so what? I've robbed myself of the opportunity.

Michael says, 'Do you remember the night before your birthday? How you felt?'

I do remember. I felt a sense of urgency—not altogether unfamiliar—that made my pulse throb in my ears, and sleep evade me. 'I was...excited, and scared about the idea of going to the library. I felt like...'

'Yes?'

'It's silly.'

'It isn't. Go on.'

'I felt like I might make a new friend.'

'You heard me, then. I whispered to you, "The library! Visit the library! Be brave there, smile and talk! Do it tomorrow!" I wanted you to meet Alfie.'

I lay awake for hours that night, fantasising about what warmth and friendship might await me here; however, when morning came, I felt like an idiot. People go to libraries for books, not friends. Besides, I had plenty novels to keep me going. 'I talked myself out of it. I'm sorry.'

'I knew you were heading for trouble after that. I stayed with you, watching and waiting.'

Whispering hope in vain.

Michael says, 'When you went to the railway, I knew. I'd seen you walk by that spot before, making plans.'

'You...saw me do it?' I wish I could disappear!

'I was there on the bank, pleading.'

I daren't look at the disappointment on his face; I can hear it in his voice. 'I'm sorry,' is all I can say, and the words mock my profound shame. I squandered his generous efforts. I'm useless! Why couldn't I just listen to him? What might've happened if I'd come down here and met Alfie? Maybe he would've distracted me from mum missing my stupid birthday. Maybe he would've kept me from going over the edge.

And never mind me, what about Alfie? Is he even half as lonely as I am? Have I deprived him of needed friendship?

I watch as Alfie shows a customer how to check books out at the self-service kiosk. He then works on the fantasy fiction section, checking and moving books to their correct places. He sighs in irritation at the misplaced books.

Someone mumbles, 'What's wrong?'

Alfie turns awkwardly to see a skinny, pimple-faced boy of about fifteen, with short blonde hair and glasses, slouched in a chair with *Harry Potter and the Order of the Phoenix*. 'What's wrong,' Alfie says, turning back to his task, 'is that people keep moving books around, and there's not enough time to fix them all.'

'That's annoying,' says the boy to his book.

'Yes.' Alfie hesitates as though wanting to make conversation.

Harry Potter, I nudge.

Alfie asks, 'Harry Potter fan, are you?'

'Yeah.' The boy looks up. Alfie has to listen hard to understand him; his lips hardly move when he speaks. He'd make a good ventriloquist. 'I've read them before, but not for a while, so...'

'Why don't you take them home to read?' Alfie seems to address the question to the adjacent bookshelf.

'I like the library. It's...quiet.'

Alfie looks puzzled. 'Isn't home quiet?'

The boy gives a humourless smile. 'No.'

'Why not?'

'My parents argue. A lot.'

'Oh.' Alfie turns back to his task. 'Sorry about that.'

The boy shrugs. 'You're new here, aren't you?'

'Yes. I'm Alfie.' He turns and extends his hand to the boy, who takes it loosely in his own for a moment.

'Nathan. Can I give you a hand?'

Alfie accepts—though he doesn't look enamoured with the idea. Undeterred, Nathan starts at the opposite end of fantasy fiction, sorting the books carefully. It doesn't take them long to complete it. Alfie checks Nathan's side and looks pleasantly surprised. He thanks the boy, who's already sat down and resumed his reading.

I don't see any other teenagers hanging out alone in the library on a Saturday. This kid is a misfit, just like Alfie and I. Is this the universe's way of stepping in with another friend for Alfie? He shouldn't miss out because I messed up, I suppose. And I don't want him to.

Alfie glances over in the boy's direction once in a while, and looks surprised to see him still there at lunchtime. 'Still here, Nathan? Aren't you bored?'

Nathan looks over the top of his book and shrugs. 'Nah. My parents are both off work today. They're having a huge argument about money. I'm keeping out of the way as long as I can. Let it blow over.'

'I see.' Alfie stands there awkwardly.

I want to help him make friends. He doesn't know it, but it seems I owe him one, too. So I try to make an idea pop into his head. *Offer to buy him a drink.*

To my surprise, Alfie says, 'Well, it's my lunch break...buy you a coffee?'

Nathan makes a face. 'Hate coffee.'

Alfie has already half turned away, looking unsurprised at the rejection.

'Wouldn't mind a coke though.'

Alfie treats the boy to a coke and a piece of mars bar cake at the café. He looks a bit like a rabbit in headlights at first, but he relaxes as they chat easily about Harry Potter, which they both love. Alfie's conversation with adults is painfully stilted, but he has an easy way with this kid.

Michael asks if I'm ready to see mum. I'm so ashamed right now I would do anything he said. Plus, I know he's right. I need to go home.

I feel a great rush as we arrive, like cold air being sucked out of the room. Everything is still, and the light grows subtly brighter, as though the sun has just broken through clouds.

Mum exhales and slumps down, exhausted. She never slouches—that's my trick. A bluebottle buzzes out the door to the hall.

What is this? What's this dark presence I feel? I try to follow the rush, searching frantically for some hideous demon, but whatever it was, it's gone. Its influence still hangs heavy in the air.

'What was that?' I ask Michael.

He closes his eyes and breathes, then opens them. 'We call them shadows.'

'What are they?'

'They're like us, only they whisper evil, hurtful things.'

'Will it hurt her?'

No answer.

'Michael?'

'It's like...'

'What? Tell me!'

'Poison. Poison for the soul.'

'Do you mean?'

'It can kill her spirit? No. But it can turn her soul black.'

'Then what?'

He looks at me and his expression brightens. 'Don't worry. It won't come to that.'

'Can we get rid of it?'

Michael smiles sadly. 'They're tricky. They disappear when we come near. The problem is...if they're getting somewhere, it's because the living allow it.'

'Allow?'

'It means your mum's been entertaining the shadow. The power to keep it away comes from her, not us.'

'Why did the shadow disappear when we arrived?'

'Fear. These people can't abide our light. It burns them.'

Our light? Did he mean to group me together with himself? He must've meant him and other whisperers, other people he knows. 'So, you could get rid of it temporarily, just by being here?'

Michael nods. 'As could you.'

I don't believe that for a second. The thing would probably gape its mouth open and swallow me.

'Unfortunately,' Michael says, 'we can't be in more than one place at a time, so we can't always watch her.'

For the next few hours, we do watch, but the shadow doesn't return.

CHAPTER 5

Helen

Helen sat on the bed with her old box of photos, pouring over the one picture she had of her parents. Her father was in his army uniform. Keeping the tattered picture in its plastic envelope, she touched it lightly, remembering the last day she saw her mother. The last day she got to be a child.

Laughter rang through the summer air as bare-footed children splashed in a burn[2] behind a row of tenement flats. Helen was amongst them, a skinny twelve-year-old. Adjacent to the tenements was a row of prefabs, erected in Gilmerton for the families of soldiers; that is, soldiers who came home.

The boys wore shorts and ill-fitting shirts, and the girls had simple dresses. Most were handed down by older siblings or recycled from old clothes and bedding. They'd made a dam, and were now paddling happily in the pool it created.

Today they'd been given a treat: sticks of rhubarb from Janet Bruce's garden. Mrs Nairn next door had given each of them the cut-off corner of a paper bag, called a 'poke', with a couple of spoonfuls of sugar in the bottom. Helen's was all finished, the poke stuffed in her pocket, but she could still taste the sharp tang of rhubarb against the sweetness of sugar. She licked the last grains off from around her mouth.

Helen was a little scrawny and under-nourished, but no more than the others. She had become aware of her looks—not that the family owned a mirror—but sometimes she would catch her reflection in the water or a shop window. This summer she was brown and freckle-faced from playing outside, her sun-bleached hair wild and windswept.

She had the beginnings of breasts starting to form – soon she'd be a woman, just like mum. She would finish school and get a job, but not for long because soon she'd have a husband of her own. He would be extremely handsome and very, very clever. She would care for their three children, and her husband would bring home lots of money for meat and potatoes and bread and milk and clothes and shoes and...

'Helen!' A voice called from an open window on the second floor – tired and stern. 'Get the boys and come in for tea!'

Helen cupped her hands around her mouth. 'Yes, Granny!' She rounded up her brothers, eleven-year-old Murray and ten-year-old Hugh.

---

[2] burn (noun): a stream

As the perpetually hungry children hurried up the stairs, a delicious smell wafted out to greet them. Granny had managed to buy their ration of bacon and they gobbled it down gratefully with a slice of bread and some watered-down milk.

'Is there any more, Granny?' asked the youngest.

Helen would likely have been furnished with a 'skelp roond the lug'³ for asking such an impertinent question, but to the golden boy Granny only said, 'Sorry Hughie, that's the lot son.' She was still on her feet, working away now at the ironing. Without looking up, she said to Helen, 'Take some milk to your mother.'

Helen rose, filled a cup and took it to the only bedroom. Since mum had fallen ill, only she and Granny slept there, while the children shared a bed in the kitchen.

Mum's emaciated frame was almost entirely spent. She had undoubtedly carried on as long as possible without acknowledging the disease. Even when the night sweats had started, she had justified it and carried on; finally Granny had caught her coughing up blood. She was sent to bed. There was no arguing with Granny.

Helen was anxious to hear whatever news the doctor had delivered that day, but mum didn't stir. Helen kissed her gently on the cheek, and quietly laid the milk on the bedside cabinet, never to be touched.

Shaking her head, Helen dropped the picture on the bed and began to pace. Why dredge that up at a time like this? There was no use moping. What was the point? When someone's gone, they're gone. You just get on with things. And why in the world, after all these years, was she still thinking of mum when things got tough? Unaware that her daughter was listening, she stopped pacing, looked at the picture one more time, and allowed herself to say, 'I miss you,' before tidying it neatly away.

Meredith

Nathan sits behind his closed bedroom door with earphones in, his chin resting on his bony knees. The argument has resumed in the kitchen. His playlist is currently on *Human* by *Rag 'n' Bone Man*.

He closes his eyes and moves his head along with the beat, mouthing the words.

But I'm only human after all,

---

³ a skelp roond the lug: a slap around the ear

I'm only human after all,
don't put your blame on me.
Don't put your blame on me.

He concentrates hard on the song, screwing up his eyes.

Downstairs, Nathan's mum shouts, 'This is *your* responsibility Gordon, that's what we agreed!' She's pointing at his chest. She's tall and slim, with long blonde hair—she should be beautiful, but her face is contorted with bitterness.

Gordon grabs her wrist and pushes her arm away. 'I said I'll sort it, all right?'

'That's great Gordon! When and how are you going to "sort it"?'

'I'll sort it!'

'What, you going down to the bookies with your last tenner? Going to sort everything out, big man?'

He bangs the table with his fist. 'Shut it, Laura! Just shut it!'

Laura speaks with resigned bitterness. 'Damn it, Gordon. How am I supposed to come up with five hundred quid?'

Gordon steps out and slams the back door, hard.

Laura lets out a howl of frustration.

Nathan lip-syncs.

Oh, some people got the real problems
Some people out of luck
Some people think I can solve them
Lord, heavens above
I'm only human after all...

Nathan turns the music off and listens. The only sounds now are his mother's sobs. He rocks gently back and forward, humming the tune he was listening to. He sings quietly *I'm only human after all, don't put your blame on me.* His pitch is perfect—I wonder if anyone's heard him sing.

With a deep breath, Nathan grabs his bag and tentatively ventures downstairs and through the kitchen.

Laura looks up and smiles, wiping her tears hurriedly. 'Off out, son?'

'Yeah.' He pretends not to hear Laura asking where he's going and who with, as he strides off into the street-lit evening.

He walks for a couple of miles right into Princes Street; he must be freezing in his T-shirt. Then he goes into McDonald's, and buys a cheeseburger from the 99p menu. He sits in the corner, nibbling it slowly. A group of laughing youths comes in, and he sinks down in his seat. Once they pass by, he ducks out so they don't see him. He walks back the way he came, hands stuffed in his jeans pockets. My heart goes out to this forlorn boy—he's far too young to be so lonely.

The universe didn't put him in the library just for Alfie's sake, I suppose.

Gordon

It was early, but Gordon was already quite drunk. He'd spent his last ten-pound note on a half bottle of whisky and walked the streets. Laura's guess at his plan for coming up with the rent was irritatingly accurate; although, if she'd known he actually *did* have a tenner she'd have had it off him. And the way she'd sarcastically called him 'big man'. It rubbed salt into an open wound: his failure as a man. A man should be able to provide for his family.

He was supposed to pay his wife eight hundred a month for the rent. This time he had come up with three hundred. He wasn't proud of it, but there was so much pressure. He had been paid, but he was in so much debt that the money was spent before it was earned. She didn't know what that was like, damn it! She didn't understand.

Laura insisted on keeping her finances separate: no shared accounts. She took care of the other bills herself, and paid Gordon's rent on to the landlord. Laura didn't know that—while the landlord would tolerate a certain amount of arrears—some of Gordon's other debts were a bit more pressing. The interest was crippling him. But all she did was nag, nag, nag.

Gordon was so sick of being reminded of everything *she* had to pay for: food, school stuff, the phone bill, this for the boys, that for the boys. He paid more than the rent when he could. If he had anything spare, it went to the housekeeping.

A body thumped into the side of him and interrupted his reverie. He was shoved into a close and up against a wall before he could even see who had him. It was a big man, even compared to him, and not one he'd seen before.

'Gordon. Message from Vic for you.' Vic was a low-life loan shark. 'You owe two hundred.'

'What the f—' Gordon doubled over as the messenger punched him in the gut. He coughed and spat on the ground. 'Look, I've already paid it for this month.' The next punch got him in the jaw, and he almost fought back before thinking better of it.

'Payments went up. Now you pay four hundred. You've got one week.' The man left Gordon in the close, seething.

Gordon didn't see his old pal Brian waiting around the corner for the thug. He knew nothing about the nod or the money that changed hands. He staggered out of the close, blinking under the glare of the streetlights. He rubbed his jaw.

If he only had some cash to get him started, he could be in the bookies right now, turning things around. He often placed bets online, but Laura had found him out again. Nag, nag, nag. Just one big win was all he needed. He just needed to start winning again.

Gordon weighed up his two options for the evening: stay out till late and slip quietly into bed, or go home and give the bitch a piece of his mind.

'Hey, Gordo!' There was Brian across the road, having a smoke outside the pub. Laura didn't approve of him, though they'd known each other since school. Before Gordon knew it, Brian's arm was around his shoulder. 'How are you, bro? Haven't seen you in ages! You don't look great pal. Come on, I'm buying you a beer!'

Without a word, Gordon allowed himself to be steered across the road and into the warmth.

Meredith

Nathan's father sits in a dark corner away from the bar, deep in conversation with another man. Gordon looks to be in his early forties; he's tall and well-built. He might be quite handsome but for a brow creased by habitual frowning. I can't decide if his eyes are grey or green, but there's an intensity to them that frightens me. His ginger stubble doesn't quite match his thick brown hair.

The other man is short and weedy, with shifty eyes. He says, 'You're a delivery driver already, pal. It's just exactly the same. You pick up a package, you drop it off. But the money...' The man grins and rubs his fingers and thumb together. 'You can make a month's wages in a day or two.'

Gordon sits straight, sobers up fast. The crease on his forehead disappears and his face becomes animated. 'I am skint Bri, no joke. Skint and scunnered.' [4]

'Well, this is the ticket. You just keep your day job, and do an extra delivery or two at night. It's easy...Look at me, pal. If I can do it, so can you.' Bri places a hand on Gordon's arm, an earnest look on his face. 'Think about it.'

'Don't need to. Sign me up bro. I'm in.'

The truth that flows through me for Gordon is urgent and intense; it grips me like a vice. It's not specific, just a feeling—utter dread, in the pit of my stomach.

Tell him no. Change your mind, before it's too late! This is a bad decision—think of your family. Turn back. Turn back!

My warnings fall on deaf ears, and I'm left holding the stranger's burden. It's like that moment in a movie when you know the killer is in the house, right on the other side of the door. You shout at the victim 'don't go in there, you idiot!' But they can't hear you—they're already reaching for the handle.

I can't let Gordon open that door. I must make him listen! I'm going to save him.

I spend another night whispering with Michael. We come in the silence when the living stop and rest. Are they listening? Is it possible that I could ever learn to make a difference in the world?

Gordon staggers home and creeps into bed. He lies on his back with his eyes open, a hopeful grin dancing across his face, then gradually drifts off to sleep.

Laura is full of anger; she needs to remember why she loves Gordon. Michael doesn't know, but suggests it to her dreams by whispering questions. *How did you meet Gordon? What made you fall in love with him?* Her breathing slows down, and her energy feels more positive. She smiles and turns over, mumbling something.

I ask Michael, 'Do people remember their dreams?'

'Only vivid ones, or maybe the last one of the night. Sometimes they forget the specifics, but the feeling lingers.'

---

[4] skint: short of money; scunnered: fed up

Michael takes me to visit Andy, a man he watches over. Andy's older than me, but younger than my old folk—I guess mid to late sixties. He has a good head of grey hair. Michael's presence throws a warm light on Andy's sparsely furnished one-bedroom flat. Pictures of a boy at various ages take pride of place on his walls and surfaces.

Michael says, 'Andy has nightmares most nights.'

'Can you stop them?'

'No. If a man's haunted, he's haunted for a reason. You can only try to help him in the moment.'

Tonight, Andy sleeps fitfully. His hair and forehead are damp with sweat.

Michael asks me to try feeling his energy.

Is this a test? I don't have a clue what I'm doing; still, I stand close to Andy, and close my eyes. At first, all I feel is anxious. What am I doing here? How can *I* do what Michael does?

'You need to get on his wavelength,' Michael says. 'It's like tuning into the same frequency. You'll sense it.'

I try again, listening to Andy's breath. It's a restful feeling, concentrating outside of myself. Just as I consider taking a guess, something shifts within me, and I know I'm on Andy's wavelength. I'm gripped by fear so suddenly that I open my eyes, flinching back into myself as if I've touched something hot.

Michael smiles. 'You found him. What's he feeling?'

Steeling myself, I find my way back to Andy, more easily this time. 'A sense of foreboding? He knows something horrible is coming, and he doesn't want it to happen.'

'Yes—that's good. Anything else?'

I want to get out of Andy's head, but I force myself to go a little deeper. The fear intensifies, white-hot now, and I gasp. 'He's powerless to stop the thing from happening. It's inevitable.'

Now I'm back to just being me, and it's strange to say I'm relieved. My own familiar hopelessness is ever present, but not terrifying.

Andy speaks in a strangled whisper, his head turning from side to side. 'No, Brunco, no!'

Michael says, 'Here it comes.'

Andy takes in a sharp breath and sits bolt upright. He swears, shivering and exhaling in sharp bursts as he gets control again. He gets up for a glass of water; he looks exhausted from more than lack of sleep. His eyes stare towards a corner of the kitchen, focussed on nothing, and his half-open mouth takes weary, reluctant breaths. He looks like he might cry if he had the energy.

Michael says, 'His nightmares are memories. Whatever he dreamed about, he's still seeing it.' Andy gives himself a shake, and turns his attention to one of the photos—a young man in a graduation gown, holding a scroll. His grim-set features break into a fond smile that reaches his eyes.

Michael whispers *peace* to Andy.

I suggest a book as a distraction; it often worked for me.

Andy has one, *The Boy on the Bridge*, half-finished by the bed. Distractedly, he reads the same paragraph several times before drifting back to sleep. But it's not the sleep of the content, nor—if I'm right—the innocent.

Next, we visit my Aunt Lizzie. She's sleeping peacefully in her immaculate bedroom. Her slippers sit together on the floor, perfectly lined up for her to step into when she wakes. Her beauty products and jewellery stands sit neatly on her dresser. She has regular beauty treatments at the salon, and gets her hair done twice a week. Why does she still need all this stuff?

She's so energetic, you wouldn't think she was eighty. But her wrinkles give it away, especially without the make-up—I haven't seen her bare-faced for years. Does she know I'm dead yet? I'm not sure it would affect her sleep. She never was much of a worrier—she's too efficient for that.

I know mum is my responsibility; I'm torn between wanting to see her, and dreading facing it. She's fine, I know she is. And the finer she is, the more it'll hurt.

So I procrastinate, checking on Stan. He isn't sleeping and still seems anxious. I'd like to see him recovered, but I really did a number on him. He's fidgeting a lot, that leg jittering for all it's worth. There's a Star Wars film on, but I don't think he's really watching it.

I do my best to help Michael calm Stan's restless soul. I feel like an idiot whispering 'peace'—not that it seems remotely foolish coming from Michael. I think it's because peace eludes me. I step back and let Michael help him.

We go from Stan's brother's place to the old folk's home. I can come here every night now if I want to, and no one can say I'm unfit for work. Well, Michael could I suppose, but it would be a different kind of unfit and a different kind of work. Fiona sits in the same chair as last night, but she's fallen asleep. She's unfit for work too, in a much worse way than me. There's nothing wrong with her health; she's a carer who doesn't care. She cuts corners at the cost of people's dignity.

At first, I would go quietly behind her, doing the work she'd missed, until that day with Irene. The poor old soul smelled strongly of stale urine, and of course she couldn't tell me anything. But I found out. Fiona had been ticking her chart every day to say she'd taken Irene for a shower, but she'd done nothing of the sort. I wasn't convinced Irene had been given so much as a clean set of underwear in days.

Irene's daughter Sandra was on holiday, so Fiona must've thought no one would notice or care. Wrong. I had never been so livid! I saw to Irene first, but I knew I had to speak up. Fiona was my senior, so I couldn't discipline her myself. I could go above her head, but in the end, I decided to tell Sandra and let her make a complaint. Of course, the manager had to interview me when the complaint came in.

Fiona knew who'd shopped her. After that, she only spoke to me to criticise or bark orders. She was never off me about how slow I was, and bothered management until they decided to assess my 'fitness for work'. That was the beginning of the end for me; I really couldn't live without my work. Not that Fiona would understand—she just wanted me out of the way so she could neglect my old folk.

I visit each of them, but the night isn't done yet. I've run out of excuses, so I go home. There's no rush of air this time, but I can feel the same dark influence in the bedroom that I felt downstairs earlier.

Even in sleep, mum exudes irritation. No doubt my suicide has inconvenienced her. She's going to have things to organise, but after that she's free, isn't she? Or is she irritated for a different reason? Is it because she can feel my presence and wants me to leave? Is there anything I can do now that'll please her? Was there ever? I don't know the answers, so I don't try to whisper. Michael puts a hand on her head, but I don't know what he's doing, and I don't ask.

After a while he seems to notice my discomfort.

'There's something I want to show you,' he says. 'It's a skill you'll be able to learn with time.' I hope he doesn't ask me to do anything difficult. He offers me his hand, and I find the squeezing sensation less nauseating than I expect.

We're in the bedroom of an older man, sleeping.

'He's a grieving widower,' Michael says. 'If you can picture the dead who've gone on, you can give them and their loved one a gift. It's a one-off gift, whose purpose is to comfort, and allow a last goodbye.

'By concentrating on the dead, you can bridge the gap from them to their loved one, allowing them to visit in a dream.'

'Wow. How—'

'You channel the loved one's longing to summon the dead from their far away places. When done successfully, it's draining. I need to warn you—afterwards, I'll drift, and I'll need to be still and quiet for a while. Okay?'

'Okay.'

'I know his wife, Stella, well enough to picture her clearly. I'm going to do that now.' He closes his eyes and concentrates. He waits patiently with his hands outstretched until the crackling and buzzing starts, like sparks in the darkness. At first it's like someone flicking an empty cigarette lighter, then there's a little blue light, then thin lines branch out from the light, like static electricity. The centre grows brighter and larger until it's as big as Michael himself.

A stout woman appears in the light, and smiles at Michael. She doesn't come all the way into the room, but stays there as though she's part of the light. Her eyes close.

Michael says in a strained whisper, 'They're talking now.' They're communicating one spirit to another; we don't hear the conversation.

Five or ten minutes pass before Stella's eyes open, glistening. She mouths, 'Thank you' to Michael, and melts back into the light.

Michael's hands drop to his sides as the light folds away and disappears. He flops down onto the floor, and I look out the window. I'm grateful to see dawn approaching — I won't need to humiliate myself trying this tonight.

Part Two
The Suicide Notes

CHAPTER 6

Helen

Lizzie passed Helen her cup. 'How are you holding up, darling?'

Helen shrugged. She wasn't in the mood for conversation.

'You poor thing. You've had such a difficult life. Your parents, Pottsy, your brothers, and now this? I hardly know what to say.'

Lizzie was right; things had been tough. At least Helen's parents left her against their will. She didn't care much for her brothers anyway. Pottsy and his child, well, they *chose* to leave her. Helen shook her head slowly, remembering, while Lizzie sipped her tea in silence.

Pottsy. He 'disappeared' in 1963. Helen snorted—'disappeared'—that made it sound like some cheap magic trick. As though he'd put on a fancy ring and evaporated in a theatrical puff of smoke. She had never suspected him for a moment. At first, she had actually been worried about him. She had waited, keeping his tea warm for as long as possible. She had put the little one to bed and phoned the office; perhaps he was working late and there had been a mix-up. But there was no answer. By nine-thirty she was imagining something terrible had happened. She hadn't waited; she'd made the stupid mistake of reporting him missing.

Two policemen had arrived at the house a couple of hours later. There was a Sergeant, a tall man who looked about ten years Helen's senior, and a young Constable. The Sergeant did the talking.

'Now, Mrs Potts,' he said. 'Has your husband never come home late on a Friday night before?' A smile played on his lips.

'No.'

'I see. Where does he normally drink?'

'He doesn't.' She had glared at the condescending cretin, then glanced briefly at the young Constable, who looked at the floor.

'Was this morning the last time you saw your husband, Mrs Potts?'

'Yes.'

'And how are things between the two of you?'

She had answered with a cold, insulted stare.

'Did you argue this morning?'

'No. We didn't argue.' Was it an interrogation?

'Very well.' The Sergeant had sighed, taking out his notebook with an air of reluctance. He'd taken down details about her husband: where he worked, his normal movements. 'Is there anything missing from the house? Clothing, for example?'

It hadn't occurred to Helen to check. She wasn't stupid, mind you. 'I wouldn't think so, but I'll check. Excuse me a minute.'

To her astonishment and horror, half of his clothes were gone, along with his passport and most of their savings. Three years of marriage were put to rest with a short note, which he'd left in the tin that housed their cash. It said, 'There's someone else. I can't pretend anymore. I'm sorry.' Mortified, Helen had pocketed the note, determined not to embarrass herself any more than necessary in front of that smug Police Sergeant.

She'd returned to the sitting room, trying not to look flabbergasted. 'There are clothes missing, and money, and his passport.'

The Sergeant said aloud, 'I'm sorry, Mrs Potts. It seems that your husband has left of his own accord.' However, the way he'd shut his notebook and stood up said, 'What did I tell you, you stupid cow? I'm not surprised he's walked out on you. Thanks for wasting our time.'

Even now, her cheeks flushed when she thought about it. Well. It was what it was.

There had been so many questions, but she couldn't think of them in that moment. All she could think of was getting the officers out of the door before her face became any redder. The sheer humiliation! That was what she hated him for more than anything.

'How about a walk, darling, if you don't feel like talking? Bit of fresh air?' Lizzie's voice yanked Helen back to the present.

Fifty-odd years, and every time she thought about that night, it still seemed like yesterday.

Stan

By the time Stacy arrived at the busy café on Morningside Road, Stan was on his second coffee and beginning to think she wasn't coming. She was working but had agreed to meet him for lunch on the understanding that times were flexible. He grinned, led her to the table he'd bagged in a cosy corner and pulled out a chair.

Stacy raised her eyebrows. 'How chivalrous,'

Stan frowned as she sat down—it didn't sound like a compliment.

He scanned the menu hurriedly and decided. Then he pretended to peruse it, throwing stealthy glances at Stacy. While she was busy choosing, he took in her features more fully.

Stacy's skin was clear and smooth. She was pale—typical Scot. Stan preferred women to look natural. There was nothing worse than fake tan and heavy makeup—might as well go for an Oompa Loompa. Stacy was wearing a little makeup, but it was subtle and accentuated her gorgeous eyes. There was a small scar above her left eyebrow, and she wore a tiny nose jewel.

'Have you eaten here before?' Stacy interrupted his observations.

'Yeah, the food's great here. Aw smell it, I'm Hank Marvin.' A pink-faced waitress appeared and took their order.

Stacy took a few moments to zone out, watching the general hubbub, and Stan picked up where he'd left off. Her chestnut hair was braided to one side, and the pleat hung over her shoulder. He wondered how it would look down. A tattoo peeped out from under the collar of her uniform; a Celtic design—classy.

His eyes wandered lower, trying to decipher her body beneath the uniform. She was quite petite, definitely slim, but beyond that, a mystery.

She must've felt him watching; she looked at him with a start.

His eyes darted back to her face, betrayed by his hot cheeks. He tried for a charming smile, sighed and said, 'You've got incredible mincers, you know that?'

Stacy looked at him quizzically, and the waitress appeared with her diet coke.

'You know, mince pies—eyes.'

Her expression moved from dawning comprehension to amusement.

Stan took a sip of coffee.

'Feeling a bit more human?' Stacy asked.

Stan nodded and shrugged.

'You've had quite a trauma—it was selfish of that woman to involve you in her suicide.'

'How could she think of me? She was that desperate to get out, poor soul. Did you hear a name?'

'Meredith Potts.'

'Well, there's a silver lining to every cloud. If she hadn't done what she did, I wouldn't be sitting here with you.'

Stacy shrugged. 'Happy coincidence, I suppose.'

'How d'you know it isn't fate?' He kept his tone jovial, but he was quite serious.

'I don't believe in that stuff.' The waitress brought their toasties, masking the conversation-stopper.

Stacy said, 'So, I still don't know anything about you, except that you're a bit of a pansy.'

Stan grinned sportingly, blood rushing to his face. 'Well, I'm twenty-eight. I'm a born and bred Londoner. That's where I live, but I stay up here a lot, with my brother and his trouble.'

Stacy looked bemused again.

'Trouble and strife—wife.'

'Ah, got you.' Stacy smiled. 'Question. Are you going to confuse me with rhyming slang all the time?'

'I won't tell you any porkies, love. It'll be worse on the dog 'n' bone. You'll catch on though. Don't get your Alan Whickers in a twist.' He had her laughing out loud by the time he'd finished. The Cockney rhymes were a great ice-breaker, and Stan couldn't resist them. Sometimes he made up new ones just for fun.

Mischief flashed across Stacy's face as she thought of her comeback. 'Awa and bile yer heid, ya chancer, or ye'll get a skelp! Ye've nae business getting folk up tae high doh wi' yer shitey English blethers!' [5]

---

[5] Scots vernacular roughly translated: 'Go away and boil your own head, you upstart, or I'll slap you! You've no business winding people up with your unimpressive English babbling.'

One or two heads turned as Stan roared with appreciative laughter.

'Brilliant! Think I've met my match. We're not gonna do England/Scotland bashing are we?'

Stacy shook her head, smiling.

'Cool. I love Scotland, actually. My favourite thing is the hills. And my least favourite—the ruddy midges.'[6]

She snorted her agreement. 'Hobbies?' She demanded, one eyebrow raised.

'Well, if I'm honest...I am a bit of a potato—potato and leek—geek. I mean, I might own a few fantasy books and films.' He looked sheepish. 'There may be one or two Star Wars movie replica items, y'know, lying around the house.'

'No way! I love Star Wars! I want to see this stuff.'

'That's all right then,' Stan joked to hide his relief. 'You've passed the test. You can get a second date.'

'What? Is this a date?' she asked with exaggerated surprise.

'I hope so.' He smirked.

Stacy smiled generously, and for the first time, Stan noticed the dimple that appeared on her left cheek.

She asked, 'So, when do you want to bungee jump with me?' There was a playful glint in her eye.

Stan blanched. He didn't want to pass up the chance to impress her, but what he'd said before was perfectly true: heights terrified him. He'd genuinely rather eat his own faeces than attempt a bungee jump, even with Stacy.

'I'm just teasing.' She giggled. 'Your face, though!' Although it had only been twenty-five minutes, there was a beep from Stacy's pocket. 'Crap. We have a shout. I've got to meet my partner at the taxi rank. Sorry.'

As Stacy strode off with the remains of her lunch, Stan called, 'See you soon, yeah?'

She waved an acknowledgement without turning back.

There was no time for the kiss he'd already imagined. Annoyingly, she'd slapped a tenner on the table before he could insist on paying.

---

[6] The highland midge is a small mosquito-like insect common to Scotland, universally hated for its tendency to swarm and bite humans.

Meredith

I want to make sure Stan's okay; I didn't mean to force this horror upon him. Michael takes me to him, and he's gone to lunch with Stacy! Wow—he moves fast.

This is a different kind of people-watching. I used to watch from a distance, but now I can get close. I hear the whole conversation, see every blink, every twitch, the slightest reddening of the cheek. The man's quite traumatised—he's stoic, but it's written all over his face.

I like Stan—the way he talks, his cheeky grin, the twinkle in his eye. He's a gentleman, a genuine sort of person, and funny. Red-blooded male too, but I don't suppose I should hold that against him.

She is beautiful after all—so slim. What must it be like, looking like that? It must feel good having men look at you in that way. The closest I ever got to that was more of a sneer, now that I think back. When Stan looks at Stacy, it's like a flower turning towards the sun. He wants to get to know her better, no doubt. She's harder to read, but she must be interested if she's here. I want to help him if I can.

Alfie may be a lonely soul, but he comes home to the most loyal friend a man can get. She's a golden Labrador called Shirley. She goes everywhere with him other than work and sits faithfully at his feet when he's home. He talks to her in an easy way; she makes a wonderful confidant.

Shirley loves Sunday. Alfie takes her for a long walk and doesn't leave for work. She's allowed to wander as far as she wants in The Meadows, one of the city's green areas, though she never ventures further than a stick's throw from her beloved master. She doesn't run—it's more of an amble, so I suppose she's getting old—but she seems to enjoy the exercise. Alfie rewards her regularly with gentle attention.

I can see how a dog works for him – no need for conversation, no awkwardness, no expectations. She simply loves him. It makes me wonder why I never had one. Of course, it's mum; she isn't a dog person. I used to ask for one all the time, but she wouldn't budge. Still, Ginger wasn't bad company when he was around.

Laura seems puzzled by Gordon's change of mood. After spending half the day in bed, he's now whistling around the house. She looks both surprised and annoyed when he slips his arm around her waist and kisses her. She makes no attempt to return his affection.

'Gordon, what's going on?'

'What's going on?...I've decided things are going to get better. I promise.'

'Well, your promises aren't worth much, I'm afraid.'

His volume rises a little. 'They will be, soon.'

Laura considers him with a sarcastic pout, hands on hips.

Gordon puts his hands up. 'Look,' he says, 'I've decided to make a change. The company is taking on a lot of deliveries and a couple of guys moved on, so I'm going to be pulling some extra shifts. I'm determined to get a handle on things. The rent won't be a problem anymore—you'll see.'

'*Sounds* good.'

Gordon doesn't bite. He just repeats, 'You'll see,' kisses her on the cheek and heads out the door.

Laura shakes her head, shrugs and carries on sorting the laundry.

Gordon's optimism does nothing to ease the dread I feel on his behalf. If I don't stop him soon he's going to dig himself an even deeper hole.

Stan

The urge to make plans with Stacy got the better of him within hours. He typed up a text:

Enjoyed lunch xx

He deleted the second *x*, then put it back. His finger hovered over the send icon, then moved away. At last, he hit send with a small sigh, his leg jittering nervously.

Half an hour passed by, and it seemed like an eternity to Stan.

Finally, the reply came.

Me too x

He keyed the question in a flash.

Next weekend, how about it? ;-)

He hoped he could wait until the weekend.

After a short pause, the reply came:

Ok x

And that, Stan decided, was a fair start.

As we do our quiet work through the night, a thought begins to form in my mind. I remember mum looking at that photo of her parents, saying she missed them. She was close to her mum when she was young; she doesn't remember much about her father, but she thinks of him fondly. Granny used to tell mum stories about him. I wonder if it would help her if we could bring them in a dream, the way Michael did with Stella.

It takes me hours to work up the courage to ask him. 'Did you ever summon her parents in a dream, like the woman last night?'

'No.'

'She misses them. I'd like to help if I can.' I'm not sure what to take from his smile.

Michael spends hours with me, patiently teaching me how to open a pathway for the dead. I make a lot of tiny sparks in the darkness before one finally begins to branch out. It reminds me of one of those science globes with the static electricity inside. If you touch it, the thin blue lines of light connect to your fingers. I struggle to make the light grow any bigger. I would've given up ages ago, but Michael persists. He explains how to do it and encourages me to keep trying. I wish I had his confidence.

Finally, my efforts to bring my grandparents take effect. My soul locks onto theirs, and I can feel them, far away but connected—to each other, and to mum. My little science globe grows larger and brighter as I feel them coming closer. I'm awed when I see them appear in the light, angels like Michael, their faces bathed in blue glory.

They're holding hands. They close their eyes, their faces turned towards mum, and I know they're talking to her. I can't believe I'm actually doing this! Don't panic, don't lose the connection. After a few minutes, mum starts to whimper, and there are interruptions like short bursts of white noise. I concentrate hard, trying to recover control, but the link is volatile now and my strength is waning. The light begins to fold around my grandparents, their earnest faces the last thing I see before the darkness returns. I fall, thought and feeling suspended somewhere above me.

Helen

Helen felt the sun warm on her back. A hundred swallows called from the telephone wires, and the burn trickled down the slope towards the old quarry. The water was refreshingly cool on her feet, the sugar sweet round her lips. She was a little girl again, but her friends were gone and everything was tinged with a golden hue.

Then mum was there at the end of the green[7], calling her name. Helen drifted towards her; elated, confused. Mum glowed with energy. Wisps of shiny brown hair wafted in the breeze. Her sky-blue eyes shone brightly and her smile was carefree. When Helen reached her, she was pulled into an embrace that filled her with light. 'Come with me girlie. Someone very special wants to see you.'

As they approached the building, Helen knew it was the block of flats they'd lived in after the war but it looked different: spacious, and empty of other families. Inside was a great hall with tall windows, at the far end a roaring fire surrounded by comfortable chairs. As they entered, a seat near the fireplace spun slowly around and Helen's heart leapt for joy as she recognised its long-lost occupant.

'Daddy!' She ran to him. He laughed as she jumped onto his lap, threw her arms around his neck and kissed him on the cheek, just as she had always planned. His cheek was scratchy with stubble, and he smelled like a thin wisp of pipe smoke after the rain. He was glowing too, vivid and tangible against the red velvet armchair. Helen turned to her mother, and asked in a small voice, 'Why are you here?'

'We came to visit, girlie,' said her mum, while her father ran his fingers through the dark blonde hair he'd passed to his daughter, 'to tell you we're okay. Better than okay.' The woman took Helen's hand in both of hers, kneeling down to look into her eyes. 'There's no death or pain where we've gone, Helen. We came to tell you how much we love you.'

'Then why did you leave me?' The child pouted as her eyes filled up with tears.

---

[7] green (noun): a grassy area

'We had no choice,' her mother said. 'We didn't want to. We've missed you so much!' The child looked up as a tear rolled down her mother's cheek.

'This isn't real!' Helen shook her head. 'You're going to leave me again!' The room darkened suddenly and began to swim and melt around the three figures and the chair.

'It's not forever Helen!' her father whispered. 'Don't give up! Don't give up!...'

She awoke in the middle of the night an old woman, alone in the back bedroom of an ex-council house in Oxgangs, his words ringing in her ears.

CHAPTER 7

Helen
Helen had lain awake since about four, listening first to the silence, then the birdsong and early traffic, then the rain. Giving up on sleep, she plodded downstairs in her dressing gown, made a cup of tea and stuck on the television. She stared at it blankly, seeing nothing but the faces of her parents.

As reality set back in, Friday's horrifying events replayed in Helen's mind. She couldn't shake the image of Meredith's disfigured face. The two women had long co-existed without having much to say to one another. It was comfortable, mind you; Helen could rely on Meredith for company.

Without her daughter, she had nothing. Her bleak future stared out from the box in front of her. It stretched across the windows, shutting out the light. It filled the air with heaviness, making her lungs work hard just to breathe.

Then it happened. Decades of uncried tears gushed out over Helen's aged features in one morning. She could no longer hold them; they were as unstoppable as the rain lashing against the window.

Meredith
When I come back to myself, mum's bed is empty and unmade. She normally makes it the second she gets up. Michael isn't here either, but I find them both downstairs.

I can't believe what I'm seeing: mum weeping like her heart's breaking, Michael watching silently. I can't think that I've ever seen her cry, let alone like this. Her eyes and nose are red, and she's making these awful wailing noises between taking gasps of air.

What have I done? Could she be this upset because of me? No. No, that's stupid. I did her a favour when I jumped. I did her a favour, didn't I?

It must be the dream. How did it cause her all this pain? I only wanted to help, but I've gone and messed with something I didn't understand. Typical me—I've put my big foot in it again.

I can't be here; I'll only make things worse. For the first time since I met Michael, I leave him, and he doesn't follow. I return to my spot at the railway, still wishing I could make it all stop.

The wind whips the rain almost sideways, but it doesn't sting my face or soak my clothes. I sit on the bank, wondering what I'm doing with Michael, trying to help people. What do I expect to achieve? I'm too clumsy, too used to solitude.

I first started thinking about suicide when I was forced to retire early. I knew my poor health was my own fault—I had tried to lose the weight, but diets made me miserable. I would lose a stone or two, then pile it back on (with extra) before it could make much difference. Every time that happened, it was harder to try again. It was embarrassing going to the doctor, who was understandably fed up with me; I cost the National Health Service a lot of money. With each failure, Mum's disappointment was harder to take than my own. I would turn to secret eating for comfort.

Losing my job was so final—it was everything to me. I felt useless, and powerless to do anything about my declining health.

I spent a lot of time considering the best way to die. There's the Forth Road Bridge—I could've joined the hundreds who've chosen to jump over the years, and the impact of landing in the water would mean certain death. They say from 150 feet it's like hitting a concrete wall. But I knew I hadn't the guts to take the plunge. I couldn't jump from that height.

I wouldn't know how to get hold of a gun.

I wasn't keen on trying to cut myself; I probably would've passed out before I'd finished and woken up in hospital.

Hanging? I was afraid of messing it up. I imagined myself dangling grotesquely from a tree, choking but alive, stuck until I was finally discovered, and—God forbid—rescued.

Poisoning. I was tempted by that one, but I didn't want a slow, drawn-out death. If I knew how to fall asleep and never wake up, that would've been perfect. Like a lethal injection. But I imagined I'd make myself sick and, if I was lucky, die in agony. Worst case scenario—rescue. Too risky.

Whatever I did, it had to be quick and effective. I could've jumped in front of a bus or a car, but trains are faster. It seemed the surest way to get it right. Just one well-timed heave and it would all be over. I used to walk here and look for hiding places right by the tracks. The one I chose was perfect—a thicket of bushes on a high bank. I was completely concealed, and I'd only need to fall a few feet for maximum impact.

I hear the low rumble of a train in the distance and I get up. What if I could connect with it? What if I could die for real this time? No more thinking or feeling or being a burden.

The engine grows louder. I brace myself.

As the front of the train comes into view, I catch sight of the driver, and I think of Stan, I don't want to traumatise anyone else. I'm beaten. Even if I did it, I know it wouldn't work. The train passes by without incident. I sit down on the ground and weep.

But it isn't the same as living, burning, salty tears. I sniff and moan, but it's just an imitation. My tears are counterfeit.

Helen

Helen was interrupted from a profound sleep by the doorbell. She registered Lizzie's voice calling from far away. 'It's only me, darling. Can you take the chain off?'

Helen's eyes were crusty and sore—was it easy to tell she'd been crying? Embarrassed, she released the chain.

'You poor thing, you look awful!' Lizzie was good at stating the obvious. Not that she meant any harm, mind you. She bustled in, wearing full make-up as always, and not a hair out of place under her hood. 'I'll get the kettle on,' she said. She removed her coat, revealing a green tweed skirt and matching silk blouse. 'First things first.'

Before long, Lizzie was on the phone to the mortuary. 'Yes, I'm her aunt,' she said. 'I'll be taking care of all the arrangements. Would you like to verify that with her mother now?...Very well.'

Lizzie nodded towards Helen, one upheld palm assuring her she didn't need to speak to them.

Helen wanted to cling to the welcome oblivion of sleep—waking and remembering was like a punch to the gut—but she was glad of the tea. It warmed her up and brought her round.

'Now,' Lizzie was saying, 'when do you think you'll be releasing the body?'

Helen headed up to the bathroom. Someone else looked back at her from the mirror. Her long white hair was unkempt and framed a blotchy face. Her rectangular-framed glasses were filthy and did little to hide her puffy eyes. She looked too thin and too old. How could Meredith be so selfish, leaving her to deal with all this at her age?

Well, no point in wallowing. She snapped herself upright and took a cool shower, letting the water cascade over her face and soothe her eyes. This crying nonsense wouldn't help anything. There were things to be done, and they had to be faced.

Helen dressed in simple jeans and a grey woollen jumper and pinned her hair into a roll at the back of her head. Clean. Presentable.

'Ah, there you are, darling!' Lizzie smiled when Helen appeared. 'They're saying the cause of death seems to be clear-cut. The police want to check a few things first, but the body should be released by mid-week.'

Helen nodded. 'Thanks, Lizzie.'

'When do you want to hold the funeral? Shall we make it Friday, just to be safe?'

'Okay.'

'Obviously, we'll need to go over the details, but let's source a funeral director first. Do you want her buried or cremated?'

Helen drew in a sharp breath. Buried or cremated? She imagined Meredith's body rotting under the ground and made up her mind. 'Cremated.'

Meredith

The rain stops, and Michael returns to my side. I grow still, embarrassed for him to see me like this. Why is he bothering with me?

We don't speak for a long time. What is there to say? We both know it's my fault my mum's upset, and there's nothing I can do about it now. I can't even apologise to her. Then I realise, I could try. Maybe at night, when she's sleeping. I could try.

I say, 'Michael?'

'Yes?'

'Can we visit some of our—what should I call them, charges?'

'Charges is good, and yes, of course we can.' He smiles, but he's watching me carefully.

I can't shake the feeling that he sees everything, my inner ugliness laid bare before him. And yet, here he is. I don't get it.

Just as we prepare to leave, we hear voices approaching. It's Stan, with two police offers: one in a white jumpsuit and the other in uniform.

The uniformed man is talking. He's young, probably under thirty, and a bit taller than Stan. He's slim-built, with blonde hair cropped short. 'Nothing to worry about,' he says. 'It's just routine, really. We need to make sure there's no sign of a struggle, just in case.'

'Stop here, Chris.' Stan stands looking at my spot on the bank. For a second I can almost believe he's looking at me. His face turns pale as he looks around. 'That's the spot,' he says, pointing at my hiding place. 'She must've been hiding there, and dropped herself down onto the track at the last second.' He swallows. 'But she never hit the track. Her timing was...spot on. She landed on the other side, on that tree.' He points to the oak tree.

The man in the jumpsuit examines the area around my hiding place, careful to find footholds on the wet, steep bank.

Chris says, 'You stated that you saw no one else but Ms Potts, is that right?'

'Yeah.'

'Okay Stan,' Chris says. 'You've done great.'

Stan

Stan was dying to get back to work, but Sergeant Chris Bain had required his presence at the railway. Tomorrow, for sure, he'd be able to get back to some kind of normality. Sharron had offered to put him on different duties for a while until he was ready to drive again.

He'd made friends with Stacy on Facebook and couldn't resist stalking her. He flicked through her pictures and made cheeky comments. It was a chance to keep the banter alive and get to know her better between dates.

She made him look like a sad old hermit; her life was full and active. She'd taken some great holidays with her friends: skiing, cycling, and sightseeing. She'd run the London marathon and other races. She'd been tagged at various concerts and events in the last few months alone.

He was naturally curious about her relationships. He'd gone back a couple of years and hadn't seen anyone that looked like a serious boyfriend. A lead weight seemed to drop in his stomach when he found an image of her cheek to cheek with any man but him—and there was no shortage of those. Maybe, Stan reasoned, she was like him; going on dates but never finding the right person to settle down with. Maybe all that was about to change.

Meredith

Nathan spends a lot of time in the library. He's there most days after school, putting off going home. His parents both work shifts and the afternoons can be tense in the house if they're both home. Laura's been having a go at Gordon this week for going out at night. He says he's taken on extra work, and she thinks he's out wasting money. In reality, he's drinking with Brian, who's still paying.

When Nathan tires of reading, he turns to sorting the books. Alfie seems pleased. He's found Nathan a few times, rearranging the books on his own. One day he went to sort out a particular section, only to find that Nathan had already been there. Alfie didn't say much, but he brightened visibly.

At closing time, Alfie puts on his coat and scarf against the October wind. He catches a glimpse of Nathan through the window, wearing only a T-shirt, heading reluctantly home, hands in pockets. Alfie's brow furrows. Why doesn't the boy wear a jacket? Does he own one?

The image of the poorly-dressed boy troubles Alfie, who spends his evening worrying about it. He tells Shirley and asks her for advice; she doesn't offer any.

I suggest that his best bet is simply to ask Nathan about it. *You're friends*, I tell him, *after all*.

I can't budge Gordon or shake the dread in my gut when I watch him. He's so full of hope.

Brian tells him the first job is a test. If he handles it well, another will follow soon after. Brian isn't issuing the jobs—he doesn't know who the bosses are, and neither will Gordon. Brian is his recruiter, and thus becomes his only point of contact in the organisation. Brian, too, gets all of his instructions via a pay-as-you-go mobile and has only one contact.

'The stuff we deliver...is it brown?' Gordon whispers in the pub.

'What do we care what's in the packages?' Brian says in a hushed tone. 'If it's drugs, it'll get from dealers to users with or without us. What's that to do with us, eh?'

Gordon takes a swig of beer. 'Nothing. Nothing at all.'

'That's right. Let's say no more about it.'

Say no more about it? How can Gordon knowingly get involved in drugs, with two boys at home? How would he feel if it was them getting addicted to the stuff? I want to shake him, but all I can do is shout at him. I might as well save my energy; he doesn't hear me.

He just nods at Brian.

Gordon gets his first job on Monday night. The text comes in; a small package. Collect from A, deliver to B. Cash collected at B. £250—almost a week's wages. Simple. No names. No questions.

Afterwards, he stands outside the bookies, hesitating. His hand is inside his jacket pocket, fingering the envelope of cash. After a while, he passes by and goes into the pub instead. Before he's finished one pint, his face brightens and he nods to himself. He downs the last of his drink and walks purposefully back to the bookies, where he places various bets on the next day's football and horse-racing.

Laura gets in from an early shift on Tuesday to find him shouting at the telly, and eyes him suspiciously. 'Why are you so intent on that football game, Gordon?'

He feigns innocence. 'I'm not, babe. Just watching.'

'Your deliveries all done, are they?'

'Yeah, but I might get a few more tonight.'

I don't know much about betting, but I understand this much: Gordon bets £240 on eight different sporting events. He wins two, loses the rest, and ends up with £150. He celebrates his wins—I don't get it.

As Gordon drives his delivery van into Dalkeith on Wednesday morning, humming along to the radio, his new work phone buzzes in the inside pocket of his jacket. He whips it out to take a quick look. He's been given a second delivery, twice the value of the last one. He smiles and slips the phone back into his pocket.

How can I stop him from taking the job? What would happen if he didn't carry out the instructions? If I could move objects, maybe I could steal the phone, throw it in the ocean. I sit in the passenger's seat and concentrate hard on that phone. I try and try, but I can't even peel back the edge of his jacket. Each time I put my hand forward, my fingertips go right into his chest, without touching.

Reply to the text and say no, I beg him. *Tell them you've changed your mind. You don't know anything, so maybe they'll leave you alone.*

His optimistic expression doesn't change. He continues cheerfully on his way, still singing.

Why can't I make him see that he's running headlong into danger?

This time at least, he stays away from the bookies. On Thursday morning he gives the whole five hundred to Laura.

She looks inside the envelope. 'What's this?'

'500 quid—rest of the rent,' Gordon says, perhaps a little too smugly.

'And how the hell did you go from having nothing to having 500 so quickly?'

'What are you, Laura, my mother? Why can't you just be happy that I sorted it out?'

'Oh, I am. I'm delirious. It's a great delight having the rent paid only a week late. It really takes the stress out of life.' Laura's volume is rising, her face growing pink. She turns her back to him while she rants, clearing up dishes.

Gordon stands in silence, his nostrils flaring as he breathes in and out, his jaw clamped shut.

Laura whirls back round. 'You still haven't answered my question. Where did this come from? Did you borrow it?'

'No.' His teeth are gritted, and his voice comes out dangerously quiet. 'I told you already. I earned it. I've taken some extra shifts—cash in hand.'

'Cash in hand?' Laura scoffs. 'From UPS?'

Gordon's face betrays his quandary for a fraction of a second before he looks straight at Laura, attempting a smile.

'Aye.' He scratches the side of his nose. He's not a very good liar.

'Don't take me for an idiot, Gordon. At least give me a story I can believe. Did you win a bet?'

Gordon's face is contorted with the effort of deciding what to say. He looks so angry; I'm surprised Laura isn't scared of him. 'Fine,' he says. 'It was a bet.' He scratches his nose again, but Laura doesn't seem to notice.

'What the hell Gordon?' Her eyes fill up. 'How many times have you lost this much so you could eventually win it once? And what about next mo—' The back door slams hard behind Gordon. 'Damn it!'

I tell Laura I'm sorry. Although he won't listen, I promise not to give up on him. But I'm afraid I can't succeed. I'm too inexperienced, too invisible. Too weak.

At night, Michael and I move like a soft mist amongst the living, feeling their joys and sorrows, helping in whatever way we can. I never do much, but Michael's influence is strong. I've seen him visibly comfort people while they sleep. When he does that, it comforts me, too. I can feel everything that emanates from him for the living. I suppose that means he can feel my emotions just as plainly as theirs. Which brings up the question again: why does he bother with me? I suppose it must be pity.

Michael has been with me a lot since I died, but now he's beginning to leave me more to work alone; that way we can cover more ground. Why is he trusting me with people? Has he already forgotten the mess I made of things with mum? He seems to hold this unfounded confidence in me; I wish I could share it. I don't tell him any of this. It's bad enough that I didn't listen to him before I died; the least I can do is try to take his advice now.

He promises I can find him anytime; I can will myself to his side by concentrating on him. We've practised it. It's just the same as moving to a specific place. When the channel opens up, I get a vague sense of how near or far he is. Sometimes—when I have a question—he just shows up as though he's tuned into my wavelength.

We've revisited everyone I'm helping to watch over—my charges.

We asked Alfie Campbell to look out for Nathan. I don't know how, but I feel sure he and the boy will need each other. I press the image of the T-shirt clad boy into his dreams—well, I try to, anyway. I don't suppose it's a jacket that Nathan needs most, but it's a symbol.

Stan has done nothing but work and obsess about Stacy. He spends too much time on Facebook, looking at the same photos again and again. It's *patience* I whisper to Stan, and I try to invite a feeling of calm, as best I can. I'm afraid his anxiety rubs off on me a bit too; I really want things to pan out for him.

I haven't visited Andy on my own; it's out of my depth. His trauma is way deeper than Stan's impatience. I'm afraid if I came alone and tried to help, I'd be pulled into the horror of his reality. Probably I would make it worse. But Michael always knows what to do. His light and warmth can cut through anything. I don't know if he realises how much his work blesses me, too. Slowly, slowly, I feel something rubbing off on me. Something pure and good.

Gordon's out of my depth too, I suppose, but I must help him. What's the use in sensing impending disaster if I can't stop it? Michael says that sometimes people just don't listen, and there's nothing you can do. It's different for him. If someone doesn't listen to him, he knows it's on them. With me...well, maybe I make things worse. If Gordon doesn't listen, maybe whatever happens is on me.

My old folk comfort me more than I comfort them. I like to be there, sitting in the quiet with those familiar souls, especially when Fiona's off. I go there most nights, and just...reminisce. I regret that I couldn't sort myself out for them: lose weight, look after my health, and stay. But at least I can visit now. Irene is close to dying. I can feel her spirit, reaching out for my world and letting go of hers.

I know there are more pressing things to attend to. I can't put it off any longer. Michael has told me it's my funeral tomorrow. I should be there, facing up to what I've done and taking care of my family. I have mum, Aunt Lizzie, and other family members I can hardly remember. Mum fell out with them years ago. There are two uncles, an aunt and two cousins on my mum's side. I don't know anything about my father's side. We never talked about him. I suppose it would be weird to have anything to do with his family anyway, after what he did to us. I wonder if any of my relatives or anyone from work will come to my funeral. I don't suppose many will.

It's late but Lizzie is still in the house. I'm grateful for the help and support she gives mum. I suppose she has her flaws, but she's been good to me all my life. She's been good to both of us.

I try to feel her emotions, and I think she's sad or lonely—which doesn't make much sense. She could be feeling sad about my death, but as for loneliness, she's always busy and has plenty of friends. There's a positive feeling too. Something bittersweet, like pleasure and pain jumbled up together. I think she gets a lot of pleasure from helping people. She'd do anything for us.

I wait for Lizzie to leave and for mum to fall asleep. There's a chill over the house—that shadow, marking its territory. Am I imagining things, or is mum's aura weakening? It seems more transparent than before.

When her breathing tells me she's resting, I think about seeing her cry. I think about why she was crying; because the dream of her parents upset her. The dream I gave her. I wait until my breast is filled with the sorrow of my blunder, then I tell her, over and over.

I'm sorry about the dream. I didn't mean to upset you.

CHAPTER 8

Meredith

Mum wakes with a look of dawning comprehension, followed by more tears. It's so unlike her; I don't know what to think. It's getting harder to believe it's all because of the dream. Let's face it: it's the funeral.

I honestly didn't think she would mind letting me go. Sometimes, I thought she actually wanted rid of me. I've convinced myself I was doing her a favour, but what if I was wrong?

She doesn't seem pleased, relieved or even indifferent now. This is a lot to deal with, especially at her age. I suppose she always thought I'd be there to take care of her. I just never thought of her as someone who'd need taking care of; my own health was failing much faster. Still, I'm the daughter, and I forgot my duty.

If only I could hide somewhere until the consequences of my actions blow over. But will they ever? Isn't that why I'm in this mess—because I couldn't face up to things?

Mum sniffs, gives herself a little shake and starts getting ready. She drinks her tea, showers and dresses. My mum is beautiful, even at seventy-nine. She's wearing a simple black wool dress, with small heels and a grey jacket, but she looks fit for a magazine. Hardly a day goes by when I don't wish I was more like her and less like my father. Mum and I have been mistaken as sisters more than once.

She's five foot seven, with a figure to die for. She's been a size ten her entire life. Her dark blonde hair has turned white now, but it's still thick and shiny. She rolls it up expertly and pins it to the back of her head, showing off her slender neck and incredible bone structure. I don't think she knows she's beautiful. She doesn't look particularly impressed with her reflection. She never wears make-up, or does anything with her nails; she's just naturally stunning.

Aunt Lizzie is the opposite, I suppose. She's not ugly or anything—I don't mean that—but she has nothing that stands out. She's always very particular about her clothes and make-up. She regularly has her nails done and overdresses for every occasion. Today is no exception. She rings the bell and lets herself in, wearing all black—a tweed suit topped with an ostentatious hat. It's adorned with black velvet roses, a net veil hanging over her face. She's had her nails manicured for the occasion—no colour—and her brown dyed bob is straightened and sprayed in place under the hat. She's wearing a string of pearls, contrasted against her blouse, and a little corsage.

Lizzie looks short and stout at the best of times, but more so next to mum. Sometimes, I think I catch a flash of jealousy pass across her face when she looks at mum. They're different, but they're both strong and self-assured in their own way. They hold their heads high and meet your gaze; I slouch and look down. The two of them were forever on at me to sit up straight. They used to correct me about a lot of things, but that's the job of mums and aunts, I suppose.

Aunt Lizzie draws breath to speak, but her eyes fill up and she flaps a hand in front of her face to fan the tears away. She clasps her hands together and moves them forward to accentuate words, a gesture she uses when talking in earnest. 'Now, darling, everything is organised, so you mustn't worry.'

Mum nods.

'I know it's going to be awkward for you if Murray and Hugh turn up, but I'll be with you every step.'

Mum takes a deep breath and says, 'Thank you.'

Lizzie waves the *thank you* away with a little shake of her head and takes a corsage from the top of her handbag. She pins it to the lapel of mum's jacket. It matches her own, a neat bunch of tiny white roses mounted on a mess of black ribbon.

We get in the chauffeur-driven Mercedes Lizzie has waiting outside, which follows the hearse to Warriston crematorium. My body is in that car, in that rose-topped coffin we're following. This is what I wanted, isn't it? But now, faced with the shock of my own casket, it makes me sad. *This* isn't what I wanted—I wanted to sleep.

Mum stares at the seat in front, a look of determination on her face.

Lizzie sniffs and talks in hushed tones. 'I can't help thinking of my mother's funeral. One reminds you of another, doesn't it? I do miss her.'

Mum leans over and pats Lizzie's hand.

Lizzie says, 'I really am touched that you asked me to speak. I hope my remarks will do justice to our darling girl.'

'I'm sure they will.'

I don't know if I can bear it. The urge to run and hide is coming over me in waves, yet I'm curious to see my own funeral. Who turns up? What do they say about me?

Michael is already here when we arrive. My casket is wheeled to the front of the little chapel. The funeral director stands beside it, staring at the back wall with practised solemnity. Aunt Lizzie speaks quietly with the organist before sitting next to mum in the front row. The organist begins to play on low volume—hymns, most of which I don't recognise.

There's a photo of me on display by the pulpit. It's quite flattering—I look younger—but it still makes me cringe. Although it's just a mugshot, you can tell from my face that I'm obese. I like my hair though. I didn't bother to wear it down often, but that day it hung over my shoulders, perfectly straight. I remember when the picture was taken; mum, Aunt Lizzie and I were out for a meal to celebrate my birthday. My fortieth, I think.

An old couple comes in with two men following behind, one young and one elderly; they stand hesitantly at the back of the chapel. Aunt Lizzie notices them and gives mum a little nudge. I barely recognise the group, but I guess the two old men are my uncles, Murray and Hugh, and the woman my Aunt Jean. The young man must be one of my cousins, roped in as the designated driver. Mum hesitates too. We hardly ever saw them; there was some disagreement way back, but mum never told me about it.

Lizzie gives mum's hand a little squeeze, and they head to the back. Lizzie smiles and shakes hands with everyone in the group. 'Thank you so much for coming.'

Mum nods, bravely making eye contact with each of the old men. 'It means a lot. Please, sit at the front.'

The group moves awkwardly past mum and Lizzie and settles in the second row. Murray and Jean whisper quietly to one another.

'Beautiful flowers.'

'Yes, a lovely picture too.'

Their faces are kind. Murray's head is bald on top, his remaining hair white. Jean's is cut short and dyed auburn—it suits her.

My heart warms to see Kyle and Nadia from work. Kyle was my favourite colleague; he's one of the kindest people you'll ever meet. Mum and Aunt Lizzie were forever trying to matchmake us, even after I told them he was gay. Mum went so far as to suggest he just hadn't found the right woman yet! Honestly. Nadia is a good sort, too. Her English isn't the best, but she works hard and she's easy going. It was kind of them to come.

The funeral director steals glances at the wall clock every few minutes, probably wondering if this can really be everyone. Finally, he steps up to the pulpit and clears his throat.

'We are here today,' he says, 'to celebrate the life,' (he reads my name) 'of Meredith Elizabeth Potts. May she find rest, and peace to her soul. Let us pray.' The invocation sounds hollow and meaningless—he reads it from a card.

The congregation sings *Nearer My God to Thee*. For the most part, it's rotten singing; I can hear the funeral director's voice above the others, but Murray and Jean are helping. They seem familiar with the hymn, and I wonder if they go to church. I listen to the words.

Nearer my God to thee,
Nearer to thee,
E'en though it be a cross
That raiseth me.
So by my woes to be,
Nearer my God to thee,
Nearer my God to thee,
Nearer to thee.

Is there any truth in it? Am I nearer to God because of my suffering? The only evidence I can find for that is Michael—when I'm with him, I think I might be nearer to God, if there is such a thing. Or is the hymn talking about those you leave behind? Does loss change them, somehow, for the better? Maybe it's just a vague way of putting that comforting cliché: 'at least she's gone to a better place.'

Aunt Lizzie takes a moment to compose herself before she speaks. 'Helen has asked me to say a few words about our darling girl. There are a lot of things one could say about Meredith. She was talented but modest. She drew beautiful sketches—never to sell or show off—but just because she had art inside of her. She was an avid reader and probably read as many books in a year as most people read in a lifetime. Meredith was unusually quiet and observant, and a sound judge of character. She was economical with words, but what she had to say was important.

'When Meredith was little, she was fascinated by nature. She loved to walk by the beach or in the woods, finding little treasures to bring home to her mum. She adored her mother,'—doubt casts a sudden shadow over mum's face at these words—'and they had many special times together. I, too, was fortunate to spend a great deal of time with Meredith throughout her life. She was a grateful, intelligent woman.

'She seemed, for the most part, a contented person,' Aunt Lizzie's voice began to crack a little. 'Why then, did she choose to end her life the way she did? Of course, none of us can say for certain, but it's my belief that Meredith was a lonely soul. She lived for her work, and when that became too difficult, she retreated into herself. We knew she was low, but we thought it would pass. I wish we had seen it coming and done something to stop her; however, we must weather our regret and remember the good times.' She pauses to dab her eyes with a tissue.

'Of course, the most important thing to remember about Meredith is that she had the heart of a saint. Nothing was too much trouble for her. By all accounts, she was an angel to the old people she looked after.' Kyle and Nadia are nodding, bless them. 'She was a loving daughter and niece to Helen and I. It's left to us, then, to be thankful for the time we had with our darling girl.' She looks at my casket with its myriad of roses. 'Meredith, we love you.' After a little pause, she faces the front again, her eyes wet. 'Thank you all for being with us today, as we remember and say goodbye.'

Aunt Lizzie returns to her seat, the organ begins to play, and my oversized coffin is slowly lowered.

This is me, leaving mum's life forever. I watch her carefully, looking for a sign; something to prove me wrong for thinking she wouldn't miss me. How I wish I was wrong! I hold my breath, but she only stares straight ahead until a heavy curtain closes, hiding the casket from view. Her lips are tight, her back straight.

A closing hymn and a benediction later, it's all over.

I didn't think there would be anyone to miss me, and I was right. Half of the few who've been kind enough to turn up don't even know me. Lizzie's speech was kind and generous. I'm glad there was someone to speak about me that way. I only wish I could've heard mum calling me darling, or saying she loved me. I used to ask her if she loved me, and she'd say 'you know I do', which wasn't quite what I was looking for.

I think of that doubtful look on mum's face when Aunt Lizzie said I adored her. Did I ever give *her* a sign? Did I say the three words I wanted so much to hear? Panic rises within me; I don't remember saying it. Why didn't I say it? What if she was only waiting for me to go first?

After the service, mum approaches the silent group of relatives. 'Thank you for coming.'

Murray lays a hand gently on mum's shoulder, his eyes filling with tears. I never expected to see such genuine concern on his face.

It's Jean who speaks. 'Helen, we're so sorry about Meredith.'

Mum nods and pats Murray's hand awkwardly with a sad smile.

No one seems to know what else to say. Each little group has brought flowers to pay their respects. The funeral director leads the thin crop of mourners to the memorial gardens, where space is reserved for me. The stone is simply engraved:

Meredith Elizabeth Potts
1960-2017

After placing their flowers, they stand in awkward silence for a while, until mum asks for some time alone. The mourners retreat, their relief palpable. The brothers promise Lizzie they'll be in touch with mum soon. Lizzie goes back to the empty chapel alone.

Here we are, mother and daughter. We're a million miles apart standing next to one another.

Finally mum whispers, 'I'm sorry I missed your birthday.' She closes her eyes, and a tear squeezes through. A real tear this time, a sorry one.

Impotently, I whisper back, aching for my voice. *I love you.*

'I got you a present, but I forgot to give it to you. I knew you weren't able to sketch much anymore, so I thought you might try painting. I found a book all about painting with rheumatoid arthritis, and I got you a set of acrylics and brushes.'

It's my turn to cry. It sounds like a beautiful gift, and one she'd really thought about. It's incongruous with her regret of me.

Mum takes a deep breath, smiles sadly and begins a slow walk back towards the chapel. I look around for Michael, but he's slipped away. I feel the sky cloud over—though in reality it hasn't—and a chill sweeps across the gardens from mum's direction. My heart lurches at the sight of another figure, a dark shadow walking alongside mum. In a flash, I'm face to face with the creature.

It's a woman—I don't know why I expected otherwise. I don't recognise her, but her face looks strangely familiar. It's hideous – ancient-looking, grey and lined under a dark hooded cloak, and contorted in a vindictive grimace as I catch her in the act of whispering in mum's ear. She stops the instant I arrive. Her eyes are completely black, and they narrow as they turn on me. Unaware of the confrontation, mum ambles on, arms folded across her slender waist.

I glare at the shadow, and she glares back. It feels like there's no warmth left in the world. Memories start to flash through my mind. Mum sighing in exasperation. *You're just like your father.* My burned skin blistered and weeping. Binging. Kids laughing at me. My teenage crush with his girlfriend. Binging again. Aunt Lizzie's livid face when I got in trouble at work. Binging again. Layla at the care home giving me the dreaded verdict. The train getting closer. Mum crying. Something snaps.

I shout, 'No!' I think of Michael, and how he believes in me. He said I'm kind, that I did well at the care home. I think of my love for mum, and how this monster can't change it. Something powerful wells up inside me, and I shine against the darkness, beams of light issuing from my heart. 'You're not welcome here!'

The shadow recoils with a pained expression.

'She doesn't want you around.'

With a mean, determined look, the creature throws back her head and laughs. It's a hollow, humourless sound that speaks of nothing but hatred. Turning away, she hisses, 'Are you sure?' Without waiting for an answer, she implodes into a dark, dissipating fog.

Did I muster enough light to burn her? Did I really make her go away? Or did she choose to leave? The beams of light are gone now, and it's hard to be sure they were real.

Where is Michael? Seeking him, I find him at Mortonhall Crematorium, his light dimmed. It isn't the first time; he visits this place often. He always brightens up when I arrive, but I'm beginning to sense that even angels have troubles.

I say, 'Is there...anything I can do?' I doubt that *I* could help *him*, but I want to.

'You possess a generous heart, Meredith. Just being around you builds me up.'

That makes no sense whatsoever. I never had Michael down as a liar, but what he's saying can't possibly be true.

'You're learning fast. You're going to be an excellent whisperer.'

I cringe inwardly, uncomfortable with compliments, craving them at the same time.

'Your light is growing brighter every day...I'm proud of you.'

'Thank you.'

He turns back to look out across the gardens, something weighing on him. I'll find a better time to tell him about the shadow.

CHAPTER 9

Meredith

Relieved that the funeral's over with, I return to my charges. Nathan hasn't been to the library for a couple of days.

Alfie catches up with him late afternoon, sorting books. 'Where've you been?'

'Looking for a job,' Nathan says.

'You need money?' Alfie's always direct; Nathan's used to it by now.

He shrugs. 'Not really, but my mum does.'

'Don't you need some things for yourself? Like a jacket?' The boy shrugs again. 'Well, any luck with the search?'

'Nope. You've got to be at least sixteen for most jobs.'

Alfie hesitates. He wants to help, so I encourage him. *Just offer—he can say no.*

'I could...buy you a jacket, Nathan.'

The boy looks surprised.

'You can meet me tomorrow and choose something you like. You've earned it by helping me in here.'

'Okay.' The boy smiles as he moves another wayward book.

Stan is positively giddy with anticipation; he has another date with Stacy tonight. There are dark circles around his eyes, but he's cheerful. He's done well getting back to work after his ordeal. His train is heading from Newcastle towards Edinburgh again. Although he isn't driving, fear flashes in his eyes when he nears the spot where I jumped a week ago today. He looks relieved to get beyond it, and the rest of the journey passes without incident.

Gordon's getting wiser in spite of his stupidity. After making two deliveries last night, he was loaded. I've started trying to help him make better financial decisions, since I can't seem to make any headway on the job. *Pay your debts. Save up. Take care of the family.* That sort of thing.

He visited Vic's 'office' (i.e. seedy pub) and paid the extra £200 before setting foot in the bookies. He didn't bet everything this time, either. I suppose it's something.

Helen

Helen was glad of Lizzie's help but relieved to finally be alone. She didn't know what to think or how to feel. It was exhausting.

As evening fell, the DO NOT OPEN box in the back of her mind shuffled and thudded until the question escaped. It bounced around until it became impossible to resist.

'Why did you do it, Meredith? Why?'

The room didn't answer. The mantel clock ticked on, regardless. Helen's eye was drawn toward something out of place—an envelope tucked under one of the ornamental plates. Of course! Meredith's note, returned by Sergeant Jamieson. She'd intended to read it later, alone, but had forgotten it was there. Stupid. She reached for the note and opened it, trembling.

Dear mum,

I don't know what I'm living for so I've decided to end my life. I think you'll be happier without me. Sorry I couldn't be the daughter you wanted.

Meredith

Helen's hands dropped to her lap. She thought of the note that had so abruptly ended her marriage. How similarly short and to the point this new one was. She snorted in disgust at the pair of them; how alike they were!

That was a comfortable reaction—she would nurse it, let it protect her from self-recrimination. She took out *his* note and read it again, comparing the two. Yes, how alike.

It looks almost as if he's been giving her lessons. He's the expert on how to destroy me, but look here! She's caught up.

The room around her dimmed and turned cold. She shivered, turned on the gas fire and began to pace.

She thought I'd be happier without her? How dare she try to blame her selfish act on me? Typical Meredith—manipulative and attention-seeking. Thought the whole world revolved around her.

She stood close to the fire, rubbing her hands, but it didn't seem to make her any warmer.

How many times could I have taken my own life, when Meredith was young? What did I ever have to live for? Nothing since Pottsy. It was like a fairy tale, and I was like a child—I knew nothing! The fairy tale became a nightmare.

Anger propelled Helen into the kitchen. She grabbed a cup and saucer and smashed them against the tiled wall. A shard bounced back and cut the side of her hand.

They're not here, but they're still controlling me. Look what they made me do!

I hope they both rot in hell.

The light in the sitting room brightened and Helen looked up. There was no dimmer switch. The chill in her bones was gone—in fact, it was too hot. She looked at the pieces of broken china and let out a sob, sinking to the floor.

They had sweet peas on them.

Stan

Stan pressed the buzzer at exactly 7 p.m. at 6 Warrender Park Terrace. He'd been there a few minutes, taking in the street with its tall stone-built flats. Even in the dark, it seemed a lovely spot, with a park just across the road. The few seconds it took Stacy to answer seemed like minutes.

Her voice came through the intercom. 'Just come up.' The front door clicked open. When he reached the landing, Stacy was waiting in the open doorway, putting on an earring.

'Sorry,' she said. 'It's been one of those days. I'll just be five minutes.'

'No problem.' He was taking her in. 'You look gorgeous.' She was wearing a casual black dress that showed her curves off beautifully, still leaving much to the imagination. Her knee-high boots were sensible but feminine. Her dark brown hair hung in loose waves over her shoulders, the layers framing her face.

'Thanks. You're looking good as well.' She winked. Stan had chosen his best jeans and a dark grey shirt with small checks. He'd had a good shave and was wearing a new Dolce & Gabbana fragrance. He'd put a little putty in his hair and teased his curls out a bit, but not too much; he didn't want to look like a poser.

Stacy ushered him into the living room; he sat down while she finished getting organised. He examined the room, trying to ignore his sweaty palms. He played a little game, guessing which pictures and objects belonged to Stacy and which to her flatmate. The place was uncluttered and practical, with a few framed black and white photographs: a close-up of rose petals, a sunset seascape with figures silhouetted at the shoreline, a portrait of a very old face, smiling. There were a few candles dotted around, and basic but comfortable furniture: a sofa, two chairs, a coffee table and a TV.

'I like your photos,' he said as Stacy returned. 'Where did you get them?'

'It's just a hobby of mine.' She shrugged and blushed.

'No way! You took these?'

She nodded.

'They're amazing—really professional.'

'Thanks.' She took his hand and pulled him up. 'Let's get out of here before my head gets any bigger!'

Helen

Helen's mind went blank as she sat curled up against the kitchen units. She took a tissue from her sleeve to blot the blood from her hand. Silent tears ran down her cheeks. When the next thought came, it made her uneasy.

Did Meredith really feel unwanted?

Her daughter *had* been wanted—very much so—until it had all gone wrong. They had called her Merry when she was a baby, before it happened. Helen adored that little bundle of joy when she thought they were safe with Pottsy. She had expected to have other children and grow old with Pottsy at her side.

Becoming Mrs Potts had given Helen a new hope for the future. She no longer needed to work, which took a bit of getting used to. She was provided for most comfortably.

She should have known; it had seemed too good to be true. But young love is blind and naive. He had seemed the genuine article, the adoring husband and father.

There had been a period of a few months—when she was pregnant with Meredith—when they hadn't had sex. He'd said it wasn't safe for the baby, but maybe he found her unattractive pregnant. She'd let it go, confident that he would come back to her after the birth; and he did. However, prior to his disappearance, he'd seemed disinterested in sex again. She'd wait for him to make a move, turning on the charm; he'd avoid it, making excuses. He was tired, it had been a tough day at work, and so on.

She didn't think much on that until he left, and Lizzie finally shared a secret. She was tight-lipped, but Helen got it out of her.

Seemingly, about a year after their marriage, Pottsy had kissed Lizzie. She hadn't seen it coming, and of course, she'd stopped him. Then, about a year before he left, he'd asked Lizzie to run away with him. He'd been drinking—something Helen believed he rarely did—and Lizzie thought he was joking until he tried to kiss her again. Of course, she backed off and refused him. He never brought it up again, and neither did she. She hadn't the heart to tell Helen at the time, until circumstance forced her to.

Helen had been stunned by her husband's duality. If he'd been willing to run away with her best friend, how many others had he tried it on with? Clearly, one of them had said yes.

Lizzie had been kind. 'Poor you! This is so unfair! You've already been through so much, darling. You deserve better.'

Helen wasn't sure then, nor was she now. *There must be a reason why people leave me. Maybe it's exactly what I deserve.*

No. Surely, it's his fault! If he hadn't left, nothing would've changed. I'd have loved him and doted on our daughter, and she might've been quite different.

But he had left. He'd left without planning anything. He'd just stopped turning up at work. The money had stopped. Helen was abruptly returned to a life of drudgery, alone with a child to support. They'd moved out of his house; Helen couldn't afford the bills. They couldn't sell it or rent it out; the title deeds were solely in his name. He had been in the very fortunate position of owning it outright, having received a sizeable inheritance from his parents. How he could just walk away from that was beyond Helen. She could only assume he'd kept significant assets concealed from her. Perhaps leaving the house was some twisted kindness on his part. In any case, Helen hadn't wanted it. She had never belonged there.

Almost overnight, she'd gone from loving and feeling loved to living with bitter disappointment. She still wished she'd never met the man; never had the child. At times, it consumed her. Little Merry had soon become Meredith, or just 'the girl'. At first a source of joy, she'd become a monumental burden.

I think you'll be happier without me. Sorry I couldn't be the daughter you wanted.

There was another voice in Helen's head now. It was strangely kind, but it hurt more than anger and blame. It rifled gently but firmly through that dusty old box in the back of her mind, where she preferred to leave certain things to rot. It pulled one of those things out, a dirty, crumpled truth squashed down out of sight. The voice smoothed out the truth until it became undeniably clear. It confronted her starkly; it would not be dismissed.

I took out my troubles on a child.

Meredith

Stan and Stacy are on a date—brilliant! It's nothing to do with me, but it's good news. The walk to the restaurant he's booked in Morningside takes twenty minutes, plenty of time to break the ice.

Stan asks, 'Were you working today?'

'Yeah. Early shift. We've been run off our feet—I'm exhausted.'

'It must be tiring, running about after fainting wusses all day.'

Her laugh is hearty and generous.

'How about you?'

'Yeah, working. I was offered a fortnight's compassionate leave, but I wouldn't do it. Better to get back on the horse, you know? I didn't want to let myself get spooked.'

'That makes sense.'

'Mind you, I'm not driving yet. They've got me doing other things. I've passed the spot twice now, and I must admit, I don't like it...'

'I don't blame you.'

'It'll get easier, though.'

'Definitely.'

'Tell me more about your day at work.'

Stacy's dealt with a cardiac arrest, a ruptured appendix and a road traffic accident today. She finishes her last story as they reach the restaurant, where they're shown to a cosy candle-lit table.

'Wow,' Stan says. 'It's a good job we're not all squeamish! What made you decide to be a paramedic?'

'Can I tell you after we order? I'm starving!'

'Great idea, love.' Stan picks up a menu. 'Let's have a butcher's.'

Stacy orders a pasta dish with char-grilled chicken breast, lemon and thyme. Stan goes for the classic lasagne. A bottle of wine is brought, and as they take their first sips, Stan repeats the question.

'Come on then, why a paramedic?'

'Well. Therein lies a tale.'

He looks intrigued. 'Go on.'

'When I was twelve years old, I had an accident.'

'Oh no! What happened?'

'I was cycling home from school and got hit by a car. I'd been cycling on the pavement, without a helmet—even though I'd been told a hundred times to wear it—and I wasn't paying attention. I crossed in front of the car. The poor woman had no time to stop.'

Stan blanches.

Stacy makes an apologetic face. 'You know how that feels.'

'Yeah. Were you hurt badly?'

'I was pretty lucky really—I broke my arm. Other than that it was just cuts and bruises, but I got the fright of my life.'

'I bet you did.'

'A passer-by sat with me until the paramedics arrived, and I thought they were amazing. I was sitting on the pavement in floods of tears, and the woman who hit me was beside herself. The paramedic who looked after me was kind. He calmed me down and made me more comfortable until my mum arrived. His name was Sean. I thought I'd be in big trouble for not wearing my helmet and not paying attention, but Sean didn't say anything. He left all that to my mum—and she gave me what for, I can tell you.'

Stan listens to Stacy talk, sipping his wine. He's captivated.

Stacy says, 'I bombarded Sean with questions the whole time. He was very patient. He explained everything as he checked me over, got me into the ambulance and strapped up my arm. He showed me how to properly clean and dress cuts. And that was it. From that day on I was determined to become a paramedic. And I *always* wear a helmet when I cycle.'

'Great story. Did you ever see Sean again?'

'Yeah!' Stacy chuckles. 'He's still on the job, so I see him quite often. He did part of my training. I think he was quite tickled to have a young protégé. Now you mention it, I think we're on shift together in the morning.'

The food arrives, looking and smelling delicious. A body definitely has its uses. I gaze wistfully as they tuck in with gusto. I catch myself ogling the melted cheese dripping off Stan's lasagne, and I'm glad Michael isn't here. Of course, if he's been watching me all my life, he knows I'm a hopeless food addict. Anyway, you can tell from a cursory glance at me—it doesn't take a mastermind.

Stacy asks about Stan's family, and he chats freely about his parents in London, and Simon, Carla and Sam.

Stan says, 'Tell me about your family.'

Stacy shrugs. 'Not much to tell. My mum lives in Aberdeen with her partner Harry, and my dad's in Glasgow.' At the mention of her dad, her face falls.

'Sorry, did I touch a nerve?'

'No, it's okay. I don't get on great with dad, that's all.'

'Any brothers or sisters?'

'Nah, just me.' She smiles unconvincingly.

Stan looks a little disconcerted, and he changes the subject. 'What's your favourite film?'

'Oh, I love loads of films.' Stacy delves enthusiastically into the topic, glad to get back to small talk. 'How could you narrow it down to just one?'

'You're right, that's impossible.'

'It totally depends on my mood. You already know I like Star Wars – also Harry Potter and The Lord of the Rings.'

'Yes!' Stan makes a fist and pulls it in towards his body in a jubilant gesture. 'You're a potato, too! I knew it!'

Stacy laughs. 'Geek?'

'Got it in one, love. See, I said you'd catch on...'

CHAPTER 10

Meredith

Being with Stan and Stacy makes me feel like there may be a point to my existence. The way he looks at her when they're together is quite rare. He makes her laugh, which must take her mind off the serious work of the day. He makes me laugh, too, and it makes me feel...lighter, somehow.

That's how I'm feeling when I catch up with Michael in a pub, until I take in Andy, drowning his sorrows. He has his own private raincloud following him, impervious to the surrounding environment. Andy's looking at the football game on TV, but I don't think he's watching it.

Michael perceives a question on my mind. 'What is it?' he asks.

'I want to know how to move things. Gordon won't listen to me, but if I could physically *do* something, he'd notice...Will you teach me?'

He doesn't answer straight away. 'It takes a long time and a lot of practice to learn that. We aren't supposed to make ourselves known to the living, so we must be careful about what we touch. We also mustn't interfere with anyone's freedom to choose. Forcing Gordon's hand isn't the answer. He's responsible for his choices, not you.'

I try to take in what he's saying, but it's hard to believe I'm not responsible. I mean, believe with my heart—my head understands. I nod slowly. 'Will you teach me?'

'We'll make a start on it soon.'

I realise we're not the only spirits here. I hadn't noticed them at first, hanging around like vultures. There are several of them, watching the living hungrily. They pay no attention to Michael and me.

'What are they doing?' I ask.

'Wasting their time.'

His vague answer only piques my interest.

Michael indicates Andy. 'He needs companionship. I've been working on this for a long time, and tonight I've brought someone here who might just be his salvation.'

I notice something strange about an old man in the corner. There's a gap in his aura, which seems to grow as he drinks. A ghostly figure standing near dives through the gap, and another face morphs into the old man's. There are two men drinking now—two men in one body. Drinking like they're dying of thirst.

Andy

At first, Andy didn't register the woman talking to him.

'Titch?' She said again, 'Is that you?'

'Bloody hell!' He jumped to his feet. 'It's a long time since any bugger called me that!' He took in her attractive face and bright eyes, and was immediately sorry for his language—incongruously sober, too.

'Remember me?' She asked.

'You're familiar lass...' He discerned the petite build, the wry smile. 'Nance?'

'Aye, it's me!' She laughed and sat down opposite him.

He relaxed a little—Nancy came from his neighbourhood. She had been like one of the boys when they were young kids. Later, as teenagers, they'd taken a shine to one another and she'd become something more to him—much more. Then she'd disappeared, he never knew where.

'I've never seen you in here before,' he said. 'I think I would've known you.'

'I don't normally come here, but a friend of mine's looking for bar work, so we've been all over the place tonight. Here she is now.'

Andy smiled politely, but he forgot the name as soon as he heard it, and was glad when the friend got a taxi home and left them to catch up. He bought Nancy a drink—she only wanted a coke.

'It's been a *long* time,' he said. 'How are you? Where've you been?'

'Here and there.'

'When you left Gracemount...'

'I went to work as a nanny for some toffs in the borders. My dad packed me off with hardly a days' notice. That's why—'

'You never said goodbye?'

'I'm sorry, Andy.'

Now it made sense. Nancy's dad had never liked Andy. No doubt he'd made it clear when he'd packed her off that Titch Laidlaw was strictly off-limits.

'Who could blame him?' Andy said aloud.

'Who?'

'Your dad—for sending you away.' He met her eyes. 'Away from me.'

Her silence confirmed it.

'I turned things around a long time ago, Nance.'

'You didn't need to change. Not for me.'

Andy scoffed. 'Trust me, I did. You must've had blinkers on.'

'I knew you were in a bit of bother with the Graham brothers.'

Andy shivered at the name. 'Aye. But I got out. There was trouble one night, and I was the only one caught. I never sold Brunco out—I did time for him. He owed me a favour for that, otherwise, he never would've let me go.'

'I remember him. "Mad Brunco."'

'D'you know what earned him that nickname?'

'No.'

Andy gave a derisive snort. 'Neither do I. It could've been so many things. It was a playground jibe that stuck, and he wore it like a badge of honour. *You* kept away from all the trouble, Nance, you don't know how bad it was.'

He was surprised by her look of concern when she said, 'Tell me.'

Andy gazed through everything in his line of sight, remembering. 'Hibs were playing Hearts at Easter Road one Saturday.[8] We gathered after the football match, about eighty or ninety of us, intent on trouble with the Hearts gangs.

'We stormed Princes Street that night—it was mayhem. The shops were still open when the battle started, and we scattered the regular folk. Fists, bricks, knives—whatever we could get our hands on. We were outnumbered but we didn't care.

---

[8] Hibernian FC is a professional football club based in Leith (in the north of Edinburgh). Home matches are played at Easter Road stadium. Nickname: Hibs; Heart of Midlothian FC is a professional football club based in Gorgie (in the West of Edinburgh). Home matches are played at Tynecastle Park. Nicknames: Hearts, The Jam Tarts, HMFC, The Jambos.

Somehow, we got a thrill from fighting. We ignored the cops. There were too many of us to stop, and any who tried would've taken punches, and worse.'

Nancy listened intently. She'd seen him plenty of times with bloodied knuckles, cuts and bruises when they were kids; all the same, he'd never shared the details.

'You used to ask me things,' Andy said, 'but you were so innocent. I didn't want to pollute you, even with a knowledge of it. Truth is, we fought like animals most weekends. You didn't back down, no matter what. You couldn't.'

She nodded. She'd come from the same rough neighbourhood; she had brothers, too.

'Anyway,' Andy said, 'this one night, Brunco was jumped by five or six of these Jambos. He took a hell of a pasting. He was on the deck. The leader of the group gets down to spit in his face. Next thing you know, Brunco sticks the heid on him and smashes his nose, and before he's had time to come round, Brunco's penknife goes straight through his eye.

'The other Jambos hesitate as the leader screams and flails. Brunco doesn't waste any time. He jumps up roaring, with three broken ribs and a stab wound, and takes every single one of them down.'

'You saw that?'

'You wouldn't believe some of the things I've seen, Nance.'

'How old were you both when that happened?'

'I was twelve. Brunco would be...sixteen.'

'Mental! He was a hard case right enough. What happened to him?'

'Heard he was murdered in the eighties over nothing much.'

'Well, I'm glad you got out.'

'I should've done it sooner. Maybe then, you'd never have left, eh?'

Nancy glanced briefly away, confirming his suspicion—he'd blown it. Her dad or brothers must've heard something.

'Anyway,' he said, 'I'm one of the lucky ones – all I'm left with is some bad memories, a jail record and a gammy leg.'

'You jammy bastard!' Nancy grinned and gave him a friendly jab with her elbow.

He laughed for the first time in a long while.

'Seriously, you were always better than that lot, Andy. You were just in the wrong place at the wrong time.'

'I wish I'd had the sense to keep out of it like you did...I missed you, Nance.'

'I missed you, too.' She frowned at his brooding expression. 'Andy, do you need to talk to someone about this stuff?'

He gave a humourless laugh. 'And who would I talk to? I was a criminal before I could read and write. Who wants to help a scumbag like me?'

'I do.'

Andy's heart skipped a beat.

Stan

By the time Stan had walked Stacy home, he was already feeling it. She could be the one he'd been waiting for! But it was so sudden—and he knew so little about her—it terrified him. He had to be careful. Falling in love too fast had been his downfall with Nora. They stood in the doorway, unsure what to do next.

'I had a nice time tonight,' Stacy said.

'Me too.' Stan's voice came out low as he wrapped his arms around her waist and pulled her close, breathing her in. Her hair and skin smelled amazing. When she didn't resist, he kissed her gently, his lips searching for a sign that she felt the same.

She began to return the kiss, and he allowed his hands to drift into her hair, cupping her head, the first steps on a thrilling journey of discovery. Stacy. As the kiss grew stronger, she ran her hands up his muscular arms. They were standing so close now that he could feel the contours of her breasts against him. He felt his body respond and pulled reluctantly back, taking a deep breath.

Not yet, Stan, he told himself. *Be a gent.*

'Goodnight, Stan.' Stacy smiled, her cheeks rosy.

He caught her hand as she turned to go inside.

'Can I see you again?' He couldn't leave without knowing the answer.

'Yeah. I'd like that.'

Meredith

Andy and Nancy exchanged numbers, and they're still deep in conversation. Andy's vigilant—he keeps glancing around as though expecting some kind of attack.

I've seen two more thirsty souls possess the living as the alcohol weakened their auras. 'Why are they doing that?' I ask Michael.

'Because they're alcoholics—they can't drink without their bodies. It's unlawful to possess a body like that there will be consequences.'

'What consequences?'

'I couldn't say.' He draws my attention back to Andy's conversation.

Nancy says, 'I had a few nannying jobs before I met my ex. I've got two grown-up bairns now, and three grandkids. How about you?'

'After you left, I got together with Mags. You know—Mags Kinnair?'

'Aye.'

'I would've waited for you, but...I didn't know if you'd ever come back. I asked your dad once, but he wouldn't tell me anything.'

'It's okay. You were right to move on.'

'It never lasted long with Mags. But we have a son.'

'Did you get married?'

'No.'

'Why not?' Nancy leans forward in her seat.

'She had the baby while I was inside.' Andy's face clouds over. 'She didn't even tell me she was pregnant.'

'She may have had her reasons.'

'Aye—she thought I was useless, and she didn't want anything to do with me. I can't blame her. My track record wasn't good. But that was when I got free of Brunco, and I swear I would've done whatever I could for Mags. I would've married her, without question.'

'That's what I thought.' Nancy sniffs. 'Did she keep you from your son?'

'No. Fair play to her, she gave me a chance where he was concerned. I got to see wee Gary a lot. I was quite involved with him, growing up, even after Mags got married. I used to get

Gary for weekends and holidays, that sort of thing.' With a tinge of pride, he says, 'he's a high school teacher now.'

'That's great, Andy. Listen, it's getting late. I need to go.'

We visit my dear old folk. Kyle's here sorting laundry, and Fiona's on shift too. I find her in one of the bedrooms in the dark—it's Gina's room. I can't believe what I'm seeing! Fiona's rifling through Gina's things by torchlight. She finds a necklace but decides it's not worth taking. Then she takes money from Gina's purse.

In fury, I rush at Kyle.

Check on Fiona! Find out what she's doing!

He pauses briefly, then carries on. So I try again.

Kyle, Fiona's up to something! Find out what it is.

Kyle gives a little shrug and moseys down the hall. When Gina's door opens, he ducks out of sight next to the bathrooms. From there he peers around the corner as Fiona creeps into Irene's room. His eyes widen. There's no legitimate reason to enter residents' rooms when they're asleep.

Kyle checks his watch. Three full minutes go by before Fiona emerges. Kyle deliberately walks by as though he just happened to be passing.

'What were you doing in there?' he asks.

Fiona's ready with a quick answer. 'I thought I'd forgotten her laundry earlier. Just checking.'

Rubbish! She's lying, Kyle. She's stealing—you need to catch her.

To my surprise, Kyle mutters, 'Stealing?' to Fiona's retreating back. Is it possible that he heard me, or did he just guess right? It's not rocket science, I suppose.

Yes! You need to catch her.

Kyle returns to his laundry, looking thoughtful. I devise a way for him to catch Fiona out, and I whisper it to him over and over. We'll soon see if he's hearing me.

'Isn't this cause for taking away someone's freedom to choose?' I ask Michael. 'How can we let this woman steal from vulnerable old people?'

'If that was our attitude, we'd be stopping an awful lot of things. People are doing far worse than that to each other.'

'Why do they get away with it?'

'Who says they get away with it? Maybe it just looks that way now.'

'What if I were to frighten Fiona—make her think this place is haunted? Would that count as revealing myself?'

Michael smiles kindly. 'I suppose it depends on how you go about it. If it's subtle enough, you might be able to do something.'

'You promised we could make a start, teaching me to move things.'

'I did. Here's how it works. You need a physical body to lift a physical object, but everything physical also exists in spiritual form.'

'Even inanimate objects?'

'Yes. The spirit object inhabits the physical. That's why the gifted can sometimes feel things from objects, left by those who've touched them. The spiritual leaves a mark. If you can harness the spirit object, you can move that, and the physical will follow.'

I listen carefully, trying to take it all in. It seems that when I stand on the ground, I'm not really doing so, I'm just choosing that space to occupy. I could just as easily stand a little below or above. It's similar to standing on the floor or sitting in a car. The seat isn't supporting me—I'm just occupying the space there. However, in a moving car, we are interacting with the physical, otherwise, the car would move and we'd stay put. Moving with the car feels natural and easy, so it's a start. Causing something to move seems impossible by comparison.

We start by learning to connect with the spiritual—each other. As spirits, it's possible for us to occupy the same physical space. Michael passes his hand through mine to demonstrate. I'm afraid I might burn like a shadow, but it's more like something electric. We can also touch because we're both spirit matter. Michael places a hand on mine, and this time I can feel pressure on the surface. Next, it's my turn. The first few times I place my hand on his, it passes through.

'You may be overthinking it,' Michael says. 'Pretend we just met. There's no reason to think you can't touch me. Shake my hand.'

I do it without giving myself time to worry, and it works!

It's a small step towards what I want to do, but Michael says it's enough to be going on with. We practise it over and over, but I still don't get it right every time. Then we rest—I'm not convinced Michael needs to, but my energy is spent.

Part Three
The Shadow Falls

CHAPTER 11

Meredith

Stacy and Sean are preparing the ambulance for their first call.

Sean runs equipment checks. 'So, what's going on with my Padawan? Is there a special someone at the moment?'

Stacy flushes just a little.

'Oh, there is!' Sean claps his hands together enthusiastically. 'I want all the juicy details. What's he like?'

Stacy laughs and gives him a friendly jab with her elbow. 'Taken, Yoda!'

'Come on.' Sean wiggles his eyebrows. 'Give me *something*. What's his name? What does he look like?'

'Stan. He's a train driver from London. Stocky, but taller than me. Curly hair.'

'Sounds gorgeous! So, is it serious?'

'Nah, last night was only our first date...or maybe second.'

Their first call comes in on the radio—Colinton Road.

Fastening his seatbelt, Sean says, 'Well Padawan, next time you see Stan, don't do anything I wouldn't do.'

'Yoda, Yoda, Yoda.' Stacy shakes her head. 'I doubt anything *I* could think up would shock *you*.'

Sean puts on a Yoda voice. 'Offended I am!'

Grinning, Stacy pulls the ambulance out past the car parks and turns on the siren.

When they arrive at the downstairs flat on Colinton Road, an old man in pyjamas lies in recovery position on the floor, a woman kneeling beside him. The man looks at least eighty. His grey hair has receded beyond a high forehead. He's of average height and build with a round belly. The woman moves out of the way for Sean.

'What's his name?' Sean asks.

'Davie.'

'Davie, can you hear me?' Davie gives a jerky nod.

The woman speaks to Stacy while Sean works. 'I'm his sister. I come by a few mornings a week. I'd have come earlier if I'd known.'

Stacy nods, smiling sympathetically. 'Of course.'

'It's hard to understand what he's saying, and he's really confused. He doesn't know this place, and he's lived here for ten years. He keeps asking for Pat, who he lived with in Australia. She died before he moved here. I don't know how long he's been lying there.'

As the woman's eyes brim with tears, Stacy lays a hand gently on her arm. 'It's great that you're here. Trust me, he's in good hands. Sean is one of the best.'

Davie struggles to answer Sean's questions. His speech comes out slurred, the muscles drooping on one side. Sean is soon satisfied that it's safe to move him, and Stacy brings a wheelchair. They need to support his weight and move him carefully; he's very stiff.

My Uncle Murray sits at a neatly laid breakfast table, with fresh fruit, toast and yoghurt. A pot of tea and a newspaper lie on the table beside him.

Jean brings the butter and sits down. She smiles, attractive in spite of the wrinkles. Maybe because of them—they're laughter lines. I like Murray and Jean, the way they look at each other with the frank familiarity of many years.

Murray's face darkens. 'I keep thinking—what if it had been Helen's funeral yesterday? How would I feel if it was too late to make things right? I shouldn't have left it so long.'

Jean says, 'You did your best. Helen always made things...difficult.'

'I don't think she meant to. Things were hard for her after our mum-'

'Because she had to keep house? You worked hard too, Murray, and you were even younger. *You* didn't resent it or take it out on Hughie. You had the same struggle and overcame it.'

'Maybe, once I found *you*. That made all the difference.'

She smiles again, takes his hand across the table. 'I know. Pottsy's disappearance was hard on her. But she still had Meredith. She could've concentrated on that.'

'She was just so angry. And now who's she got? No one.'
'She has Lizzie.'
'But she needs family, Jean. She needs us.'
Jean sighs. 'That sounds fine, but would she want us?'
'I don't know. But I've got to try.'

'Then try we will.' Jean's expression is a blend of admiration and worry.

'Remember when Helen asked us to take Meredith in after Pottsy left?'

'Of course.'

'D'you ever wonder if we should've done it?'

My heart does a somersault. Mum didn't want me—I knew it.

I need to talk to Michael.

He's in a hospital room with Davie, the man Stacy picked up this morning.

'I didn't know you watched over him,' I say.

Michael nods, then catches my expression. 'What's wrong?'

'I heard Murray and Jean say my mum didn't want me. She asked them to take me in.'

'Listen to me. You've had it rough, with your mum. But you must understand, it's not because of anything you've done.'

'How can it be someone else's fault?'

'She was so angry with your dad, and I'm afraid you took the brunt of it. That's your mum's mistake, not yours.'

I feel childlike hysteria rising within me. I don't know where I'm finding the courage to speak to Michael like this, but I shake my head. '*I'm* the mistake! If she never had me, she could've moved on. Or, if I was more like her, if I was good—'

'You *are* good!'

I don't answer. I go back to my spot by the railway to brood.

Helen

Helen woke later than usual. She sat down with her morning tea and the crossword, but she couldn't concentrate. She was thinking of the last time she saw Meredith alive. The way her daughter had hovered, unwelcome, for a hug, and how that summed up their relationship.

The relief she'd felt when Meredith walked out the door was long gone. Had she known it was goodbye, she'd have done better. If she could only live that moment again. Her blood turned cold.

You were cruel. She was trying to say goodbye.

For the first time since Pottsy left, Helen began to feel ashamed of how she felt about Meredith. Yes, the girl was difficult, and they were very different, but they were family.

Let the sins of the father be visited upon the child, was that it?

Mind you, it was a long time since Meredith had been a child. *She* could've changed, taken better care of herself and learned to be more sociable. Helen fumbled for some reason to blame Meredith for their unsatisfying relationship, but it was no use. It all started with a parent and child. The responsible party was pretty unequivocal.

Face it—you might as well have pushed her in front of that train yourself.

Helen wasn't a fan of feeling things, much less of crying, but it was too late. The floodgates were opened. A new regret swept over her, a misery for which she could blame no one but herself.

Meredith

I return to Michael in the hospital, grateful he let me be. We turn our attention to poor Davie.

'They don't know how long he'll be in hospital,' Michael says. 'He's lost a lot of muscle control—it could be a stroke. He won't know anything until after the doctor's rounds.'

Davie's sister—her name is Angela—keeps having to explain where they are and why.

Michael says, 'Can you feel his energy? What can you perceive?'

I close my eyes, breathing in my surroundings and breathing out my worries. Then I concentrate on the man in the bed. 'He has a strong will,' I say. 'He's very anxious, but also determined. Impatient, too.'

'Insightful,' Michael says. 'Feeling people's emotions can help you understand truth.'

It seems a strange thing for him to say, at the point where he would normally offer comfort to the living.

Before I can formulate a question, he says, 'I think your mum's feelings may be softening. Let's go and see how she is.'

Mum would normally be out walking by now, but she's still in her dressing gown. My suicide note sits on her lap and great tears roll down her cheeks. Knowing I've caused this threatens to overwhelm me; I challenge my instinct to run. Instead, I slow myself down inside.

Softening, Michael said. There's something different about these tears.

These are real sorry tears, like the one she gave me at my memorial site when she apologised for missing my birthday.

Michael says, 'She's beginning to understand the hurt she's caused you over the years. She has to feel this—it's part of grief.'

Her tears come hard and fast now, a river of regret like I've never seen.

I say, 'I didn't mean to cause her all this pain.'

'You need to stop blaming everything on yourself.'

'I left her.'

'We all carry regrets, and that's yours. Your mum has regrets too, for her part.'

If I had only known this before I jumped…I wipe a tear from my cheek. 'If she really has regrets about me…that's a gift.'

'She does. Can't you feel it?'

It's an effort to shut out my own emotions, but I focus on hers. 'Yes,' I say. 'She has regrets…and I'll answer them with gifts of my own.' I hold Michael's gaze for a moment. 'I am a whisperer, after all.'

Michael brightens at my reaction; perhaps he was expecting me to disappear again. Buoyed, I take his hand and move us to Murray and Jean's house.

I say, 'I'll start by spending more time with my Uncle Murray. He seems like a good man; he wants to help her. I can't be there myself, so I need others to step in. She needs family.'

'You're right.' Michael beams at me. 'It's a great idea. I'll leave you to see what you can do here, and I'll see you soon.'

Mum seems to be on Murray's mind.

'What's it all about, anyway,' he asks Jean, 'the feud? I can hardly remember where it started, now.'

Jean stands at the sink, peeling potatoes. 'Helen took umbrage when you defended Pottsy.'

'I just couldn't believe he'd run off like that. Fat lot I knew.' Murray took a large saucepan from the cupboard and filled it with water.

'Then she was unhappy with your reaction when she asked us to take Meredith.'

'I was really shocked that she asked. I should've been more understanding. I should've kept in touch with my sister.'

'You tried, but she made it difficult.'

'Well, that's all in the past now.'

'Yes, but I don't want you to be disappointed if you get more of the same. The last thing you need right now is unnecessary stress. Have you forgotten how cantankerous she can be?'

'I remember. I used to put off visiting her. Once when I dropped in after a long absence, she accused me of not giving a damn. We argued, and she told me to get out and leave them alone. I've hardly said two words to her since then, until now.'

'You see? It wasn't your fault.'

'I don't know, Jean. I could've tried harder—to be honest, I was relieved when she said that. It was just the excuse I needed to stop trying.'

Jean plants a kiss on her husband's bald head. 'You're a good man, Murray Stevens.' Murray looks doubtful.

Sunday dinner is a family tradition—what a lovely thing! Mum and I never had family dinner. We had a table, but we just ate our meals on our laps in front of the TV. Being part of this could only do mum good.

Invite Helen, I whisper. *Give her a call.*

Helen

Lizzie was making the Sunday afternoon tea. She called out from the kitchen. 'Where's your cup, darling?'

'I broke it.'

'Oh, that's a shame. Which one are you using now?'

Helen joined Lizzie. 'Doesn't matter.' She brought the plate of cupcakes to the table, while Lizzie brought the tea.

'There we are,' Lizzie said.

'Thanks.' Helen chose a cake, wishing Meredith could enjoy one. The phone rang, and she rose to answer. 'Hello?'

'Helen, it's Murray. How are you doing?'

'Okay, thanks.'

'I've been thinking about you a lot, and I know it's short notice, but would you like to come over? We'll be having Sunday dinner in an hour or so.'

'That's good of you, but I'm with Lizzie just now.'
'Bring her along.'
'Not today. Thank you.'
'Maybe another day?'
'Maybe.'
'Alright, good...Bye, then.'
'Bye.' Helen hung up the phone and returned to the table.
'Who was that, darling?' Lizzie asked.
'Murray.' Helen poured some tea. 'I'm not fond of this cup. I broke my favourite one, you know.'

Meredith

He did it! He invited mum after I suggested it! I'm not sure I can keep putting these things down to coincidence. Then again, who's to say if he would've done it without me? He wanted to reach out before I whispered.

If only she'd said yes.

But we won't give up that easily, will we Uncle Murray?

'She sounds different,' Murray tells Jean. 'Sad, you know? Like the fire in her belly has gone out.'

'Maybe next week.' Jean pats his hand.

My cousin David comes in with his girlfriend Gail and their two children. The kids run to hug their grandparents.

Jean wipes her hands on her apron, laughing at their enthusiasm. 'Be gentle with grandad!' she calls.

The kids slow down a little and give their grandad sheepish cuddles.

Jean says, 'Bella, darling!' She hugs the girl and kisses her cheek. 'Harry!' Now it's her grandson's turn. 'How is everyone?'

Bella is twelve and Harry's nine. They're absolutely gorgeous. If we'd stayed together as a family, I could've helped look after them sometimes. I would've liked that.

Auntie Jean makes roast beef, mashed potatoes, roast carrots and parsnips, sweetcorn and gravy. My stomach growls. Murray sits in the living room with Gail and the kids, and David lends a hand in the kitchen.

'How is he?' David asks.
'Not too bad, son.'
'How are you?'

'I'm okay.' She turns her face away so he doesn't see her eyes well up.

With the family seated in the dining room around a big table, Jean quietly serves the food, others getting up to muck in with this and that. Afterwards, the kids lie on the floor to draw pictures. Bella's style is beyond her years—she draws her grandad sleeping in his chair, and it's a surprisingly good likeness. Bella and I could've been friends. I could've helped with her drawing.

If there was such a thing as heaven, I think it would look like this—families together.

Nathan comes down for school in a new jacket. It's perfect for a teenage boy: black, hooded, and rainproof. Laura's look of surprise turns to concern.

'Nice jacket, son.' She says.

'Thanks.'

'Where did you get it?'

'Friend,' Nathan says, shoving two slices of bread into the toaster.

Laura looks at him quizzically. 'What friend?'

'Alfie.'

'A school friend?' She asks.

'No, from the library.'

'He goes to a different school?'

'Alfie doesn't go to school, mum. He *works* in the library.'

Laura looks surprised, but not alarmed. 'Oh right. How old is he?'

'Dunno...about ninety! I help him out a bit in the library, so he got me this to say thanks.' Nathan's toast pops and he spreads it with butter.

Laura shrugs. 'Cool. It *was* on my shopping list you know, and you could've worn that old one of your dad's.' Nathan makes a face of comedy disgust, kisses Laura on the cheek, and heads out the door, munching.

Alfie's had a great idea—I heard him tell Shirley. He wants to get Nathan a paid job in the library. You wouldn't think it to look at the man, but he's so kind and thoughtful.

At the end of a shift, Alfie finds his manager, Monika, in the staffroom. 'Have you got a minute?' he asks.

'Sure,' Monika says with a thick Polish accent, putting down her laptop. 'Am just doing budget stuff, so boring.' Monika pats the seat next to her, but Alfie doesn't sit.

He says, 'There's a boy, Nathan, who's been helping me sort the books.'

'I've seen this boy. He is here a lot, yes?'

'Yes. He's looking for a job, and...'

'Yes?'

Alfie takes a deep breath. 'Could you use a junior assistant?' Monika looks thoughtful. 'He's nearly sixteen, so he wouldn't need to be paid a lot. I'm sure he could—'

'That's actually a good idea. There's some budget to use, this could work. Leave it with me, Alfie.'

Alfie nods stiffly, a small, secret smile etched on his face as he turns to leave.

CHAPTER 12

Helen

Confronted with her failure as a mother, Helen didn't know what to do. It followed her around like a puppy (or a child), demanding to be fed. This was her day for housework, so she tried keeping busy to shake it off. By noon, she'd been for a long walk, picked up a few groceries, and cleaned the house from top to bottom.

She fought back the tears and kept going hot and cold. Was she coming down with something nasty?

Lizzie would come if she asked, though it wasn't their usual day. But Helen didn't like being seen upset, not even by her best friend. Crying was an embarrassment, a sign of weakness. Maintaining control of one's emotions was somehow comforting.

But alone, the tears kept coming, heedless of her wishes. Meredith's dead face kept flashing across Helen's mind. That, and the growing realisation that she was the whole cause of it. The shame burned her eyes, challenged the safety of her facade.

No wonder she left me, the old woman thought miserably. *I'm a horrible person.*

Meredith

Andy sees Nancy twice more within a week of 'bumping into her' at the pub. Michael knows him well! Nancy's so compassionate, and there's a real connection between her and Andy. You can almost feel it in the air. She's retired, and he works part-time in ASDA, so it's easy for them to get together. Nancy reminds him of dark times and he gets jumpy around her, as though worried for her safety. I can't imagine anyone wanting to hurt her.

I visit home often. I sense the influence of the shadow more than once. Who is this dark soul, and why does she whisper hateful thoughts? What has she been saying to my mum? How much of it can mum take? Her aura's growing thin. What happens if it cracks—is she vulnerable to attack, like the old man in the pub?

I try to fill the space around mum with light, to whisper positive things, but it's hard. She keeps crying, and doesn't seem to hear me; the sense of rejection is all too familiar. Sometimes I even wonder if I'm in hell already, doomed to follow mum around forever, unnoticed.

Then I remember she's having regrets about *me*. At least, I think she is. I know I shouldn't be glad to see her upset, but it's a guilty pleasure to know she cares this much.

Mum is stoically keeping herself busy. To see her out and about, you wouldn't know what she was going through. She's quiet and dignified at walking group, yoga class and book club. Aunt Lizzie phones and visits more than usual and Michael helps out, too. I'm grateful mum has others to lean on, and I can go elsewhere. It's easier with the others; it takes my mind off myself, similar to the way a good book once did.

I'm learning from Michael all the time, but it turns out I'm not as patient as I thought. I'm getting the hang of touching spirit matter, but I haven't come close to seeing it clearly within an object. When Michael isn't around, I sit next to Fiona and channel all my rage towards a mug or book on the table beside her, trying to knock it over. Sadly, rage doesn't seem to help. All I see is the mug and my fingers reach straight through it, every time. Good job she can't see me; I must look like an idiot. Wait till Kyle is on shift with her. We'll catch her out eventually.

I watch Davie's anxious struggle unfold. He moans and mumbles, getting frustrated when his body doesn't respond as he hopes. He sleeps fitfully. I pour oil on troubled waters, unsure if I'm helping.

But amazingly, tonight as I whisper, he becomes visibly still. His breathing slows and regulates.

Michael bestows one of his warmest smiles and says, 'Well done, Meredith!'

For a moment I forget I'm supposed to cringe, not glow.

Andy

Andy always sat with his back to the wall. He preferred it that way; it meant no one could sneak up behind him. Logically, he knew the chances of someone doing so were slim, but he couldn't shake the feeling.

With Nancy, it was stronger. He had to look out for anyone that might do her harm. He saw the look of concern on her face when she caught him looking around, but he didn't care. What mattered most was keeping her safe.

He couldn't believe it. After all these years, he was having coffee with Nancy Gordon. She was as gorgeous as ever; the same easy sense of humour, the eyes he'd fallen in love with in his youth, the same body, improved by a little extra weight. Her hair, once strawberry blonde and naturally wavy, was now white, poker straight and cut to her shoulders with a fringe. That had made her difficult to recognise instantly, but she'd hardly changed—she was still his girl.

A middle-aged man with a beard stood suddenly and strode towards them.

Instinctively, Andy stood too, a fist pulled back at the ready.

In a flash, Nancy raised both arms to protect her head, eyes tight shut.

The man looked from Andy to Nancy, wide-eyed, and hurried past them towards the toilets.

Andy breathed out and looked at Nancy, then in horror at his still-clenched fist. His voice came out in a hoarse whisper as he sat back down. 'Nance. I would never hurt you.'

Nancy opened her eyes, let her arms drop. 'Why did you do that?'

'There was a man behind you. I thought he was going to...'

'What—hurt me?'

'It seems stupid now. I'm sorry.'

Nancy's smile was tender. 'You wanted to protect me?'

Andy was earnest. 'Of course.' His eyes darkened. 'Why did you react like that?'

Nancy only shook her head slightly, her lips tight.

He heard his volume rising. 'Who hurt you, Nancy?'

'Sh—someone will hear. Can we go, please?'

Meredith

The doctors and nurses are optimistic about Davie's recovery—speech and muscle control are gradually improving.

His more recent memories are still vague. Angela keeps explaining things to him. She brings photographs of him with her grandkids. He nods, but his face shows no recognition. He keeps forgetting their names.

Practicing sounds and movements is painstaking. The physiotherapist told him to be patient, but that isn't his strong suit. He keeps trying the exercises she showed him for his left side and swearing when the muscles don't respond.

'When can I get out?' he asks Angela, who has to strain to understand what he's saying.

'Soon,' she says.

'I need a beer.'

Angela rolls her eyes.

'And a fag. Can you bring in my smokes?'

'No. It's not allowed in here.'

After Angela leaves, he lifts his left arm slightly, palm down, and tries to turn his hand over. Just as before, it only turns about forty-five degrees. 'Bollocks', he says—only it comes out 'bwhaaacks' – followed by a guttural howl of frustration.

Nathan comes home to his parents arguing again. He turns around at the back door to leave and stops when he hears his name.

Gordon growls, 'Of course I noticed Nathan's jacket, but I thought it was *you* that gave him it.'

Laura's answers are muffled by the closed door.

'What friend?...He works there?...How old is he?...Laura, that's no right!' Gordon's voice grows louder. 'This old man sounds like some kind of weirdo!...That's MY son. MY son. He had no right!'

Laura shouts, 'It's perfectly innocent Gordon! Nathan's not an idiot.'

'I'm not saying that. It's not him I don't trust. You should've told me straight away!'

Nathan takes a deep breath and opens the kitchen door. 'Alfie's a good guy dad,' he says. 'He's not a weirdo.'

Gordon suppresses his rage. 'I'll be the judge of that.'

Michael and I whisper assurances to Nathan as he sits upstairs worrying. We can't promise him that his dad—who's already stormed out of the house—won't interfere, but Alfie will be okay. He wouldn't throw away Nathan's friendship over his hot-headed father.

Sure enough, poor Alfie is startled when Gordon marches into the library and reads his badge. Gordon's intimidating—about six foot tall, and strongly built. His face is rough with stubble, his hair messy.

'So, you're Alfie,' Gordon says.

'Y-yes.' Alfie takes a step back.

'What do you want with my son?'

'Y-your son?'

'Nathan.'

'Oh.' He still seems confused by the question, the rage. 'He's a nice lad.'

Gordon grabs Alfie by the collar and pulls him close. 'Listen to me, bookworm,' he says, 'you better not be some kind of pervert. If you lay so much as a finger on him, you'll answer to me.'

'I'd n-never hurt Nathan,' Alfie says. 'And I'm not a pervert.'

Gordon releases him, looks him up down, then produces a wad of notes. 'Just making sure.' He counts out fifties. 'And about the jacket...' He slaps £200 on the helpdesk. 'Don't buy anything for my son again. He doesn't need your charity. Understood?'

Alfie nods, gulping. He watches Gordon strut out of the library, then collapses into the nearest chair and begins to cry.

My heart goes out to Alfie. How could anyone be cruel to a soul so utterly devoid of guile? I stay with him into the evening, and he's much quieter than usual.

Shirley looks worried—she whines softly, questioning him. When he sits on the sofa and cries, she lies by his feet. I wish in this moment that I could be Shirley—to be seen, to touch. I could lay my face on his feet, close my eyes and go to sleep.

Andy

I pass a couple holding hands and laughing—they don't notice me. It's dark now, and I'm not much to notice even in broad daylight. I'm only twelve, but I look younger. I was mucking about with some pals—burning stuff—but I've been summoned.

Brunco stands at the corner with a group of older boys, deep in hushed but heated conversation. He beckons me as I approach with a quick raise of his head. 'Titch,' he says in that threatening tone I know so well, 'get over to mine and grab my crossbow and quiver from under the bunks.'

I just look at him, trying to hide my terror.

'There's no one in—my dad's working and my mum's over at Mrs Taylor's. Get your arse up there! Bring them to our spot by Main Street, got it?'

I nod.

He smacks me in the head. 'Well bugger off, what are you waiting for? We're busy here.'

My footsteps sound conspicuously loud as I clunk through the streets till I reach my own. But I stop one block of flats short of home, where the Grahams live. The concrete steps in front of me disappear as I climb. I want to make my legs stop moving, but they won't. The first time I opened that door, I never knew what I would see. The light was on at the landing, so I didn't notice it was also on in the flat.

Now I know exactly what's in there, but I go in anyway, again and again. Why do I always go in? Even when I get to the top of the stairs and hear the grunting and whimpering— meaningless but for the sick feeling in the pit of my stomach—I still put out my grubby little hand and open the door.

It's Brunco's older brother, Tam. Rab never hurts girls or women. Ever. Brunco and Tam spare no one. Tam has a girl pressed up against the back wall now, arms pinned and legs splayed. His trousers round his ankles. He turns, his face menacing, and utters a string of profanity at me. The white face looking fearfully over his shoulder isn't who I expect. It's Nancy! Her cheek is bruised and her lip bloodied, and she looks at me to save her.

But all I can do is turn around and run.

Gasping for air. Sweating. What time is it? I check the alarm by the bed—2 a.m. *It was only a dream*, I tell myself. *Only a dream, only a dream. Nancy's perfectly safe.* But it takes me a while to really believe it.

There'll be no stiff hiding[9] from Brunco tomorrow, but it's small comfort.

---

[9] a stiff hiding: a good beating

Meredith

Nathan avoids the library, mortified, until Friday. He needs to make sure Alfie's okay; he can't put it off forever. With a little encouragement he goes in, but he sidles past Alfie and wanders the aisles. He finds some books to sort.

Before long Alfie joins him, and by sorting books, they can talk without meeting one another's eyes.

'So,' Alfie says, 'I met your dad.'

'Did he give you a hard time?'

'A bit.'

'Sorry.'

'It's okay. He was only looking out for you.' Alfie was really shaken up—but look how easily he forgives!

Nathan asks, 'Are you okay?'

'Fine. You?'

'Yeah.' Nathan's tight muscles relax a little. 'I'm good.'

'So...see you soon?' Alfie asks, finally meeting his young friend's eyes for a brief moment.

'Yeah.' Nathan nods, relieved. Everything is back to normal.

I wish I could say the same for Gordon and Laura. Gordon's betting big now—he's never had so much money in his life. He meets up with Brian in the pub before going home. A handshake turns into a macho half hug like they're brothers.

'This is amazing, Bri,' Gordon says once they're out of earshot. 'The money...'

'You're welcome,' says Brian. He guzzles down his beer. I don't like him.

'I'm a thirsty man, though. I keep thinking I better just have one or two, for the driving, you know, even on my days off from UPS.'

'Ach, you normally get a days' notice. Plenty time to sober up.'

Gordon grins. 'Bloody right!' he says, and disappears for a whole tray of pints and shots.

Go home, you idiot!

But he doesn't; not till he's had his fill. He staggers into the kitchen at home after closing time. He thinks he's alone, but Laura's sitting at the table with the lights off.

'Where've you been, Gordon?'

He recoils, almost falling out of the open door.

'Oh it's you, babe, I nearly wet myself!' He locks the door and switches on the light.

'Where, Gordon?' She catches a whiff of booze. 'And how can you afford to drink so much?'

Gordon says, 'This is the first drink I've had for a week,' but it comes out slurred, and convinces no one.

'Is someone else treating you?'

He only looks at her stupidly, squinting in the light.

'Some woman, maybe?'

'A woman!' he scoffs. 'You know me better than that, darling.' He sways up behind her, slips a hand into the top of her dressing gown and says, 'You're the only one for me. Come upstairs and I'll prove it.'

Laura pushes him off, her face contorted in disgust. 'I've got a better idea,' she says. 'You sleep on the sofa tonight. We can talk about this when you're sober, and when you're ready to tell the truth.'

'I *am* telling the truth—every word!'

But she's already grabbing a duvet and pillow out of the cupboard and dumping them on the sofa.

'Laura, don't be like that!'

'Goodnight.'

Gordon gazes longingly at his wife's behind as she stomps up the stairs.

Helen

Helen curled into a foetal position against the cold, holding the blankets close. Her toes were like ice. She tried to practice mindfulness, focussing on her breath, but moments pressed themselves upon her consciousness one by one, refusing to let her rest. First, that broken face, accusing her. Then mum's tender smile, then granny, frosty and demanding, then Pottsy kissing her cheek the last time he left the house.

Everything and everyone conspired to keep her uncomfortable, churning and churning until slowly, painstakingly, her mind began to fog over.

The burn has become a raging river; she's drowning in the violent rapids. Each time she comes up for a gulp of air, she immediately falls back again. Through the foamy struggle, she sees her father on the bank. She calls out to him; he shakes his head as he passes by, disgusted. Next comes her mother. Again she calls out; mum looks back as she passes, her expression tearful and disappointed. Then her brothers, but they're just children. They don't even notice her as they run by, laughing. Next comes her husband, scorn etched upon his face as he wanders casually on. Last of all, her daughter, bruised and bloodied, answers her cries with the brutal truth.

'You're not worth saving.'

CHAPTER 13

Stan

Friday evening finally arrived. Stacy came to Simon's door at six thirty, giving Stan just enough time to grab a shower and get ready.

Sam ran to answer the door in his onesie, Stan following behind. Stacy grinned when the door was flung open, revealing the excited little boy. 'You're Stacy!' he said, as though it was news to her. 'I'm Sam!'

'Nice to meet you, Sam.' Stacy bent down and put out her hand to shake the child's small, chubby one, but he flung his arms around her instead. She returned the unearned hug, laughing.

Stacy was insisting on taking Stan out this time—to an Indian restaurant, to enjoy some of *his* favourite food. He would've been willing to eat just about anything to spend the evening with her. He'd happily pay too, but she seemed to find that mildly offensive.

As they were walking to the restaurant, Stan took Stacy's hand. He felt almost giddy with excitement at her touch. She was letting him show the world they were together.

During the meal, he tried to dig a bit deeper. 'So,' he asked, 'how do I compare to past boyfriends?'

Stacy looked taken aback. 'I'm not comparing you, really.' She smiled, showing the dimple on her cheek.

'Girl as gorgeous you, I bet you've had plenty offers.'

'Oh, you have no idea.'

Stan felt his face fall.

'Proposals every other weekend—it's exhausting.' They burst out laughing.

Stan tried again. 'Really, though, was there ever anyone serious?' Stacy hesitated, so he blundered on. 'I nearly got married once, and I can tell you, "trouble and strife" would've been the understatement of the century.'

'Lucky escape?'

'Definitely. Her name was Nora, and she—'

'You don't need to tell me.'

'I want to. She was gorgeous—not like you, mind—but she wasn't right in the head. She manipulated me, separated me from my family. I was miserable, but I didn't want to go back on my word.'

'Stan—'

'I finally ended it. I couldn't live like that, like a prisoner.'

Stacy nodded. He hoped she'd share something personal, but she didn't. Maybe she wasn't ready yet.

After they'd finished eating she took him to a classy bar with live acoustic music. The vibe was perfect. With his stomach satisfied, he still hungered. He held her hand at every opportunity, letting his eyes linger on her and watching her body language. She returned his smiles and leaned in towards him when they were talking.

Sitting together on a bench in a booth, there were a few people who'd see if they kissed; Stan threw away his inhibitions – he didn't care who saw. In fact, he kind of wanted the whole world to see.

Although it made him uncomfortable, Stacy paid for the drinks. It was worse since she only had one glass of wine because of tomorrow's shift.

One thing he insisted on was seeing her safely home. This time the pull to be intimate with her was even stronger, and he sensed that she felt it too; however, they'd known each other two weeks, and he respected her too much to rush in. Part of him was afraid of taking that step. Would it change things? Should he wait for the 'l' word? If he waited too long, would she lose interest?

Whatever the answers were, he knew that tonight was too soon. He made sure to show Stacy how he felt but again pulled back before things went too far. He left her in her doorway, sparkly-eyed. He walked the two miles or so back to his brother's, just to mull things over in the cool of the night.

Meredith

Davie's doing better. He walked right to the end of the ward and back this morning. He winced and grimaced the whole time, but with the aid of a stick, he did it. He spent the rest of the morning watching TV, waiting for news of his release.

The consultant appears and checks the folder. 'How are you doing?' she asks.

'Fine.' His speech is laboured but it's clearer now. The muscles on one side of his face are still drooping.

'And how did you find the walking?'

Davie shrugs. 'No bother.'

'That's great.' She makes a few notes. 'I think we can discharge you on Monday. That'll give us time to organise everything. You're going to need home support and medication, and you'll be expected to attend outpatient physiotherapy. Okay?'

Davie nods, looking bored.

Angela visits after lunch. 'They're going to ring me when you can leave,' she tells him, 'and I'll pick you up.'

'Where are you taking me?'

'Home, Davie.'

'Australia?'

'No. *Colinton.* You've been there for ten years.'

He scratches his head, his brow furrowed. 'Why would I do that?'

'Because Pat passed away. Don't worry, I'm sure once you get settled it'll feel like home again.'

Davie scoffs. 'As long as there's beer.'

Mum has afternoon tea with Aunt Lizzie on Sundays, but today she calls to cancel.

'Can we give tea a miss? I'm not feeling up to it.'

'Darling, I quite understand. You need time to grieve. What's happened is just...unimaginable. If you change your mind later, or if you want someone to talk to, just call me right back.'

'Okay. Thanks.' Mum hangs up the phone with a sigh of relief. There's a change in her usually confident demeanour. She's slouching in her chair, and her head hangs down. She's dressed, so I assume she's been for her walk. Her hair looks more tousled than usual. There are a few dirty cups gathering in the kitchen; she normally washes things straight away. Her bed is made, but not with her usual meticulous care.

I wish I could help. I've made such a mess of things.

Michael says she needs to work through things in her own time. There's no point in trying to whisper this pain away. Some pain needs to be felt before things can improve. I'm sorry, mum.

Stan

Stan and Stacy spent Sunday afternoon cycling up the coastal route to North Berwick. Stacy did this kind of thing regularly—she loved the outdoors—so Stan was pleased to find that he could keep up. It was a cold but clear day and he enjoyed the fresh air. It took them the best part of two hours to get to North Berwick. They had a bite to eat in a quaint little café before taking the train back to Edinburgh.

Stan was heading home to London that night, and Stacy was night shift Tuesday to Thursday. Stan was on lates all week, so it would be Saturday before they could see each other again.

'It's gonna be a long bubble and squeak—week,' Stan said. It was probably weird, but seeing his girlfriend windswept and sweaty just made him fancy her more.

'What if I come down to London this time? I'm off Friday night so I could come down on the train with you.'

It sounded amazing, but Stan didn't want to be presumptuous. 'D'you mean, we go out for a Ruby, and I drop you at your hotel, or d'you mean...you stay at my place?' he asked.

'Thought you'd never ask!' Stacy grinned. 'I'll stay.'

Stan felt like the luckiest guy on the planet.

'And what's a Ruby, when it's at home?'

'Ruby Murray—curry!'

Meredith

Murray phones Hughie on Sunday evening.

'Did you invite Helen for dinner?' Hughie asks.

'Aye. She didn't want to come.' He doesn't mention that he's asked her twice.

'No surprises there, then.'

'Well, no,' says Murray, 'but I can understand her needing a bit of time alone. I think she'll come around eventually—she wasn't rude about it.'

'First time for everything.'

'I've never known Helen to sound so defeated. Just remember, she's our sister. No matter what she's done or not done in the past.'

Hughie sighs. 'She's had nothing to with me since she got married. She's not *my* sister.'

'Please, Hughie.'

'She didn't even turn up at Jessie's funeral! I know it's been a long time, but I can't see past it.'

'I know. That was very wrong. I think she was too wrapped up in her own affairs—she's had a hard time—'

'Haven't we all?'

'Your right. I'm sorry. I can't excuse the way Helen's treated you over the years. But I don't know how long I've got...'

The line goes quiet.

'If I can get Helen back on side, will you give her one more chance? For me?'

'Okay—for you. I hope this crusade to get the family back together doesn't cost you too much.'

'How d'you mean?'

'Well, you can try with the patience of a saint. But Helen's Helen, at the end of the day.'

'I'll get through to her, you'll see.'

You're right, Uncle Murray. Stick to your guns—she'll come around.

Davie

Angela picks Davie up from the hospital and takes him home. She makes a disapproving face when he coughs and spits on the ground outside. She stays a while to get him settled. She collects his dirty clothes, puts the washing on, and cleans a few dishes.

'There,' she says. 'You're all set. Before I go, I'll pop out and get you some groceries. Milk, bread, butter...' She checks the fridge and cupboards. 'I'll pick up a few ready meals. Anything else you want?'

'A packet of fags and some beer,' he says gruffly.

'I'm not sure that's a good idea – why not just leave it now you've gone without for so long?'

'I *need* a drink. Come on, what harm is there in a few beers? Just pick me up a couple of six packs and a twenty-deck.' Seeing her weakening, he says, 'I'll be out shopping soon anyway, and I'll buy what I like.'

'Fine.' She rolls her eyes. 'Good thing I've brought my wheelie bag.'

While Angela does the shopping, Davie paces and fidgets. He looks disapprovingly around the flat. Once the errand is done and Angela's gone, he gets straight down to business. He cracks open his first tin of Stella. It makes a hissing sound and he closes his eyes, takes a whiff.

He switches on the TV and turns to a sports channel. He takes his first swig of beer, lights a cigarette and inhales the smoke deeply.

By the time he's onto his second tin he looks more relaxed, and as he chugs down the third, he looks satisfied, like an animal with an itch that's found the perfect tree to scratch itself on.

Meredith

Andy meets up at lunchtime with his son Gary in Deacon Brodie's. He swells with pride the moment Gary comes in; his grave, brooding expression brightens at the mere sight of him. Gary looks a bit like Andy: fairly slim built, and about six foot tall. I can't tell what colour Andy's hair was before it went white, but Gary's is dark brown and similarly full. The main difference between them is in the face. Gary's features are sharper than his father's, but not grim set; his muscles are relaxed, and he greets his dad with an easy smile.

'Pint of bitter for my son please, Norm,' Andy says, slapping Gary on the back. 'And what would you like to eat, Gary?'

'Just a cheese toastie, please.'

Norm, pulling the pint, nods in acknowledgement. The drink is served and the pair sits at a nearby table.

Gary asks, 'How are you, dad?'

'I'm well, son, thanks—doing well.' I've never seen Andy this animated. Not that he is, compared to other people, but compared to himself he's positively hyper. 'How's work?'

'Same old. Seniors have mock exams in a few weeks, so we're busy getting ready for that. I'm running an after-school club for the ones that struggle with physics.'

'That's great, son! You're such a genius.'

'Hardly.' Gary laughs.

Norm brings his toastie.

'This looks great. Thanks, dad, I'm starving.' Gary tucks in, the hot melted cheese oozing out the sides of his sandwich. 'So, what've you been up to?' Seeing Andy grin, he asks, 'What? What is it?'

'I've met someone.'

'That's brilliant, dad! What's her name?'

'Nancy. I knew her before. A long time ago. She's amazing, son.'

'I'm dead chuffed for you, can't wait to meet her. Fancy having dinner with us at the weekend?'

'Definitely—just let us know when you're both free. And how's Freya doing?'

'She's good. Yeah, just busy with the gallery. The usual.'

'And Mark?'

'Fine dad, fine. He's been with us for the October holidays, but he's away back to his dad's. He seems to be doing well at school, and he's no bother at ours.'

'How's your mum?'

'She's okay. Her surgery went fine. She said there were women in the unit a lot worse off than her. She was lucky they caught it early. She's just had the all clear, but she has to go back in a year.'

'That's great son. I'm glad she's okay.'

'Well,' says Gary, finishing his pint, 'thanks for lunch, dad. Better get back to it. Class in ten minutes. I'll give you a shout about that dinner.'

They hug, and after Gary leaves his dad's face gradually clouds over again.

Gordon's day job is quick becoming an inconvenience. He doesn't need the money—it's pointless when he can make a month's wages in a few days. He's in the bookies most nights, and of course, the pub.

Sitting in their usual dark corner, he says, 'Bri, I'm quitting UPS.'

'No, no, mate,' Brian says, 'you can't do that. Boss expects us to hold down a legit job, as cover. Why d'you think I'm still tiling? It's not for fun, I can tell you.'

Gordon looks disappointed, but shrugs. 'Makes sense.'

Brian glances around, leans in and speaks in a hushed tone. 'You've done well. The boss wants you to branch out a bit.'

'How d'you mean? I'm quite happy doing deliveries.'

'Look, Gordo, if these guys want you to do something, you do it. This isn't Edinburgh City Council, man.'

This can't be good! What do they want him to do now? *Say no, Gordon! Show some guts.*

But he only says, 'Fine. What's the score?'

'You'll get a text with instructions as usual. Don't look so worried, you'll be fine. It's just a message for someone, that's all.'

'A message?'

'Aye.'

Gordon looks uncomfortable. Well, what did he expect?

'Someone's stepped out of line. You've to teach him a lesson.'

Gordon's a big guy and I'm sure he packs a fair punch. I can see why they'd choose him for a job like this. I just wish they hadn't.

Brian says, 'You'll get an address and picture, and twenty-four hours to do it. Then you take a pic after it's done, send it by reply, and you get instructions for payment. Gordo, get it done, and they'll pay you five hundred quid. It'll take you twenty minutes. If you do well, they'll keep giving you deliveries. You might even be up for a promotion.'

Gordon nods, but says again, 'I'm quite happy doing deliveries.'

I've been conspiring with Kyle—he's back on night shift with Fiona. He hasn't said a word about his suspicions; instead he waits till everyone's settled. He tucks Irene in, and quietly leaves fifty pounds on her chest of drawers. He's marked the notes so he can identify them later. All we need to do is wait.

Michael gives me another lesson on moving things.

'Take your time,' he says. 'It took me years to get the hang of this.'

Not a chance—he makes it look so easy. There's a box of tissues on the table in the sitting room. I stare at it for hours, trying to connect with the spiritual. Finally, there's something. I get a glimpse of a fourth dimension to the box, like a blueprint occupying the same space. It's only a flash; I can't hold it long enough to touch it. The box is just as it was before.

Kyle's good. He lies down on the sofa and pretends to fall asleep. Sure enough, Fiona leaves the TV on but gets up for a wander. She goes into one other room before Irene's, unaware that Kyle is watching. It's bold of her to do this regularly; she must know there's CCTV in the hallway. Kyle resumes his position on the sofa before Fiona returns. He waits a while, then gets up and casually wanders to the loo before checking Irene's room. Of course, the money is gone.

Now you know for sure. The question is, what are you going to do about it? How are you going to deal with her?

Kyle's bold, too. Careful to avoid the cameras himself, he checks Fiona's coat pockets when she's at the loo, and rifles through her handbag till he finds the notes she took from Irene. He takes them back, but he doesn't say a word.

CHAPTER 14

Meredith

Laura wakes up at lunchtime and comes downstairs in her dressing gown. She finds Gordon in the kitchen, making bacon rolls.

'Hi, babe,' he says cheerfully. 'Thought you might like a bacon butty after the night shift.'

'Yeah, smells good.' She makes to boil the kettle, but Gordon ushers her into a seat.

'I'll make the coffee.'

'What's the occasion?'

'Do I need an occasion to look after my gorgeous wife?' he asks.

Laura looks suspicious but says nothing. She's awful thin—she looks like she could do with a bacon roll.

After they eat, Gordon says, 'I've got a surprise for you.'

'What, better than coffee and a bacon roll?' she asks.

He leads her upstairs by the hand and pulls a gift-wrapped box with a big bow on top from under the bed.

He says, 'I'm sorry things have been a bit weird. I want you to know how much I love you. You, Laura, and no one else.'

Eyes wide, Laura carefully unties the ribbon and opens the box. She gasps at the sight of its contents—a stunning emerald-blue satin dress. She takes it out and holds it up in awe. It has capped sleeves, a ruched waist and a fabulous tapered outline. She drops her robe and slips into the dress.

Gordon zips it up at the back and stands behind her while she looks in the full-length mirror.

The dress is perfect for Laura. She's like a supermodel. It stops a couple of inches above the knee, showing just enough of her long legs. It accentuates her wide hips, the fabric resting on the bones either side of her flat belly. The colour is a beautiful contrast against her blonde hair. She looks astonished, lost for words. Bewitched.

'Wow,' says Gordon. He clears the hair from one side of her neck and kisses it gently. He whispers in her ear. 'You look amazing.'

Laura smiles shyly, in a girlish way.

It's just a dress, Laura! What about the truth?

She pulls up the hem of the skirt and finds the label. It says Talbot Runhof. 'Where did you get this?'

'Harvey Nichols,' says Gordon, as though they shop there all the time.

'I mean, how did you pay?' Her voice is almost pleading. 'Did you have a big win?'

'You could say that, sweetheart.'

Her face betrays her quandary. Does she probe further, and risk losing this fairy tale dress? 'We can't afford this, Gordon. We should be paying a debt or something.'

'Are you kidding me?' His voice is so soft—I'd be glad if this whole dress thing wasn't so messed up. 'This dress was made for you. Just look.'

Laura doesn't answer.

'You work so hard, babe. When do you ever get anything for yourself?'

Laura's eyes fill up and she smiles at him in the mirror.

'Now you just let me do this, and don't try and talk me out of it.'

A pause, then she nods.

Gordon pulls a wad of notes from his pocket, folds them up and slips them gently into the neckline of Laura's dress. 'I'm taking you out for dinner at the weekend,' he says. 'Somewhere special, where you can wear this. Why don't you go and choose some shoes and a bag, hm?'

Laura is still looking at him in the mirror, wide eyed.

'Enjoy your day, sweetheart,' Gordon says, brushing his wife's cheek with the back of his fingers. 'There's something I need to do.' He leaves her glued to the mirror.

Mum phones Aunt Lizzie after lunch. Normally on a Tuesday afternoon, they're both out with their walking group, the Roving Ramblers. It's most unlike mum to miss a walk; she loves exercise and fresh air.

'I'm going to give this afternoon a miss,' mum says.

'Oh no, darling, you must come! You'll feel better if you get out and about. Our darling girl wouldn't want us to mope too long, would she?'

'It's not that,' mum says, 'I really feel quite unwell.'

'What's the matter?'

'Something viral, I think. I've got a headache and I'm tired. I keep going hot and cold.'

'Oh dear. Would you like me to come and drive you to the doctor's?'

'No thanks. That's kind of you, but I just need some rest.'

'Alright, darling. Well, let me know if you need anything.'

'I will.'

Gordon

Gordon was no shrinking violet, but he had no inclination to be anyone's thug. However, his new employer had been good to him. The work was easy, and the money was amazing. For the first time in years, his wife had looked at him without disgust or disappointment. If he played his cards right, he reckoned he could soon have Laura eating out of his hand. No more Spanish Inquisition every time he went out or made a bit of cash. Not if she felt the benefits too, enough to realise it was better not to ask. But he wouldn't let her think it was another woman. No way.

He only looked once at the picture of the boy on his phone. He was little more than a kid, not much older than Gordon's boys.

It didn't take long to find the West Pilton flat where the target lived. He parked a few hundred yards down the road and walked back. His own house was no palace, but it would look like one here amongst the dilapidated buildings with their boarded-up windows. There were a few large items dumped on the pavement or in the unkempt front gardens: a mattress, a sofa, a broken washing machine. Reaching the target's block, he passed a kid's bike and scooter in the overgrown garden. There was takeaway rubbish, beer cans and cigarette ends on the inside stair.

He found the flat on the second floor, rang the bell and waited. No answer. There was no way Gordon was dealing with this shite twice, so he kicked the door in. The kid was there—he jumped up from the sofa. He put his hands up in a conciliatory gesture.

'It was an accident,' the kid said. 'I never gave anything away, I swear.'

Gordon grabbed him by the scruff of the neck and put him up against the nearest bit of bare wall.

A woman's voice called groggily from an adjoining room. 'John – what's going on?'

Gordon's heart lurched.

'Nothing mum – it's just a friend,' John said. 'Go back to sleep.'

Gordon hauled the boy across a threadbare carpet towards the front door, past the only furniture: a small sofa, a coffee table and a TV unit. How dare he have a woman in there, making this difficult? He yanked the boy out, slammed the door and thrust him against the landing wall.

'I've got a message for you,' Gordon said. 'You hold your tongue about your work. You trust no one. This is your only warning.'

Gordon's instructions were: Beating. No weapons. No hospital. Mess face. Since a busted face was required, Gordon hit the boy nowhere else. The first well-placed punch burst his lip, which immediately swelled to twice its usual size; the second was landed in the perfect position to blacken his eye. Gordon waited a few seconds for the eye to swell up, catching his breath. The boy stood frozen against the wall, as though expecting to be shot.

Gordon whipped out his phone and took the requisite picture. He said, 'Don't give me a reason to come here again,' and promptly left.

Before he could get to his van, he bent over, retching and heaving until the contents of his stomach spattered onto the pavement.

Meredith

Mum hesitates when the doorbell rings, as though she might pretend to be out. But she heads to the front door and looks through the peephole. She opens the door to a delivery woman with a large bouquet.

Mum sets the flowers by the kitchen sink. They're from Murray, bless him. He's chosen an exquisite white arrangement—roses and lilies, set off with various greenery. I wonder why he chose white flowers—was it to let mum know he remembered me, because of the white roses at my funeral?

Or because white is a symbol of peace and surrender? Maybe it was both. Or maybe I'm reading too much into it. Either way, how unimaginably thoughtful.

Mum reads the little card. It says, 'Thinking of you. Hope to see you soon. Love, Murray.' She raises her eyebrows in an expression of pleasant surprise, but leaves the flowers in their box and returns to her armchair.

She's staring blankly at the TV again. It's almost lunchtime and she's not even dressed. Maybe she really is unwell.

Later in the afternoon, the phone rings, and she's still sitting there. She lets the answering machine take it. 'Hi Helen, it's Margot. We missed you at yoga class today. I hope you're okay. Let me know if I can help with anything, and hopefully, we'll see you next week.' There's a click, then a beep, and mum just sits there, staring through the TV, a cup of tea going cold beside her.

Davie

Angela refuses to buy Davie any more beer. 'It's time you were getting out anyway,' she says. 'You're becoming a recluse.'

I doubt he would've found the motivation for milk and bread, but for beer, there's no question. He takes the walking stick, lights a fag, and heads towards Holy Corner[10] and the shops beyond.

He's only slightly lop-sided now; a little unsteady on his feet, but the stick helps. He coughs and spits on the pavement.

He stops suddenly, staring at a building across the road. His expression is far away, as though remembering a long-forgotten past.

He shakes himself and takes his journey in earnest. He enters the first off-license he comes to and grabs what he needs, keeping his head down like a wanted criminal. He struggles home as quickly as his old legs can carry him. He keeps checking over his shoulder until he reaches the flat and locks the door behind him.

He goes straight to the kitchen and opens a beer, taking a deep slug before he's even removed his coat.

---

[10] Local nickname for a small area of Edinburgh where Bruntsfield meets Morningside. A crossroads with a church on every corner gave rise to the name.

A couple of tins later, he shakes his head and chuckles to himself. 'Leave the past where it belongs you stupid sod,' he says. 'She's probably dead by now.'

Meredith

Kyle's on shift with Fiona again, and he's ready for confrontation.

'You're a thief,' he says.

Fiona scoffs. 'You don't know *anything*.'

'I know you neglect the residents and cut corners, but stealing from them? That's low.'

Fiona shrugs. 'You can't prove anything.'

'I can,' Kyle says, 'because I planted fifty quid in Irene's room the other night, with another member of staff as my witness.' Nice touch about the witness, Kyle! 'Then you took it. I found the notes in your bag, easily identified because I marked them. I removed them from your bag in front of the same member of staff who watched me leave them in Irene's room.'

'And who is this mysterious "member of staff?"'

'You'll only find out if you force my hand, Fiona. Here's what you're going to do. You're going to resign within one week. If you don't, we'll make sure you're sacked. And you'll never work in the caring profession again.'

Fiona's lips tighten. 'You don't understand,' she says. 'I need this job, Kyle.'

'You should've thought of that before you stole from the residents.'

'It's not for me.' Fiona's eyes well up and her cheeks turn red. 'I need money for my son.' She turns her face away. 'For bail.'

'That's tough,' Kyle says, his expression softening, 'but it's not Irene's problem. What I've said stands. You resign within the week. But to show there are no hard feelings, you can keep the fifty.' He takes the money from his pocket and holds it out.

Fiona looks from the notes to Kyle and back again, her expression full of bitterness. 'Screw this!' she mutters, but she takes the money. She grabs her things and walks out without another glance at Kyle.

Alfie brightens to see Nathan in his favourite reading spot; he has exciting news for the boy. There's a smile on my face, too—they spread.

'There's a job opening here,' Alfie says. 'Junior assistant, part-time. They're looking for a young person to train up. You're practically doing the job already, so you should definitely apply.'

Nathan grins. 'That sounds great!'

'Here.' Alfie passes him an application pack. 'The deadline's next week. I can write you a reference if you like.'

'Thanks, Alfie.' Nathan takes the paperwork, finds a table and gets stuck in.

Alfie returns to work, but etched on his face is a secret smile that only I can see.

Davie finds his courage to go out again. The beer seems to help. He takes a deep breath outside and holds his head high. Nothing to worry about.

He wanders along the road and into a shop for a newspaper. He takes it to a neighbouring café and orders coffee and a scone. He opens the paper and peruses the headlines but becomes distracted by a petite twenty-something brunette at a nearby table. The woman is well-dressed in a suit and heels, with close-set eyes. She sits up straight, her head held high, typing on a laptop. Davie peers at her over the top of his newspaper, his eyes narrowed.

He makes for the toilets, which allows him to get a better look. Trepidation turns to relief on his face, then back again. The woman looks up and catches his eye.

He steps backwards and bumps into someone's chair, then shuffles out of the café as quickly as possible, forgetting to pay, hiding his face under his hat. He stumbles towards home, checking over his shoulder every thirty seconds. He stops by a building site that smells of fresh cement and leans his hands on the wall, taking great heaving breaths. His face turns very pale.

When he recovers enough to walk home, he locks and bolts the door from the inside. He watches it for a long time, as though it might be knocked in at any moment.

Helen

Fed up with the mess, Helen lifted the dirty cups and saucers from her little table and washed the dishes. Ginger yowled and bolted upstairs.

'What's wrong with him?' She finished the washing up and emptied the water from the sink, shivering. Maybe the dishes could drip dry, just this once. She planned to sit down again with her blanket, but there was a dirty cup still on the table. 'Damn.' She was so sure she'd lifted them all. She took it to the kitchen, gave it a quick wash and left it drying with the others.

Before sitting down, she needed the toilet. 'Damn.' She headed upstairs and found Meredith's door open, Ginger curled up on the bed. 'Did you push that door open?' She lifted the cat out of the room and closed the door with a click.

Downstairs again, Helen's heart skipped a beat when she reached her chair: the same dirty cup sat on the table. 'What the...?'

Am I losing my mind?

Stan

Stan took Stacy to his place, tense and eager with anticipation. Having just come off his shift, he showed her around – which didn't take long in his one-bedroom flat – and fixed her a drink. 'I need a shower love, so just make yourself at home.'

By the time he was dressed, she'd rifled through his entire film collection and was onto the books.

'You really *are* a potato Mr Marshall! I haven't heard of half of this stuff – I mean really, how many superhero movies can they make?'

Stan laughed nervously. 'Infinite, really. There are millions of graphic novels that haven't been made into films yet.'

'Oooh, *graphic novels*? Is that what these big boy comics are?'

'Watch it. I'll have you know I'm a sensitive soul. How about you make yourself useful and put on some music?'

'Bring it on.' She laughed.

Stan switched on his bluetooth speaker as she started looking through playlists on her phone. 'You can connect to this—it's called Frodo.'

'Nice.' Stacy grinned.

It was hard to think about food, but Stan brought the takeaway menus and set them on the coffee table. He lit a few candles and dimmed the lights. The first track started—Adele *Set Fire to the Rain*.

Stacy moved next to him on the sofa, close.

'What do you want to eat?' he asked, putting his arms around her.

'Not hungry.' She leaned in for a kiss.

Stan returned it, exploring slowly, but promising everything. He was almost overwhelmed by desire, and at once anxious about his performance.

Stacy let him take the lead, and he took his time, savouring every moment. He allowed himself to smell her hair and skin, to feel her close. He gave her time to respond to his kisses. His hands teased, touching lightly until he finally allowed them to wander.

He gave Stacy everything he had; body and soul, he was hers. He watched her reactions, listened to every sound, and attended to her wants. He made love to her like his life depended on it. There was no one else in the whole world but the two of them.

Finally, they lay on the bed, catching their breath. Stan barely managed to stop himself saying *I love you*.

Meredith

Stacy's been at Stan's overnight! I'm so happy for him, I can't stop smiling. When I saw where things were going last night I left them to it, but I couldn't resist checking in this morning. They're just glowing.

I think I've had a little something to do with that! Let's face it, if it weren't for me, they wouldn't have met. I've done what I can to encourage it since.

Stan can't keep the smile off his face either. They goof around with his movie replica toys and carry on like a pair of kids. They go out for a huge cooked breakfast at Stan's favourite cafe. Bacon, sausage, eggs, toast, beans, hot coffee and great company. Stacy loves Stan's banter, and he keeps it coming.

'What are you thinking?' she asks.

'I'm thinking about getting you back up the apples to bed.'

Stacy giggles. 'What?'

'Apples and pears. Stairs.' He causes further confusion and hilarity a few minutes later, when he says, 'I love your bacons.'

'I didn't make the bacon.'

'Bacon and eggs—legs.'

After breakfast, he takes her hand and shows her around London. She's been before but enjoys the tour anyway. They take the tube and see the sights: The Houses of Parliament, Big Ben and the London Eye. They wander around Camden market.

Somehow, I find myself thinking of Alfie, and I leave for the railway.

CHAPTER 15

Meredith

Andy and Nancy meet Gary and his wife Freya at their favourite Indian Restaurant, just across from Haymarket station. Introductions done, Gary and Freya go inside first. Andy glances up and down the street before following, one hand sitting protectively on Nancy's back. Andy pulls out chairs for Nancy and Freya before sitting with his back to the wall. Once he's scanned the room, he relaxes a little. Nancy watches him do all this, her brow furrowed. She looks around the room too, then back at Andy.

'So, Nancy,' says Freya in her Irish accent, 'Gary tells me you've got family.'

'I do,' Nancy says. 'A daughter, Claire, and a son, Malcolm. Claire has three wee ones—Hannah, Bailey and Evie.'

'Sounds like Claire has her work cut out!' says Gary.

Nancy says, 'Aye, she does! What about you two?'

'I've a son, Mark,' says Freya. 'He's fourteen. He's only with us for holidays and weekends, but he gets on great with Gary.'

'Aye,' Gary says. 'Mark's a good lad.'

Andy stiffens when the waiter approaches to take their order. What does he think is going to happen?

Gary asks Nancy, 'So, what about you two? How did you meet?'

'At school, would you believe? We were in the same year. We grew up near each other in Gracemount. I was a bit of a tomboy when I was wee, and we used to play together—well, all the kids did, I suppose.'

A shadow passes over Andy's face. His memories of childhood in Gracemount are not so rose-tinted. His expressions flit between anxiety, pride for Gary, and adoration for Nancy, who's still talking.

'We went out together when we were teenagers, didn't we Andy?'

He smiles at Nancy, full and warm, his angst forgotten in that moment. 'Aye, we did.'

Nancy says, 'I hadn't seen him since I left Gracemount at seventeen until I bumped into him in a pub a couple of weeks ago! After fifty years! Can you believe that?'

Andy takes her hand under the table. 'It's like you never left,' he says.

There's love mingled with sadness in Nancy's eyes.

'Aw!' Freya turns to Gary and says, 'I hope we're that smitten at their age!'

The food is served and the conversation flows. Andy's keen to tell Nancy all about Gary's achievements—his promotion to head of his faculty at the high school, his doctorate, and how well-respected he is.

Gary blushes a bit, but I suppose he's used to it.

'That's amazing, Gary,' says Nancy. 'No wonder your dad's so proud.'

Gary's smile is bashful. 'He's always got behind me. He's a great dad.'

Nancy smiles, her eyes welling up.

Gary says, 'You know, Freya runs her own art gallery.'

'Is that right?' Nancy sounds impressed. 'Are you an artist yourself, Freya, or a businesswoman?'

'Oh, a bit of both, I hope!'

'Yeah,' says Gary. 'She rents out some studio space, and sells other artists' work, but half the space is dedicated to her own stuff. You should see it, Nancy, she paints with oils: big, bold paintings with vivid colours.'

'I absolutely must see it. Andy, you'll need to take me along very soon.'

Tonight is the night Gordon has promised Laura dinner and dancing. She's organised food for the boys, showered and laid out her new dress. She's chosen gunmetal grey stilettos, a matching beaded clutch bag and a cashmere shawl. Looks like she's going along with it, then. And yet, the whole outfit is laid out with tags still attached—the option to take it back.

Gordon finds her standing in her robe, hair wet, just looking at the dress. He's bought himself a black Armani suit, and a shirt, tie and shoes worthy of it. He's been for a haircut and shave from the Turkish barber, and he's bought a Dior fragrance. He greets his wife with a kiss, hangs up his things, and goes for a shower. She watches him silently. When he comes back, a towel around his waist, he finds her still standing there, gazing at the dress. He dresses quickly in jeans and a T-shirt.

'It's okay, we've plenty of time,' he says. 'I need to pop out for twenty minutes before I get ready. There's something I need to do.'

'Where's the money coming from, Gordon?' Laura asks, but only half-heartedly. The anger's gone from her voice.

'Do you like it?' Before she can answer, Gordon produces a box from his wardrobe and passes it to Laura.

Inside is a stunning diamond necklace and earring set. The tiny jewels sparkle under the light, leaving Laura speechless.

Gordon says, 'You deserve this, sweetheart. It's high time you were recognised for all the hard work you do.' He moves closer, lifts some of Laura's hair and whispers in her ear, allowing his lips to touch her softly. 'That'll look so sexy with the dress. Why don't you take these labels off your things, and get ready, hm?'

She turns, surrenders herself into his arms and lets his mouth find hers.

His keen, lingering kiss promises more before he whispers, 'That's my girl,' and promptly exits, leaving her smouldering, guilty.

If you accept all this, Laura, you become complicit. Whatever he's doing, you're saying it's okay with you.

Laura takes a few deep breaths, finds a pair of scissors, and with trembling hands does just as Gordon suggests. She blow dries her hair and heats it into loose curls. She dons the dress and shoes and looks in the mirror from every angle, the girl within smiling and giggling to herself. It's a big change from the jeans and jogging bottoms she wears around the house.

By the time she's applied make-up and perfume, Gordon's back, getting into his suit. It's a big change for him, too. With his hair neatly cut and his close shave, he looks almost refined. Laura's distracted from her own appeal by Gordon.

'Wow,' she says as he knots his tie, 'you look...'

'Respectable?'

She laughs. 'I was going to say handsome.'

'I should be to go out with you. You look incredible—you're going to turn heads.'

There's that girlish smile again.

'Here.' Gordon takes the diamond necklace from its box, and his wife lifts her hair. They both turn towards the mirror as he delicately places it on her neck and fastens it at the back.

The diamonds wink and shimmer with the slightest movement. They both gaze into the mirror, transfixed. Then she adds the earrings.

Gordon calls for a taxi. Laura makes to speak but he says, 'Stop worrying. I'll take care of it. Just relax and enjoy yourself. Tonight is for you.'

He takes her to the Tower Restaurant, and they're seated at a table for two by the window. Gordon was right—heads do turn when Laura walks in. I like seeing her happy; I want them both to be happy. I want them to enjoy nice things and spend time together. But at what cost? This is all false, an illusion that could fall apart at any moment.

There's a live pianist, and candles on the tables. This is the first time I've seen Gordon and Laura look into each other's eyes. There's something new, an excitement you don't get from twenty-odd years of marriage. Is it possible I could be wrong about everything? Could Gordon keep doing deliveries without any harm to him or his family? Even if he could, what about the other families—the ones whose kids, or worse, parents are using the drugs?

I watch them order delicious meals: steak for Gordon, oysters for Laura. They eat, drink wine, and relax more and more as the evening goes on. They talk about their boys, what colour to decorate the living room—anything but Gordon's new job.

'Maybe we should take a holiday,' Gordon says. 'It's time we got away somewhere, just the two of us.'

Laura's face shows a mixture of confusion and delight.

'Where would you like to go? How about a cruise?'

She gets on board with the conversation, but I think she's just humouring him. It's too soon for Laura to be confident that there's more wherever this money came from.

Gordon leaves a ludicrous tip behind when they leave. He's really enjoying the novelty of throwing his money around. I've seen enough. I'm going to leave them to their dancing, and whatever comes next.

Stan and Stacy are in bed at Stan's place. He gets up to make coffee and returns with two steaming mugs. He wraps an arm around her waist and moves in for another kiss. He pulls back after a few seconds and looks at her with a sigh, hesitating.

'What?' she asks.

'I love you.'

Stan waits anxiously, but Stacy doesn't say it back.

She breaks away, sits up and sips her coffee.

Stan's face shows the same panic that's rising within me. Has he put his foot in it? But how could he hold it back, if that's how he feels?

'You've gone quiet. Was it not...good, for you?' he asks.

'Oh, it was,' she says. 'It's not that.'

'What's wrong, then?'

There's a pause. 'Stan, what are we doing?'

'What d'you mean, love?'

'I mean, what are you looking for out of this relationship?'

'Are you ready to hear the answer to that?'

'Look, you've said those three words, you might as well be out with it.' She sounds irritable.

Poor Stan looks crestfallen. He says, 'I'm sorry if those little words upset you, Stace, but I can't help the way I feel.'

'What do you want me to say?'

Stan lays a hand gently on her shoulder and moves around to look into her eyes. 'I want you to say you love me, too.' Her face says it's impossible; her eyes tear up a little. 'You asked what I'm looking for – it's *you*, Stace. I've been looking for you my whole life. I want us to grow old together. I want kids.'

Stacy exhales sharply. 'I...don't know what to say. I like you a lot. I like being with you. But I didn't know you felt so strongly...it's just so full on.'

'I get it.'

'I mean, I thought we were just having fun.'

'We *are* having fun, ain't we?' He grins, trying to lighten the mood.

She smiles sadly.

'Why does this change anything?'

'Because...I don't want to hurt you.'

Stan says, 'You won't.'

'I will. I already have. I can see it in your face.'

He turns away, looking like his heart might break. 'Don't push me away,' he says. 'That would hurt more.'

'Can we just sleep on it?' she asks. 'It's been a long week.'

'Course love. I can sleep on the sofa if you like?'

'No, you're okay here.' She smiles but turns her back to him as she lies down.

As I've watched Aunt Lizzie, and our friend Davie, I've had the strangest impression that there's some connection between them. Truths flow through us and we pass them on; I feel these two need to meet, though I've no idea why. I watch their movements, and I arrange a 'coincidence'.

Aunt Lizzie plans to wear her grey tweed jacket to the Scottish Women's Institute AGM; so she drops it at the dry cleaners on Morningside Road. On the way there, she passes the surgery where Davie has an appointment, the day after the AGM. It's a bit of a long shot—they could easily miss each other, but it's a chance. I ask Michael to help me out with the physical work, and he changes the date on the job slip for Aunt Lizzie's jacket.

The days and nights are long watching over mum. I'm powerless to ease her grief, but it's my duty to watch. It's the least I can do. She's restless but resigned at the same time. She's falling into a pattern of tossing and turning at night and sleeping more during the day. Lizzie believes her to be unwell, but I'm not convinced. She isn't showing any outward physical symptoms. She's hardly taken any painkillers, either.

She detests 'idleness', as she'd call it, but here she is surrounded by half drunk cups of tea, dirty dishes in the kitchen, and her bed unmade. She hasn't even showered in days.

On the positive side, she's stopped crying. Now, she's mostly just sitting there, falling in and out of sleep, staring at the wall, not even bothering to switch on the television.

The phone's gone a few times, but she doesn't answer. She just lets the answering machine take it. There's one from a friend of hers, from her book club—they're all concerned about her. I suppose they've heard about me, and what I did. There's one from Aunt Lizzie just checking in, assuming she's still ill and telling her to get well soon. The last one is from Murray, inviting her to Sunday dinner again. He says he's going to keep asking till she says yes—and there's something so endearing in his voice, I don't know how she can resist him.

Murray's determined already, but I keep visiting anyway. I remind him of mum, keeping her present in his thoughts.

Stan wakes to the sound of the shower running, realising with a jolt that Stacy's still in his flat. Excitement on his face quickly turns to dread.

He dresses quickly, makes coffee and sits on the sofa, his leg jittering.

Stacy comes out of the bathroom, also dressed, drying her hair with a towel. 'Morning,' she says pleasantly.

'Morning love.' An awkward silence.

'Look Stan...sorry if I was cold last night.'

'You don't need to apologise for being honest.'

'You just took me by surprise. If I were to settle down with someone, it would be someone like you. It's just that I'm not looking to settle down.'

'That's okay,' Stan says. 'Take as long as you need. I can wait.'

'I'm not sure time would make any difference.' She sighs. 'Anyway, I'm going away for a while. I've been offered an opportunity, and I've decided to take it.'

'Where?'

'I'm going to Lusaka, Zambia, as a health centre volunteer. There's an HIV and AIDS epidemic, and they're short of workers.'

'That's...good.' He nods. 'How long for?'

'Six months, initially.'

'Are you running away from me, Stace?'

'No—I've been planning this for a year. It's on my bucket list.'

'Why didn't you tell me sooner?'

Stacy says, 'I didn't think it was a big deal.'

Stan raises his eyebrows.

'Thanks for this weekend – it's been fun.'

'What does that mean? Am I gonna see you again?'

'We want different things. I think we should call it off.'

'No we shouldn't! Talk to me – let's work it out.'

'I don't want to talk. I need to go.' She collects her things.

As she reaches the door, Stan says, 'At least let me see you off. We could still travel together—I'm heading back up today anyway.'

'That's not a good idea. I'll see you around, Stan.'

This wasn't how it was supposed to work out. I'm so sorry, Stan.

Andy wakes on Sunday morning to the smell of grilled bacon; Nancy is up, dressed, and cooking. 'Morning gorgeous,' he says, kissing her cheek as he pulls on his dressing gown.

'Morning.' She smiles and gives him a wink, reminding him without words of some private encounter of the previous night. 'Hope you're hungry.' He grins like a schoolboy, inhaling the smell of the fried food.

'Starving,' he says, boiling the kettle.

'So, what do you think of my brood?'

'They're great, Nance. I thought they wouldn't like me...but they're not judgemental, are they?'

'No!' She scoffed. 'No airs and graces here!'

'I just mean, they're easy going...like you. It was like they'd known me for years. Like I was part of the family.'

'You are.'

'If they knew everything about my past, they might not want me joining their family.' He looks down and says, 'You might not, either.'

Nancy turns to face him. 'I don't care what you've done. I can see what kind of man you are now and that's all that matters.'

'Is it?'

'Well, isn't it? Don't you think people should get second chances when they've made mistakes?' Nancy watches Andy's face, biting her lip.

'Yeah, I believe in second chances.'

'Well, then. You can tell me what's bothering you when you're ready—or just forget it. It won't change the way I feel.' Andy looks doubtful, ashamed.

'Okay.' he says. 'Wee Evie's a cracker! I can't believe how many words she knows.'

'Aye, she's clever—and quite a wee character.'

'How old did you say she was?'

'Just two and a half.' She passes him a plate of steaming hot breakfast.

He inhales the aroma and says, 'If I didn't love you yesterday, I certainly do now.'

She laughs at his enthusiasm as he tucks into a greasy sausage.

CHAPTER 16

Meredith

Laura sings around the house while she cleans and tidies. She pops her head into Nathan's room and finds him playing with a shiny new iPhone. 'When did you get that?' she asks.

Nathan shrugs. "Few days ago."

'Who from?' He hesitates. 'Was it dad?'

'Yeah, but he told me not to say anything.'

'Why?'

He shrugs again. 'Probably in case you thought it was too much.'

She smiles. 'I don't think that. It's cool with me.' In a casual tone, she asks, 'Did dad say anything about where the money came from?'

Nathan shrugs again—the teenage answer for everything.

Laura asks, 'How's your friend Alfie doing?'

'He's fine.'

'He hasn't asked you to go anywhere with him, or tried anything weird?'

Nathan rolls his eyes. 'Mum, stop. Alfie's a good guy.' He was still fixed on the phone, both thumbs going. 'He might've found me a job.'

'Oh really? Do tell.'

'Part-time junior assistant at the library. I've filled out an application.'

'That's great! I hope you get it, son.'

The shrug. 'You never know.'

The house is in quite a state—relatively speaking—when Aunt Lizzie arrives on Sunday afternoon. She unlocks the door, gives a knock, opens it and calls 'hello?' Mum hasn't taken the chain off, and I don't expect her to answer. She'd be mortified for Lizzie to see her unwashed, let alone see the house in a state of disarray.

However, mum drags her feet to the door, releases the chain, and returns to her chair. Lizzie comes in behind her, taking in the fact that she isn't dressed.

'You didn't phone to say you were still ill, darling, so here I am.' Aunt Lizzie puts one of her prize Victoria sponges on the kitchen bunker and clocks the undone dishes. 'Just as well, by the look of things!' She comes back to the sitting room and finds mum's collection of half drunk cups of tea. She clasps her hands together in earnest. 'Really, darling! If I'd known you were so under the weather, I'd have come before now to give you a hand.' Mum only looks wearily at Lizzie. 'Oh, you poor thing! We must get you to bed.'

After inspection, Aunt Lizzie insists on changing mum's bedding before coaxing her to lie down.

Mum obeys but lies in bed staring at the ceiling.

Aunt Lizzie offers to make food and drink, but mum declines weakly.

'Not to worry, darling, once you're rested you'll get your appetite back. I must insist that you try to take some water, though.' The water is brought and left by the bed, but mum doesn't touch it.

Aunt Lizzie goes to work downstairs, collecting and washing dishes. She opens the fridge and cupboards, tutting and muttering when she finds nothing but a half-finished pint of milk and a packet of biscuits. 'How does she expect to get well without eating?'

After running around with a duster and the hoover, Aunt Lizzie goes out for groceries and returns with a loaf of bread and fresh veg to make soup.

I watch her fondly. She's like a busy bee, my Aunt Lizzie, always working away at something. Her mother was a lady, just like her. Aunt Lizzie used to try making a lady of me, but I'm too awkward. It was always, 'Sit up straight. Say "please" and "thank you". Speak clearly. Hold your head up.' It wasn't so bad, though. She always called me 'darling' and she loved me, lady or not.

I'm glad you're here, I say. *Thank you for taking care of mum.*

Stan's on my mind—I don't know if I can help, but I need to try. Mum's asleep now. Her aura has grown so pale, it's like a thin layer of smoke. She's safe for now, and Aunt Lizzie's here. I can go to Stan and come straight back.

He's at Stacy's door! I try to stop him—I don't want him to suffer any more rejection—but he won't be deterred.

She visibly deflates when she sees him standing there.

'Can we talk?' Stan asks, his expression miserable.

Stacy sighs. 'I really don't have anything to say. I'm sorry.'

'I don't get it. I thought we had something good going on – something great. And now I'm getting the cold shoulder? What did I do wrong?'

Stacy says, 'Nothing. We're just in different places.'

'I need real answers, love. I don't understand.'

'Please, just go,' She closes the door firmly and returns to the sitting room with red cheeks and an elevated heart rate. She sighs and collapses onto the sofa next to her flatmate, Jules.

'What's with this guy?' Stacy says. 'Why can't he take no for an answer?'

'Persistent, is he?' Jules asks.

'I'll say. He's a nester. He needs to find someone who wants to settle down: marriage, kids, a mortgage. It's not for me.'

'Yeah,' Jules says between munching on crisps, 'he sounds horrible.'

'It's not funny, Jules!' Stacy jabs her friend with an elbow. 'I'm not turning into my mum. You can go through a whole life together and still end up hating one another.'

'Hey.' Jules sits up straighter and turns to Stacy. 'Just because your parents made a hash of things, doesn't mean you will.'

'That's what I used to tell myself, before Jake.'

'Oh, what's that cheating scumbag got to do with Stan?'

'Nothing. I don't know. He's just too full on, you know?'

Jules says, 'You'll work it out.'

'Already did. I'll head out to Zambia, and he'll forget about me. He'll be on to someone new long before I'm back.'

Stan is still there on the other side of the door, as though walking away might sever some invisible tie. My heart goes out to him, but I can't think of any words to whisper. I just hope he can feel it.

Mum's standing in the sitting room, making an awful choking noise. Aunt Lizzie cowers by the door, whimpering. The room feels like fire raging against a blizzard. Michael stands face to face with mum—very close, his light white-hot.

He roars at mum. 'Get out!' My stomach does a somersault—I've never seen Michael angry before. I move round to look at mum's face, then I see it.

The shadow!

She has the shadow's colourless eyes and grey skin. Mum screams.

Afraid he's hurting her, I shout, 'Stop it!'

Michael doesn't pay any attention to me. He dives through a gap in mum's aura. Mum screams louder, pieces of three faces merging grotesquely into one. I watch, terrified, for seconds that feel like hours, until black dust spews out of mum's head like a swarm of tiny insects and vanishes into the air. Right behind the dust comes a dazzling beam of light that materialises into Michael. He flops onto the floor. Mum collapses into her armchair.

Aunt Lizzie looks white as a sheet, her eyes wild. 'What the hell was that?' she demands.

Mum looks at her friend uncomprehendingly.

'Was that supposed to be funny?'

'What?' Mum puts a hand to her head, wincing.

'That voice you put on. Those things you said. Was it some kind of joke, darling?'

'No, I...don't know what you're talking about.'

'Well. I need to go.' Without further ado, Aunt Lizzie turns on her heel and walks out, nose in the air.

Mum sits for five minutes, wearing the same confused expression. She totters up to bed, holding onto furniture and walls, and crashes out in her clothes on top of the duvet.

I stay the night, terrified the shadow will return before Michael wakes.

It's the day of Davie's appointment, and Lizzie has to collect her jacket a day late from the dry cleaners. I feel a bit guilty about the telling off she gives the poor woman in the shop.

'Such incompetence! It's inexcusable, really. What a terrible inconvenience!'

The woman's cheeks turn a deep shade of puce, and she apologises profusely and waives the cost.

Aunt Lizzie is hardly placated but leaves the shop with a parting shot. 'You just lost a life-long customer!'

I calculate she's a little early to bump into Davie. (I want her to pass the surgery at the right time—Angela always has him there fifteen minutes before the appointment.)

I call on Michael again—he approves of the whole thing, which is encouraging. I'd be afraid to interfere on my own. He's amazingly skilled when it comes to doing things without being discovered. He bumps a passer-by, who spills coffee over Aunt Lizzie's skirt. She's most displeased, and the incident delays her a full five minutes, by the time she's finished having a go at the reprobate with the coffee and dabbing her skirt with tissues from her handbag. She mutters to herself as she bins the tissues and moves on just when I want her to.

Sure enough, Aunt Lizzie passes by the surgery as Davie and Angela arrive. They're about to cross the pavement right in front of her. They stop to let her pass. She glances up with a curt nod, followed swiftly by a double-take.

'David, is that you?' she asks.

His eyes widen; he opens his mouth but doesn't answer.

'Good Lord, it's been so long!'

'Davie,' Angela says, 'the lady's talking to you.' She addresses Lizzie. 'I'm sorry, he's not very well. I'm Angela.' She extends her hand, and Aunt Lizzie shakes it warmly.

'I'm Lizzie. We go way back.' She turns back to Davie. 'I didn't know you were back in the country,' she says. 'You should've looked me up. We've plenty to reminisce about, hm?'

Davie's face has turned ashen grey, and his breath is coming in short bursts.

'Oh my dear man, you don't look well at all.' She turns to Angela and says, 'I must insist on catching up with him when he's up to it.' She takes a notebook and pen from her handbag and exchanges contact details with Angela, who seems pleased with the prospect of Davie having an old friend visit.

Aunt Lizzie takes her leave, and Angela struggles into the surgery with her ailing brother.

Stan's time passes painstakingly, in sleepless nights and endless cups of coffee. He tries to engage Stacy on Facebook, but her interaction is minimal – a like here and there, no comment, no reply. I should've seen this coming and warned him to hold back. I thought I was doing him a favour but I've set him up for heartache. It's just like the way it is with mum—I can't whisper away what he's going through, try as I might.

Stan can't give up yet; he's in too deep. He calls her; she doesn't answer. He leaves a message and sends a text.

We need to talk. Please.

I watch Stacy. She's busy making plans for Zambia—travel arrangements, vaccinations and so on. It looks like she's really going.

Nathan doesn't realise the library job was created with him in mind. It's his first ever interview. He paces outside the library after school, checking the time every few minutes. He produces a can of Lynx and sprays it on his clothes, but he reeks of nervous sweat.

His eyes widen when he finds four other young people waiting. He takes a seat between two of them, fidgeting nervously. A name is called—not his. Alfie passes by, giving him a sly thumbs up, and he grins. *Someone has to get the job Nathan – why not you?*

Two more interviewees are taken in before Monika opens the door and asks for Nathan. 'Hello, Nathan. I understand you spend a lot of time here, yes?'

Nathan nods.

'Why is that?'

'I like the library,' he says.

'Alfie tells me you are helping him a lot. You are good with alphabet, yes?'

Nathan shrugs. 'I like sorting the books.'

'That's good. Have you thought about what you want for career?'

'I've tried to, but I'm not too sure yet.'

Monika nods. 'Maybe you learn more here – maybe you like to be a librarian?'

'Yeah...I think maybe I would,' Nathan says. 'I mean, definitely. Yes, I want to be a librarian.'

Monika chuckles and notes something down on her clipboard. 'Is good to meet you, Nathan. I'll be in touch—probably later today, okay?'

Nathan nods. 'Thanks.' He leaves the room, relieved it's over.

He doesn't go home—job aside, he chooses the library. He sits and reads, still working his way through the Harry Potter saga. He sorts books. He exchanges nervous glances with Alfie.

It's only half an hour before Monika comes to tell him the good news. The job is his! Nathan's face is a picture—he's really pleased.

Alfie's chuffed for him, too, and they go out for doughnuts after his shift. Nathan starts part-time next week. He chats excitedly to Alfie about it; he's unusually animated.

'It'll be great to earn some money of my own. I can help my mum...if she needs it. I can't wait to tell her!'

Alfie listens quietly to his chatter, a knowing smile dancing across his kind eyes.

I've been practising trying to isolate spiritual objects night and day. Occasionally, I see them, but they're so hard to hold onto! I still don't understand what it is I'm doing right or wrong. I should be improving by now.

How can I achieve anything with just words? How do I know if anyone can hear? If Stacy can, she doesn't listen. Gordon and Laura, the same. I try, I really do, but I can't see any progress. They're all in a quandary, at some level—what if it's my fault? Maybe things would unfold exactly the same with or without me. If I could just move something solid, I could prove to myself that I'm really here. I could change something.

I go to Michael to ask for his help. It takes me a moment to realise we're across the road from Aunt Lizzie's house, a couple of doors down. Michael is intent on a rough-looking old man getting out of a beaten-up Vauxhall Astra. He's a hulking creature with sun-weathered skin, whose body looks like it's seen better days. His T-shirt reveals toned shoulders and arms but does nothing to hide the gut hanging over the waistband of his jeans. His white hair is shaved short, and he sports matching white stubble. Above his lip is an ugly scar that runs right up the side of his nose. His forearm bears a faded tattoo—an eagle's head. There's a deadness to his eyes that chills me.

The man picks up a pair of binoculars from the passenger's seat. What on earth is he doing here? He walks to Aunt Lizzie's house but doesn't go to the door. Instead, he walks around the side of the house to the back garden. He finds a spot behind the fruit trees where he can see Aunt Lizzie in the kitchen. She's busy baking—she bakes a lot. (Not that she eats all the cakes herself—she enters competitions and brings her wares when she visits.) The spy in the garden lowers his binoculars and shakes his head, looking thoroughly bored.

He hides in the garden till Aunt Lizzie finishes her cupcakes and does the washing up, which takes an hour and a half. He doesn't seem to feel the cold.

When Lizzie heads out to her women's meeting, he follows her. He loiters outside and tracks her home again when it's over. By this time, darkness is falling. After a few minutes of watching lights come on, he mutters a few expletives and something about a debt before driving off.

Part Four
Box of Secrets

CHAPTER 17

Meredith

Mum wakes with renewed energy. It's a relief to see her out of bed at a reasonable time! She drinks her morning tea, takes a shower and dresses herself. She even pins up her hair. She looks in the mirror and takes a deep breath.

She wraps up warm against the cold and puts on her walking shoes. Thank goodness she's finally getting back to normal! She heads out to Colinton Mains Park and twice around its circumference, nodding to the dog walkers. She hasn't noticed she's almost eighty years old. She doesn't let the hip slow her down; if it becomes painful, she takes tablets, but she always says walking helps.

She walks back towards the house via the shops. First, she stops at the local chemist and collects a prescription that's been waiting for over two weeks. She speaks to several people, remarking on the weather and thanking them politely when they express their condolences.

Next, she joins a queue at the Spar. The weekend is about to start; chocolate, booze and cigarettes are in high demand. Sweets and cakes are flying out the door too; it's Halloween and the kids are expected to be out in force tonight. I assume mum is here for food—some item Aunt Lizzie forgot when she last stocked the fridge—but she chooses a half bottle of gin. I believe she was fond of the occasional gin and tonic in her younger days. I haven't seen her drink in a long while, but who can blame her for wanting one now? At least she's actually *doing* something.

Gordon comes home whistling and passes Laura an envelope full of cash.

'What's this?' she asks.

'November's rent,' he says, 'and a contribution to the housekeeping.'

Laura counts the money. 'Gordon, there's two grand here!'

'I know that. Listen, I'm different now. I can provide for you and the boys, the way I always should've. You could even give up your work if you want.'

Laura looks from the money to Gordon, eyebrows raised. 'Wow, that's...I like working in the children's ward. I wouldn't want to give it up. What would I do with myself?'

'Whatever you fancy. Why don't you reduce your hours a bit, then? Is there any flexibility?'

'I don't know. And what if we need the money, after all?'

'We won't.'

'Gordon, it's great that you're doing this for us, but-'

'Less questions asked, the better,' he says.

Laura's voice is an urgent whisper. 'I'm just worried you're going to get in some kind of crazy trouble! You're not...hurting anyone, are you?'

'No, of course not.' He scratches his nose. 'You know I'd never do anything like that. And I'm not in trouble...but I'm taking out some insurance.'

Laura's face is aghast.

'Just in case,' he says, hands held up in a placatory gesture, 'so you'll be taken care of.'

'You're like someone else. You couldn't even scrape together a month's rent, and now you're taking out insurance?'

'I was advised to, by a friend.'

'Who, that Brian? Well, at least he's good for something. Look, I just want to know you're safe.'

'Safe as houses. I promise.'

Laura waits till she's alone, picks up the phone and dials. She listens to it ring.

'Martha Jones.'

Laura says, 'Really mum, you don't need to be so formal! It's only me.'

'Ah, Laura! It's not formal. It's the proper way to answer the phone.'

'Ok...Mum, can we talk? I'm a bit worried about Gordon.'

'Oh dear. What's wrong?'

'Will you promise to keep this to yourself?'

'Of course, dear.'

'He has a bit of extra money, and I'm not sure where it's coming from.'

'Well, did you ask him?'

'Yeah.'

'And?'

'Well, first he said he was getting extra shifts, but it didn't add up. Then I thought maybe he'd won a bet...'

'But?'

'But the money keeps coming.'

'And what, you think he might be doing something illegal?'

'I'd like to say no, but the amount of cash, mum. Always cash in envelopes. And he's so...different.'

'Different good? Different bad?'

'Good! He's dressing sharp, and he looks ten years younger. He's happier and, frankly, paying his way and more for the first time in years.'

'Hm. Well...I suppose the big question is, do you really want to know?'

Laura asks, 'How d'you mean?'

'Well, if you find out the truth about what he's doing, what then?'

'I suppose that would depend on what I found out.'

'Exactly. The more you know, the more likely you'll be forced to do something about it. Whatever he's into, there's a good chance you couldn't do anything to stop it. Digging could even be dangerous for you and the boys.'

'I hadn't thought of that.'

'Well, I'd think on it, dear. You should make the best of your situation.'

'You're right—I'll think about it. Thanks, mum.'

'You take care.'

'I will.'

Andy

Nancy let out a sudden howl of anguish in the dark street. Andy followed her gaze and spotted Evie's tiny, darkly-dressed form tottering onto the road in front of a moving van. Nancy was running full pelt towards her, leaving Hannah alone on the pavement. With a jolt, Andy looked down and realised Evie had let herself out of the buggy.

The driver wouldn't see her! Nancy was too far away, Andy himself farther still. Instinctively, he crouched down and put an arm around five-year-old Bailey, covering the boy's eyes to shield him from witnessing the inevitable impact.

Evie was in the middle of the road, the van almost on her. Nancy shouted, 'Stop!' and waved her arms trying to get the driver's attention.

It happened so fast—no one could be sure how. The child moved quickly across the road to the far side, the van missing her by inches as it passed by. The driver—who hadn't seen the little girl – slowed down as he approached the hysterical woman in the road, honking his horn. Nancy ran to Evie and pulled her into an embrace, her chest heaving. Before Andy, Bailey and Hannah had caught up, her tears were already flowing—tears of terror and relief.

Andy was pale and sweating, shaking with the knowledge that he'd almost killed Nancy's granddaughter. He was supposed to be looking after her, and he let her get away. It was some moments before he could even speak.

'I'm so sorry, Nance!' Andy said, laying a hand on her shoulder. 'She let herself out the buggy! I never noticed—I'm so sorry!'

'No harm done,' she said, struggling to get her emotions under control.

Evie looked up at her granny's face, peeping out from under her witch's hat. 'What's wrong, Granny?' she asked.

'You ran in the road sweetheart, and Granny was worried you'd get run over. You must never, *ever* cross the road by yourself.'

'Sorry, Granny.' The child buried her face in Nancy's neck.

'Can we try another door?' asked Bailey, keen to get on with his guising.

Hannah looked expectant.

'Aye.' Nancy sighed, strapping Evie back into her seat. 'Let's go.'

What had almost happened didn't bear thinking about. The panic kept resurfacing as they walked. Andy kept seeing the tiny witch tottering in front of the moving van, impact a certainty. Then the weird part—some strange trick of the mind. The child, in a flash, shooting across the road a few inches above the ground and landing gently at the far side.

Meredith

I can't believe this—I saved a life! I must find Michael and tell him what happened. I saw the little girl as clear as day. There was no time for doubt, no room for failure. I didn't think about it, I just acted, and then she was safe!

If I concentrate on Michael I can instantly move to him. Right before moving, something clicks to let me know where he is. Not this time. Something's wrong; the connection is lost. Why? Now that I think about it, I haven't seen him since yesterday, when we practised isolating objects with so little success. Has he finally got tired of trying to make a decent whisperer of me?

I feel for him again but I can't find him. The night draws near, and Michael isn't anywhere.

He couldn't have gone on without warning, could he? He said it himself, you'd know it was coming. No, he must've done something to block me; he doesn't want to be found. I knew it couldn't last – why would a shining creature like Michael take me under his wing? Maybe I was just an assignment.

Or maybe I'm way off base. Not finding Michael could be down to me. I feel weak after saving Evie. Maybe I just need some rest.

Mum sits on the bathroom floor, rocking back and forth, hugging a small wooden box and moaning incomprehensibly. Scattered on the floor in front of her are several items: an empty gin bottle, the lid, two Co-Codamol boxes, and four plastic sheets cleared out of all their pills.

Silently, I scream, 'Michael!' I must find him. He'll know what to do.

I look everywhere I've ever been with Michael. I flit in a fraction of a second from place to place, person to person: Mortonhall, the railway, Waverley Station, Stan, Stacy, Alfie, Nathan, Gordon, Laura, Lizzie, Murray, Hughie, Davie, Andy, Nancy, and everywhere we've ever whispered in the night.

Michael is nowhere.

I whisper furiously to mum, over and over. *Phone for an ambulance!*

It soon becomes obvious that she's going to do no such thing. She just sits there, rocking and moaning to herself. Makes sense. She's never listened to me before. Why should she start now?

I visit my aunts and uncles, trying to persuade them to check up on mum. It's hopeless; it's after midnight and I can't wake anyone.

There's nothing to do but wait. Oh, where is Michael? How could he watch over me my whole life but not be here when it really matters? It was stupid of me, I suppose, to think he was a friend. What's it been, four weeks?

With every passing minute, I expect mum to cry out in agony, start vomiting, pass out or simply die. And what then? What would we say to one another? I'd probably be the last person she'd want to see. I want to see her, though. If she dies, at least we can be together. I'm so selfish! Am I actually *hoping* she dies?

It's going to be a long night.

After an hour of sitting on the bathroom floor, she crawls into bed with her little wooden box. What's inside it? Do I want to know?

I wait for something to happen but there's no obvious sign of poisoning. She gasps the air, letting out little sobs, but slowly her breathing regulates until she falls asleep.

The long night passes uneventfully. I keep checking she's still breathing, uneasy and hopeful at the same time. This could be a sleep she never wakes up from. I wish I could pop on a computer and Google 'Co-Codamol poisoning'. I know nothing about it, so I've no idea when it's safe to relax, or when to stop hoping she might pass into my world.

Mum wakes about eight and still seems okay. She parts the blinds and stands by the bedroom window for a long time. She shakes her head incredulously and puts the wooden box – I've never seen it before last night – in the back of a drawer, out of sight.

I try whispering again, in a last desperate attempt to help. *Call for an ambulance. You need to be checked out. Call for an ambulance!*

Mum shakes her head again, and puts her hands in her hair, watching the drawer as though the box might jump out and bite her.

Call someone—anyone! Call for help! Lizzie? Murray? Call them!

Mum shouts, 'Stop!' She closes her eyes tightly and shakes her head. 'Leave me alone!'

It's like I've been physically punched. It's the same as always—she wants rid of me.

Andy

A new nightmare has taken first place in the charts. In this one, Andy pushes a tiny girl in a buggy, but she runs away. He reaches out to catch her but he can't move. It's like he's weighed down, chained to the spot he's standing on. The little girl runs into the road, and she's going to die, and it's his fault. The van hits her with a sickening thud, over and over again, while he screams her name.

Andy woke up pale and sweaty. He caught his breath and became aware of Nancy beside him. 'Sorry,' he said. 'Did I wake you?'

She laid a hand gently on his arm. 'You were shouting Evie's name again.'

He closed his eyes. 'I almost killed her, Nancy.'

'No, you didn't. It was just one of those things. Kids are fast. It wasn't your fault. Anyway, Evie's fine. She's forgotten about it already.'

Andy turned to Nancy, tears in his eyes. 'How can you just forgive me?'

'There's nothing to forgive.'

'Why do you want to be around me? What if...'

'What is it, love?'

'What if I make bad things happen?'

Nancy twisted round to look into Andy's eyes, taking both of his hands in hers. 'Why would you say a thing like that?'

He didn't answer, except with great heaving sobs.

Nancy put her arms around him and let him weep, shushing him like a frightened child and saying, 'It's okay, it's okay,' until the shivers finally subsided.

Helen

It was a surprise when Lizzie came – it must've been Sunday afternoon.

Lizzie took one look at Helen. 'Darling! What on earth is going on?'

'Nothing. It's just these bugs. I can't seem to shake them.'

'You don't look well.'

Lizzie's offering was chocolate cupcakes. *Meredith's favourite*, Helen thought as Lizzie began bustling around the kitchen. A memory stirred – Lizzie being angry with her.

'What did I do wrong, last time you were here?' Helen asked.

'Nothing, darling.'

'You were upset with me.'

'Oh, don't worry yourself. It must've been something I ate.'

'Lizzie, I...I'm starting to forget things.'

'Oh, pish posh. Nothing to worry about darling. Par for the course at our age, I'm sure.' Lizzie brought the tea and joined Helen at the table.

When Lizzie picked up a cake and took a bite, Helen said, 'Don't forget your plate,' passing one over. 'What would your mother say?'

Lizzie shot her an angry, suspicious look, pursing her lips beneath a thin chocolate moustache.

What's got into her?

Meredith

Davie was the wrong person to come to from a moping session by the railway. I could use cheering up, but I won't get it here. He wakes up back in hospital. Another stroke—he looks miserable. He's able to speak but difficult to understand. He can't walk, either – he's badly lopsided again.

He sleeps fitfully, babbling a bit about nothing that makes much sense. I'm watching, but I've fallen silent. What difference does it make? He gets hold of a nurse and speaks to her in urgent tones.

'See baybe brunway!'

'Baby? What baby?' says the nurse.

'No baby. *She* bade be brun way!'

'She made you run away?'

'Yeah.' He waits expectantly, as though the nurse is going to do something about it.

'Well, never mind, you're back now,' she says, patting his arm. 'Everything's fine.'

Davie sighs and lies back on his pillows, exhausted with the effort of talking.

I wonder who *she* is, and what he ran away from. Most likely he's just an old man losing his mind.

Aunt Lizzie pours over her old photographs. There are two black and white ones of her parents, looking stern. People didn't smile for photos in those days. The rest are all of Lizzie, or Lizzie with her mother. She touches the pages lightly and smiles fondly. Here's an infant in a smock. Now a chubby toddler in a variety of frilly dresses. There's one of a little girl, around eight, with her mother on the beach. She's wearing a strappy summer dress. Her mum has an arm around her, smiling, and they're both holding an ice-cream cone.

'My lemon dress,' Aunt Lizzie whispers.

The number of photos begins to tail off when the girl gets older – twelve, maybe. There's only one more of the mother, and she looks thin, drawn. Aunt Lizzie touches the page with a trembling hand.

After that, there are a couple of school pictures of a teenager. No more of her mum. She never talked about her much, but I know they were close. I think Lizzie was fourteen when her mum died.

She dons her funeral outfit and calls for a taxi. She asks the driver to take her to the cemetery, via the florists. This is a tradition of hers on the anniversary of her mum's death. They were so close that neither death nor time can take away her dedication. I wonder if my mum will visit my grave next year?

Aunt Lizzie places the flowers neatly by the gravestone and stands quietly – back straight, head held high, hands clasped together.

'I've never forgotten you, mummy,' she says. 'I remember everything you taught me. I'm every bit the lady. Are you proud?'

Helen

Helen sat with the little wooden box on her lap and took out the tattered black and white photograph.

It was the only picture of him she'd kept. It was taken on their wedding day, in 1959. He was dashingly handsome in his dark suit, wearing a dapper smile as he stood arm in arm with his bride. She'd felt like a princess in that long white gown with its embroidered detail; luxury she was unaccustomed to wearing. They both looked so young, so optimistic, the prospect of a wonderful life together stretched out before them like a red carpet.

How could it all have been a lie? The facts were there: the note; the missing clothes, money and passport; the reluctance for intimacy. And yet, that had only been brief. For most of their time together he was a passionate, considerate lover. Had she simply been naïve? Like any married man in those days, he was regularly out on his own. He worked late occasionally and went to the cinema the odd weekend. But he never seemed guilty, like he had secrets.

Even if he *had* been hiding an affair, how could he leave so spontaneously? How could a normally organised person up and leave without selling the house or giving notice at work? And how could he be so duplicitous as to leave in the morning as though it was just a normal day? Even if he had fallen out of love with her, why didn't he say so?

If the marriage was farce, why waste all that energy chasing after her in the first place? He'd come looking for her after they first met at the Palais, she'd learned later. He'd been there every weekend, waiting to bump into her again.

One thing is certain. I didn't know him at all.

Perturbed, she put the photograph back in its box, her reservations left hanging in the air.

CHAPTER 18

Andy

Sixteen hours a week in ASDA made ends meet; the state pension wasn't enough. Andy should've saved for his retirement when he was a bricklayer, but who thinks about getting old before it happens? ASDA was nothing special, but at least it was honest. The checkout was okay; people were friendly and the time passed quickly.

Nancy had become part of his life again after a long separation. He was full of regret about many things, but Nancy was the exception. He couldn't regret anything he'd done with her – other than losing her. She made him want to be better, and he needed that desperately. He had to become good enough to cancel out the bad. With Nancy, that almost seemed possible.

He'd been worried about her seeing him shirtless—he'd avoided it when they were teenagers. What would she think of the marks? Reminders of what he was, where he came from. There were bald cigarette burns on his chest—a punishment from Brunco. Not that it happened often, but Brunco had been wound up that night, and taken it out on a twelve-year-old Andy. He remembered Brunco sitting on him, pinning his arms to the ground. Andy hadn't cried. Not till later. He also carried two stab wounds, on his back and shoulder. Those had happened later, during the football riots.

The scars would tell Nancy he was no good and warn her off. But when she saw them, she only touched them lightly and looked up at him with sad eyes. Why did she always look at him like he was good? Would she feel the same if she knew *everything*?

Andy didn't deserve Nancy, but he needed her all the same. He made a decision. He was going to put all his cards on the table, and to hell with the risk. He couldn't offer Nancy much, but offer it he would.

Stan

Stan ordered a large bouquet for Stacy and had it delivered with a card he wrote himself. He imagined her reading it and calling off her trip, but he wasn't really expecting that. He wanted her to know exactly where she stood with him. The card said:

Dear Stacy,

I've never cared about a woman the way I do about you. I know you think it can't work because we want different things. All I know is that I need to be with you. Nothing else matters. I've scared you off by being too full on, and I'm sorry. I just need you to know that I can wait. If you change your mind – next week, next month or a year from now, just call me. I'll be here.

Love,

Stan

That done, Stan concentrated on his work. There was sadness in his eyes as he smiled at the passengers, taking their tickets. He chatted with a few in a stoic effort to be cheerful. There was a gorgeous Lithuanian girl on her way to Edinburgh for a job—Lina. She was slim, with brown eyes and great skin. If that didn't help him get his flirt on, nothing would.

It was no use—Stacy had his whole heart.

All the same, he wrote down his name and number and passed it quietly to the pretty Lithuanian.

'In case you need a friend in Edinburgh,' he said, giving her one last lonely smile. Nothing wrong with making friends.

Meredith

Gordon stands on the platform at Waverley, holding a sign that says *Lina*; a crowd spills off the London train. He looks uncomfortable. He's been given no information other than where to take the girl. He's convinced himself it's an innocent favour for the boss—Brian didn't correct him. It pays an awful lot for an innocent favour—twice what he gets for delivering a kilo of heroin.

A stunning young woman, maybe twenty, steps out from the crowd, points to herself and says, 'Lina.'

He gives a curt nod and turns to lead her to the car park, tight-lipped. In the van, Gordon hardly says a word.

Lina looks out the window at the floodlit buildings. 'Scotland,' she says. 'I come for job.'

Gordon follows his strange instructions, taking her to a certain park, sitting her on a certain bench and telling her to wait.

He doesn't look back as he walks away. It's not his business to see what happens next, and the less he knows the better. He's only doing his job, right? I've heard all his justifications. If anything bad happens, it would happen regardless of him. Anyway, an adult woman who can travel here from Lithuania can take care of herself. All Gordon has to do now is head to the meeting place for payment.

Could his unease somehow save him?

These are very bad people, Gordon. You don't want to get involved in this. I whisper unheeded warnings over and over.

Sitting in the pub with Nancy, back to the wall, Andy stiffens. The scar-faced man who spied on Aunt Lizzie is walking straight towards them. He slides onto the bench next to Andy and slaps him on the back.

'Titch Laidlaw! How's things?'

'Rab,' Andy says. 'Fine. You?'

Rab's face darkens. 'I've had some bad news about my brother Tam. It's not a conversation for a lady.' Rab indicates Nancy.

Nancy says, 'Anything you need to say to Andy, you can say in front of me.'

Rab gives her a long look. 'Fine. Laidlaw, Tam's been done for by that old bastard Joe Nelson.'

'Don't know him,' says Andy.

'It was last night. A fight broke out in the Crown, and they got moved out onto the street. Tam was there with a couple of his boys, and Joe with some of his. Now Tam's dead.' Rab stares at the far wall with his cold eyes, his nostrils flaring.

'I'm sorry to hear it,' says Andy.

Rab looks at him with a sudden intensity. 'I'm getting some of the guys back together and making big plans for Joe. You in?'

Andy says, 'No. I'm sorry about Tam, but I won't fight.'

'Just one more fight, Titch, for old times' sake.' When Andy doesn't answer, Rab's expression hardens. 'Have you forgotten that you grew up under the protection of the Graham brothers?'

'No, Rab. I haven't forgotten a thing,' Andy says. 'Now, I did Brunco a solid and he let me go. That was a long time ago, but I know you'd want to honour Brunco's word.'

Rab deflates a little. 'Aye. Of course. But don't you miss the old days?'

'No, Rab. I don't.'

'Alright well, if you change your mind, I'm in the Stag most nights.'

Andy nods, and his tense muscles don't relax till Rab leaves.

'Wow,' says Nancy. 'He must be desperate if he's crawling pubs looking for people to rope into his fight.'

'Aye. Most of the old gang settled down years ago, but a few of these older guys are still angry and violent. The fight that ended Tam could've been about nothing much. Someone insults the wrong woman, looks at the wrong person in the wrong way…The chances are that once Rab catches up with Joe, one of them'll die or come close. And they'll pull whoever else they can into the fray.'

'Hey, it's not your problem. You stood up to him.'

Andy lifts his glass with a trembling hand, puts it down again. 'It's just the sight of him, you know? I've seen him and Tam once in a while, but I prefer to avoid them. I've never seen either of them in here before.'

'Well then, you probably won't again.'

'I hate stuff like this; it's like nothing's changed.'

'A lot's changed, Andy. You've changed.'

He looks at her with a kind of awe. There's love, need, and shame all wrapped up together in that expression. Then he says, 'Stay with me.'

'Tonight?'

'Every night. Will you be my wife, Nancy?'

She smiles sadly.

Andy's face falls.

Nancy says, 'There's something I need to tell you…'

'It's okay. I come with too much baggage. Why would you-'

'No, that's not it. If you still want to marry me after you hear what I've got to say, then my answer is yes.'

Andy

His heart stopped in his chest. 'What is it?' What could be so devastating that she'd think it could change his mind?

Nancy wiped a tear with her sleeve. 'I've wanted to tell you ever since we met up. Well, a lot longer than that. But saying it out loud…I haven't talked about it in decades. It hurts too much.' Her eyes welled up. 'I'm afraid you're going to hate me.'

'I could never hate you.' Andy knew the agony of secrets. 'How about we go for a walk, find somewhere quieter?'

Nancy nodded, and he led her by the hand out into the street, and towards the park.

Nancy took a deep breath. 'The day my dad packed me off, it *was* to separate us.'

'It's okay. I know.'

'No, you don't. I was pregnant, Andy.'

Speechless, Andy collapsed onto the nearest bench. Nancy sat beside him, not meeting his eyes. She said, 'My dad was so angry when he found out. I was afraid of what he might do. I should've told you. I should've stood up to him, but I was so young...'

Everything went dark. Andy tried to make sense of what he'd heard. 'What happened next?'

'I was sent to stay with friends of my dad—strangers. They kept me hidden. I had the baby in their house. It was a girl. They never even let me hold her.' Nancy sobbed. 'They took her away.' She struggled against tears to get the words out. 'She was to be adopted by a nice family. A married couple.'

Andy shook his head—it couldn't be true.

'After that, it was like I said. I nannied. It was okay as long as I didn't have a girl of that age. I thought about her every day. I thought about both of you.'

Nancy looked at Andy's face, but he couldn't speak. Couldn't think.

She said, 'Once the thing was done, there was no going back. I decided there was no point in making you suffer. I never came home again, never spoke to my dad again. I tried to move on and forget it ever happened. But there isn't a day goes by that I don't think of it. I never stopped loving you, Andy. But I can't live this lie anymore—not with you. Can you ever forgive me?'

Andy looked at Nancy and didn't know what to think. He stood up, opened his mouth to speak, and changed his mind.

'Andy?' Nancy looked up at him with pleading eyes.

He put up his hands, turned and walked away, leaving her sobbing on the park bench.

Meredith

Stacy gets in from the shops at lunchtime.

Jules can't wait to tell her about Stan's flowers. 'Come and see,' says Jules, leading her into the kitchen.

Stacy looks at the bouquet and sighs.

Jules rolls her eyes. 'Read the card.'

'I don't want to.'

Read it, Stacy! Just read it!

Jules picks up the card. 'I'll read it for you then–'

'No. Look, it makes no difference what it says. I'm leaving today.'

Don't go!

Jules presses the card into Stacy's hand. 'And what if it's too late when you get back?'

'Good—that's what I want. Will you just leave it, please?' Stacy pops the card into a kitchen drawer.

'Fine.'

While Stacy eats lunch, I badger her about Stan. She ignores me, phones for a taxi and brings her suitcase out to the hall.

It's over. I failed.

Mum is sitting in silence, apparently ruminating about something. And there's that little wooden box on the table beside her chair. She tried to kill herself, and nothing happened at all. It doesn't make any sense.

If mum had that box during my life, it's been well hidden. Why? What's inside? Why does she keep taking it out from its hiding place?

Without much hope, I muster my power to isolate the spiritual object concealed within the box. I give it a long time, but on this occasion, I don't even get a glimpse. The box sits there stubbornly, solid and impenetrable. How did I manage to move the child, then? It was the crisis, I think. Being driven by pure need and having no time for doubt. I can't recreate that now. It was a fluke.

Davie drifts in and out of sleep, mumbling his jumbled nonsense. There's one word he keeps repeating, but I can't make it out. Two syllables...it sounds like 'compress,' but that can't be right.

Nothing I do seems to make any difference to him—or any of them. I'm trying with all my strength to whisper *peace*, but he's more agitated than ever.

Not that my 'strength' is up to much. I'm not feeling peaceful myself, so how could I pass it onto him?

I make one last feeble search for Michael, but I know I won't find him; he's gone. Wherever he is, he's not coming back to me. And who can blame him? Whispering is almost impossible without him; I can't do anything right

Without Michael, I'm nothing.

As evening falls, I haunt my spot on the railway bank. For a while, I actually thought I was doing okay, but it always comes back to this. Me, alone on this bank, wishing for a way out.

My achievements as a whisperer...let's see...I've alienated my mum even more than I managed to do in life. I've failed to reconcile her with her brothers. I've made her so lonely that she wanted to die, too. And to my shame, I was disappointed! Disappointed when she lived, because I wanted her for myself.

Then there's Michael. He's the best friend I ever had, and I've driven him away.

I've set off to save Gordon, who hasn't listened to a word I've said. I've encouraged an unlikely friendship between Alfie and Nathan, which would've happened anyway. I've done nothing to ease Davie's suffering. I've traumatised an innocent train driver, then proceeded to cajole him into a relationship that's broken his heart. I've watched things fall apart between Andy and Nancy; if I'd left them alone, they might've done fine.

Everything I touch turns to dust.

An idea gradually comes into focus. I'll do what I always do when things get on top of me.

I'm in Deacon Brodie's again. I'm one of the hungry dead, watching and waiting. I find a miserable lone drinker at the bar – a short, bony woman of about forty, with a prominent chin. The aura is weakening. Soon I can use that body to do whatever I want. I wait as the woman becomes more inebriated and the aura breaks down until finally, an opening appears above the head.

I don't hesitate. I dive, squeezing myself into the tiny body, and feel a sudden rush of sensation that makes my head spin. I look at my hands, wiggling the fingers and giggling stupidly. I lift the glass and put it down again, amazed at how it feels to be seen, to affect the world around me. I shout out and smash the glass onto the floor, not caring that people are looking, not fearing the bartender starting angrily towards me.

I stagger onto the street, my footsteps loud in my ears, and concentrate on finding a takeaway. There's a handbag over my shoulder, and raking through its contents I find a purse with twenty-odd pounds in it. A few minutes later, I stumble into a Turkish kebab shop on Cockburn Street. The smell of fried food is intoxicating; I want to eat everything. My voice comes out strange, but I manage to buy a large portion of deep-fried pizza and chips and a two-litre bottle of coke. Regardless of onlookers, I sit down at the side of the road and open the box. I can smell the cooked oil, the melted cheese, the vinegar! It's glorious.

I grab the pizza like a starved animal and stuff it in my mouth, chewing only as much as I need to, anxious to get to the next bite. I tear and tear at the soft white bread inside. It's half gone already and I start on the mountain of chips, taking handfuls at a time. The smell of the food is so familiar, the way the greasy potato slips down my throat, leaving behind a thick coating of oil and salt. When the chips are half finished I gulp down some of the coke, fast so I can get back to my meal. While I polish off the rest, a familiar pressure grows more painful in my stomach, but I'm compelled to keep eating. While I eat, I think of nothing but the food and the act of consuming it. I don't even know my own name. I gobble every last morsel of pizza and each crispy scrap of batter, washing it all down with the rest of the coke. I lie prostrate on the cold pavement, groaning with pain and pleasure.

Then comes another familiar sensation. Guilt. Regret, with an added dimension. Not only have I done this to myself—I've done it to the drunken stranger, too. I'm disgusting. I look up and see passers-by stealing glances at me.

My host exerts herself. She somehow manages to get us both up and hail a taxi. Luckily we get out of it on her street before we vomit on our shoes. I deserved that. She didn't. How do I get out of her? Who's in charge of the body? Everything feels confused. We enter the house as one and fall down on the bed. Then I pass out of time and space into stillness.

CHAPTER 19

Meredith

I'm in a spotlessly clean, white room. There are no doors, windows or light sources to be seen, yet somehow there's a bright glow all around. I sit on one of the ivory upholstered armchairs, the only two pieces of furniture in the room. There's something different about the chairs. When I realise what it is, my heart does a little summersault. I'm seeing the spiritual objects! I jump to my feet and push a chair to the corner of the room, then back again. I can move them!

It was too easy. I sit down again, scrutinising the empty chair. There is no physical element to the object. What is this place?

I need to check on mum—what if she tries to hurt herself again? I concentrate on home, but nothing happens.

I don't move.

Let's try somewhere else. I think of the railway, but I can't feel the path. I think of Stan, Gordon, Andy, Davie, but I can't find anyone.

I can't leave this room. I'm a prisoner. I call out, but only silence answers.

Is this hell? Am I doomed to stay here forever, alone with only my thoughts for company?

A stunning woman appears in the room, with long shining hair and bright blue eyes. I shrink back in her presence, as when I first saw Michael. Unlike him, the woman is dressed in white—but still no wings. Her face shines like the sun, her lustre making the room brighter. There's something familiar in her face, but I can hardly look at it, and it's not possible that *I* could know *her*.

When she speaks, it's as soft as snowflakes, yet penetrating as if it had been the roaring of a great lion. 'Meredith,' she says, 'I'm Veronica. I'm here to help you.' I look up, and then at the floor. I can't hold her gaze—I feel so dirty. She sits in the empty chair and waits.

What am I supposed to be thinking? Which of my many questions should I ask? I say, 'My mum! I left her – I'm sorry!'

Veronica raises a hand. 'She's alright. She's not going to hurt herself.'

'And the others. I left them, but…I didn't mean to. I just can't *help* with anything. I didn't know what else to do.'

Veronica smiles but says nothing.

I ask, 'How long have I been here?'

'A week has passed on earth.'

I don't know what to say next; my thoughts race with fears and suppositions about where I am and why, and what Veronica wants with me.

Finally, I manage another question. 'Have I gone on?'

'No, girlie,' Veronica says, 'this is the in-between. D'you know why you're here?'

'I did something bad.'

'D'you understand why it was wrong to possess that woman?'

'I made her eat till she was sick.' I'm mortified, my shame naked before Veronica's glory.

'She's recovered now, but she's been quite ill. She has no memory of leaving Deacon Brodie's that night, or how she got home.'

'I'm sorry.'

'The dead roam the earth, Meredith,' Veronica says, 'but there are certain things we may not freely interfere with. The body of a living person is one of them. You see, there are two main laws that govern us. The first law is that we do not reveal ourselves to the living. If we were supposed to get all the answers on a silver platter, the mysteries of life and death, it would be so. There are reasons why the living and the dead are separated. The second law is that we do not interfere with anyone's freedom to choose. Our choices shape us, and they must remain ours.'

'So…I broke the second law?'

'Yes. But as you know, many have done so in this manner, and many will yet make the attempt. Please don't think of this as a punishment; it's more of an education. You're here to learn what's expected of you.'

'If I did it again, would I be punished?' I ask before I think it through—I'm such an idiot! Veronica will think I'm planning a second offence!

'Those who deliberately persist in breaking the law must eventually be removed from the earth. But you must be strong, girlie. There's important work for you to do before you go on.'

'What work? What can *I* do that's important?'

Veronica smiles, warming the room. 'You underestimate yourself, child. You must continue bravely on your path. Keep trying to help, seek truth, and you'll find your way. When you do, you'll change everything.'

My goodness, Veronica makes me sound positively heroic! However, I daren't contradict her.

As though reading my thoughts, she says with raised eyebrows: 'You've already begun.'

'I don't understand. I haven't changed anything.'

Veronica gestures to the wall in front of us, which lights up in a full colour moving picture.

Evie is larger than life on the screen, busily rocking a dolly and singing 'Ally Bally Bee'[11]. Her sweet little voice fills the air. Her blonde hair falls around her face in loose curls, her chubby wee fingers patting the dolly's back as she says, 'Shhh, baby, shhh.'

My heart melts.

'You saved her life,' Veronica says. 'How can you say you haven't changed anything?'

'Anyone would've done it,' I say.

'But you're the one who did. You were the only one who could. For every decision, there are two paths. Would you like to see the one where you don't save her?'

'No. Don't show me the wee one dead, please! So this,' I indicate the screen, 'is reality?'

'Yes, this is Evie right now.'

Evie drops the dolly and runs to the kitchen. 'Mummy!' she calls. 'Mummy, I need a wee wee!'

The woman at the sink must be Claire. She dries her hands and kneels down to look at her daughter. The adoring smile on her face shows me I *have* changed everything—at least for Claire.

---

[11] *Ally Bally Bee* is a traditional Scottish lullaby

'Clever girl,' Claire says. 'Come on then.' She takes the tiny hand in hers and leads the toddler to the bathroom.

The picture fades out, and a thought occurs to me. 'Didn't I break the law by moving the child? Wasn't it her choice to run on the road?'

'If she'd been grown up, yes, but little children don't know right from wrong. Keeping her safe was the best course. Andy and Nancy are already having trouble believing what they saw.'

I'm sad at the mention of their names. 'I couldn't help them. They fell out over Nancy's secret.'

'The secret had to be shared. How could she keep a thing like that from Andy and hope to give him her heart? Look.'

The screen lights up again. Andy sits next to the bed of a frail old man.

Andy says, 'Do you know who I am?'

The old man nods.

'What's my name?'

The old man's voice is hoarse and unfriendly. 'Titch.'

'I only just found out about the baby. How could you keep that from me all this time?...I did wrong by Nancy back then, and for that I'm sorry.'

'Bit late for that.' The old man chuckles and it turns into a nasty coughing fit.

'I'm not finished. What you did was worse. You separated us from each other and our child. I would've married Nancy. We would've done okay.'

More laughter, more coughing.

'Nancy never got over it. You hurt her, didn't you?'

The cruel smile falls from the old man's face.

'How hard did you push her to do what she was told? What did you do to her, Clive?'

'I did what any decent father would do—what had to be done. I paid a heavy price for it. She never forgave me.'

'She's come back to me, and we're getting married.'

Clive raises his eyebrows, his lips pursed.

'D'you know she has grandchildren? You tell me everything you know about our daughter. You owe us that. You do that for me, and maybe I can get Nancy to visit you.'

Clive considers as the picture fades into another.

A dilapidated sign stands outside Chongwe Clinic, Lusaka. The waiting room is like a sea of men, women and children. Two youngsters wearing 'volunteer' badges are conducting preliminary triage. They identify those whose need to be seen looks most urgent and mark their names on a clipboard.

A woman approaches one of the volunteers. 'I have been waiting all day,' she says. 'When can I see a doctor?'

'Soon,' he says.

'Bah, soon! That is what you said this morning.' She puts up her hands and returns to her seat.

Another volunteer is busily passing out water in plastic cups—there are no vending machines like in our hospitals.

In the clinic, Stacy is working with a woman who's crying out in pain and sweating profusely. There are already two bowls of vomit on the table. A young volunteer is shushing a baby.

Stacy says to her, 'Tell Paul this woman needs more medicine.' Stacy wipes beads of sweat off her forehead.

The volunteer leaves the room, and the patient starts convulsing and foaming at the mouth. After half a minute, she becomes still.

Stacy checks her pulse.

The volunteer returns with Paul, who passes Stacy a bottle. He says, 'Supplies are coming soon. We will increase the dose and have faith that there will be enough.'

The girl asks, 'What do we do with the baby? There's no information, no next of kin.'

Paul says, 'Take her to the orphanage.'

'No!' Stacy cries.

'It's okay,' says Paul, 'she can collect her when she's well.'

Stacy says to the girl, 'Make sure you tell them she's not staying. Put this band around her ankle. Put her name on it—Madeline.'

Paul puts a hand on Stacy's shoulder, and another on the girl's. 'I thank God you have come to help us.'

The picture fades, and Veronica says, 'This is an eye-opener for Stacy. She's doing fantastic work out there.'

'Why are you showing me this? It doesn't help Stan. I made a mess of things for him, bringing them together.'

'It isn't over yet. Time and experience can change many things.'

'Stan's so miserable without her! He was better off before.'
'Was he? Are you sure?'
Suddenly I'm not sure.
'If the two of them had never met, wouldn't Stan still be searching? Now he knows exactly what he wants. It's a start.'
'I suppose.'
'Your feelings were true—why should you doubt them now? We don't know yet how the story ends.'

Next, the screen shows Alfie at the vets with Shirley.
The vet says, 'The cancer is aggressive and advanced—it's spread into her organs. Surgery isn't an option. Chemo could slow it down, but it won't cure her.'
Alfie nods gravely.
'I'll give you tablets for her, and I'll see you again soon. We could let nature take its course, but if she's in pain it may be kinder to put her to sleep.'
My heart swells with emotion—I've lost cats before, and really missed them. I can only imagine how awful it must be for Alfie to face losing his beloved dog.
He leaves the surgery, downcast, looking at his faithful friend. Her walk has become slow and laboured. 'I'm sorry,' he says. 'Let's make the best of it, eh?' He gives her an affectionate pat.
'Alfie will have no one!' I say, distressed.
As if in answer, the screen shows Nathan, working in the library. He smiles to himself as he works. Alfie's taught him new things. He sorts the returned books, checking the system and placing them on the shelves. He tidies up, vacuums carpets, cleans toilets and makes cups of tea. He seems happy; he's found a place in the world.
Veronica turns to me. 'You see, Alfie will have someone, thanks to you.'
'I didn't bring them together,' I say. 'They did it on their own.'
'No. Without your encouragement, it would've gone like this.'
The screen changes to that first meeting. There's Alfie, irritated, sorting the books into the correct order.
There's Nathan, reading Harry Potter. 'What's wrong?'

'What's wrong,' Alfie says, 'is that people keep moving books around, and there's not enough time to fix them all.'

'That's annoying,' says the boy to his book.

'Yes.' Alfie hesitates as though wanting to make conversation.

'This is the part where you gave him a gentle nudge,' Veronica says. 'Harry Potter—d'you remember?'

I nod.

In this version of events, there's no nudge. Alfie turns back to his task, and Nathan to his reading.

'That's what would've happened without you,' Veronica says. 'And never another word between them.'

I'm stunned. 'Can you show me what would've happened...'

'If you'd followed Michael's whisperings, and met Alfie?'

I nod, a single tear escaping down my cheek.

'Oh, girlie. That wouldn't help you now.'

More silent tears cascade down my face.

'Keep your chin up. Things can still change.' She winks.

Next, the screen shows my dear old Irene, in bed at the care home where I once worked.

Veronica says, 'You made sure she wasn't taken advantage of. You protected her dignity. You got to know Irene, not just as she is now, but as she was, and will be again. You treated her as that young woman, temporarily trapped in an old woman's body.'

The screen changes to an earlier time. Irene sits in her chair, and I brush her hair while we sing along to 'Love Me Tender'.

I help her get her teeth in, fix her scarlet lipstick, and tell her not to do anything I wouldn't do.

With a mischievous smile, she pinches my cheek and calls me Daisy.

I can't help smiling at the memory.

'She's dying,' Veronica says. 'They don't expect her to last long. They've called Sandra and she's on her way.'

'I need to go!' I say. 'I need to be there to help her when she passes!'

Veronica puts her hands up. 'Don't worry, Irene is well taken care of.

Again, the picture changes. This time, it's my Uncle Murray, pacing his sitting room with the phone.

'Helen,' he says. 'It's Murray again. I told you I wouldn't give up, and I meant it. When are you coming for Sunday dinner? Consider it an open invite, okay? If you want to come tomorrow, next week. Any time. Helen? Will you pick up the phone?...Okay, I'll see you soon.' He hangs up and sits down.

Jean walks by and pats him on the shoulder. 'You're a good man, Murray Stevens.'

'You see, Meredith,' Veronica says. 'He's not giving up, and neither should you.'

Veronica says, 'Now, to Gordon, girlie. You're not to blame for his choices. If he doesn't listen, that's up to him. You may be unable to help him directly, but you can still help those around him. He's resisted your warnings, but see how uneasy he's become.'

There he is on the screen, now having a drink, now placing bets and watching races. He's trying to cheer himself up, but he looks anxious—I'm surmising it's because of the girl. He phones Brian to meet him in the pub for lunch.

Once they've eaten and the second round of drinks are brought, Brian speaks in a low voice. 'How's it all going, brother? Better life now, eh?'

'Aye, I suppose,' Gordon shifts uncomfortably in his seat. 'Look, mate, my last job, was...different.'

Brian holds up a hand. 'Let me stop you right there, bro. We don't speak about the details. Not even to each other. Not unless we're told to.'

Gordon hisses, 'I need to talk Bri! What if I don't want to do this anymore?'

Brian looks alarmed. 'Gordo, mate.' He puts a hand on his friend's shoulder and looks him square in the eyes. 'You don't quit this job. There's only one way you get out of this game. D'you understand me?'

Gordon gives Brian a scrutinising look. His eyes harden. 'Got it.' He necks his pint, and with one last glare at Brian, leaves.

Veronica says again, 'You're not responsible.'

I think Michael said something similar.

The screen melts back into the clean, white wall, and Veronica says, 'You've done a lot of good as a whisperer. Look at me.'

Sheepishly, I raise my eyes to meet the beautiful face.

'Do you know me, Meredith?'

I look harder. 'You're my granny!' I say, only just realising it. 'You're so different to that one picture we have, and when I made the connection for you and mum, for her dream, I was concentrating so hard, I...I see it now, I'm sorry.'

Veronica smiles. 'Don't worry yourself, girlie. I only wanted to thank you for what you did for us. It takes considerable skill to make that connection, and it's not everyone who has the opportunity to go back, like your grandfather and I, so thank you.'

If I had any blood it would all rush to my cheeks. 'You're welcome,' I say. 'I'm only sorry I couldn't hold onto the connection a bit longer.'

'It wasn't you who broke it, child. It was your mum.' She's quiet for a moment, as though searching for the right words. 'You've done right by her, Meredith. You've set events in motion that may yet save her.'

'Save her from what?'

'I must go,' Veronica says. 'You're doing well, girlie. Don't give up. You're free to leave.'

Emboldened by her revelation, I say, 'Granny, wait!' but she's already fading. 'Do you know where Michael is? Can't you tell me what to do?'

Without Veronica, the room feels dark and cold. I'm left with my thoughts, now dominated by a healthy curiosity about my purpose.

CHAPTER 20

Meredith

Once I gather myself, I go straight home. The shadow has returned. She leaves a mark on a place, and the air is heavy with her bile. Mum is watching TV, and the little box she's been nursing is somewhere out of sight.

I replay the things Veronica showed me in my mind. I focus all my energy on what she said until I convince myself that things will get better. I surround mum with my light, such as it is, and I whisper kind words. Gradually, the muscles in her face seem to relax a little, and I choose to believe I'm not imagining it. I'm helping. I picture my Granny Veronica giving me an approving smile.

Davie lies lifeless in his hospital bed. The shadow has been here, too. The room feels devoid of all hope—the light devoured. Why? Why would the creature bother the old man?

I look around, expecting to see Davie's spirit near, but there's only his body. I search the ward, the hospital. The dead are here, but he isn't among them. Back on the ward, a nurse is talking to one of his colleagues about Davie.

'Must've had another stroke or something. You've got to go sometime, I suppose.'

The lady nods, shrugs. 'I'll get the doctor.'

A doctor breezes in a few minutes later, and upon taking a cursory look at the patient, is about to fill in a form when she notices something about his face that warrants a closer look.

Before long, Davie's room has been cordoned off and staff instructed not to enter. I overhear snippets of conversation. Davie's death is being treated as suspicious until it can be proved otherwise. The doctor has referred the case to a coroner and wants the room undisturbed pending the autopsy and any resulting inquest.

Helen

Lizzie breezed in on Sunday afternoon, just as Helen was thinking of going for a shower. 'How are you bearing up, darling?' Lizzie asked, giving her friend a hug and walking past her into the sitting room.

'Okay,' Helen said. 'How are you?'

'Fine, thank you. I've come to chivvy you along a bit. It's time for you to get back to normal.'

'Normal?' Helen scoffed.

'Yes, as normal as things can be without our darling girl. Speaking of, have you done anything with Meredith's room yet?'

'Not yet.' Helen was a little taken aback, though used to Lizzie's business-like manner.

'I thought I could give you a hand—sort through her things, box them up and so on. Any thoughts?'

'I...hadn't really thought about it, but if you'd like to make a start, that would be fine. Thank you.'

'Not at all—you've enough to worry about. Why don't you get yourself organised, and we'll go for a walk later.'

It wasn't a question, but Helen didn't mind. That was just Lizzie. Some fresh air and company would do her good.

Meredith

Davie's hospital room is a hub of activity. Crime scene tape blocks the area, and an officer stands guard near the door. Others are busy in the room, recording every detail before collecting the physical evidence. It's like something from the TV – each wears white overalls, blue gloves and a face mask. The pillows and bedding are carefully bagged, hard surfaces dusted for prints, and every inch of the room scoured for potential evidence.

'Who'd want to murder *him*?' a short, plump nurse is saying in a conspiratorial tone. 'He was half dead anyway!'

'I know, it's mad,' says her companion.

The charge nurse appears briskly in the office doorway. 'Vera, Craig, enough chat,' she says. 'We still need to finish the drug round.'

The nurses scarper, rolling their eyes.

'Now Sergeant,' she says, returning to the office. 'What can I do for you?'

In the office is Chris Bain. I recognise his blonde hair and blue eyes—I saw him once before, with Stan, at my spot by the railway. He was with the British Transport Police then. When he introduces himself, he says he's with MIT—the Major Investigation Team.

Chris has had a list compiled of everyone who had access to Davie's room on the day of his death, consisting of staff members, visitors and patients. There were six nurses and care assistants and eighteen visitors. Everyone on the list must be investigated and ruled out, he tells the charge nurse and—though she keeps checking her watch and looking around as though itching to get on—she assures him of the ward's cooperation.

Chris is young and ambitious; he's very thorough in his work to identify all possible suspects. I see both Aunt Lizzie and Angela on the CCTV visiting the ward, and someone else I recognise. An old man, strong and rough, with a scarred face. That's Rab Graham—was he visiting Davie? Or was he following Aunt Lizzie around again?

If I hadn't brought Aunt Lizzie and Davie together, she wouldn't have been here. Now, she could be a suspect in a murder case! My pattern of self-blame starts, but I catch myself. I try to think of what Veronica would say, or Michael if he were here. I did Aunt Lizzie a favour in bringing her together with her friend. If I hadn't done so, she never would've seen him again. For all I know, his imminent death was the very reason why they needed to meet.

In any event, there's nothing I can do about it now.

I'm lost without Michael, but Veronica has got me thinking. What work waits for me? How can *I* 'change everything?' If I could make a real difference, even to one person, I think I could be content. I remember Evie, playing with her doll, oblivious to her recent danger. It's true—I saved her! Evie will always be there, living and growing proof that I *can* change things. From now on, whenever I doubt myself, I'm going to hold onto that.

I return home to find Aunt Lizzie in my room, going through my belongings. Here she is taking mum's place again – not that I'm ungrateful. It's kind of her to take care of us.

She finds a bundle of late library books. 'I'll return these for you, darling,' she whispers and puts them to one side. Most of my clothes are in bags and boxes, ready to be donated. Aunt Lizzie pauses while folding the last of them and gives a little sob.

'How did you get like this, my darling girl?' Lizzie asks an oversized dress that lies on the bed. 'You were so lonely, so unhappy! We should've made you happy.'

No, Aunt Lizzie. It's me who did this. My happiness is my responsibility. It's time I got to work.

I faithfully visit all the souls I looked in on with Michael, always returning to mum. I keep wondering—what does she need to be saved from? She has a pile of new books beside her bed—'What Happens When We Die', 'Is there life after death?', 'How to talk to the dead', and 'Near Death Experiences'. I've never seen mum entertain anything like this before—she would've called it nonsense. Does she want to make contact with me? My heart flutters at the thought.

I visit my uncles often, speaking mum's name to them.

When I have nothing to do I search public places for someone in need: the library, the train station and the city centre. I watch and listen, whispering peace and love to the living day and night.

Meredith

Alfie puts on wellies and an old jumper and takes a spade from the shed. Sobbing, he begins to dig.

Another whisperer appears beside me—a woman. She's slim, with green eyes and long hair that shines like fire. She looks at me in surprise, and I feel like I've been caught somewhere I shouldn't be.

'Hi,' she says.

Is this what a rabbit in headlights feels like? I try to smile.

'I'm Mina.'

'I'm Meredith.'

'What a beautiful name.'

I look at the ground.

'Have you been helping him?'

'Trying to,' I say, clocking her wedding ring. 'I'm...quite new. I didn't know he had help already.'

'He's had no one but me for a long time.'

I nod. I get it—I've stepped on her toes.

Alfie sniffs, and Mina moves closer to him, bathing him in her powerful light. She looks on him with great compassion and they weep together.

I'm about to leave when Mina calls, 'Wait.' She's beside me again. 'How do you two know each other?' she asks.

We watch Alfie finishing the dog-sized grave, his face smeared with dirt and tears.

'I saw him in the library, but...he doesn't know me.'

'Not yet.' She smiles. 'You know how short life is. He'll know you soon enough.'

'I don't know,' I say. 'I'll go on some time. Anyway, I'll leave you to it.'

I'm already squeezing into the channel when I hear her say 'I'll see you around?'

I spend many hours with Stan, trying to soothe his troubled heart. The truth flows through me (after that little nudge from Veronica): *it isn't over yet; don't give up.*

He has a disturbing call on Wednesday afternoon.

'Stan? Is Lina.'

He looks confused. 'Lina,' he says finally, 'we met on the train last week. I gave you my number in case you needed a friend up here. How are things?'

'Not good.' She sounds afraid. Is this the girl that Gordon picked up off the London train? 'I need help. Job not good.'

'Not good? How d'you mean?'

She begins speaking rapidly in Lithuanian, through tears, but Stan can't understand a word.

'Hey,' he says, 'slow down love.'

She stops, breathing sharply, sniffling.

'Where are you right now?'

'Where?' she says. 'Eh...I walk, I buy food. But I must return now.'

'Return where?'

'I must not tell...you cannot go there. I need to go to my home! Can you help?'

'I can try love, but you need to tell me where you are.'

There's a sudden urgency to Lina's voice right before she hangs up. 'I try to meet you soon.'

Stan is wide-eyed.

What can we do? I remember Veronica telling me—if I can't help Gordon, I can still help those around him. Maybe the police could trace the call and find her, make sure she's okay?

Call the police, Stan. This is serious.

Andy and Nancy are at the jewellers, where she chooses a pretty ring with one small diamond. The sales assistant disappears through the back to fetch the sizing rings.

'Are you sure you want to do this?' Andy says.

'Yes! I'll marry you tomorrow if you like. Use a plastic ring, for all I care.'

Andy grins, then his face turns serious again. 'Let's wait a few weeks or a month, just in case you change your mind.'

Nancy gives him a jab with her elbow. 'I'm not going to, you big tattie[12].'

'Okay.'

The sales assistant returns to fit Nancy's ring. That done, Andy pays for it and arranges to collect it in a few days.

Andy brightens and relaxes whenever he looks into Nancy's eyes. There's no judgement there, yet his constant self-recrimination follows him around like a dark raincloud. *Be patient,* I tell him. *Your time will come.* It occurs to me that he and I have something in common—we both need to give ourselves a break.

Chris

Detective Sergeant Chris Bain spent the morning finishing up his initial report on the hospital death. There were a number of potential suspects, but only one with a criminal record – Robert Graham. His list of offences was extensive and went way back: countless charges of assault, robbery, breaking and entering and possessing weapons.

The coroner's preliminary report said the cause of death was asphyxiation. The victim had been suffocated, a pillow pressed against his face. He was found to have ingested fibres matching those of a pillow from his hospital bed. It was likely that he'd scratched the perpetrator during the struggle; trace evidence of someone else's skin epithelial was found under his fingernails.

The forensic team had also found trace evidence of sweat on the pillow from no less than four different individuals. This

---

[12] Tattie (noun): potato, used in this context as an affectionate insult

could've been transferred by the killer and/or by hospital staff and visitors, who prepared his bedding or moved his pillows to make him more comfortable. The killer may have worn gloves, thus leaving no trace of DNA on the pillow at all.

Chris was new to MIT, and this was his first big case—a chance to prove himself as a detective. If his report was up to scratch, he hoped to get assigned to the case full-time. He checked it a second time, making sure it was comprehensive and concise. He listed the next steps at the end, to show the DI he could take the initiative. With a mixture of trepidation and satisfaction, he filed the report.

That done, he went onto the system to process enquiries in priority order. He selected the first, began to read the notes made by the call handler and frowned. There wasn't much to go on but it seemed that a young woman was in trouble. He'd need to visit the man who reported it to take a statement.

Meredith

They're saying Davie was murdered! I should've been here. If only I hadn't done what I did to that poor woman, maybe I could've prevented it. However, no point thinking on that now. No point.

The official cause of death is asphyxiation. Angela, my Aunt Lizzie and Rab Graham are all on the long list of possible suspects! Who would stop an old man's breath?

Stan has a visit from Sergeant Bain at his brother's house. It takes them a minute to figure out where they've seen each other before.

'New job, then?' Stan asks.

'Yeah,' Chris grins. 'Major Investigation Team. Bit more interesting—still plenty paper to push around, as it turns out.' He rolls his eyes.

Chris takes Stan's statement about meeting Lina on the train from London, offering her friendship in a new place and the phone call he received later. Chris listens politely, taking notes and asking the occasional question.

'Can you get her number from your recents?' he asks.

'Yeah,' Stan says. 'I already wrote it down. Here.' He passes Chris a piece of paper. 'I tried calling her back, but she didn't answer.'

'If it's a contract phone we'll be able to trace it to whoever is paying for it,' Chris says, 'and that may help us to locate your friend. In the meantime, if she calls you again, let me know straight away.' He passes Stan a business card. 'This is my direct number. We may be in a hurry to get to her. Still, let's hope it turns out to be nothing at all.'

Stan nods.

I think I could find Lina, see what's going on, but it frightens me too much. Besides, it's not like I could tell anyone.

Gordon

After a few more of his regular deliveries, Gordon was starting to feel better again. True, the pay was only half of what he got for moving the girl, but it was plenty for him. Anyway, with two drops in one evening, he was doing great. He could save half of it, place a juicy bet, drink himself under the table and buy something expensive for Laura. In one day.

The presents made everything better. His wife was no gold digger – she wasn't like that – but she seemed to enjoy the new Gordon. There was no feeling quite like this. He could provide for his family, their needs and wants. He could give money to his boys if he wanted. He could satisfy his wife in every way. It was like a brand new relationship—it made him feel young again.

Still, Brian's words haunted him, popping into his head involuntarily.

There's only one way you get out of this game.

Some friend. *Fingers crossed*, he thought. *No more girls.*

Meredith

Alfie's dog is so tired now. She's not interested in walking anymore, and she's off her food. He takes the day off for the appointment. Everything's ready. He carries Shirley into the surgery and waits, trying to hold back the tears. He needs support—where is Mina? I can always go if she shows up.

I follow them into the surgery, and when the dog goes to sleep, her spirit rises and comes to me. I bury my hands in her fur and she nuzzles my leg. I wish Alfie could see this.

He carries her body back to the car in a blanket, still warm. We follow.

In his garden, he places her gently in the grave and goes for the shovel. Mina returns, but before I can leave she takes my hand. We watch silently as Alfie covers the dog's body with soil. There are no dry eyes, except Shirley's. She whines at Alfie's feet, looking from him to the grave and back again. Then she comes back to sit by me.

Mina says, 'It looks like you've got yourself a pet.'

I say, 'I don't know how long she'll stay. What happens to them, usually?'

'Same as us, I think. They go on when it's time.' She nods towards Alfie. 'She'll want to wait for him. You can keep her company.'

'I'd love to,' I say, though I'm afraid to get too attached.

CHAPTER 21

Meredith

I've been watching Aunt Lizzie in case that horrible Rab comes back, but there's no sign of him. Instead, the policewoman who's picked up Davie's case arrives at the door with Chris Bain.

Lizzie—who's busy kneading dough for the SWI bread-making competition—tuts and goes to the door, wiping her hands on her apron. She looks surprised to see the police.

The woman introduces herself as Detective Inspector Trisha Macdonald. She looks young for a DI – mid-thirties, I think. She's of average height, with long dark hair expertly pinned up, and wears a smart grey business suit and sensible heels. No wedding ring.

Once they're comfortably seated and have politely refused a cup of tea, Trisha gets down to business. 'Ms Jacobs, I need to ask you a few questions in connection with the recent death of a man in hospital.'

'Is this about my friend David?' Lizzie asks. 'His sister told me he'd died, poor man.'

'Did you visit the hospital last Saturday, 15th November between the hours of 6 pm and 8 pm?'

'Certainly.'

'What time would you say that was?'

'I arrived about 6.45.'

'Did you pass anyone on your way in?'

'Yes, my friend's sister Angela was leaving just as I entered the ward.'

'Thank you. Which ward were you visiting?'

'Ward 42 – neurology.'

Chris makes notes as the interview progresses.

Lizzie checks her watch, tight-lipped, impatient to get back to her bread.

Trisha asks, 'And who were you visiting on that ward?'

'My friend, David.'

'How do you know him, if you don't mind me asking?'

'Not at all. We've known each other since we were young. My father was an architect, and David was a building contractor – they often worked together.'

'Very good.'

'I'm saddened by his passing. At my age, you lose so many of your family and friends...' Lizzie's eyes well up a little. 'It's difficult.'

'I understand,' says Trisha. 'Just a few more questions and we'll be on our way. When you visited David, was there anyone else in the room?'

'No. Why, Inspector? Why all the questions? What's happened?'

'That's what we're trying to understand,' Trisha says with a polite smile. 'Can you describe your visit – how he was, your conversation?'

Lizzie straightens up a little. 'The conversation was difficult. I couldn't understand him very well. I did my best to make small talk. It was awkward, to be honest; I couldn't bear seeing my friend like that. I just held his hand. I was only there for five minutes.'

'Did he say anything that made you think he could be in danger?'

'Dear God, no,' says Lizzie. 'As I say, he wasn't making any sense, but there was nothing like that.'

'Ms Jacobs, did David seem like he wanted to die?'

'I can't say, Inspector. He was quite agitated. He certainly wasn't himself, but whether he wanted to die...'

'Did he ask you to help him die?'

'No.'

'And did you see anyone else enter the room? Anyone at all?'

Lizzie pauses again. 'I didn't see anyone inside the room. There were plenty of people milling around, but who went in the room, I couldn't say.'

Trisha nods. 'Anything else you can think of that might be relevant?'

'I don't think so, Inspector.'

'Your cooperation is much appreciated, Ms Jacobs. People like you make my job so much easier.' Trisha smiles warmly.

'No problem.' Lizzie nods, her head held high.

'I would just love to be able to rule you out of our enquiries to save troubling you again.'

Lizzie smiles politely.

'Now, if you're willing to give us an oral swab for DNA, we could eliminate you very quickly.'

'What?' Lizzie's head draws back, a look of incredulity on her face. 'Is that really necessary? Am I a *suspect*?'

'Ms Jacobs,' Trisha says. 'I don't mean any offence. Now, I can see you're a very respectable member of society.'

Lizzie straightens up.

'I'm sure you were simply in the wrong place at the wrong time. That's why we need to rule you out. I'll be asking everyone who was in that room for the same thing.'

'Well.' Lizzie considers. 'That's very intrusive. Am I obliged to give this sample?'

'Not at all, Ms Jacobs.' Trisha smiles again. 'It was just to save you hassle. I thought that, since you have nothing to hide, you'd want your part to be over as soon as possible. But it's no problem, we can always do it later if need be.'

Lizzie thinks for a moment.

Trisha waits—there's a threat in her eyes but she's still smiling.

'I don't have anything to hide,' Aunt Lizzie says, 'but you've no right to march in here and take my DNA. I should be happy to give you a sample at such time as I'm legally obliged to do so.'

'No problem, Ms Jacobs,' Trisha says. 'I quite understand.'

They rise to leave, and Aunt Lizzie rises too, looking relieved.

Trisha notices some scratches scabbing over on Lizzie's left arm. She says, 'Those scratches look sore.'

'Not really,' Lizzie says, nonchalant. 'They're healing up fine.'

'A while ago was it?'

'Maybe a week. It was my friend's cat. Why are you so interested?'

'Just making conversation.' Trisha smiles again.

Lizzie does too, but her eyes narrow.

'What's her name?' Trisha asks.

'Sorry?'

'The friend with the cat.'

'Oh. Helen—Helen Potts.'

'Well, thank you again. If you should think of anything else that may be relevant, give us a call.'

After the officers leave, Aunt Lizzie peers out of the window in the front room, just in time to see the curtain-twitcher across the road disappear from view. She sighs. If there's one thing my Aunt Lizzie hates, it's nosy neighbours. I've heard her complain about them often enough. (Not that she's above a bit of neighbourhood gossip herself.)

Lizzie gets on the phone to Angela immediately, the dough forgotten. 'What on earth is going on, darling? I've just had the police at my door!'

'They've been to see me, too,' Angela says. 'I can't believe it, Lizzie. They say Davie didn't die of natural causes. The post-mortem confirmed it-someone suffocated him.'

Lizzie's eyes widen. 'Impossible! How can they be sure?'

'I don't know, but that's what they said.' Angela sniffs. 'My brother was murdered.'

'Now, who would want to hurt a harmless old fellow like that?'

'That's what the police asked, but I don't know. I don't know anything. I just want them caught so I can put my brother to rest.'

'You poor dear. It's bad enough losing your brother, but having to deal with a murder investigation, too.'

Angela sobs. 'It's awful. I think I'm a suspect! They asked me for a swab.'

Relief flashes across Aunt Lizzie's face. 'Don't worry, darling. They asked me for one, too. I'm assured it's all just routine. The truth will out, in the end.'

'That was brilliant!' Chris says to Trisha in the car. 'The way you manipulated her—I think you almost got the swab!'

Trisha gives a sly smirk. 'Well, it's going to be important in this case, and if we wait till the point of arrest to take swabs, it'll be harder to collect enough evidence to make said arrest. Bit of a potential Catch-22 I fear.'

Chris nods appreciatively, taking it in like a sponge. 'Smart,' he says. 'If that didn't make her give it up, nothing will.'

'It's useful to see what kind of reaction you get from asking. You might get the sample—that's a bonus—but if not, you still get the reaction. I mean, how would you react to that question if you were guilty?'

'People react in all sorts of ways, I suppose. You'd be mad to give the sample, but you might give it just to make it look like you were innocent.'

'Interesting, isn't it? It's nothing we can use, of course, but it gives you a feel for people.'

'I've got a feel for Lizzie Jacobs. She thinks we're impertinent for turning up at her door!' I laugh along with Trisha—that's my Aunt Lizzie alright.

Alfie sits at home and weeps inconsolably. He doesn't eat. Shirley stays with me when I'm not with Alfie, but when I come here she sits by his feet, whining softly. I don't want to get in Mina's way but Shirley needs to visit home.

I feel Alfie's energy and my heart breaks, too. This will pass, but right now his grief must be felt. I can only share what light I possess with him and hope he can feel he isn't alone.

Shirley is still here with you, I tell him.

I don't know Mina's here until she speaks. 'How is he?'

'As well as can be expected.'

She says, 'I'm glad you're here. If I knew he was taken care of, I could...step back.'

'Oh, I didn't mean to-'

'I miss my husband.' There's a faraway look in her green eyes.

'Alfie's not your husband?'

'Alfie? No, he's my son.'

Of course! Why didn't I see it? The auburn hair.

'You know,' Mina says, 'he's a lot like his dad. He needs people to be very direct, and to accept him as he is.'

I look at him. 'He's perfect as he is.'

Mina's smile reaches the depths of her eyes, full of wonder. 'You're right.'

I blurt out, 'Does he have a wife, waiting somewhere?'

'No. Women never noticed him.'

'Idiots.' I'm not joking, but Mina laughs, and I feel myself relax.

It's Rab Graham's turn. He knows the drill, and he doesn't bother to feign politeness for the police. He opens the door, turns around and walks back inside, allowing them to follow.

He's not the sort of man to offer them tea and biscuits. I expect if he had a fiver for every time he'd been asked: 'Where were you on the night of whenever between the hours of this and that,' he'd be a rich man.

'Don't remember.' He says, arms folded, scowling like a huffy teenager.

'Let me help you out, then,' says Trisha. 'You were at the Western General, ward 42.'

'Was I?'

'You were seen coming and going on the CCTV camera.'

'Great work, detective.' Rab claps his hands slowly. 'I was there. So what?'

'Who were you visiting?'

'None of your business.'

'Look, Mr Graham, this is a murder investigation. If you choose not to cooperate, it's not going to look good.'

Rab looks Chris up and down, a look of hatred in his eyes. He turns his gaze back to Trisha, but only her face.

'I ask you again,' Trisha says. 'Who were you visiting?'

'An old pal, Davie,' Rab says. 'He was asleep. I sat with him for a couple of minutes, then I left. Whoever got done in, it had nothing to do with me.'

'Are you sure he was just asleep?'

'I don't know, I'm no doctor. I never checked his bloody pulse.'

Trisha says, 'Davie's dead.'

A pause.

'You don't seem concerned, Mr Graham.'

Rab shrugs.

'Maybe he wanted to die? Maybe you helped him?'

'No.'

'How do you two know each other?'

'We grew up in the same neighbourhood. He's lost his marbles lately, but I owe him a debt. So I visit.'

'How much do you owe him?' Trisha asks.

'It's not that kind of debt.'

'What kind of debt is it, then?'

Rab's eyes harden. 'It's personal.'

Trisha sighs. 'Did Davie have any enemies?'

Rab hesitates for a second. 'I'm not answering any more questions.'

Trisha gives him a hard stare. 'Who were his enemies, Mr Graham?'

'No comment.' Rab's tone is final.

Trisha sees it's a lost cause, and the officers leave.

'Chris,' Trisha says as they arrive back at the station, 'check the DNA database. There might be a sample from Rab Graham already. We'll see if that throws anything up relating to the crime scene.'

'Will do boss,' Chris says and turns on his heel.

Helen

Murray turned up on Saturday with more flowers, and his grandson Harry. Helen gave a little start when she opened the door and saw the lad and couldn't help straightening up ever so slightly when he called her 'Auntie Helen'.

'Come in,' she said, leading the way back to the sitting room. She felt herself blush when she took the flowers—how rude it must seem that she'd ignored Murray's efforts so far. Helen was glad she had showered and dressed, but Murray wouldn't see how dysfunctional she'd been lately.

'Thank you.' Helen attempted a friendly smile. 'They're lovely. The other ones were, too. You've been kind, and I'm sorry I haven't been responsive. Things have been...' The truth was too much and too weird.

'I know,' Murray said. A sympathetic smile played on his lips. 'Don't worry about it. How are you holding up?'

'You just need to get on with it. What else can you do?' She sat them down and offered them drinks, even producing a plate of biscuits. Harry tucked in cheerfully, oblivious to the awkwardness between the two adults.

'Listen, Helen,' Murray began, 'I just want you to know...I'm sorry for what's happened between us, in the past.'

It was so long ago now, the reasons for the grudge were growing fuzzy in Helen's mind. 'Forget all that,' she said. 'Let's leave the past where it belongs.'

Murray nodded and bestowed another of his generous smiles.

Helen felt a rush of emotion but didn't know how to express it.

'How about Sunday dinner tomorrow?' he asked. 'It'll just be Jean and I, and this young man's family.'

'You should come, Auntie Helen,' the child piped up. 'My Granny makes the best Sunday dinners ever!'

'I'll come.' Helen smiled. 'But you better not let your mum hear you say that.' She turned to Murray. 'And how are you?'

He hesitated. 'Doing okay,' he said. 'Jean's looking forward to seeing you. We'll catch you up on all the family tomorrow.'

Not long after Murray and Harry left, Lizzie appeared, ranting about the police. 'Honestly darling, they treated me like a common criminal. I've half a mind to make a complaint!'

'You should,' said Helen, boiling the kettle.

'They even asked me about these silly scratches on my arm, can you believe the nerve?'

Helen shook her head. Her mind was on other things, but there was an appropriate response when Lizzie was like this. 'Outrageous,' she threw in for effect.

'It was Ginger, of course, who scratched me.'

'Oh, did he?'

'Yes, darling. Remember I was here last weekend? Sorting Meredith's things?'

Helen nodded.

'Well, poor Ginger, it wasn't his fault. I didn't know he was there, you see, under Meredith's bed, and I stood on his tail. He jumped up and clawed at me. It was my fault, and you had enough to worry about—that's why I didn't mention it.'

Helen nodded again.

'I'm surprised you didn't hear him yowl—he was most displeased with me. You will tell the police that, won't you, if they come snooping?'

'Why would they come snooping?' Helen asked.

'Oh, I shouldn't think they would,' Lizzie said with a wave of the hand and opened the fridge. 'Just thought I'd mention it. *If* they come snooping, you must tell them Ginger scratched me.'

'Why? What's going on?'

'They didn't say—nothing serious, I should think. Now, what do you have by way of a biscuit?'

Lizzie opened the cupboard and helped herself to the biscuit tin, choosing a kit-kat and pouring milk in the tea.

After they sat down to their tea, Lizzie rose to leave. 'Well, I'll see you tomorrow darling, usual sort of time.'

'Oh,' Helen said, remembering. 'Can we make it another time? I've been invited for Sunday dinner with Murray's family.'

'But we *always* have afternoon tea on Sundays.' Lizzie looked a little injured.

'I know. I'm sorry, but he's been asking me for weeks on end.'

'You're very forgiving. He hasn't been much of a brother to you.'

'I'm not the only one with things to forgive.'

'What talk is this? You were never in the wrong. Have you forgotten what that man said about Pottsy? That it didn't *sound* like him, as though you were just *imagining* that your husband had run off?'

'It was just an opinion, Lizzie. I was wrong to get so angry. It wasn't Murray's fault.'

'Well, you know what's best, I'm sure,' Lizzie said, nose in the air. 'I'll see you some time.'

Part Five
Seeds of change

CHAPTER 22

Chris

Keen to get a decent amount of leg-work done, Chris worked overtime through the weekend. He interviewed hospital staff—some at home, and some at work. He spoke to the patients—the ones who theoretically could've been involved. A few had spoken to Davie, but not at length. He'd kept himself to himself. Anyone who did speak to him reported the same thing—he was anxious and talking nonsense. He'd got himself quite worked up about something.

Vera, a nurse, said, 'He was going on about running away or something? I think he was a bit confused. It took me a while to make it out, but he said "she made me run away". Strange thing to say, I suppose, but I've heard a lot of strange things in here.'

Chris noted everything down. He got a bit of Davie's history on a visit to his sister, Angela. He'd emigrated to Australia in 1963 and returned to Edinburgh some ten years ago.

Chris asked Angela, 'Would you say he was running away from anything, either when he left Scotland, or when he came back?'

Angela said, 'Before he emigrated, I didn't see much of him, and he never told me anything. He left a wife and child.'

Chris took down the limited details Angela could give him about the family. She remembered their first names, but not the wife's maiden name. She knew the year they were married, so he'd be able to check the register. She also said that Clements was an assumed name he'd taken on when he emigrated.

'Why would he do that?'

'I have no idea.'

'Did you keep in touch with his wife, after he left?'

'No. She wouldn't have anything to do with me. She moved away and left no forwarding address.'

'Would you say he was running away from his family?'

'I don't know, sorry.'

Chris's phone rang. He put it on silent and apologised. 'Did he keep in touch with you from Australia?'

'Yes, we wrote to each other occasionally. Christmas cards, that sort of thing.'

'And why did he come back?'

'His Australian wife, Pat, passed away. He had no one else, so I asked him to come home. At least here, he's got me and my family. After a while, he did come back, and we saw each other a lot more after that.'

After Chris was finished at Angela's, he got in the car and checked his phone. Five missed calls and three texts from Connor. He sighed. He didn't have time for this. The texts said:

Fone me pls
Bro I need u
Help

Connor only ever got in touch when he wanted something. Chris didn't need to read the texts to know that. It was never quick and easy, so it would have to wait. He replied:

Working, phone you later

He put the phone away, determined to ignore its constant vibrating and get on with his work. He still had two nurses to see at home, and he'd need Sunday to write it all up. He wasn't about to let Connor throw him off his game.

Meredith

Mum finally accepted Uncle Murray's invitation! There, Uncle Murray—we knew she'd come, didn't we? It isn't as awkward as it might be. The family do their best to include mum in the conversation. They don't bring up my suicide, but they don't pretend I never existed, either. Shirley lies at Murray's feet—she doesn't normally do that with anyone living, other than Alfie.

Jean tells mum, 'Gail's a primary school teacher.'

'Mum works at my school, Auntie Helen,' Harry says, 'but Bella goes to High School now.'

'And how are you getting on in High School, Bella?' mum asks.

'Good, thanks.' Bella smiles sweetly.

'What's your favourite subject?'

'I like P.E. best. We've been playing football this term, and I've joined the girls' team.'

'That's great! Do you play other schools?'

'Yeah, it's good fun.'

Mum helps Jean bring the dishes to the table: beef, gravy, roast potatoes, Yorkshire puddings, carrots and sweetcorn. I miss my body—it looks delicious. The best mum's eaten since my passing is Aunt Lizzie's soup. She's been living on ready meals.

There's something a little different about mum—it's subtle but unmistakeable. Her aura is whole again, and clearer than before. Her demeanour is different, too—the anger has softened.

When the meal is done, mum helps Auntie Jean to clear everything away, and they wash the dishes together.

Jean says, 'Murray's been awful worried about you.'

'Has he?'

'Aye. After Meredith...he felt terrible about losing touch. He's been anxious to make things right before it's too late.'

'Too late?'

'He has leukaemia. We don't know how much longer he'll be with us.'

'Oh.' Mum holds back tears. 'I'm sorry.'

Mum's never been open before; I know I can keep working with Murray, to bring her into the family. Murray can help her, even in a short time—he already has.

When she gets home and settled, she lights a candle in her bedroom, turns out the lights and sits in front of the mirror, breathing deeply. She sits like this for a long time before she closes her eyes and whispers, 'Mum? Where are you?'

I realise with a jolt, she hasn't been reading the books for me—it's Veronica she's looking for. It makes sense, I suppose, after the dream. If mum knew I was here, she'd speak to me, wouldn't she? I'm sure she would.

I focus on my love for mum, as we are now, and my longing to be with her properly. I send it out to her on the air.

'I can feel you, mum,' she whispers. 'You're here. Please, talk to me.'

I can't. I'm sorry!

Chris

On Monday morning, Chris knocked on Trisha's office door and popped his head around. She was poring over his report—good. He'd taken the liberty of finding out how she liked her coffee and picked up two cups from Costa on the way in. His was extra strong—he'd had a late night with Connor.

'Come in, Chris,' she beckoned. 'I gather you've had a busy weekend.'

'You don't know the half of it.'

'Woman trouble?'

He felt his cheeks turn red. 'Nah, I'm single. It's just my brother—he's trouble enough.' He passed her a cup. 'He got what he came for and he's off, so I probably won't see him for another six months.'

'He sounds delightful,' Trisha said with raised eyebrows. 'Thanks for the coffee. So, what else have you got for me?'

'There's no sample for Rab Graham on the DNA database. His last arrest was 1996. Whoever did it wasn't up on DNA sampling or didn't deem it necessary for whatever reason.'

'Okay, he's definitely a suspect, but I feel we'd need more evidence to detain him, at this stage. We'll need to wait for forensics, keep digging, go through a process of elimination. What's the most likely scenario?'

'Most likely it's a case of assisted suicide. By all accounts, the old man was in a state of agitation for some time prior to his death. He could've persuaded someone to help him.'

Trisha nods. 'If that was the case, who would be most likely to agree to that?'

'His sister?'

'Probably. But she can't have done it. Because, if she had, Lizzie wouldn't have been able to come in after her and talk to him, would she?'

'No,' Chris said. 'Angela gave a DNA sample as well, quite willingly. She didn't seem to be hiding anything.'

'If Davie was asking for help to die, wouldn't he have asked Angela first?'

Chris nodded, comprehension dawning. 'And if she said no, he'd have asked Lizzie. And if that's the case, why has everyone denied that he asked to die? Angela would've told us.'

'Exactly. This isn't euthanasia. This is someone committing murder and hoping it'll go unnoticed because the victim was an old man with one foot in the grave. So, we need to answer two questions. First, who *could* have done it? And second, why *would* they?'

Chris said, 'First question. Forensics have narrowed the time of death down to a two-hour window. I've eliminated four of the six members of staff who had access—they can all prove they were elsewhere for the duration. Of the eighteen visitors to the ward that evening, fifteen of them said they were visiting other patients on the ward. I'm in process of double-checking that everyone is who they say they are, and that said visits took place. That only leaves the patients. I've been able to confirm that there were twenty-three patients on the ward including our victim, and ten of those had visitors with them. It's difficult to confirm that the visitors were there for the full duration, but we can safely eliminate six of the ten. Of the twelve who didn't have visitors, only three of them were well enough to have slipped in unnoticed.'

Trisha looked impressed. 'You've got through a power of work.'

Chris's cheeks reddened again.

'So, what potential suspects does that leave us with?'

'Assuming everything checks out, there are our three visitors—Angela Summers, Lizzie Jacobs and Rab Graham; two staff members, Craig Hall and Brenda Lee; and seven patients not yet eliminated.'

'What do you think about Angela?'

'She definitely visited before Lizzie, so she can't have done it. If she had, Lizzie would have reported him dead, or said something similar to Rab.'

'I agree. It has to be Lizzie, Rab, or one of the staff or patients. Did the staff offer DNA samples?'

'Craig did, but Brenda refused.'

'Okay. Let's see what forensics come back with. Who stands out at the moment?'

Was Trisha testing him? 'Well, Rab Graham is the most likely suspect. It occurs to me that Davie might have asked Rab to help him die, in payment of his 'debt'. He may not have wanted to put the task on his sister, or a female friend?'

'It's possible, but I must say, by all accounts, Davie wasn't much of a gentleman. Sounds a bit chivalrous for him.'

'True. Plus, the skin under the victim's fingernails suggests he was fighting. Why would he do that if he wanted to die?'

Trisha said, 'Survival instinct could've kicked in. We should keep an open mind. So, what are our best lines of enquiry?'

Yep, she *was* testing him. Beads of sweat started to form at his hairline. 'The scratches on Lizzie Jacobs' arm could be something. I could track down her friend to verify her story.'

Trisha nodded approvingly.

'Other than that, I think we should go back and do some digging around the victim, maybe look for links to any staff or patients. His kid would've been too young to remember him, but I can look for the wife, see if she's still living. She may be able to shed some light on his absconsion. Apart from anything else, she has a right to know what's going on.'

'Absolutely. You're spot on, Chris. Track down the wife first, and we'll see her together. Find Lizzie Jacobs' friend with the cat as well. Keep going with the patients and visitors in your spare time—check the relationships between them and look for anything that doesn't feel right. Assign some of it to Rogers and Callaghan, if you like. Keep an open mind.'

Chris nodded, still so pleased with the 'spot on' that it was hard to remember the rest.

'I want to go over your reports in more detail, in case there's anything we're missing. It's possible that the whole absconding to Australia thing could be connected to his death.'

Meredith

Alfie comes home from work and fixes himself some tea and toast. I've been bringing Shirley here regularly, and he seems to feel it. He hasn't thrown out her bed, and she still uses it.

He sits down with a sigh and switches on the TV. Pet rescue—fantastic. He changes the channel and watches some medical drama instead. Once he's finished eating, he takes a photo of Shirley out of a kitchen drawer and sits back down.

I close my eyes, feeling his emotions. He's so lonely! Alfie has a hold of himself now, but I start to cry. The feeling is so familiar that I'm not sure if it's coming from him or me. I kneel in front of him and reach out to touch his hand, but mine slips right through. I try again and again, but I can't reach him. Shirley nuzzles up next to me and I put my arms around her, sobbing into her fur.

When I finally look up, Mina is there. I don't know how long she's been watching. I stand up and dry my tears hurriedly.

'You know,' she says, 'there's marriage in the afterlife, too.'
'Really?'
'Of course. Why not? We're still us, after all.'
'Your husband—has he gone on?'
'Yes. I want to go to him, Meredith. I feel a pull. Will you take care of Alfie for me?'

I'm afraid, but I say, 'Yes.'

Mina smiles with tears in her eyes and takes my hand. 'I won't worry about him anymore, thanks to you.'

I smile, more tears threatening. I ask, 'Would you like to talk to him, one more time?'

'There's hardly a day goes by I don't wish he could see me and hear my voice.'

'I can make it happen after you go on.'
'Can you really? That's a special skill.'
'Is it?'

'I only ever knew one other who could do it.' She embraces me like an old friend. 'Goodbye, Meredith,' she says. 'I don't think we'll meet again here.'

And with that, she's gone.

Chris

Chris ducked out for a sandwich and an espresso, then settled down at his desk to carry on the work of tracking down the wife. He'd found the couple's marriage and the child's date of birth in the national records, which gave him the wife's maiden name. He'd checked for a divorce post-1963 but found nothing.

He'd spent hours scouring the electoral roll, under her married and maiden names. There was no telling whether she was still in Scotland, let alone Edinburgh. In Edinburgh alone, there were two dozen to wade through. He narrowed it down to three that were over seventy. Since there were no phone numbers, he'd be visiting them all, unless he struck lucky. He noted the details down and armed himself with the photos Angela had given them—one of Davie as a younger man, and a recent one.

He could be in for a long evening visiting old ladies. If this didn't turn anything up, he'd look for the daughter to find the wife.

Meredith

The police turn up at the door after mum's morning walk. She invites them in, looking baffled.

'Mrs Potts, we just have a few questions for you,' says Trisha.

Mum's brow furrows. 'What's this about?'

'It's confidential, Mrs Potts. But nothing to worry about—just routine, really.' After taking mum's details, Trisha says, 'I know it seems a strange question, but do you own a cat?'

'Yes – Ginger,' Mum says. 'He's upstairs.'

'May we see him, please?'

Mum raises her eyebrows. It's bizarre, but she fetches our old cat and brings him down. He sits on her knee, eyes closed, purring softly, his expanding mass spread out around his little face like a giant pompom.

Trisha asks, 'Are you aware of Ginger scratching anyone recently?'

'No, he never scratches.' But remembering, mum says, 'Wait, now you mention it, he did scratch my friend Lizzie.'

'When did it happen?'

'I don't know...She came to clear out some things upstairs. It was a Sunday.'

'Last Sunday? The twenty-third?'

'Yes. No, the week before.'

'The sixteenth?'

'I think so. Yes.'

Chris takes notes while Trisha asks, 'And what happened, exactly?'

'The cat was under the bed, and Lizzie stood on his tail, so he jumped up and scratched her.'

'Mrs Potts,' Trisha asks, 'Did you *see* Ginger scratch Lizzie?'

'No, but she wouldn't lie.'

'Did she mention it to you, at the time?'

'I...no.'

'When *did* she mention it?'

Mum looks worried now. 'I don't...it was...' She screws up her eyes. 'It was Saturday, just there. I remember because we changed our plans for Sunday.'

What in the world has Ginger scratching Aunt Lizzie got to do with a murder investigation?

'Very good, Mrs Potts.' Trisha smiles politely, and Chris writes something down. 'Has Ginger done anything like that before?'

He hasn't. I actually did step on his tail once, and all he did was lumber off a few paces. He could hardly even be bothered to yowl. Aunt Lizzie must've really hurt him.

Mum's getting agitated. 'What is this? Are you thinking of arresting my cat, Inspector?'

Trisha smiles. 'I know it's an unusual line of enquiry, and I'm sorry, but we had to ask. How long have you known Lizzie?'

'Let's see...about sixty-three years.'

'Then perhaps you also know David Clements?'

'No,' mum says. 'I've never heard that name.'

'What about David Walker?'

'No, sorry.'

I leave them to finish and go upstairs to my room. I picture Aunt Lizzie, that day when she was in my room, sorting through my things. What was she wearing? No matter how hard I try, I can't recall the details. I can't say whether she was scratched or not.

Next door, in mum's meticulously tidy room, something is different—it's that wooden box. Mum often keeps it close to her person, but it sits on her bedside table now—taunting me, challenging me.

I know I've glimpsed spiritual objects before, and this one seems important in ways I don't yet understand. I know you're in there, blueprint box. And if I can see you, and hold you, I can push your lid right open and look at your secrets. Obediently, the box reveals itself to me. It's the longest I've ever gone, but still only a second. Panicking, I flail at the thing and push it back a few inches before I lose sight of it. Damnit!

I hear Trisha saying, 'Mrs Potts, can I ask you to keep this conversation to yourself, for the moment?'

Mum swallows and nods before closing the door.

I follow the police, and Trisha says to Chris, 'What do you make of that, then?'

'It *could* be true about the cat. But to be honest, I'd be surprised to see *him* go to the bother of scratching his own arse.'

Trisha bursts into laughter. 'You're right,' she says.

'Is it worth asking Ms Jacobs about it again?'

'Not yet—we'd only get the same answer, and it'd put her back up. Why don't we sit on it for a while and do some more digging into the victim's life? There's a mystery there. Maybe if we find the wife or others who knew the man, we'll be able to uncover a motive.'

I go back inside, thinking I might muster my strength for another crack at the box, but mum is there. She's perched on the edge of the bed, her head watchfully inclined towards the box, rocking gently back and forth. Does she know it's moved? Can she tell?

Don't be scared, mum. The box is just where you left it.

But she looks at the box as though, if opened, it could spew forth horrors beyond imagination.

CHAPTER 23

Meredith

'Any joy?' Trisha asks.

'Unfortunately not,' Chris says. 'I've had some lovely chats with the old women I visited, but none of them were Davie's wife.'

Trisha sits back in her chair with a sigh.

'I've had a look for the daughter, but no joy. She didn't marry in Scotland, and I can't find her living in Edinburgh or the surrounding area.'

Trisha nods. 'Let's have the support team widen the search, then. You've done enough—it's a needle in a haystack. In the meantime, we need to find someone who knows about Davie: his emigrating to Australia or anything about his life that could help us find a motive. How d'you think we should proceed?'

Chris takes a deep breath. 'We could try Angela again, see if there's anything we've missed. She might be able to put us in touch with other relatives or friends.'

'It's worth a shot.'

'There's his funeral. If we make sure it's well publicised, someone might turn up there who can shed some light on it. Other than that, we could appeal to the public for information.'

She gives an approving nod. 'I think we'll need to. But we'll see if Angela turns anything up first. And let's pay Lizzie Jacobs another visit—she and Davie may have had mutual acquaintances.'

Aunt Lizzie is vacuuming the carpet when the police arrive and is less than appreciative of the interruption. When she sees who it is, her face falls. She glances furtively around—the nosy neighbours will be having a field day.

'Didn't you get everything you needed the first time?' she asks, ushering them inside.

'Sometimes more questions come up as a case unfolds,' Trisha says. 'We need to know more about your friend and his life.'

'Fine.' Lizzie sighs. 'What can I help you with?'

'How long exactly have you known David—you said since you were young?'

'Gosh...since I was about fifteen, I think.'

'How often were you in touch with him in the last ten years?'

'Not at all until very recently. I didn't know he was living in Edinburgh. He absconded to Australia fifty-odd years ago.'

Absconded? Fifty-odd years? I never heard that before. He had a wife and daughter. Is that why Michael was watching him? Was Davie the no-good father who left us behind? His name isn't Potts – I can't remember what it is, but Potts I would've noticed. He had it changed, didn't he? Yes, there were two names. Could he have changed it more than once? What if he was some kind of criminal with multiple identities? Now that I think about it, I don't even know my father's first name. He was always referred to as *him*, *your father*, or when mum and Aunt Lizzie were talking, *Pottsy*.

Mum didn't know either of Davie's names, but what if they showed her a picture of him—would the colour drain from her face? I don't know what my father looks like. She hated him so much, she tore him out of every picture in the family album. She made it like he'd never existed.

'What do you mean, absconded?' Trisha asks.

Aunt Lizzie says, 'He left suddenly, without explanation I believe. I heard about it from a mutual friend.'

'What's the name of that friend, Ms Jacobs?'

'Well, more of an acquaintance, really. His name was John...Brown, I think. Dead now, I'm afraid.'

'How did you reconnect with David recently?'

'I bumped into him in the street by pure coincidence,' Lizzie says. 'It was just a few days before he died. And that was the first of me knowing he was back in town.' She gave a little sob. 'I'm so glad I got to see him, one last time.'

Why would she care so much about an old acquaintance? Had they been close?

'Prior to that,' Trisha asked, 'when was the last time you saw him?'

'Good Lord, now you're asking! That was a long time ago, before he emigrated.'

'Can you tell me anything about why he left the country?'

'Sorry, I don't know anything of substance. I remember my father complaining. David had been contracted for another building job with father's company, but he left before work was due to start. Father thought he was off with a woman—which wouldn't surprise me, to be honest.'

'Why is that?'

'Well, David was a flirt. He had a bit of a reputation.'

'Were you ever in a relationship with him, beyond friendship?'

'Good Lord, no! The man was married, I believe. He did try as I said, he was a flirt—but he soon gave up on it.'

'Ms Jacobs, it's important that we find out as much about David and his life as we can. We're looking for anyone who knew him, at any time in his life. Can you point anyone out that might be worth speaking to?'

'Gosh, other than Angela and John, I don't know anyone who knew him. I'm sorry.'

Trisha nodded, while Chris finished up his notes. 'Is there anything else you can tell us about David, Ms Jacobs, anything at all?'

'Nothing, I'm sorry.' As Lizzie lets them out the door, she says, 'If I think of anything else I'll give you a call. Good luck, Inspector.' She closes the door behind them and peers out of the front room window. This time, there are a number of curtains twitching. Aunt Lizzie's nostrils flare. What an affront!

If Davie *was* married to my mum, and Aunt Lizzie knew it, why didn't she tell that to the police? Why would she want to hide it? She wouldn't, would she? If he *was* my father, mum knew nothing about Australia, either—unless for some reason she kept it to herself. It's probably just a coincidence. More than one married man ran away from Edinburgh in the sixties, no doubt.

What do I care, anyway? What difference does it make if he is or isn't my father? Who was my father, but a no-good toe-rag who ran off? What little I know about him comes back to me now. Every time I was in trouble: *you're just like your father.* Anytime I asked about him: *he doesn't care about us, Meredith. He left us.*

I don't care, but I go to Davie's house, anyway. Angela is there, and her mobile rings—it's Lizzie phoning to compare notes.

'They've been back to me as well,' Angela says. 'They're digging into his past, but there wasn't much I could tell them.

I'm having a look around the house, but I don't know what I'm looking for. The police are applying for a warrant to search the place.'

'I couldn't help either,' Lizzie says. 'I'm sorry.'

Around the house, there are a few family photos, mostly of people I don't recognise. There's one of Angela with what I assume to be her husband and kids. The rest are children at various stages of growth. There's only one of Davie that I can see – standing on a beach with a woman that looks twenty years younger than him. She's still not a patch on my mum.

Australia.

'Angela darling, why are they asking about my relationship with him?' Lizzie asks.

'I think they're just trying to learn about him.'

'Are we suspects?'

'I'm sure they'd tell us if we were,' Angela says. 'Don't worry, Lizzie. Let the police do their jobs.' Angela sobs. 'I just want to bury my brother.'

'Of course. I'm sorry. Talk soon.'

Chris

Chris was keen to compare the DNA samples to see if it would eliminate anyone. He received notification that the samples were on the database, whereupon he could instruct the lab to compare them with DNA from the crime scene.

It was late afternoon when he knocked on Trisha's door, the results in his hand.

She was on the phone but gestured towards the chair on the other side of her desk.

He waited till she'd hung up, his left leg twitching a little. Without preamble, he gave her the news.

'The DNA results came back. We found a match for two of the four samples from the pillow – Craig who was Davie's nurse, and Angela, the sister.'

'Okay. What about the other two?'

'The charge nurse refused to give a swab – one could be hers. Same goes for Lizzie Jacobs and Rab Graham. We're also checking out the care assistants who changed the bedclothes the day before. The fourth sample is the most interesting one. It matches the skin under the victim's fingernails.'

Trisha leaned back in her chair. 'Most likely our killer, then.'

Chris said, 'Most likely. If we could only get DNA samples for the rest of the suspects.'

'We can't do it without an arrest warrant, unless we detain a suspect, and we'd need reasonable grounds for that.'

'That thing about the cat,' Chris said. 'Is that reasonable grounds?'

'No way. Not on its own. Can you imagine the comeback if we moved too quick and we were off base? We don't know that someone else wasn't scratched, too. The killer could've lost traces of skin without being much marked. We could've interviewed someone who was covering scratches up.'

Chris sighed and nodded.

'I want everyone in the incident room first thing tomorrow. Let's get an update on all lines of enquiry.'

Gordon

Gordon was heading out for a night with the lads, a large wad of twenties in his wallet, whistling a cheery tune, when he saw the girl. He stopped whistling. She sat alone on a bench in a grassy area by the road, with a mobile phone and what looked like a business card. Her posture told him she was in some kind of distress; she kept glancing fearfully around. She was wearing only a short skirt and a tight T-shirt, and it was a damn cold night. Gordon's jacket was already off as he approached, ready to make sure she was okay. He had no qualms with punching some clown of a boyfriend in the face either, if need be.

Whoever she was trying to call, she wasn't getting through. She pressed a button on the phone and muttered at it in a foreign language. As Gordon got closer, she looked up at him, her cheeks smeared with tears and mascara, shivering.

Gordon stopped in his tracks, noticing two things: one, it was Lina, the girl he'd moved for his employers; and two, she'd been beaten. He was too close not to at least offer the jacket.

She froze too, when she saw his face.

He put up a hand to signal that he meant no harm, placed the jacket gently on her shoulders, and walked quickly on, hating himself.

Stan

After an early shift, Stan took a nap. He was doing more and more of that these days. When he woke up it was dark, he was hungry, and there was a missed call on his phone. His heart skipped a beat when he realised who it was from – Lina. He checked the time; it was two hours ago. 'Nightmare,' he muttered, and jumped up to call Chris.

Chris couldn't tell him much. 'Unfortunately, it's a pay-as-you-go phone,' he said, 'so we can't trace it to an account holder. It isn't switched on all the time, and it has no GPS either, but we've been able to pinpoint her likely location to a particular area. We're doing our best to find her—that's all I can tell you.'

'Thanks. I'm only sorry I missed the call.'

'Listen, Stan, I know you're worried, so I'll check in once in a while and let you know if they find her.'

'I'd appreciate it, Chris.'

'And if you hear from her again, try and get her out in the open somewhere, and call us.'

'Will do.'

Meredith

Alfie is sleeping soundly, Shirley lying at his feet. I feel for Mina, and I can't find her. She's gone. Time to keep my promise. I concentrate on her green eyes, her freckled face, her auburn hair, and I make sparks in the darkness. I feel the pathway open up to the world beyond, Alfie's love pulling her closer. How must it feel to be loved like that?

My little orb of blue light grows larger and brighter until Mina appears inside. She smiles at me and closes her eyes. I hold the connection while they talk. After a short while, she looks at me again with that warm, beautiful smile, and melts back into the light.

I stay with Alfie all night, listening to him breathe. It feels peaceful here—Alfie and Shirley are straightforward, undemanding. I like being with them.

In the morning when Alfie wakes, he jumps up and goes straight to the kitchen. He finds a pen and notebook in a drawer. He scribbles down one word.

Meredith.

I don't know why I'm at Davie's funeral. This guy probably isn't my father—but he could be, and if he was, I suppose that would count for something. Some things fit, even if I can't make sense of it. He's started to represent my father, in my mind. I wish I could've asked him, before he went on. That fits too—if he didn't want to see us in life, why would he be any different in death?

There aren't many people here. It makes me feel a bit better about my own funeral. Davie's is held in a small chapel in the funeral director's building. Angela sits at the front with a younger man, probably her son. Aunt Lizzie sits behind them, wearing the same outfit she wore for my funeral, right down to the audacious hat. That horrible man, Rab Graham, is sitting right behind her—I don't like it. He hasn't dressed smartly for the occasion but wears his usual jeans and T-shirt. Next to Rab sits a man with an unwashed, shifty look—I don't like him, either.

There's one other stranger here—an old man. He has sun-weathered skin and a bald head with a ring of white hair. He sits at the back alone. Other than that, there's only Trisha and Chris.

After a short service, there are sandwiches and cakes in another room. Nobody seems keen to stay long. The police quietly question the stranger. His name is Phil, and he was in the building trade with Davie before he went to Australia. Phil doesn't know anything about why he left, though. He saw a notice in the newspaper about the funeral and decided to pay his respects, even though he hasn't seen the man since 1963. They used to have a good laugh, Phil says, back in the day. He can name a couple of other men in the building trade who knew him.

Mum celebrates her eightieth birthday with Murray, Jean, Hughie, Lizzie, David, Gail, Bella and Harry. Murray has organised a sit-down meal in a family restaurant. There's a play area for the kids, and mum enjoys watching them. Bella's too old, officially, but she's small enough to get away with it. After a while, a shadow passes over mum's face.

'Are you okay?' Jean asks her, on the way to the ladies. 'You seem a bit distracted.'

Mum smiles, only partially forced. 'I'm okay. Only...something strange happened to me a few weeks ago, and I can't stop thinking about it.'

'Something strange?' Jean asks. 'How d'you mean?'

Mum considers, then says, 'Ach, forget it. You'd think I was crackers.'

Jean smiles kindly, 'Ok. I'm sure you're not, but there's no need to share if you don't want to.'

I guess mum's referring to her failed attempt to poison herself. It didn't even seem to hurt. How is that possible?

Murray and Jean treat mum as though she's always been part of their lives, even sharing their grandchildren.

With Uncle Hughie, it's going to take time. They can't go back to the way things were: tense and bitter. Instead, they must build something new.

'How are you?' mum asks Hughie over dinner.

'Fine,' he says, 'considering that it's coming up for thirty years since Jessie passed.'

'I'm sorry.'

Hughie raises his eyebrows.

Mum asks, 'So, what's been happening with you?'

'I'm doing a half marathon for Marie Curie in April. I can send you a link if you want to donate.'

'Of course,' mum says. 'Half marathon? How many miles is that?'

'Thirteen.'

Mum exhales, impressed.

'I go pretty slow,' Hughie says, 'I'll be happy just to finish the race.'

Mum is invited to Sunday dinner every week at Murray's house, and she says she'll come. Murray looks almost as pleased as I am, and Hughie looks as surprised as Murray looks pleased.

My cousin David drops mum home when the meal is finished, with flowers and chocolates. There's a new, softer way about her as she thanks him. This time, she arranges the flowers in a vase and gives them pride of place on the sideboard.

'There, mum,' she says. 'I'm making an effort. Are you happy?'

It's weird, but maybe I can be mum, for now.

Yes, I say. *I'm happy.*

Chris and Trisha are at the hospital going over the CCTV again.

Trisha tells Chris, 'It's always worth looking again, and with another set of eyes. We might pick up something new.'

They watch the visitors entering and leaving the ward the night Davie died. They check off each one—their name and who they visited. You can see them outside the secure doors, then they pass beneath the camera as they enter, and again as they leave.

The first of Davie's visitors is Angela, who rings the buzzer and waits, unbuttoning her coat, before passing through the doors. About forty minutes later, Aunt Lizzie arrives with her coat over her arm, and about five minutes after that, Angela leaves the ward. Aunt Lizzie leaves the ward ten minutes after Angela with her coat on. This has all happened by 7 pm.

It's almost 7.30 when Rab Graham shows up, wearing jeans and a T-shirt. You can't see his face very well; he has his head down looking at his phone. He's not in the ward five minutes before he leaves. He stops in view to hold the door for someone and turns his head. The left side of his face is exposed for a second.

'There,' Trisha says. 'Pause that. Zoom in on his face. Can you enhance it?'

In that frozen image, you can make out that Rab has a fresh-looking injury to his left eye. It's bloodshot, and there are dual red marks like cuts or scratches from eyebrow to cheekbone.

'That's interesting.'

'Yeah,' Chris says. 'Can we see him go in again? Maybe we can establish whether he has that on the way in?'

Trisha nods, and the security man replays Rab entering the ward. They slow it down, freeze frames, but whatever way they try, they can't get a good look at that left eye.

'Damn!' Trisha says. 'It's impossible to say whether that happened on the ward or not.'

Chris sighs. 'We keep digging, then.'

CHAPTER 24

Meredith

I never thought I'd see him again, but he appears at mum's when she's getting ready to leave for Murray's. Michael. He's different. He's shining a bit less brightly than before. Or am I imagining it? Shirley gives him a sniff and nuzzles his leg.

'You have a dog now?' Michael asks, patting her back.

'She's Alfie's. I'm just keeping her company for now.' I crouch down to cuddle the dog as she returns to me.

Michael says, 'I didn't leave you by choice. I was...detained.'

'D'you mean you went to...the in-between?'

He looks shocked. 'You know it?'

'Yes. I've been there, too.' I wait for some show of disappointment, but it doesn't come. Emboldened by his newly-exposed vulnerability, I ask, 'What did you do?'

Michael hesitates, his expression dark. 'I took away someone's freedom to choose.'

'You...broke the second law?' I can't picture Michael possessing someone else's body like I did. It's hard to imagine him doing anything wrong at all.

'Yes,' he says, 'and the first.'

'Someone *saw* you?'

'Not exactly.' His tone makes it clear the discussion is over. 'Anyway, it's done.'

'You've been gone a long time,' I say, my hurt feelings bubbling under the surface.

'I know, and I'm sorry. But I'm here now, and there's still work to do. Hm?' He smiles in that warm way that's so familiar to me. 'Now, what did you learn while I was gone?'

The answer surprises me, but I feel myself straighten up and the words come easily. 'I'm not wasting my time. I've become a half-decent whisperer.'

Michael looks deflated for a split second, then he brightens. He's disappointed with me. It wasn't the answer he was looking for.

'That's a wonderful discovery,' he says. 'I always knew you'd be great at it.'

I can't quite face the compliment, though it seems genuine. What am I really supposed to be learning? How do I stop letting him down?

Michael says, 'You've grown while I was gone. Look at yourself, how bright you shine!'

I hold out my arms, looking down at everything I can see. A bright glow surrounds my entire person. Something else too – I look smaller, slimmer. 'I'm changing! I'm more like you!'

Michael beams down at me, and in this moment, I think I can do it, whatever *it* is—my purpose.

Veronica's strange words echo in my mind. *You underestimate yourself, child. You must continue bravely on your path. Keep trying to help, seek truth, and you'll find your way. When you do, you'll change everything.*

As we watch Sunday dinner at Murray's—mum's new family tradition—I fill Michael in on her progress with Murray and Jean, and even Hughie. He seems pleased.

I slip home and try again to open the box. I remember Evie, and the feeling just before I moved the child. I focus on that spiritual object with all my might, but I still can't hold onto it longer than a second. I don't flail this time—I don't want to frighten mum. I just want to know what's in there.

Michael finds me, and I ask, 'Will you open it?'

He smiles sadly, shakes his head.

I don't understand—he's moved things for me before.

'I can't, Meredith. After what I did, I'm on my last warning. Trust me—it's best if I touch nothing.'

I'm getting to know my Uncle Hughie better. Today he's running. He's worked his distance up to about ten kilometres in his personal training, and now he's running his first official 10K in Dunbar with his friend, Rita. He worked as a primary school head teacher before he retired, and Rita was one of his teachers. She's a seasoned runner; it was her who inspired him. He's training for a half marathon in memory of his late wife, Jessie.

He's handsome for an old man—tall and slim. His curly hair is completely white, but there are still flecks of reddish brown in his beard. He has a sad, kind face. I can tell from the lines around his eyes that he's found plenty to laugh about through the hard times.

Rita is a good ten years younger than Hughie. She's petite—probably five foot tall. She wears her hair in a short bob, dyed light brown to cover the grey. There's a compassionate spirit manifest in her eyes—I like her instantly.

At the start line, Rita smiles and winks at Hughie from under her hat.

He grins and says, 'Don't let me hold you up, mind.'

'Don't be daft,' she says. 'You won't.'

The whistle blows and they're off across the grass and out towards the street.

The cold is bitter, but they won't feel it after a couple of miles. By the time they pass through the streets and reach the rugged coastline, their cheeks are pink and their bodies warm, in spite of the biting sea breeze. Rita jogs easily alongside Hughie; the race isn't a third gone yet. Most of the others are ahead of them, but it doesn't matter to Hughie. He's only racing against himself. He's hoping to raise £500 for Marie Curie, and he's willing to work for it.

Hughie flags towards the middle of the race; his feet slow down a little. Michael and I move along beside them, cheering him on with everything we've got. It seems to buoy him. When Rita looks back, he gives her a grin and a nod, and drives his feet on.

As they reach the final stretch, noses red, eyes watering, Hughie has a glint of triumph in his eye. He looks sideways as Rita, then with a determined expression, propels himself forward faster. He keeps it up for the last kilometre or so, through the woods, and Rita jogs along with him, her expression unchanged. Did she even notice they'd sped up?

At the finish line, Hughie gets a personal best—1 hour 4 minutes! He catches his breath—Rita can already talk normally.

After showering at the running club, Hughie offers to take Rita out for a meal. They follow their noses to an Indian restaurant in Dunbar. They're shown to a cosy table for two and given menus. Their appetites are large after their long run, and they enjoy three courses and take their time.

They talk easily, and sit in silence without awkwardness. She's his best friend. After they've finished talking about the race, they fall silent, enjoying the food.

An expression of deep thought comes over Hughie's face. He fiddles with his wedding ring, then glances up at Rita with a forlorn expression.

'What is it?' Rita asks, munching enthusiastically on a piece of naan bread.

He smiles sadly.

Rita asks, 'Thinking about Jessie again? You still miss her a lot, don't you?'

Hughie nods, and they take hands across the table. 'It's not just that,' he says. 'I'm thinking of you, too.'

'We've been over this Hughie. I've told you enough times, I'm content with friendship.'

Hughie looks into Rita's eyes, searching. 'You're so good.'

'Anything more would make you feel unfaithful to Jessie. I understand.'

'I haven't been fair to you. I can't shift the guilty feeling whenever I think of you,' he looks down and adds, 'which is a lot.'

Rita smiles shyly. 'I think of you a lot, too. I love spending time with you. We've managed fine like this for many years, haven't we?'

'Aye, but you deserve better. You could've found someone else. Someone who could—'

'Shh,' Rita says. 'I'm happy here with you, like this.'

I see the love and longing in Hughie's eyes—he needs to give his heart to this woman. Whatever he's got into his head about Jessie's feelings, it may not be the truth. He needs time to change his thinking, and there can't be much of that at his disposal.

A beautiful spirit comes to me at home. She reminds me of Veronica—white and shining, young and full of vitality. A month ago I would've cringed at the sight of her, but now, I smile into her brown eyes. She's looking at me in the same way, like an old friend.

'I found you!' she says.

She has the better of me. I gaze a moment longer, taking in her healthy but slight figure, voluminous hair, perfect teeth and cherry red lips. 'Irene?'

Her smile widens.

'You look so different!'

'So do you, honey,' she says, coming forward to embrace me. 'There's more to us than meets the eye, isn't there?'

I can't argue with that.

'Meredith, I'm so glad I found you. I'm on my way out, but I wanted to thank you first.'

I listen, trying not to get embarrassed.

'You cared for me when I was ill. At the time, I didn't even know your name. But now, I remember everything, and I'll love you for it forever.'

'I only did what any decent person would do.'

'No, you did more than that. You saw *me,* not an old woman with dementia. You defined me by what you could learn about my life, and you treated me with such love and respect! Thank you, sweet Meredith.'

Tears are running down my cheeks, and she reaches out a hand, wiping one away with her thumb. There are no words for this exchange—to have such a glorious creature love me as a friend.

'My daughter's okay,' Irene says. 'She's glad I've been released from suffering. It's been a while since I knew her. Will you do one more thing for me, sweetheart?'

'Anything.'

'When I'm gone, will you bring me back once more, so I can say goodbye?'

'I will,' I promise.

A light whiter than anything earthly I've ever seen appears behind Irene, widening into an archway. There are stairs just inside, glittering like crystal. A voice is softly calling her name from somewhere within. It's a quiet voice, but so penetrating, so familiar. In this moment, I wish that voice was calling my name, that I could walk into the light. Irene starts up the steps, turns to bestow one more adoring smile on me, and fades into the light beyond.

I tell Michael about Davie's death and the investigation. I don't mention my suspicions about Davie—they're too vague, too unfounded.

As the Christmas trees appear in the windows and the shops get busier, Trisha and Chris become increasingly frustrated with the investigation.

The man from the funeral, Phil, puts them in touch with two others who knew Davie, but they can't help. All they can say is that he smoked, gambled and liked booze and women.

Chris uncovers a couple of tenuous connections, but nothing to arouse any real suspicion. Brenda Lee, the charge nurse, lives near Davie on Colinton Road but maintains she's never seen him there. One of the patients worked with Angela before she retired but doesn't know Davie.

They've released a public appeal, and even offered a cash reward for any information about the man. The helpline is busy with bogus callers looking for a little boost for the Christmas fund. Of the few passed to Chris and Trisha, only one has anything to say that interests them.

'We were involved, for a while,' she says, 'in the early sixties.' She has dyed hair, far too dark for an old woman, and wears mascara, rouge and lipstick. She's thin and dressed like someone half her age: skinny jeans, black boots and a hoodie. If you saw her from behind you'd expect to see a much younger face, and you'd get a fright when she turned around. Her name's Theresa Bain.

Trisha proceeds with the interview. 'When you say "involved", Ms Bain, do you mean sexually?'

'Yes.'

'Can you tell me roughly when and how long that went on for?'

Theresa thinks. 'A couple of years. Early sixties, definitely. I didn't see him for a few months, and someone said he'd skipped town. Wasn't surprised.'

'Why not?'

She shrugs. 'He was no good, always borrowing and gambling. Thought he was probably running away from debts.'

'But you don't know specifically why he left?'

'No.'

'Where did the two of you meet, Ms Bain?'

'The Black Bull.'

'And did you know he was married?'

'Yeah. So?'

'Do you know his wife? Could you put us in touch with her?'

'Sorry, no.'

'When did you last see Davie?'

'Back in the sixties, before he left Edinburgh.'

Theresa isn't able to put the detectives in touch with another soul who knew Davie. She says they've all died or moved away. She came for the cash reward. After the interview, Chris does a bit of digging.

'Theresa Bain,' he says to Trisha.

'What about her?'

'She was a known prostitute in the sixties. The Black Bull was where men went to pick up girls.'

Please don't let that disgusting man be my father.

Andy broods alone and brightens whenever Nancy catches him. Gary tells her not to worry—he's always been like this. Gary helps Andy move in with Nancy—she has the bigger house, and it's more homely than Andy's place. It's all decorated for Christmas like Santa's grotto.

Andy advances his relationship with Nancy apologetically, counting himself wholly unworthy. Each time she tries to broach the subject of setting a date for the wedding, he makes excuses to put it off. No matter how many times she says she's sure, that his past doesn't matter, his eyes betray doubt. Quietly, he pays another month's rent on his flat.

I tell him as often as I can that Nancy's true, and everything will be okay. I speak to Nancy, and we start scheming to organise the wedding without him, as a surprise. A surprise and a gift.

Andy's been planning a surprise too, but it isn't going how he hoped. The information he got from Clive led to a dead end. He couldn't find any illegitimate births under the name of Gordon for that year in the national records, and he wasn't sure what to do next. Would Clive give him false information, after all this time?

Talk to Gary, I suggest. Maybe he can help.

As December takes over, Stan mopes wearily. He spends too much time on Facebook, looking for some encouragement from Stacy, but she never replies to his comments, likes his posts, or answers his messages. He sends one now and then, asking how she's doing.

He decorates his flat for Christmas, makes plans with his brother, and tries to cheer himself up with a bit of shopping, but I can see his heart isn't in it.

Your story isn't over yet. Chin up, Stan.

I think of Stacy for his sake, and wonder what she's doing. I concentrate on her, expecting to find her in Zambia, but she's much closer. She's in Aberdeen, and something's wrong. Her mum has passed away unexpectedly—a heart attack. Stacy's full of angry questions.

Her mum's there, just out of sight, searching for her own answers. For Stacy, I can only whisper courage – the kind that lets you fix your face and do what needs to be done, until you can be alone to cry.

Stacy plans a funeral, contacts family and friends, and supports her mum's partner Harry. He's grateful she's there to choose the coffin and floral arrangements. Other than the necessities, they don't speak much to one another. They're each lost in their own grief.

Stacy's dad doesn't show up at the funeral, and she's furious.

'It was her *funeral*, dad,' she growls down the phone, through clenched teeth. 'You couldn't take one day off for *that*?'

'Sorry, Stacy. I couldn't get the time off.'

'Couldn't? Or wouldn't?'

Silence.

'Thought so. You might've made the effort, for me. But you had more important things to do.'

'Stacy, I...'

'Save it, dad.' She hangs up on him, her cheeks red.

Harry has the good sense to stay out of the way.

Mum's more like her old self, attending her yoga classes, book club and walking group. The Roving Ramblers go out in all weathers, and she loves the fresh air. She gets a good catch up with Aunt Lizzie and the others. She talks about Murray, Bella and Harry quite a bit. She always went to church on a Sunday morning—the Church of Scotland along the road—and she's doing so again. She hangs on the minister's every word, questions in her eyes.

She goes to Uncle Murray's for dinner every week now. David picks her up; it's a standing arrangement. Aunt Lizzie wasn't exactly chuffed about changing the routine—they're creatures of habit, these two—but she agreed to have afternoon tea on Mondays instead.

I love these family times, but they fill me with regret. Why did we miss out all those years? I wish they could see me, and I could talk with them face to face.

Seeing mum happier, I sometimes think she's better without me, that I was right to go, but I fight the self-pity. It doesn't help anything. And I don't think that's really why she's happier. It's the family. Her feelings are changing. Things could've been better between us with time. Unfortunately, we've run out of that.

She's still talking to Veronica. She feels someone listening, but she doesn't know it's me.

When it becomes too much I leave her, forget myself, and find something I can help with. I think about little Evie and sometimes visit just to watch her play.

Nathan watches Alfie at work. Since Shirley died, Alfie isn't the same—he's so sad. Nathan feels it too. His friend is quiet and prefers to go home than sit in the cafe at the end of a shift.

Laura's warned Nathan never to go to Alfie's house, 'just in case'—but he would, if he knew where it was. Laura's still a bit weird about Alfie. It's the job of parents to be cautious but Nathan keeps telling them—Alfie isn't like that at all.

On the face of it, things seem great at home. His parents are getting on better than ever, and there's plenty money. It's shaping up to be a great Christmas.

But I know better. I know what Gordon's doing. Laura does too, but she chooses to stick her head in the sand.

Andy

Nancy and Andy were about to eat dinner when the news came on the TV. She'd made a lamb roast—it smelled delicious. Andy was at the breakfast bar opening a bottle of wine and letting the newsreader's voice wash over him.

In Edinburgh, a man has died in hospital under suspicious circumstances. Police are conducting a thorough investigation and at this point are unwilling to release full details. However, they have released these photographs of the victim...

Andy stopped where he was, a glass of wine smashing on the tiled floor.

Detective Inspector Trisha Macdonald is appealing for anyone who has ever known the man to come forward.

The DI was now on the screen, saying: 'There's a great deal of mystery around this man and his life. If you know anything about him, even if it doesn't seem relevant to this investigation, we urge you to come forward.'

Nancy helped Andy to a chair and switched off the TV. 'Sweetheart,' she said, 'you look like you've seen a ghost.'

For several minutes, he couldn't speak. He could only sit there, ashen-faced.

'Nance...' he said finally, in a hoarse whisper. 'I need to tell you something. Something I've never told anyone.' He told her the whole story, from the beginning. The story of why the dead man left the country.

When Andy had finished the tale, he couldn't hold back the tears.

Nancy sat quietly with him, holding his hand until he was more in control.

'Do you think I'm going to hell, Nance?' he asked.

She placed a hand on his arm, not caring that the lamb was now stone cold. 'No,' she said, looking into his eyes. 'You were just a child, Andy. You didn't know what you were doing.'

He melted into her arms, great tears rolling down his cheeks and onto her shoulder. How could she marry him now? How could she ever look at him the same way again?

CHAPTER 25

Meredith

Stan gets ready for a late shift. He's grown a beard—it suits him. After showering, he gets into his work clothes and fixes his hair, curls flicking out behind his ears and flopping over his forehead. He adds a bit of fragrance and looks in the mirror with satisfaction.

'Look out girls,' he tells his reflection. 'I'm back.'

He's more like the original Stan today. He's back in the driver's seat, humming a cheery tune.

At Edinburgh, Emma is working at the station. Stan clocks her and with a look of decision, he marches right up to her. He turns his charm up full throttle, chatting and making her laugh. He watches the curve of her lips, making no effort to hide it.

'I think a good catch up is long overdue,' Stan says, standing a little closer than is necessary. 'How about dinner some time?'

And in a matter of minutes, he has a date set up for the weekend.

Stan leaves for his break with a spring in his step.

I haven't the heart to try and talk him out of it.

Andy

Andy avoided the TV. Whenever the news came on he switched it off or left the room. He wasn't going to give Trisha Macdonald the chance to ask him again.

What good would it do, speaking ill of the dead? The chances of something that happened over fifty years ago having anything to do with the current investigation were slim to none.

He'd shared his secret with Nancy, and he felt better. Much better. Miraculously, she still loved him. He couldn't understand it. He felt so dirty when he thought about the things he'd done. The only thing standing between him and moving on was the police appeal, which he stoically ignored.

Gordon

Gordon's heart had missed a beat when he saw the instructions for his Friday evening job. Once again, here he was, waiting at the station. This time the sign said *Justina*.

Another young woman stepped off the train and found him. This one was wearing a warm coat, but he could still see her curves. Under her woolly hat was dark brown hair cut in a bob, and her skin was beautifully tanned. He walked her to the van, trying not to think about what might happen to her.

'My friend Lina help me find job here,' Justina said. 'She text me. She tell me job very good. Good money, nice people. She send me pictures—Edinburgh Castle.'

Gordon smiled distractedly as he began to navigate the city streets. *There's no way Lina said any of that,* he thought, *not by choice.*

'Where are best places for nightlife here?' Justina asked. 'Good clubs?'

Gordon only shrugged and grunted. He thought of his wife and wondered how he'd feel if anyone tried to hurt her. What if he had a daughter? These girls were someone's daughters. Judging by what he got paid for moving one of them, they were a lucrative source of income. And they thought they were coming here to be with friends, make good money and party.

In a split second, Gordon made his decision. He swerved onto a side street, changing his route.

'Justina, listen to me. Lina is in trouble with some very bad people.'

'What do you mean?' Justina breathed. 'She text me.'

'They must've forced her to. Or used her phone. The job is bad. The people are bad. They hurt you. No nightlife. Do you understand me?'

'Yes,' she whispered. 'What can I do?'

'I can give you money and take you back to the station. Go home.'

Justina sobbed. 'I cannot go home without Lina! You tell me they hurt her?'

'I think so. I don't know them, or where to find them...but I saw her on Bruntsfield Place the other night, so they might be keeping her somewhere near there. Bruntsfield Place, can you remember that?'

'Bruntsfield Place,' she repeated. 'What is your name? Why are you helping me?'

'That's all I can tell you. I'm sorry.'

Gordon dropped the girl at a police station, told her to go inside and tell them everything, and steeled himself for what he had to do. It was worth a try. It was this, or leave his family, disappear. Maybe if they thought he was unreliable, they'd give him a good beating and he could just go back to delivering parcels.

He doubled back and resumed his original route. Heading down Fountainbridge, he accelerated up to forty, took a deep breath and swerved the van left, smashing it hard into a brick wall. Heart pounding, unsure of whether he was hurt, he opened both doors, abandoned the van and staggered off down the road. Breaking all the rules, he sent a reply text.

Girl made me crash van on Fountainbridge. She got away. What now?

Stan

Out with the lovely Emma, Stan was facing a relentless internal struggle. She was gorgeous; there wasn't a thing wrong with her. He did his best to be charming and enjoy the company, but Stacy still had his heart. It made no sense to save himself for someone that didn't love him back.

Knowing it logically didn't make moving on any easier. He surprised Emma with Ed Sheeran tickets he'd got months ago. He'd originally planned to go with his brother, who'd bowed out gracefully and told him to take the girl.

The concert was amazing – they were blown away by the music.

'He's so awesome!' Emma said as they left the SEC[13] in a sea of fans, holding hands so they didn't lose one another.

'Yeah! Even better live,' said Stan.

The small talk was easy enough on the train back from Glasgow. Stan learned a bit about Emma's parents and sisters before she laid her head on his shoulder and closed her eyes. He put an arm around her and enjoyed the smell of her hair, promising himself he would get her safely home that night and be off. Nothing more. Not until he could get Stacy out of his head.

Meredith

Laura checks the time—1 a.m. Gordon often comes home late, but not this late. She's learned not to ask questions. She

---

[13] Scottish Event Campus – a famous Glasgow venue

knows he gambles and drinks, but she accepts it, now that he can afford to.

She fingers a scrap of paper he gave her only days ago, with the combination to the safe stashed at a trusted cousin's house.

'That's where you'll find everything you need,' he'd told her, 'if anything ever happens to me.'

'What do you mean?' she'd asked. 'Are you in trouble?'

'No, but it's best to be prepared, just in case. There's insurance and some money. I wouldn't want you to struggle.'

She checks the time again: almost 1.30 now.

I flit between her and Gordon, panicking, wishing I could do something. I can't save him now, if I ever could. And I can't comfort her. She can sense what I know. You can smell it in the air.

She lies on her back, eyes wide open, waiting.

Stacy volunteered for night shift. She's been doing that a lot since she came home—it lets her sleep during the day and avoid everyone. The time passes quickly going from one shout to another. The city never sleeps – there are always comings and goings and cries for help.

A jogger dials 999 just before 6 a.m. after finding an unconscious man propped against a tree, eyes closed, bleeding heavily. The jogger reports that he's still breathing and has a weak pulse, but by the time Stacy and her partner Bill arrive, there's nothing.

They lie him down and Stacy starts chest compressions while Bill prepares the defibrillator and ventilation equipment. Stacy clocks the victim's wedding ring.

Someone loved him, I tell her.

She looks at the wound, and tells Bill, 'It's a gunshot.' She asks the distressed jogger, 'Can you apply pressure?'

He nods, and Bill passes him a cloth to use.

Stacy works and works, giving it everything she has. Minutes go by. 'Come on, stay with me,' she pleads.

Finally, Bill says, 'I think we should stop.'

'We've got to save him,' Stacy gasps, fighting back tears and thumping the dead man's chest. 'Come on!'

'It's too late,' Bill grabs Stacy by the wrists.

Tears spill out over her cheeks.

Bill helps her up and leads her away from the body. He knows about her mum. 'I think it's time you clocked off.'

Bill's right. It was too late before they arrived. Gordon was standing there, looking at himself, at his body, and back again. He watched the whole thing, and as they gave up trying to resuscitate him, he noticed me. He put up a hand to shield his eyes. A man came to take care of him, so I left.

I go to my spot by the railway to think. That's two of my charges murdered on my watch. I know who shot Gordon. I saw it happen. It was Brian. He did it with tears in his eyes—it was kill or be killed. I couldn't stop him, or turn Gordon to the right or left before it all went too far. Now there's a widow and two fatherless boys. A world of emptiness. I'm glad I didn't have to explain anything to him. What would I say, 'Hi, I'm Meredith, the guardian angel who let you die?'

My thinking is skewed—this isn't my fault. I did my best. If Michael couldn't stop me from taking my life, does that make it his fault? Of course not. A few people's choices contributed to this, but I'm not one of them. Gordon died doing something heroic. He saved a girl, so maybe he did listen to me in the end. We don't know how his final act might change the world.

Stan

After a good lie-in and a late breakfast, Stan popped his computer on to browse Facebook. Clicking on his notifications, he saw that Emma had tagged him in a photo. It was a cosy selfie of the two of them together at the gig. *Crap! Stacy will see it.* He wasn't ready to go public – what would Stacy think if she saw the photo? Should he untag himself? But then what would Emma think?

Calm down Stanny boy. Everything's cool, he told himself. Still, for the rest of the day, he kept gravitating back to the laptop, checking the picture to see if Stacy had reacted or commented. Nothing. He checked whether she was online and she never was. He looked at her timeline. She hadn't posted anything since before Zambia. Did she even have internet access out there? *Probably not,* he told himself. *She won't see this.*

Meredith

Jules has given up trying to get Stacy off the couch. She's been miserable since she came home, working all the hours God sends.

'If you can't beat 'em,' Jules says. She grabs a tub of Ben & Jerry's and two spoons, and plonks herself on the sofa next to her flatmate. She passes a spoon to Stacy, who takes it but doesn't eat.

A couple of minutes go by before Stacy speaks, 'I should be going back to Zambia,' she says, 'but I don't want to put all those miles between me and mum. Stupid, isn't it?'

Jules shrugs. 'No, I get it.'

'I saw some awful things out there, Jules, even in a few weeks. If they had more workers, more supplies, they could save more people.'

Don't worry about Zambia now, I say. *You need some rest.*

Stacy says, 'I lost someone yesterday at work.'

'I'm sorry.'

Stacy shrugs. 'It's happened before. I'm used to seeing people dead or dying but for some reason, I can't stop thinking about this one. He was older than us, but not bad looking. He was well-dressed – designer jeans, high-end trainers and a carefully-laundered shirt. It was soaked in blood. Somewhere, someone was waiting for him to come home, wondering what had happened to him.'

Jules listens, wide-eyed.

'It was so final, you know? One minute, he had his life ahead of him; a bullet to the gut later, he had nothing. Why? Why would someone take a life like that?'

'Who knows?'

'I don't envy the police having to inform the wife. And what if he had kids?'

Jules says, 'It's terrible.'

'What a Christmas for the man's family.'

'Maybe you're just feeling things deeply, you know, because of your mum?'

'Yeah.'

There may yet be a silver lining to this cloud in the form of a handsome train driver. I want to help Stacy see sense, but she isn't ready. When the time seems right, I'll give her a little nudge.

Christmas comes and goes with its mandatory festivities—but not for Laura, Nathan and his brother Callum. The presents sit under the tree, forgotten. The police ask Laura a lot of questions, but she doesn't know anything. I'm glad she didn't go digging now—she really can't help them. There's nothing incriminating in the house, except some ridiculously expensive items of clothing and jewellery. They're not stolen, so the police don't confiscate anything. Of course, Gordon's work phone wasn't found on his body, only his regular one. The police have taken it but they won't find anything. Brian may be on there, but there's no reason to suspect him above any other. Gordon's final gift is waiting for Laura at the cousin's house, when she's ready to collect it. She won't have any more financial worries. That's one thing I was able to help him with, at least, and I'm glad.

Alfie's dragging himself out of bed in the morning, and often forgets what he's in a room for. He stands staring at walls for minutes at a time before he catches himself. His house seems empty and silent. He has his work, and his young friend, but now Nathan disappears from his life, too.

Alfie has a Christmas gift for Nathan, and he brings it to the library on the 23rd, but the boy doesn't show up. It's a collector's set of Harry Potter books. It's not like Nathan to fail to turn up, especially without explanation. Alfie stands in the busy library, the day before Christmas Eve, with the same lost expression he wears at home.

He spends Christmas alone, watching films. He looks for Nathan when the library reopens, but he still doesn't come. Alfie phones and texts, but there's no response.

Don't worry. He'll be back.

Mum is invited for Christmas dinner with Murray, Jean, Hugh and Rita. Aunt Lizzie is quite miffed—she and mum have been having Christmas dinner together *forever*—until mum tells her she's invited too. A creature of habit, Aunt Lizzie insists on making a roast for New Year instead and seems somewhat placated by mum's agreement.

Andy

Christmas with Nancy was like no Christmas Andy had ever had. He remembered Christmas as a kid – his present, along with his brothers and sisters, consisted of an orange and a pair of socks. Some years they got a toy, something to share like a football. There were no decorations. The best bit about Christmas was the dinner – it was the finest meal they got all year, but it still didn't come anywhere near this. His dad would save up for months so they could have a chicken—in those days, that was special.

They were a family now: Nancy, him and the kids. The house sparkled with fairy lights and tinsel. Nancy cooked up a delicious turkey dinner. Of course, the kids couldn't wait so presents were opened whenever they arrived, before dinner was even ready. Evie squealed with delight when she opened her new baby doll and pram. Andy had to put it together for her right away.

Everything was perfect, except the bad taste in his mouth. He was really trying to move on from the past, but it held onto him like a vice. He wanted to believe that with Nancy, he could spend his twilight years in peace. But was there really any peace for the likes of him?

'What are you thinking about?' Nancy asked him later in the evening when everything was quiet.

He took her hand and pulled her down onto the sofa beside him. His belly was full, and he was warm and sleepy. 'I'm thinking I love you,' he said, and kissed her on the cheek.

Stan

Stan awoke to the sound of his phone ringing—Lina! 'Lina, where are you?' he asked.

'I go to church,' she hissed. 'Church on Bruntsfield Place. Can you come?'

'I'm on my way,' he said, already pulling on his jeans. 'Stay where you are!' As he was leaving the house he called Chris Bain's mobile. 'Chris, it's Stan. You said I should call if I heard from Lina?'

'Yeah?' Chris sounded like he was just waking up too.

'She just phoned, asked me to meet her at the church on Bruntsfield Place.'

'I'm on my way.'

Stan couldn't believe the difference in Lina when he saw her – she wasn't the same girl. She looked thin and tired, and the side of her face was bruised. She must've come out in a hurry, because she was in pyjamas and slippers, with just a thin jumper. Stan found her cowering in a doorway around the back of the church. She jumped when she saw him, then looked at him with big, pleading eyes.

'Can you help me? I want to go home,' she said.

Stan put his own jacket on Lina and offered to get her a hot drink and some food, but she begged him not to leave her. She was terrified that whoever she'd escaped from would find her. It made Stan nervous, and he readied himself for a fight just in case. But the only person who came was Chris. Stan explained to Lina that the police could help, that she could trust Chris. He wasn't in uniform, but he showed her his ID card.

She looked at Chris, panic rising in her voice. 'Justina! You must find my friend, Justina! They trick her, I think she come here.'

'It's ok,' Chris said. 'Justina is with the police. She's safe.' Chris thanked Stan, helped Lina into the back of a police car and promptly left, leaving him jacketless on the stone steps of the church doorway, and running late.

He thought of the important women in his life: his mum, his sister-in-law, Stacy. And Emma. Of course, Emma. He couldn't bear it if anyone hurt them.

Meredith

Uncle Hughie turns up at Rita's door with a huge bunch of roses.

'Wow! What's the occasion?' she asks. 'Didn't you get me enough for Christmas?'

'No,' he says. 'I didn't.' They sit, and Hughie takes a deep breath.

Rita looks confusedly expectant.

He opens his mouth and closes it again.

Rita waits patiently.

Finally, he starts. 'I had the most vivid dream, Rita. You'll think I'm crackers...'

'I won't.'

Another deep breath. 'I saw Joosie. Everything about her was so real. We danced, just like we used to, and we talked.'

'What did she say?'

'She said "I like Rita. You should marry her."'

Rita takes a sharp breath and bursts into tears.

'Oh love!' he says, dropping to his knees and taking both of her hands in his, 'will you be my wife?'

'Yes!'

Once they've recovered themselves, Hughie bursts out, 'I wish she'd told me that thirty years ago!'

They laugh through tears, and so do I.

Chris

Lina and Justina were together now, at a safe location. The police would send them home once the investigation was complete. Chris and Trisha were supposed to be full-time on the murder case, but it was drying up. There really wasn't much to do, so Chris was lending a hand and keeping an eye on them.

Detectives had established that the dead man had dropped Justina at the police station. He'd been sent to collect both girls at the train station when they arrived in Edinburgh. His job was to take them to another location, where someone else collected them. There was nothing on his body or in his van that could lead the police to the gang running the operation.

Lina showed them the place where she was held, and frustratingly, it was empty. Completely cleaned out. It smelled of bleach—these scumbags knew what they were doing. The property had been rented out to a man that didn't exist. Fake identity, rent paid in cash, the lot.

These two girls were safe, but what Lina had been through would haunt her for life. And how many others were there?

Chris shook his head. 'Welcome to Scotland,' he muttered.

Part Six
The Whisperer

CHAPTER 26

Nancy & Andy

Nancy loved the January sales. It was her tradition to start the new year with new clothes.

Andy hardly said a word on the way to the retail park.

She parked the car and glanced over at him. No point asking what he was ruminating about. He'd been quiet ever since he'd shared his secret – staring off into space and shaking himself out of it, forcing a smile when he caught her watching. But the smile never reached his eyes.

'You okay?' she asked.

'Aye, fine.' He turned with that same dead smile on his face. 'Let's go shopping.'

'Andy.' Nancy put a hand on his arm, looking straight into his eyes. 'When are you going to forgive yourself?'

He looked away, exhaling sharply. He shook his head slightly. 'How, Nance? I don't know how,' he said.

'Listen, love...Why don't you go to the police and tell them what you told me? Maybe it's nothing to do with his death, but who knows? At least you'll leave no stone unturned. You'll feel better.'

Andy snorted derisively. 'They'll probably arrest me.'

'I doubt it.'

He was quiet for a moment. 'You're right. I know I've got to do it.'

'Then let's go now. The shopping can wait.'

Meredith

I keep an eye on Rab Graham—he came too close to my Aunt Lizzie, and he's always drinking and talking filth. Today is no exception—he's blind drunk by mid-afternoon. He sits in his local, staring darkly at the football match on the TV, his mind elsewhere. I gather there was a punch-up the other night involving two groups: one consisting of Rab and his pals, the other Joe Nelson's lot. They were kicked out of the pub and Joe jumped in a taxi. Rab's been telling anyone who'll listen that Joe Nelson is a pansy. He takes one last swig of beer, and staggers out into the sunlight, squinting.

Everyone who passes him in the street gives him a wide berth. He walks—if you can call it that—to the local cemetery where his brothers are buried. He stands by their graves, a solitary figure, his shadow lengthened out behind him. He holds his hip flask out over Tam's freshly dug grave, swaying like a man at sea.

'Cancer,' he slurs, 'or a heart attack, fair enough. But Joe bloody Nelson?' A torrent of filth describing Rab's opinion of Joe follows. 'I could've gone to the pigs about Joe, but that's not how it's done! Anyway, jail's too good for that old bastard! I want to hit him, Tam. I want to make him squeal, make him apologise. Look at his pathetic face as he dies.' He moves the flask over to Brunco's side. 'It's only me now, boys. But we're still the Graham brothers—we're still a team. When this is over, I promise yous...only me or Joe Nelson lives. This has gone on too long.

'Tam,' Rab growls, 'when Brunco got done in, we found the scumbag and made him beg for death. Same goes for this clown, right? I'm old, but I'm not finished yet. I'm going to find the bastard and send him home in bits – just like old times.' He holds out the flask and shouts, 'For you!'

He takes a hefty swallow, then raises the flask again. 'Nobody messes with the Graham brothers, eh lads? Here's tae us.' He pours a little over Brunco's grave, then Tam's. He turns on his heel, draining the flask and striding away as purposefully as a man can when he's too inebriated to walk in a straight line.

One last hurrah.

I don't watch what happens next, but a few hours later, he saunters into his local, not even bothering to go home and wash off the blood. He's terrifying to behold—spattered with blood, face and knuckles cut and bruised. A space immediately clears around him as he sits down. The barman goes through the back and phones the police – this is bad for business.

It won't take much detective work to figure out what happened to Joe Nelson. Rab doesn't care—he's proud of it. One of the two men who cuff him says: 'Robert Graham, you are wanted for questioning, under suspicion of the murder of Joseph Nelson. You do not have to say anything, but anything you do say may be given in evidence.'

'Aha!' Rab roars, as they drag him roughly out of the pub. 'Now you're finally making some sense, ya useless fannies!'

Chris

Chris pulled a very old file for Trisha – Andy Laidlaw had been able to tell them where the man he called 'the suit' had lived back in 1963. Chris had checked the records, found out who owned the house, and it turned out the man had been declared dead in 1970. The 'investigation' surrounding his disappearance made light reading. 'Have a look at this,' he said to Trisha, slapping it triumphantly on her desk.

Chris disappeared while Trisha read the file, and returned a few minutes later with two cups of coffee. He sat down and took a sip, trying not to look smug.

'Interesting stuff...' Trisha muttered, the cogs turning in her mind. 'I want to interview the wife first thing tomorrow.'

Chris nodded and made to leave.

'Chris?'

He stopped in the doorway.

'I think you've earned a break. Have a coffee with me.'

Meredith

Relieved that Rab Graham is still in custody, I check on mum. She'd normally be out with the Roving Ramblers on a Tuesday afternoon, but she's home. She's pacing a lot and making copious amounts of tea that's mostly left to go cold. What's wrong? I look around the house for clues and find only one. On the table next to mum's chair lies the little wooden box, open and empty.

What was in that damn box, and where is it now? I should've been here to see it opened. I try to whisper calm thoughts to mum, but instead, I become agitated too. It's nothing to do with the shadow, not this time.

I find Michael at Mortonhall, silent and still. He comes here more and more these days, as though his whole will is being poured into whatever draws him here. I know it's selfish, but I want him to forget this place and guide me through whatever's happening to my mum. Gently but firmly, he tells me to watch and wait.

Watch and wait! Watch and wait? I'm tired of waiting. I'm tired of secrets. I fly to my Uncle Murray and pester him to check up on mum.

Mum skips her Wednesday yoga class and takes a call from Uncle Murray.

'I was just thinking about you,' he says. 'How are you?'

'Fine, thank you,' mum clips. 'Sorry, I have a headache.'

'Sorry to hear it.' He hesitates. 'Helen, is there anything you need?'

Mum takes too long to answer—between that and me, Murray must know something isn't right.

'Are you struggling to cope again?' he asks, 'after Meredith and everything?'

That's my fear. Mum tried to take her own life once. Would she do it again?

She says, 'No, that's not it. Oh, I wouldn't know where to begin, Murray.'

'How about the beginning?'

Mum smiles sadly.

Tell him mum—you can trust him.

She says, 'There's something going on, but I'm not even sure what.'

Tell us!

The words tumble out of her mouth quickly. 'To tell you the truth, the police came to see me yesterday, asking a load of questions about Pottsy's disappearance.'

There's a stunned silence on the other end of the line.

'It seems there may be some new information about what happened to him.'

'Wow, after all these years!' Did they give you any answers?'

'None. It seems someone has come forward with information, but the police want to corroborate it before they give me any details. I don't know if it's reliable, Murray. I'm terrified to get my hopes up.'

'And what would you be hoping for, if you did?'

'Well...It's daft, I know, after all this time...' Mum takes a deep breath—she's not in the habit of confiding in anyone, let alone Murray—'but I'd be hoping he didn't run off. I'd be hoping it wasn't his choice to leave me.'

I know Stacy's been dreaming of Gordon. I heard her tell Jules. So I've changed the dream a little, just to nudge her in the right direction. I'm sorry for it, but I think she'll be glad in the long run.

Now she has the same dream, over and over. The dead man, propped up against the tree. She puts her hand on his abdomen and turns it around, the palm covered in blood. She looks into his face, the eyes wide open, and she knows him.

Stan.

After another dream, she opens up her laptop and goes on Facebook for the first time since she came home. She types his name into the search box. And there it is, right at the top of his timeline. A picture of him with his new girlfriend.

Chris

Trisha doesn't notice when he first pops his head around the door. He has a minute to watch her before she senses it and looks up. A smile playing around the corners of his mouth disappears abruptly when their eyes meet.

'Guess who got arrested last weekend?' Chris says, coming into the room. 'Rab Graham. He's accused of murder—some revenge thing. They took a mouth swab.'

'Brilliant,' Trisha says. 'How long till it's analysed and on the database?'

'I'd say a few more days, at most.'

'So, all we need to do is wait, and we can check it against the data from the crime scene for Davie Clements.'

'Exactly.'

'And how are we progressing with collecting the old photos?'

'I've got most of them. Just one more visit to make.'

'Perfect—let's get Andy Laidlaw in as soon as possible. We're almost there, Chris.'

Meredith

'The nerve of those youths outside!' Aunt Lizzie rants as she enters the sitting room. 'Honestly, things were better in the days of corporal punishment.'

Mum nods vaguely.

'At least children had some respect for their elders!' Lizzie bustles into the kitchen with a box of cupcakes. 'I've been baking, darling, thought I'd just drop a few cakes in for you.'

'Thanks,' mum says. 'Stay and have tea, if you like.'

'Well,' Aunt Lizzie says, already taking off her coat, 'I know Friday isn't our usual day, but why not?'

When they get settled down at the table, Aunt Lizzie notices mum's brooding demeanour. 'Helen darling, whatever's the matter?'

'Oh.' Mum waves a hand dismissively. 'Nothing, I'm sure, I just had a strange visit from the police earlier in the week.'

'You poor woman, what could they possibly want with you.' It's a statement, rather than a question. 'You must tell me all about it.'

'It was that Detective who came before. Macdonald.'

'What on earth did she want, darling?'

'Well, it's weird, but...she asked me about Pottsy.'

Lizzie's eyes widen. 'What on earth for? It was all so long ago.'

'I know. She said it could be relevant to a current investigation. It doesn't make sense.'

Lizzie maintains her impeccable posture as she sits at the little dining table, practically on the edge of her seat. She'd never admit it, but she loves a scoop.

'They had me go over the whole story again, of how he disappeared and—'

'So insensitive!' Lizzie interrupts, 'making you relive his leaving you.'

Mum looks up, a sad, far away look in her eyes. She hesitates, then says in a small voice, 'What if he didn't leave me?'

Aunt Lizzie looks at mum with pity. 'Oh, you poor thing! After all this time? Darling, the evidence is irrefutable.'

Mum shrugs weakly. 'They took his picture, the only one I kept, and his note.'

So that's what was in the box—my father.

'You kept that silly note? Oh, Helen – you poor soul.'

'I...' Mum exhales, stifling a sob. 'It was daft, I suppose. I kept it as a reminder...to stay away from men. Can we talk about something else?'

'Of course, darling, but finish the story. Did the police say anything else?'

'Only that there may be new information. They need to corroborate the evidence before they can tell me any more.'

'New information—preposterous! How is that possible?'

'I don't know. It's probably nothing.'

'Quite right. Darling, don't get your hopes up about this. I don't know what the police are thinking, opening up old wounds like that. They can't help you.'

Mum nods, but there's still hope in her eyes.

After everything mum's been through, the police dragging up my father's disappearance is the last thing she needs. What if it turns out to be just as she's always believed, or worse? She'll relive the abandonment all over again.

Andy

Nancy came home to find Andy sitting in silence.

She took off her bag and jacket and knelt in front of him, gently taking his hand and looking into his face. 'What's happened, love? You're deathly pale.'

Andy gave a tiny shake of his head and his eyes focussed on Nancy. 'The Inspector asked me to go down to the station. They showed me a bunch of old photos, wanted to know who was who.'

Nancy nodded encouragingly.

'They threw in some random people but it didn't put me off—I remember perfectly, like it was yesterday. I wish I *could* forget.'

'And were you able to identify the ones they were looking for?'

Andy nodded slowly, his eyes wide. 'The foreman, the suit and Mrs Jones. They had pictures of them all. They took me out in their police car. They wanted me to show them where it all happened.' His voice became a whisper. 'The trees are so much bigger now. Everything's different, but I still know the exact spot. D'you think she came back – Mrs Jones? She could be looking for me.'

'She'd be very old now, Andy. If she's still alive, she'll be arrested soon.' Her smile warmed him and brought him back to the present. 'Now, let's pop the kettle on.'

CHAPTER 27

Lizzie

I've never said it out loud, but do you know what I call you, in my mind? I call you Cinders, darling. Think about it. Our friendship was unlikely, to say the least. Our lives were poles apart. When we met, I was the daughter of a prominent architect, in private school with a promising future ahead of me. You were a penniless orphan who left public school at fourteen to scrape a living. Of course, money never mattered to me, and you proved yourself a faithful friend. In the beginning.

We were both seventeen when we met at the Palais de Danse on Fountainbridge. I loved the hand-cranked revolving stage at the Palais; when the band needed a break it would turn around and the next band would immediately start playing, so the dancing was never interrupted—d'you remember that?

The dance floor was heaving that night, couples and friends jiving energetically. From our seats on the mezzanine, my friends and I had a bird's eye view. Around the periphery, small groups were straining to hold conversations above the music. Clusters of girls sat along one side of the hall while the boys sat on the other. Brave souls ventured to the other side in search of a partner.

The view was fine, but we were more interested in a group of uniformed American Air Force men sitting nearby on the mezzanine. One of them walked purposely over and took Dawn for a dance. She let him take her hand and stifled a giggle as he led her down to the floor. She was a silly sort of girl.

That was when it happened.

A girl at the next table suddenly stood, pointed at me and shouted 'Hey! She just stole a handbag!'

Well! I thought she must've been pointing at someone behind me, so I turned to look at the common red-haired girl I was back to back with.

The redhead was looking for a bag and starting to panic. 'Is that true?' she demanded. 'Have you got my bag?'

'No!' I was affronted—my cheeks turned crimson. The very suggestion that I would have any need to or any thought of stealing was deeply insulting.

As a bouncer drew near, the redhead stood and shouted, 'You did so! What's that under your seat?'

Mortified, I looked, and there was a black handbag. I had no idea how it had got there. 'I didn't take it.' I said, passing it to the redhead, who snatched it and checked its contents.

'Oh, you didn't?' She said. 'Then where's my money, eh?' Then to the bouncer, who was now standing next to us, 'This cow stole all my money!'

I shook my head vehemently, feeling like my face was on fire. I looked around for my accuser, hoping she might realise her mistake, but she'd gone.

I was glad the loud music masked the conversation from those not in the immediate vicinity. I then had to endure the humiliation—with the angry redhead—of following the bouncer to the office.

It wasn't until we arrived there that I noticed you, following a few paces behind. You were attractive but plain, your knee-length dress fashionable but clearly homemade. I couldn't help noticing you wore no stockings, you poor thing. The dress accentuated your tiny waist, but you never had much of a chest. Your dark blonde hair hung in loose waves around your shoulders, framing your face with its unnaturally high cheekbones. Your hands were rough with work, suggesting you didn't dance often; like Cinderella at the ball. That's where you got your name.

You were hesitant.

'I had thirty shillings in that bag!' The redhead was still roaring, although the din was now somewhat muffled. 'A whole weeks' wages! And I better get it back!'

As the bouncer ushered us into the office, you approached him and cleared your throat. 'I saw what happened,' you said. 'That girl had nothing to do with it.'

You saved the day, darling. According to you, my accuser was an accomplice to the crime. Her friend had subtly removed the money from the bag and dumped it under my chair, barely even slowing down as he walked past. You, apparently the only person who noticed, rose to say something. The accuser called out to pass the unwanted attention onto me, and promptly left in the ensuing commotion. You saw both thief and accuser but made no attempt to follow them. They were expert at disappearing into a crowd.

You know, I still dread to think what would've happened if you hadn't stepped in that night. The police were called to the incident but thankfully I was no longer a suspect. Can you believe that redhead didn't even apologise?

The coffee was on me, of course. I ushered you back to my friends, and we told our story at the surrounding tables, until my good name was clear. You were agreeably obliging, even relating the tale to the handsome Americans. I never forgot it.

Now, to Pottsy. I had known him since childhood—family connections, you know. I never should've introduced you, but in those days I knew nothing of your manipulative streak.

You never understood him at all. How could you possibly think a man like that could love a...a *servant* like you? D'you have any idea how many times he turned up at the dancing to find me? He was positively obsessed with me! Certainly, he asked about you and why wouldn't he? A polite gentleman like that? He felt sorry for you, as I did. Your life was so different to ours.

Dear God, he was handsome! Sometimes during our deep conversations, I'd forget to listen to what he was saying. His eyes were simply mesmerising and he was deliciously tall. When we danced, I burned with hunger: his lightest touch on my waist, our hands linked, his hard muscle under my fingers. I could feel his desire for me, a longing so strong it didn't need to be spoken. Oh, but he was so proper! He'd hardly touch me, I knew, until we were married. Not even a kiss. Of course, that only made it more exciting, our yearning almost unbearable. It made me his more completely than you can imagine.

I waited patiently for him to speak to Daddy, but he never did.

When you told me your news, I couldn't believe it. Not until I heard it from him. Even then it seemed like a sick joke. What in the world would a man like that—a man of means, handsome and intelligent—want with a girl like *you*, Cinders?

I developed a theory. He must've got you pregnant. Now *that* I could understand. His hunger for me had to be staved off somehow, until he could indulge in the real thing. But if there was a child, he'd marry its mother even if it broke his heart.

Imagine my confusion when there was no baby until you'd been married eighteen months.

How did you do it, Helen? How did you bewitch my lover? Did you pretend you were with child, to trick him? Did you cry about all the hardships common to your kind, making him mistake his pity for something more?

Well. That man's honour wouldn't let him touch me after he married you. We kissed once and our powerful urges grew stronger. That taste of the forbidden was more than he could bear. He left promptly.

You know I love you, darling. We were the best of friends. We *are* the best of friends. But you must understand—what Pottsy and I had, it was magnetic. Unstoppable. I knew then I'd never marry, so I asked him to come away with me.

He refused. I know why—because of your hold on him. You and the baby. (He loved that baby, didn't he? She was his joy, his compensation). He denied himself any pleasures with me, and the life we should've enjoyed together. I tried to make him see sense, and he said something awful. It struck me like a knife to the heart.

He looked at me with those impossibly gorgeous eyes and said, 'I don't love you, Lizzie. I never will.'

Of course, I know now he was only trying to put some distance between us, to make the pain more bearable. It wasn't true.

Looking back, it should've been you who disappeared. I should've ended you right there and taken what was mine. But I was young and foolish. And extremely angry.

So I took him from you.

I took him where you'll *never* find him. I took back what you stole from me. With interest.

I showed you what rejection feels like. I let myself in with my key, took his things, and left the note. It wasn't a lie, but a mercy of sorts. I told you the truth about his feelings, since he was incapable of doing so.

He left me no choice—if I couldn't have him, no one could. It broke my heart to say goodbye to him, you know. I loved him in ways you could never understand.

I was there every step of the way, a shoulder for you to cry on. When that pompous policeman came, I shared your indignation. When you left the room, I knew what you'd find. It was easy to imply you were a bit ditsy, without saying much at all.

After the police left, I shared your shock and disbelief about the note.

It didn't seem like *your* Pottsy, the man you thought you knew.

I listened silently.

You said you never had reason to suspect he was interested in other women.

'No,' I agreed, but I changed my intonation slightly to betray uncertainty, and when you looked up, I let a secret pass briefly across my face. Then I made a show of working hard to hide it from you.

You took the bait. I practically had you begging me to tell you what I knew.

I apologised with real tears in my eyes; I knew I should've told you at the time, but I didn't want to cause you pain. I wanted to believe you'd married a good man, so I gave him the benefit of the doubt.

I'll never forget the look of realisation on your ignorant face when I, oh so reluctantly, told you about our kiss and his plans to take me away. I hid my love from you, but I gave you a glimpse of his.

You were forgiving. You couldn't blame me for trying to protect you.

I told you I'd convinced myself it was just a one-off, that he wouldn't try it with anyone else.

I let the silence stretch while you took it all in. I could see you searching for more evidence, so I helped you find your doubts.

'Thinking back,' I asked, 'was there anything between the two of you that didn't seem quite right?'

You didn't think long before you nodded. You never shared the details, but I saw your eyes harden. The beginning of your hatred.

I gently reminded you that your parents had abandoned you, to reinforce the pattern. *Oh, you poor thing! You've been through so much! First your parents, and now this!*

I've enjoyed watching you nurse your bitterness, year after year. Every time you bring him up, I'm the sympathetic friend. But I feed your hatred. I enjoy watching the distance between the two of you grow, even now.

I severed your love. I bought his house from you when you finally inherited it, and I made you think it was all your idea. You were right—you didn't belong there. You couldn't face dealing with all the legalities, so I made my offer—a generous one. I said it like it had just occurred to me, not like I'd been planning it for years. You were able to bypass the estate agent and have the thing done and dusted in no time. You were grateful to me for taking that burden off your hands.

Your only stipulation was that I should never expect you to visit the house. Our arrangement suits me—I visit you, and I keep Pottsy to myself. You see, I feel his presence in this house. We live here together. His suit hangs in his wardrobe still, but thanks to your meddling, it may need to go now.

I comfort myself with the secret that belongs to me alone. It pleases me to leave you groping in the dark.

Meredith was like a little piece of *him*, wasn't she? Especially when she was little, before she put on all the weight. But even then—she had his eyes. Those incredible eyes. If only she'd lost the weight, she could've been stunning.

She was like a daughter to me, and in a way, she *was* my daughter. Pottsy was the love of my life and she was his child. I felt responsible for her. You wouldn't believe it after what you did, but I felt responsible for you, too. You were his weakness, that's all. But he did care for you in his way and I think he would've wanted me to look after the two of you. We've been a strange little family, haven't we?

The first seven years were hard on you. The insurance wouldn't pay out without a body or a legal declaration of death, and the house was in his name alone. You began to hate the house, so you moved out and rented from the council. You had to toil to get by. Still, you were used to that. I don't suppose your kind minds a bit of menial work. Daddy took care of me when he was alive, and left me a sizeable inheritance. I worked because I wanted to, not because I had to. I tried to help you financially, but you were too proud.

The one thing you accepted help with was our darling girl. How I loved her! For years I cared for her while you worked—I practically raised that child. When she came home to me on weekends and holidays, everything felt right with the world. Our little girl back in her own room, living the way her father would've wanted. Of course, I couldn't shower too many gifts on her to take to your house; you would've gone ballistic. But at home, in my house, she had *everything* a girl could want.

She was happy with me. She always grew sad and quiet around you. It was your anger, you see. You were so bitter about Pottsy, you began to hate his child. You were impatient and dismissive with her. I sometimes wondered whether I should find a way to make her mine and only mine. But you were always so grateful for the help; it made me feel good. I had my social life to think of, too, of course.

When things became too fraught between you and our darling girl, I knew I had to step in. She was fourteen at the time. The two of you were always at odds with one another, and she was home with me so often that moving in was only a small step. You thanked me; you were relieved.

Throughout those teenage years, I made sure we visited you regularly. As I said, darling, I've always felt responsible for you. I think I get my generosity from mummy; she just couldn't stop giving. She taught me from the Bible: love your enemies, do good to those that hate you. No one ever hurt me like you did, and—other than Pottsy—I never loved anyone more than I love you.

The arrangement with Meredith worked well, until the unfortunate business with that disgusting Graham boy from the office. It was me who got Meredith her first job when she left school, remember that? She never would've managed it on her own; she was both lazy and shy. You used to get very cross with her, when all she wanted to do was sketch or sit with her nose in a book. You wanted her to learn the value of work.

She became a typist in the housing office I used to manage. She wasn't very grateful and although she reported to one of my juniors, I had to keep a close eye on her, to begin with. That's how far I'm willing to go for the two of you, do you see? I wanted her career to be a success, even though she wasn't exactly management material.

Well, there were quite a few young people working there at the time. I loved my girl, but I wasn't oblivious to her looks. Men don't like fat girls—plain and simple. She always used to pine after that boy she played with at school—was it Jeremy? Gregory? Anyway. Nothing ever came of that long-running crush, and I suppose curiosity got the better of her.

She was eighteen. A group of laughing teenagers surrounded Graham at his desk, and I had to send them all back to work. They were extremely sheepish. Meredith was left out of the conversation, but that was no surprise. However, she looked upset that day and avoided my gaze. I grilled one of the junior managers, until he told me what had happened. I couldn't believe it! My darling girl had had a one night stand with that half-wit Graham! He did it for a bet, and everyone knew but her. No doubt he was sharing all the tawdry details with the others when I broke up their little party.

Well! I've never been so humiliated! To think that *my* girl was the laughing stock of the office! It was too much. I called her in, and I gave her the telling off of her life. She never forgave me for it, I fear. Things weren't the same after that. But I wasn't in the wrong.

She stopped confiding in me. She pushed me away, and all because of that revolting pock-faced boy. I let her move back in with you. All those years, I had been adored by my darling girl. Adored. But when she grew up, I was just Aunt Lizzie again. She even found a new job. I didn't think she had in her.

But we were still a family. I kept visiting, and in time, Meredith would come home once in a while. I only had to drop the right hint; she was a dutiful girl.

There was only one other who knew my secret. Even in the sixties, he was a blundering ignoramus, but in his dotage...well, he was a gibbering wreck of a man. I took care of him all those years ago. I paid him handsomely and sent him out of the country. For some foolish reason, however, he returned to Edinburgh some ten years ago. I don't know why he came back, or why he thought I'd allow it.

He was always too cowardly to do anything ridiculous, like going to the police for example, but lately, he'd become unhinged. There was no telling what he would do. He was paranoid. I don't know where it came from; I think he was losing his marbles, you know? After I discovered he was back, I visited him in hospital, just to make sure he wasn't going to be a problem. And what did I find? The buffoon trying to repent on his death-bed.

He started going on about things best forgotten, in a voice too loud. I don't remember him having a conscience before but suddenly he wanted to confess! Over fifty years later, can you believe that?

Well. You understand why I had to silence him. I did the old man a favour, really; he was in quite a state.

And now you, Cinders. You used to be loyal to me. I saw doubt in your eyes when I told you what Ginger did! When did you start questioning your best friend? I mean, how *dare* you?

Have you noticed what I've done for you over the years? The sacrifices I've made? I've helped you choose friends wisely. I've kept you apart from anyone that wouldn't be good for you. Even your brothers. I suppose you think you *chose* to fall out with them? No. I separated you. You and Meredith were *my* family, not theirs. *I* took care of you. Not them. And now, you march back into their lives out of the blue? And you choose to see them on *our* day of the week?

You've been like a faithful dog in a lot of ways. But if that dog turns and bites you, there's only one thing to do.

Why are the police sniffing around about Pottsy after all this time? What did you tell them? I bet you'd sell me out, if you could. There's a part of you, even now, that can't accept the truth.

He didn't love you; you were just a plaything.

I've kept you around all these years. I've let you grow old, and I wonder now if that was the right decision.

Cinders, I think it's time for you to die.

CHAPTER 28

Meredith

It's Saturday lunchtime, and Mum gets ready to go out with the Roving Ramblers. She takes her painkillers—walking improves the hip, but she's still more comfortable if she takes the pills. She packs a flask of tea and a few snacks. She wears jeans and a few layers on top, gathers her jacket, hat and gloves, and puts on her walking boots at the door. She's beautiful, my mum. She's the exact opposite of me—tall and lean. I would've been happy to look half as good and be half as fit, at half her age.

Heading outside, she sees Margot next door raking leaves in the front garden.

Margot waves.

Mum nods and smiles.

There's a cold wind, but it's a good clear day. Mum takes the bus and meets Aunt Lizzie at Waverley station.

Lizzie says, 'We're rather thin on the ground today, darling. Geoffrey and Lorna are both down with the flu, and May had to take her cat to the vet. I've just had a call from Val, too—some family crisis.'

'Oh, shame,' mum says. 'I hope everyone's alright.'

'They will be, I'm sure.'

'I'm going to get a magazine—d'you want anything?'

'No, thank you.'

Mum picks up a copy of *Women's Own*—Kate and William plastered all over the front page, again—and waits in the queue.

Aunt Lizzie takes a call. She hangs up just as mum returns. 'You'll never guess! That was Gilda—Tom's down with the flu as well, so she's staying home to play nurse. Honestly, men are pathetic.'

Mum smiles. 'Well, there's a lot of it going about.'

Aunt Lizzie checks her watch. 'Where is everyone?'

'Who haven't we heard from?' mum asks.

'Let's think...there's just Heidi, Cyril and Brenda. Hang on.' Aunt Lizzie finds Brenda in her contacts and puts the phone to her ear, waiting. 'No answer,' she says after a minute. Next, she tries Heidi.

'Heidi, it's Lizzie. We're waiting at Waverley, are you coming?...Oh, no! Did you get it looked at?...What did they say?...Alright darling, see you soon. You take care now.' She hangs up and says, 'Heidi twisted her ankle. She has to keep the weight off it for a week or two.' She checks her watch and tuts. 'Well, Cyril and Brenda are too late now. The train leaves in five minutes.'

Mum and Lizzie board the train to Dunbar.

Mum opens *Women's Own* but looks out the window, lost in thought.

Aunt Lizzie looks at her in a strange, secret way.

The walk down to Dunbar harbour from the train station takes about ten minutes. Mum and Aunt Lizzie both walk smartly, but to my amazement, I can keep up with them effortlessly. Shirley trots along beside me—she's probably thinking the same thing.

Mum and Lizzie remark on the weather—the sky has clouded over beyond the little moored boats. It takes more than a bit of wind or a threatening shower to put *them* off; they've been doing this in all weathers for decades. This walk is an easy one for them, too—they take on Munros[14] in the summer.

Aunt Lizzie looks quite different in her walking clothes. She still wears full make-up—eyelashes caked in brown mascara, lips pink and shiny. Mum's features stand out all by themselves.

The path climbs steeply up from the harbour towards the leisure centre, and they go in single file, concentrating their energies on the walk until the path levels out again. There are no other walkers in sight. A lone jogger passes by—it takes hardy folk to brave Scotland's coastline in January.

Heading down the steps to the promenade, Aunt Lizzie shouts to be heard above the rush of the wind. 'How are you bearing up, darling?'

Mum gives a little shrug and shouts back, 'You just have to get on with it.'

'Quite right. One mustn't let the emotions get out of control. And what about Pottsy?'

'What about him?'

---

[14] 277 mountains in Scotland, each at least 3,000 feet high

'Have you laid the thing to rest, stopped digging for something you won't find?'

Mum doesn't answer.

'I'm worried about you, Helen. You're brooding, and it isn't healthy.'

'I'm alright, Lizzie.'

'Are you, though? You seem so down. Please, Helen, you must stop doing this to yourself.'

'Is there anything else you know that you haven't told me?'

Lizzie looks shocked. 'Of course not, darling. I'm on your side. Only I don't want to see you set up for more disappointment.'

They walk in silence for a while. A light shower falls but the wind whips it sideways, mixed with spray from the ocean. White waves froth and slap into the wall below. Mum and Aunt Lizzie are both deep in thought. We're coming onto the clifftop path, and mum is on the outside. There's a dangerous, determined look in Lizzie's eyes. Mum *is* safe, isn't she? Shirley barks in mum's direction, looks up at me and whines.

I close my eyes and see Michael at Mortonhall. I open up the channel—I can do this so quickly now, it's almost instant. The squeeze, a pull, and I'm there. He gives me a questioning look. I don't try to explain, I just take his hand and bring him back.

Michael takes in the scene, and asks me in an urgent tone, 'What did I miss?'

'Nothing, I...something doesn't feel right.'

He nods grimly. 'You were right to fetch me.'

As we follow mum and Lizzie, the rain stops and the sun tries to break through.

Michael watches Lizzie, intent on every twitch. It's like I'm not here.

The clifftop path is deserted other than our little group. We reach a curve in the path. The cliff meets rock and sand some forty feet below, around the edge of a little bay.

Lizzie stops, so mum stops too.

Michael growls at Lizzie, 'I'm warning you!'

I stare at him for a second—the only time I've seen him this angry was when mum had the demon.

Lizzie pays no attention. She moves closer to the edge, taking in the view.

The shadow appears down the path from us, watching like a vulture.

The clouds blow over, leaving a blue gap where the sun shines through.

Lizzie looks down over the edge of the cliff and says, 'Oh, Good Lord!'

Mum comes forward to see what it is.

Lizzie takes two steps back and her face hardens.

She's going to push mum right over the edge!

As Lizzie lunges forward, Michael rushes into mum and knocks her sideways.

Lizzie trips over mum's feet, stumbles, and goes over the edge herself.

Everything is quiet and still. Nobody moves.

Lizzie rises back up over the cliff edge, and she speaks to Michael. 'My love! You waited for me!' Her ugliness is revealed—she's like an old witch with pallid skin, and eyes as black as her soul.

Michael stares with a mixture of disgust and pity.

She tries to come closer but flinches back. Then she notices me. 'My darling girl! I've missed you so much. You look beautiful!'

I don't answer. I'm not her darling girl.

She turns to the shadow down the path, squinting to see. 'Mummy? Is that you?'

The shadow doesn't move.

A pained expression passes over Lizzie's face and she's sucked into her body on the bay below.

The shadow disappears in a puff of ash.

'Mrs Potts? Mrs Potts!' Trisha calls, jogging up the path with Chris.

Chris rushes to mum's side.

Trisha peers down at Lizzie and whips out her phone.

I turn to Michael, whose gaze is fixed intently on mum. 'You and Lizzie?' I ask, incredulous.

He shakes his head vehemently. 'I knew her, but I *never* loved her.' His eyes glisten.

'Thank you for saving my mum.'

He smiles his sad, Mortonhall smile and says—still looking at her—'I couldn't help it.'

Something clicks into place.

'Dad?' I whisper.

The great soul embraces me and I melt into his light.

I feel for the first time like I belong somewhere. Looking into his eyes, I wonder that I've never seen the likeness before. They're my eyes!

Michael speaks with greater urgency. 'I'm going to the in-between for this—I can feel the pull. I'm afraid they'll send me on! Oh, Merry, there's so much I ...'

'Dad!'

He's fading, and I can't hear him, and he's gone.

I drop to my knees, sobbing. Merry? I called him dad, and he called me Merry.

I'm left on the clifftop with mum and the two detectives. Mum's bad hip has taken quite a bump and she's injured her ankle. Trisha organises two ambulances, and help from the Coastguards. A chopper comes from North Berwick to rescue Lizzie from the bay. They work on her for a while before she's moved. I suppose she's clinging to life, but I won't go down. She's not my concern anymore. She's airlifted out, while mum is helped onto a stretcher and taken to an ambulance waiting at the golf course.

Overwhelmed, I go to my spot by the railway. Snowflakes begin to float down and land silently. They're so beautiful—I reach out to touch them, but I can't.

Mum almost died – again. Another guilty wave of disappointment. I miss her so much.

I can't shake the look on Aunt Lizzie's face right before she tried to push mum. If she could do that, she could kill Davie. All these years, we thought we knew her! She was like family to mum and I. We needed our real family, not her.

And Michael! Why didn't he tell me who he was? What on earth happened between him, mum and Lizzie?

I sit for a long time, watching the snow. I lock my gaze onto a single flake as high as I can see it, and follow it all the way to the ground. I do the same again, and this time I see its blueprint as clear as the snowflake. It's like a light switch going on. I watch as it drifts closer.

I catch it on my finger and it melts away.

CHAPTER 29

Meredith

After a few shell-shocked days in hospital, mum's discharged with a plastered foot, a prescription for pain relief and a set of crutches. She had someone call Murray and Jean, and they came straight away.

Trisha and Chris took a statement from her, but they didn't push. They've been respectful of her fragile state. We're both anxious for any information they have about dad. Mum agrees to a visit from the police as soon as she's home. David takes care of transport, and Murray stays to support mum.

'Mrs Potts,' Chris begins, once they're all seated. 'This is going to be difficult for you to hear. Are you sure you're up to it?'

'Yes!' Mum sounds a little hysterical. 'I want every detail you have about my husband—whatever it is.'

Chris nods, takes a deep breath. 'We've been investigating the murder of a man in hospital—David Clements. Lizzie Jacobs was under some suspicion, but there was insufficient evidence to detain her for questioning. After some time, a man called Andrew Laidlaw came forward in response to a public appeal. Mr Laidlaw is a credible witness to the murder of a man in 1963. We believe that man to be your husband. We believe he was killed by Lizzie Jacobs and David Clements.'

Mum looks lost.

Murray sits on the arm of her chair and puts an arm gently around her shoulders.

'Lizzie?' Mum whispers, bringing a hand to her mouth. 'Lizzie? How?'

Chris' forehead is shiny with sweat; he looks at Trisha pleadingly.

Trisha gives an imperceptible nod and takes over. 'Mr Laidlaw's testimony states that Mr Clements assisted Ms Jacobs in tricking your husband into the woods. She then stabbed him repeatedly, and the pair dissected his body and buried it. Mr Laidlaw was very young. He was paid to help, but he had no idea what was planned.'

Mum sits up straight with a determined expression. 'Can I read this testimony?'

Chris and Trisha exchange glances.

'Please. I've been living this lie for a very long time. I need to know the truth.'

'There's a recording,' Trisha says. 'We can go down to the station and play it for you. But I must warn you, Mrs Potts, it's very disturbing.'

'My husband had to suffer it, Inspector. The least I can do is hear the truth.'

Murdered? I wasn't unwanted! I have a father, and he didn't leave us. He was taken.

Andy

I was just a kid at the time. I was thirteen, but tiny for my age. I was one of eight, and we lived in a tenement flat on Burnhead Grove. It was a shite life. By that time I'd already been working for the Graham brothers for years – they ran a gang of criminals in the Gracemount area. My handler was Brunco Graham. Him and his brothers were crackpots. They called me Titch. They sent me into the posh areas casing and used me to get into houses. I could squeeze through small windows or cat-flaps and let them in.

At that time they were just starting the building work on Mortonhall Crem. I used to pass the site all the time. A posh lady got a hold of me one day, pulled me into the woods next to the site. She told me to call her Mrs Jones. She gave me sweets and cigarettes. That was amazing to me – we never had much to eat, and we often ran out of food completely about Wednesday, starving till payday. When we did eat, it was basic – soup, bread and milk. Sweets were heaven. I loved a smoke too. Brunco would give me one, sometimes, when he was pleased with me.

Anyway, this Mrs Jones said she'd pay good money for some easy work. I was to watch two men. She showed them to me. I didn't know their names, but one was the foreman on the building site. The other was a business type – I called him the suit. All I had to do was watch these guys and report everything back to her: where they went, when, who they met, and what they did.

I bit her hand off for the job. I knew Brunco would give me the hiding of my life if he found out, but I couldn't resist. It sounded easy. I could make myself practically invisible. It turned out that Mrs Jones was completely unhinged, but I swear I had no idea.

The suit was like clockwork. He lived on Southhouse Road in a fancy detached house. Monday to Friday, he walked to the bus stop on Burdiehouse Road at the same time each morning and got on the green bus into town. Every night at the same time, he got off the green bus on the other side of the road and headed home the same way.

The foreman was different – he was a clown. He had a wife and child too, but he wandered about after work: the pub or the bookies, mostly. Once or twice a week he went to the Black Bull for prostitutes. I watched him week after week, coming out of there with different girls. Sometimes he would take them to a cheap hotel room, sometimes just up a close. One time, I saw a big man put him up against a wall and threaten him over money.

When I told Mrs Jones everything I'd found out, she was pleased. She gave me more money than I'd ever had. Once, she gave me a whole packet of cigarettes, and a few times, a crown[15]. I had to hide it all in my secret den in the woods. Brunco would regularly shake me down, and what was mine was his.

Then Mrs Jones gave me another job. On a certain night, I was to trick the suit, get him to come to a particular spot in the woods that she showed me. I was to say my dad had collapsed on a walk and ask him for help. When the suit was nearly at that spot I was to shout 'Please help him mister – I'll run and get my mum!' I was to get away from there as quick as I could, and not look back.

After we practised, she gave me twenty shillings – a pound! D'you know what that could buy in 1963? She said if I did well, I could come back the next day at the same time, and she'd give me the same again. I'd never seen that kind of money.

But I never went back the next day.

I did like she said. I brought the suit. I never knew what they were going to do. I was that chuffed about the money, I never even thought to wonder. The foreman was in the spot, lying on the ground like he'd fainted. I shouted what I'd been told and

---

[15] A crown was a British coin in the old system, before decimalisation in 1971. Its value was five shillings or ¼ pound sterling.

made to run away, but I never left. I was a curious wee shite. I hid behind a tree, and I saw everything.

The suit bent over the foreman, tried to rouse him. Mrs Jones jumped the suit from behind, stabbed him three times in the back. The foreman scrambled out from under him and sat against a tree, whimpering. She turned the suit onto his back and sat beside him for a while. I thought he was dead, but then he made a weird noise. She went for him again, stabbed him all over the chest and stomach I don't know how many times. She was like an animal. The foreman was rocking back and forward with his hands over his ears.

When it was all over, she started bossing the foreman around. He did everything she said. He brought a wheelbarrow with black bags in it, and a saw. She made him saw off the arms, legs and head. She did some of it herself because the foreman kept getting upset. He kept swearing and gibbering. He said they should've dug a bigger grave so they didn't need to do that. She told him to get a hold of himself and took the saw off him. Finished the job. There was a lot of blood—it was some mess.

Once that was done, they bagged the body parts and wheeled them over to the building site. I followed them there. I saw exactly where they buried him. It was in the trenches. Mrs Jones had the foreman put earth down on top of him. He used a JCB to dump stuff on the grave, then he was down there for a while with some hand tools and a roller, while she held a torch. She handed him an envelope when he was done, and told him to finish the crem and get organised—change his name, start a new life somewhere far away. She said if he didn't, she'd ruin him.

I avoided the place after that, used to go the long way round. I'm truly sorry for what I did. I never saw Mrs Jones or the foreman again, until he showed up on the news, dead.

CHAPTER 30

Meredith

The last fortnight has been punctuated by the juxtaposition of grief and solace. Lizzie has sustained traumatic injuries. She's in a coma, a police guard at the door. If she wakes, she'll be arrested.

Forensics confirmed that Lizzie forged dad's note. That along with Andy's statement is enough to charge her. It also provides an obvious motive for her to kill Davie. Her DNA matched samples from the crime scene; both from the pillow used to suffocate Davie and from under his nails. Even now it's hard to picture her squeezing the life out of the old man. Hard, until I think of her face just before she tried to push mum.

Rab Graham has been cleared of any involvement in Davie's murder, but he did provide a little information as a bargaining chip. (Whether it helped him any, I don't know.) Davie had sent him to spy on Lizzie because he was terrified she was after him. Rab thought it was funny at the time, and put it down to Davie's deteriorating mind.

As for dad's remains, Andy pointed out the exact spot where they were buried, but they're going to be difficult and expensive to access. Mum's anxious to lay him to rest.

Trisha explains some of the complications of the excavation. A forensic dig has to be done by hand so the machinery doesn't cause undue disturbance to the evidence. The first stage is to go in with something called Ground Penetrating Radar (GPR), in order to ascertain whether the lengthy and expensive procedure can be justified. It scans the earth using sonar pings to identify anything below the surface, such as evidence of a cavity. If the GPR turns anything up, Trisha hopes to get authorisation for the dig.

Because the site is under the foundations, they'll only be able to dig an area of one metre at a time. It'll require a process to strengthen the foundations called underpinning. In addition, at this time of year, there may be adverse weather conditions that could further complicate the dig. Trisha assures mum that she's determined to recover dad's remains.

They've gone over mum's statement about what happened with Lizzie on the clifftop, but they can't quite make sense of it.

Forensics uncovered signs of a struggle involving three people, but mum only saw Lizzie up there. She's been talking to Veronica about it—she thinks that's who saved her.

Helen

Making sense of the truth was thoroughly exhausting—but things came gradually into focus.

Helen wept for Pottsy, now that she could. She grieved his loss as though it had been yesterday. There were no words to express her regret over burning his things: the letters, the photographs, and his clothes. Her brothers borrowed her one wedding photo and had it blown up and framed for her. It hung in the living room now, in pride of place.

She'd put up a few of Meredith, too. And before she'd finished grieving for her husband, she'd begun doing so for her daughter. She finally understood how her choice to believe the lie had damaged that relationship.

She visited Mortonhall and stared at the building, shivering, wondering precisely where the mutilated remains of the man she loved were laid. Memories of another life came flooding into her mind, their meaning restored, cascading into her soul like a river flowing to the ocean. Those precious moments she'd once dismissed were hers to hold again.

She opened her mouth to tell him, but all that came out was a hoarse 'I'm sorry,' followed by a flood of tears, and 'Dear God, Pottsy, I'm so, so sorry!' Her words were whipped away on the freezing wind.

The money had never meant anything to Helen, but now she wanted to put it to good use. First, she took a little for herself; she had the kitchen done and bought some furniture to brighten up her home. She found a few good causes to donate to and changed her will so that the residue – which was still substantial—would pass to her brothers, or to their spouses or descendants if they had passed. She also left a gift for each of Murray's children and grandchildren, who'd become an important part of her life.

Being part of the family again was wonderful. Sunday came around and with it another dinner at Murray and Jean's. Helen didn't know what she would've done if Murray hadn't reached out—Lizzie had been all she had.

Hughie and Rita surprised everyone by announcing they'd snuck off and got married, and the group—Helen included—congratulated them heartily and toasted their good health.

She did want to make things right with Hughie, but she'd never been the wordiest of people; it wasn't easy to get things out.

'Hughie...' she began.

His face cracked instantly into a warm smile.

'What?'

'I don't think you've ever called me that!'

It was true—when they were young, she'd always called him 'Hugh' or 'Golden Boy'. 'Hughie,' she said again, 'I—'

He threw his arms around her, squeezing her so tightly it almost hurt.

Slowly but surely, she returned the hug. (Hugs were not exactly her strong suit.)

Meredith

Jules leans on the worktop and asks, 'What are you thinking about?'

Stacy gathers the words. 'Stan, shot and dying in my nightmare. How would I feel then, Jules? How would I feel if something happened to him, and it was too late? I get it now, how short life is – one day everything's fine, the next day...well, look at my mum.' Jules nods sympathetically. Stacy reaches into the drawer for Stan's note, the one that came with the flowers after she ended things with him.

Dear Stacy,

I've never cared about a woman the way I do about you. I know you think it can't work because we want different things. All I know is that I need to be with you. Nothing else matters. I've scared you off by being too full on, and I'm sorry. I just need you to know that I can wait. If you change your mind – next week, next month or a year from now, just call me. I'll be here.

Love,
Stan

Stacy stifles a little sob. 'He wasn't asking for anything. He just wanted to be with me.'

'So call him—work out the details.'

'It's too late. He's found someone else.'

'How d'you know that?'
'Facebook.'
'Show me.'

Stacy looks up the picture of Stan and Emma and shows it to Jules.

'Has he updated his relationship status?'
'No.'
'It's just a picture.'
'But they look cosy, don't you think?'
'I think it's time you speak to Stan and get things straight.'

Stacy tests the water with a short text.

How are things? X

Hughie does a double take when he checks his JustGiving page. His target amount of £500 for Marie Curie has been exceeded by 4087%! His eyes flit to an anonymous donation—£20,000! He doesn't know anyone with that kind of money. He gets straight on the phone to JustGiving customer services, assuming it's a mistake.

He explains the problem to an operator called Sam, who puts him on hold to look into it.

'Mr Stevens?' Sam returns to the call two minutes later.
'Yes?'
'Sir, the donation is no mistake.'
'I don't understand.'
'When large donations are made, it's our policy to check things out, make sure it wasn't an accident. This wasn't.'
'I see. Who was it?'
'I'm sorry Mr Stevens, I can't tell you that. The donor wants to remain anonymous.'
'Eh, okay. Thank you.' Hughie looks stunned. This is an honour to Jessie, and fuel for his footsteps.

Stan

Stan went to meet Stacy unencumbered. Emma didn't deserve to be strung along, so he'd reluctantly stopped taking her out.

His stomach was doing summersaults waiting for Stacy outside Sir Walter's café on Princes Street Gardens. He was wrapped up against the cold, but he doubted he'd feel it anyway.

The gardens were a hub of activity, the sky clear blue beyond the castle. Stan swallowed, hardly daring to hope she was really coming.

Then he saw her walking towards him, as stunning as ever. She wore a neat winter jacket tied at the waist, her brown hair hanging in waves between a cosy scarf and a woolly hat. She gave a shy wave, and as she got closer, she looked different. She looked tired – *well she just came off night shift, you idiot* – but that wasn't all. There was a deep sadness in her big hazel eyes. It was like the happy-go-lucky had been knocked out of her.

It was all Stan could do not to wrap his arms around her. Nothing had changed for all his efforts to 'move on'. He breathed in her familiar scent and smiled gently, waiting for her to speak.

'Hi,' she said. She hugged him quickly, then pulled back to look at him. 'How are you?'

'Same as before,' he said. He caught her gaze as she tried to look away. 'What's been happening with you?'

'Lots,' she said, her eyes were welling up. 'Stan...I know I hurt you, I—'

'Shush,' he put a finger to her lips, his eyes intense as he drank in her features. They would talk and eat soon, but the question was urgent. Stan gently took her hands in his, searching her expression.

She continued to look up at him, all animosity gone. There was the ghost of a smile at the corners of her mouth, although her eyes still sparkled with unshed tears. She stepped closer and kissed him decisively on the lips, then looked into his face for a reaction.

'That's what I was hoping,' he said, and grinned. Letting go of one of her hands, he led her by the other. 'Come on love, let's get something to eat and you can tell me all about it.'

Meredith

I don't think Alfie gets many dinner invites—far less that he would accept, but tonight, he's sharing a meal with Nathan's family. They've been through a terrible time grieving the loss of Nathan's dad, and Alfie paces outside a full ten minutes before he rings the doorbell.

He passes Laura a bunch of flowers.

'Aw thanks Alfie, they're lovely!' she says, beckoning him inside. She shows him to the living room where Nathan and his brother are watching the X-Factor.

Nathan grins. 'Wait till you see what we have for you!' The boy jumps up and bounds upstairs. He reappears moments later with a tiny black Labrador pup, wearing a pink bow on her head. Shirley barks at the newcomer.

Alfie takes the pup and holds her up to his face for a closer look. 'Hello there, wee girl,' he coys

Laura appears in the doorway, smiling.

'She's perfect,' he tells them. 'I didn't feel like replacing Shirley, but one look at her and I've changed my mind!' He mumbles to the puppy as she sniffs at his face. 'Yes I have. I have.'

As they sit down to enjoy spaghetti bolognaise, Laura raises her glass. 'To our new friend, Alfie, who is always welcome here, and to dad...' she stifles a little sob, 'who will always be with us, in our hearts. Cheers.'

No hint of animosity shows in Alfie's eyes as he drinks with his friends to Gordon's memory.

Andy sleeps better than he has in a long time. He's seen a doctor about his problems and learned there's a name for what he suffers from. It's caused by trauma. There are medicines and treatments that could make things better. Nothing can wipe away the memories, but sharing his darkest secret has diluted its potency. Talking is new, but thanks to Nancy, he's open to it now.

Nancy surprises him with the wedding on Valentine's Day. Nothing fancy—just a service at the registrar's and a family meal. The kids and grandkids are there, and Gary gives a speech. Andy's sister Jenny and his brother Jimmie join the celebration, and Gary reads cards from his remaining siblings. His sister Eilidh lives in Cornwall now and the journey would be too much, but she sends her love and best wishes. Wee John (who's sixty now) lives in Belgium, and Ella is recovering from a fall, but they each send their love.

Andy enjoys the party so much, he forgets to worry for a while. He even sits with his back to the room talking to Jimmie. Nancy steals glances at him, a knowing smile playing on her lips.

There's one more surprise. Gary takes a phone call and heads outside. He comes back a few minutes later with a woman. She's petite, but a little taller than Nancy. She looks a lot like Claire, but she has Gary's eyes.

'Nancy, dad' Gary says, to get their attention, 'this is my sister Catherine.' Nancy's eyes widen and brim with tears.

Catherine says, 'Hi.'

Nancy takes hold of her hand. 'Catherine.'

Andy asks, 'How did you find her?'

'Facebook,' Gary says. 'The wonders of modern technology. 'I'll let the three of you talk—you've a lot to catch up on.'

CHAPTER 31

Meredith

I've taken dad's place at Mortonhall, watching the dig. It takes months, but finally, they discover human remains, right where Andy said they were. A reporter is sniffing around, pestering the team. For mum's sake, I hoped the case wouldn't attract media attention. If the police refuse to give information, they won't get the details, will they?

The reporter's photographer friend is furiously taking snaps from the other side of the police tape. I know I shouldn't, but I choose a rock from the gardens. I know beyond all doubt I can control it. I see the spiritual object as clearly as I ever saw anything. I lift it calmly and the physical rock moves with it. No one notices. I get closer to the photographer and hurl the rock at his camera. Bullseye! The lens cracks and the power dies.

'Hey!' he shouts, whipping around. 'Who threw that?' He swears and rants, and even accuses the police of sabotage. He's escorted from the grounds with his reporter friend.

Chumps.

I'm taken to the in-between, where Veronica waits.

I ask, 'Is this because I threw that rock?'

'No, girlie, I don't think we need to worry about that. This is a gift for you—answers to your questions about Michael. He can't come back, but he's written you a letter.'

'I take my letter and sit gratefully to read it.

Dear Merry,

There's so much I've wanted to tell you! I didn't know where to begin. I could've tried to explain things, but I was afraid you wouldn't believe I was your father. The way you used to look at me when you first died, or not look at me. Like we came from different planets.

I didn't want to add to your burdens. You were so utterly devoid of hope when you first came to me, with so much to overcome.

I was afraid, too, that you'd see me as the father you've been taught to hate. I wanted you to get to know me, as I really am. I made a vow that I'd wait for you to discover the whole truth: who I am, and what happened to me. Only then could you really know me, and how much I love you.

I wanted to stop you from jumping in front of that train! I wanted to more than I can say, but you were so fragile! If I stopped you, I would've been sent to the in-between for a long time, and how would you've managed? I couldn't be parted from you, in the state you were in. In that moment, when I saw you were going to do it, I couldn't watch. I had to leave, gather my strength.

With your mum, I shouldn't have meddled the way I did. I knew I'd go to the in-between, and that you'd have to manage without me, but I couldn't help it! She was going to take the pills and drink the gin, and I couldn't let her. I flushed the lot down the toilet. I thought you were strong enough to be alone for a while, and I let you down. I'm sorry. I could never bear to see your mum suffer.

You came through it all the same! You made me proud.

I hope I've answered all your questions, Merry. If not, Veronica may be able to help. Until we meet again, goodbye sweetheart.

Love,
Dad

Veronica indicates the wall, and as before it becomes a screen.

Dad walks towards Lizzie's house—our house—wearing a suit and carrying a case. He's hardly in the door when he's accosted by a toddler no bigger than Evie, shouting 'daddy!' and grabbing one of his legs.

He smiles and scoops me up, abandoning the suitcase. 'Merry!' he says in the same excited tone and kisses my rosy cheeks.

I giggle. It's a beautiful sound.

Mum appears in the sitting room as dad carries me through—she's young and stunning, even in an apron covered in flour. She greets dad sweetly and they kiss over my little head.

The scene changes to night, and mum lays me down in my cot. She wears a familiar hard-set expression.

Dad sits as a spirit beside me, singing softly.

Ally bally, ally bally bee,
Sittin' on yer daddy's knee

I sit up and look straight at him. 'Daddy,' I say.

He puts a hand down to touch me but he can't do it, so he keeps singing.

After I fall asleep, he weeps.

Dad's remains are fully recovered at Mortonhall. All the evidence supports Andy's testimony. There's even an old kitchen knife with his bones. The limbs were severed with a saw, and forensics can tell by the details—the angle, the number of cuts and so on—that a woman and a man did it together. Dad's positively identified using his dental records.

Mum can finally give him a proper burial.

That done, it seems a good time for the two of them to talk.

Helen

Helen looked for Pottsy everywhere. She listened in the silence and sometimes fancied he was there. But there was only one time he answered – the dream.

She was young again, sitting in the house on Southhouse Road, and he returned from work, wearing his suit and carrying his briefcase. The moment he saw her, he dropped the case and rushed to her. She stood to meet him, and he wrapped her in a tight embrace.

His touch was real, the smell of his skin exactly as she remembered.

They talked, and he explained everything. Now she understood—he had always wanted her, and no one else. He'd suffered from erectile dysfunction, and was too embarrassed to say. She'd assumed it was something to do with her, and doubts had been sown that grew like noxious weeds over the decades.

When she woke, she spoke to her daughter. 'Merry?'

There was no audible answer, but something stirred inside.

'I've seen your dad! He says we'll be a family again one day.'

CHAPTER 32

Murray

I'm looking down on my body, lying in the hospital bed. I can't feel any pain. There's Jean, sitting beside me holding my hand. Tears are streaming down her face. She's surrounded by a bright glow—an aura. The doctors and nurses have it too.

I'm okay, sweetheart.

I'm confused by a growing warmth behind me—it's dark outside but I turn to face dazzling sunlight. Its source gradually comes into focus in the centre; is she an angel? Dark hair hangs over her shoulders, framing a vibrant face. She has high cheekbones and piercing blue eyes. There's a softer appearance to her mass, but she's manifestly real. Her perfect figure is covered by a long dress, and her feet are bare. There's a dog at her heel, bathed in the same light.

She's looking straight at me. I can hardly hold her gaze—it's breath-taking and terrifying at the same time. I'm convinced that by simply looking, she can penetrate the depths of my soul. She can see everything I've ever done wrong! In awe, I turn my face away. Who is this other-worldly creature, and what does she want with *me*?

'Hi, Uncle Murray.' She smiles. 'I'm Merry.'

Merry

One of my favourite things about whispering is when someone whispers back. There they are, warm and breathing and alive, thinking of the dead, wondering...where are you? If I speak to you, can you hear me? Sometimes, with a little faith, they reach out and touch you. You feel them thinking of you, saying your name, and you rush to their side. You can't answer – at least, not in the way they expect – but if you know what you're doing, and if they're open, just sometimes, you can touch them back.

Stan lies the sleeping baby gently down in his cot, kissing his fluffy head, and creeps back into bed where Stacy sleeps deeply, her breath even and warm. He can hardly believe that she's his wife as he takes in her gorgeous features in the moonlight, and lets his eyes run over the curves of her body.

'Thank you, Meredith Potts!' he says softly into the night, his eyes glistening. 'If the next one's a girl, I think we'll name her Meredith.' A little thought pops into his head as he closes his eyes.

Merry for short.

Acknowledgements

Without the kind support of family and friends, I never would have seen this project through to completion. Like many a new self-publishing author, I've turned to good old mum for help, and she was the first to see the manuscript. She saw the earliest version and gently steered me towards improvement. Jacqui Eccles, a wonderful friend, avid reader and woman of astounding talent has encouraged and advised me through the whole process. She's donated oodles of time and energy to helping with the manuscript. Jacqui you're the best—I couldn't have done it without you!

The skills and knowledge of certain others was invaluable at the research stage, and the following wonderful people were interviewed and quizzed:

- Louise Lauchlin, for her knowledge of forensics (see, I told you it wasn't a real murder)
- Ann & Bill King for their memories of Edinburgh life
- Chris Brown for his knowledge of the building trade
- Bob Laird for sharing childhood experiences
- Margaret Swift who also shared valuable memories

My special thanks to the advance readers who agreed to review my book at launch. Your feedback was invaluable! I must mention Becky Stephens by name—I was touched by this fiction editor who offered helpful professional feedback to a complete stranger. Thank you Becky!

Last but by no means least, I'd like to thank my husband, Grant, for his never-ending patience in putting up with me and my time-consuming projects! Your support and wisdom have been amazing. You are my reason, for everything.

About the author

Amy King had two life-long ambitions. The first, to be a parent, was achieved after a challenging ten-year wait. She's now a full-time mother of three with one ambition—to become a successful writer (as in, one who actually makes a living). She's somehow managed to keep all three kids alive (thus far) and release her first novel, *The Whisperer*.

A belief in better things to come gets Amy through life's inevitable challenges. As a writer, she explores the depths and heights of human experience, giving you characters to connect with. Already onto the next book, she's hoping success comes sooner than ten years this time. Meantime, she'll happily settle for getting a book in your hands and helping you feel something beautiful and personal.

Amy dyes her hair ridiculous colours, and cannot grasp the fact that she's getting older.

Find Amy online at www.airelandking.com.

Printed in Great Britain
by Amazon